"How could you?"

The words came out breathless and seething. "How could you do this to the people who care about you?" To her?

"Maybe I *am* thinking about you." Silas's tortured gaze bore into Tess's. "Maybe that's why I have to go."

The quiet admission immediately disarmed her.

"You know all the reasons I can't stay here, Tess. You know why I can't be this close to you. Not anymore."

Who cared what she knew in her head? In the last two years, her heart had only beat like this for him. And if Silas spent months away from her—if he left and something happened to him—her heart might never beat like this again.

"I have to go. I have to get away or…" He shut his mouth and shook his head.

"Or what?" Tess stepped toe to toe with him. "Or *what*?" she asked more forcefully.

A decisive smolder took over his eyes. He reached for her, sliding his hands around her waist, pulling her close to him, making her heart sigh with pure relief.

"Or I'll do something reckless," he murmured, dropping his hungry gaze to her lips. "Something I haven't been able to stop thinking about doing for one damn long month."

PRAISE FOR
SARA RICHARDSON

"With wit and warmth, Sara Richardson creates heartfelt stories you can't put down."
—Lori Foster, *New York Times* bestselling author

"Sara Richardson writes unputdownable, unforgettable stories from the heart."
—Jill Shalvis, *New York Times* bestselling author

"Sara [Richardson] brings real feelings to every scene she writes."
—Carolyn Brown, *New York Times* bestselling author

The Summer Sisters

"This is sure to win readers' hearts."
—*Publishers Weekly*

One Night with a Cowboy

"Richardson has a gift for creating empathetic characters and charming small-town settings, and her taut plotting and sparkling prose keep the pages turning. This appealing love story is sure to please."
—*Publishers Weekly*

Home for the Holidays

"Fill your favorite mug with hot chocolate and whipped cream as you savor this wonderful holiday story of family reunited and dreams finally fulfilled. I loved it!"
—Sherryl Woods, #1 *New York Times* bestselling author

"You'll want to stay home for the holidays with this satisfying Christmas read."
—Sheila Roberts, *USA Today* bestselling author

First Kiss with a Cowboy

"The pace is fast, the setting's charming, and the love scenes are delicious. Fans of cowboy romance are sure to be captivated." —*Publishers Weekly*, Starred Review

A Cowboy for Christmas

"Tight plotting and a sweet surprise ending make for a delightful Christmas treat. Readers will be sad to see the series end." —*Publishers Weekly*

Colorado Cowboy

"Readers who love tear-jerking small-town romances with minimal sex scenes and maximum emotional intimacy will quickly devour this charming installment."
—*Publishers Weekly*

Renegade Cowboy

"Top Pick! An amazing story about finding a second chance to be with the one that you love."

—Harlequin Junkie

"A beautifully honest and heartwarming tale about forgiveness and growing up that will win the hearts of fans and newcomers alike."

—*RT Book Reviews*

Hometown Cowboy

"Filled with humor, heart, and love, this page-turner is one wild ride."

—Jennifer Ryan, *New York Times* bestselling author

No Better Man

"Charming, witty, and fun. There's no better read. I enjoyed every word!"

—Debbie Macomber, #1 *New York Times* bestselling author

BETTING *on a* GOOD LUCK COWBOY

BETTING *on a* GOOD LUCK COWBOY

SARA RICHARDSON

A STAR VALLEY NOVEL

FOREVER

New York Boston

Copyright © 2023 by Sara Richardson

Cover design by Daniela Medina. Cover photographs © Rob Lang Photography; Shutterstock. Cover copyright © 2023 by Hachette Book Group, Inc.

Forever
Hachette Book Group
1290 Avenue of the Americas, New York, NY 10104
read-forever.com
twitter.com/readforeverpub

First Edition: June 2023

Forever is an imprint of Grand Central Publishing. The Forever name and logo are trademarks of Hachette Book Group, Inc.

The publisher is not responsible for websites (or their content) that are not owned by the publisher.

Forever books may be purchased in bulk for business, educational, or promotional use. For information, please contact your local bookseller or the Hachette Book Group Special Markets Department at special.markets@hbgusa.com.

ISBNs: 978-1-5387-2590-0 (mass market), 978-1-5387-2591-7 (ebook)

Printed in the United States of America

OPM

10 9 8 7 6 5 4 3 2 1

*This book is dedicated to the Oldham family
at the Wind River Wild Horse Sanctuary.
What a legacy you've built.*

AUTHOR'S NOTE

Hello, dear readers,

Thank you for picking up a copy of *Betting on a Good Luck Cowboy*. Before you start reading, I wanted to let you know that this book deals with some difficult issues, including animal abuse and grief over the loss of a loved one. I have done my best to handle these topics with sensitivity and discretion, but do understand that they could be intense and triggering for some readers. As with any story I write, the characters are all on a path toward wholeness and healing, and there is always the promise of their happy ending lighting the way. Please be sure to take care of yourself as you join them on the journey.

Best wishes,
Sara

CHAPTER ONE

Tess Valdez had experienced many firsts since bury-
ing her husband two years ago, but this one might be
the toughest.

Staring at herself in the hotel's bathroom mirror, she
pulled up the side zipper on her brand-new cocktail dress
and exhaled against the sense of dread building behind her
ribs. It wasn't the dress. No, the little black off-the-shoulder
number happened to be fabulous. The red cowgirl boots she
wore on her feet completed the ensemble, making it the
perfect outfit to wear to her brother's rustic yet swanky
engagement party at one of the nicest hotels in Jackson.
She looked good.

But this would be the first party she'd attended without
Jace by her side—the first large-scale celebration she'd have
to walk into alone...

"Tess?" Her friend Lyric knocked on the bathroom door.
"You almost ready? I told Thatch and Silas we'd meet them
in the lobby five minutes ago."

"Almost ready." She didn't know how to be ready for these new firsts. Truthfully, she never felt ready. But she'd gotten through them—the first full night in her bed without Jace, the first Christmas for her and her daughters without him, the first family vacation on their own.

But tonight, everyone would be watching her. Tonight, she was stepping outside of her comfort zone.

Glancing in the mirror, she smoothed her hair once more. She couldn't very well hide in the bathroom forever. So, Tess did what she'd had to do many times before. She put one foot in front of the other.

"Sorry," she said when she opened the door to see Lyric standing on the other side. "I wasn't sure about this dress." That was an easier explanation than confessing the real reason for her hesitation.

"Seriously?" Her friend sashayed over to her wearing an incredible floor-length red number with a plunging neckline. Her friend's sleek black hair had been elegantly knotted at the crown of her head. "That dress is exquisite. Trust me."

"*Your* dress is exquisite." That was the only adjective to describe Lyric. Her friend was graceful and wise and thoughtful. Since they were nearly the only two single women from Star Valley attending this party, they'd decided to bunk up together tonight. "My dress is pretty. But I'll take it." Tess snatched her clutch purse off the dresser. "I'm not sure I remember how to go out and be a grown-up."

For the last two years, her two main companions were under ten years old. Sure, she'd spent time with her brother and his two SEAL friends who'd moved to Star Valley to help take care of her and the girls after Jace had died. And she, Lyric, and Kyra got together every so often too. But hanging out was different than attending a fancy party.

Maybe she should've stayed home with Morgan and Willow instead of letting her parents travel out to babysit.

"I'm not much of a partier," Lyric reminded her. "But I can't wait to celebrate your brother and Kyra's engagement."

"I can't either," Tess said as she finally stepped out into the plush hallway. "I'm thrilled for them." She'd already learned it was possible to be happy and lonely at the same time. "Some of Jace's family will be here," she continued as they waited for the elevator. "Aiden felt like we should invite them."

For over ten years, Jace's family had been hers—and Aiden's by proxy. "I haven't seen a lot of them since the funeral." Her husband had had too many cousins and aunts and uncles for her to know any of them well. "I guess I'm a little nervous."

"Stick with me." Lyric held her hand as they stepped into the elevator. "We'll do this together. You and me and Silas and Thatch. And Aiden and Kyra when they're not busy dancing or gazing lovingly into each other's eyes."

"I don't know what I would do without you all." They'd gotten her through, these friends who'd become her family. They'd gotten both her and her daughters through.

"We're going to have a blast," Lyric assured her.

The elevator came to a stop and they stepped into the hotel's main lobby. Tess wasn't sure she'd ever stayed anywhere quite this nice. As a ranching family, she and Jace never had the money to splurge for fancy hotels. She hadn't needed expensive lodging, because they were just as happy camping in the high meadow back at the ranch.

Tess admired the massive antler chandeliers dangling from log beams overhead and the enormous stone fireplace that provided a focal point for the space. Yes, she had certainly found herself in a new era of her life.

Silas and Thatch stood at the bar on the other side of a baby grand piano, both dressed in jeans, crisp button-up shirts with sport coats, and their cowboy boots, naturally.

"Sorry we're late," Lyric said, leading Tess to the men by the hand. "Tess wasn't sure about her dress."

Silas tilted his head and gave her a long, smoldering appraisal—because he had long ago perfected the smolder. "I'm damn sure about that dress, Tess. Damn. Sure."

"Yeah. Looks great." Thatch's opinion would've meant more if he could've managed to tear his gaze away from Lyric and roll his tongue back into his mouth. But she also thought his crush was cute.

As for Silas, Tess knew how he operated. The man was full of smooth lines and charm and, yes, intense smolders. And he handed them out to nearly every female for free. Most women found him difficult to resist because he had one of those chiseled handsome faces, not to mention blue eyes full of mischief and thick dark hair with an unkempt wave—who wouldn't want to run their hands through hair like that?

But Tess prided herself on not being most women.

"I knew I should've worn the blue dress." She shot him her sassiest smirk to show him she wouldn't fall for his wizardry. Though she'd be lying if she said she hadn't been tempted a time or two.

Matching her smirk, he thumped his fist into his chest directly over his heart. "Why you gotta wound me like that?"

No matter what, Silas always seemed to lure a laugh out of her. He'd been the only one who could make her smile in the months following Jace's death. "Easy, Beck. Save that charisma for the women who'll actually appreciate it. I'm sure the party will be crawling with them."

Aiden and Kyra had gone all out for this shindig. Last she'd heard, there were 136 people on the guest list.

"Well, those other women won't look as good as you look in that dress." Silas said the words without the smolder this time, which gave them a more genuine ring.

"Hey, Lyric." Thatch moved in on her friend. "I've been dealing with this sciatica thing and wondered if you could recommend some stretches."

Tess snorted. That was a new approach. Had Thatch really stooped to asking for yoga advice? A month ago, her friends had opened up a holistic health clinic in Star Valley, offering medical care by Kyra and yoga classes and naturopath services from Lyric. But as far as Tess knew, Thatch had never had any interest in yoga before.

"Sure. I can recommend some things to try." Lyric led him in the direction of the ballroom talking about a pose called half lord of the fishes. Either her friend was clueless or she continued to ignore Thatch's blatant interest in her.

"I guess we should get in there too." Silas offered her his arm. "Ready?"

"No." Instead of letting him escort her away, she sat on a stool and ordered a martini. A little pregame libation would potentially relax the nervous fluttering that seemed to be gaining momentum.

"Ooookay." Silas slid onto the stool next to her. "What's wrong?"

"Nothing." Tess sipped the drink the bartender set in front of her and coughed. Whew! Martinis were a lot stronger than she remembered.

Silas swiveled his stool to face her fully, his expression calling bullshit. "Tess."

The way he spoke her name said so much—that he knew

her, that she wasn't allowed to lie to him...not after all they'd been through together. Lying to Silas was impossible. She didn't even know why she tried.

"I don't know how to act at things like this anymore." She played with the toothpick that held the skewered olive in her drink. "Everyone stares at me." Most people still saw Tess the widow. But she was someone else now. Someone who was still finding her way and figuring herself out but also someone who had walked through hell and survived. "I wish I could just have fun without anyone watching me or judging me or feeling sorry for me."

There was no official twelve-step program for grieving your spouse. And yet, a lot of people sure seemed to offer their insight and advice on how she should be living. "You need to get out there again," her mom had insisted before she'd left the house earlier this afternoon. "It's been two years, honey. Jace would want you to move on." And then there was Jace's family. His sister asked Tess if she was dating anyone every time they talked on the phone, and when she told her no, Kelly sounded relieved. "Oh good. I don't know if I could handle that."

Sighing, she forced down two more gulps of martini. Gah! Her whole face grimaced. The vodka started a fire in her throat.

"All right." Silas stood and downed the last half of her martini, likely so she didn't have to. "Then that's my mission tonight."

Even though her drink was gone, she didn't budge. "What's your mission?"

"Fun." He tugged on her hand until she stood too. "I am going to make sure you have too much fun to care if someone's watching you or judging you."

"So, you think I'm a charity case too." She picked up her purse, but before she could leave a tip, Silas threw a ten-dollar bill down next to her empty glass.

"Yeah, but you're a hot charity case, so I don't mind."

Tess punched his shoulder but the effort was futile. Silas happened to be all muscle.

"Come on." He threaded her arm through his and prodded her toward the ballroom.

Music already played, the bass thumping out into the hallway.

"There's one catch to this mission tonight. You have to pay attention only to me," he told her outside the doors. "Keep your eyes on me, and you'll have the time of your life. I promise."

"God." She rolled her eyes. "Are you sure there'll be room in there for me? What with your ego taking up so much space and everything?"

Silas laughed. He always laughed when she gave him a hard time, which made her laugh too.

"See? You're already having fun." He gently nudged her. "Remember. Eyes on me," he whispered on their way through the door.

A crowd already packed the ballroom. Most people were dancing in front of the stage set up for the live band, but there were also guests sitting at the tables on the outskirts of the room, drinking and enjoying hors d'oeuvres.

"Hey, Sis." Aiden ambled to meet them, holding tightly to his fiancée's hand.

"I'm so happy you're here!" Kyra hugged her tight. "This is going to be so much fun! You look ravishing, by the way."

"Told you," Silas murmured a little too close to her ear. The goose bumps his voice roused down her arm annoyed her. "Congrats, you two." She hugged her brother. "I can't wait for the wedding." That would be a new first too. Attending a wedding without Jace, listening to the same vows Jace had said to her when they thought they'd have forever.

"What a great party." Lyric joined their little posse. True to form, Thatch wasn't far behind.

"We'd better get out on the dance floor," Thatch said to Silas. "Show them all how it's done."

"But all of your clothes are staying on tonight, boys," Kyra warned sternly. "I've heard all about you two, and this is an *elegant* affair."

Silas shook his head. "Man. You strip at one Navy buddy's drunken wedding reception—at the bride's request, mind you—and everyone holds it over your head the rest of your life."

"That was five years ago," Thatch added. "We've matured since then."

Tess laughed. "In all fairness, the bride did beg them to do a striptease. And it didn't go further than their boxer briefs." Thankfully. She'd attended that wedding with Jace and things had gotten a little wild after midnight. She decided not to mention that Aiden had been right there with Silas and Thatch. SEALs really knew how to let loose and party. "But I won't vouch for their maturity since then."

Silas made the dagger-to-the-heart motion again. "Come on." He tugged her arm. "Let's go dance and I'll show you how much I've matured."

"We'll join you soon," Kyra promised. "We still have a few more people to greet."

"Count us in." Lyric sidled up to Tess's other side with Thatch and the four of them made their way through the crowd to the front of the stage.

The band had started playing "Little Bitty" by Alan Jackson.

"Perfect." Silas took Tess's hands and pulled her into a two-step. "I've been working on my moves."

She was already laughing too hard to answer. He had moves, she'd give him that. With one hand on her waist and the other clasped around hers, Silas led her around the dance floor, two-stepping and twirling and spinning her until she had no choice but to look only at him. God, she'd forgotten how fun it was to dance—to move with the music, to get her heart rate going with the beat.

At the end of the song, he dipped her low and she didn't even have a chance to catch her breath before the band struck up a lively rendition of "Let's Go to Vegas" and they were off again, dancing and laughing until she was almost dizzy.

Lyric and Thatch had disappeared in the crowd somewhere, but that didn't even matter. Silas was taking good care of her.

She lost track of how many songs they danced to before she had to stop.

Silas was out of breath too. "Are you having fun?"

She couldn't remember the last time she'd smiled and laughed for this long. Her cheeks ached as much as her feet. But it was the best kind of ache. "I'm having fun."

"I'm glad." He squeezed her hand. "I'll go get us some drinks. What'll you have?"

She shot him a sheepish frown. "Water?" If they were going to continue dancing like this, she'd need to hydrate.

"You got it." He stepped away. "Be right back. Stay put."

"I will." She wasn't sure she could walk very far right now anyway. The boots might've been a mistake.

"Tess?"

The voice behind her made every muscle in her neck tense. She turned, already bracing herself. "Hi, DeAnn." She should've been on alert, watching for Jace's cousin. Jace and DeAnn had been close after growing up just down the street from each other in California.

"Wow." The woman looked much the same as she had when they'd all been teenagers, except her dark hair was shorter and she smiled less. "I'm so surprised you're here. I mean, I know Aiden said you were coming, but I wasn't sure."

"Of course I'm here." She grasped at her fading smile. DeAnn had visited her six months after the funeral and had seemed to criticize everything Tess had done that weekend—with the girls, with the house, with the ranch. Because she didn't do things exactly like Jace had done them. "It's my brother's engagement party," she reminded her.

"I know. But things have been incredibly difficult since Jace passed away, haven't they?" DeAnn's mouth pinched. "It would've been understandable if you didn't feel like partying."

DeAnn lived in the camp of people who thought Tess should still be holed up at home the way she'd been for a good two years. "The girls and I are doing better," she said politely.

"You seem to be doing more than better." DeAnn didn't even try to disguise the judgment in her tone. "I saw you dancing with Silas Beck. Wasn't he Jace's best friend?"

"Yes." So what? Her face was getting hot. "He and Thatch and Aiden have been my saving grace over the last two years." And she had every right to dance with whomever she wanted to dance with.

"God, I still miss Jace so much," DeAnn said through a sigh. "I do everything I can to keep his memory alive with my boys."

"So do I." But she couldn't keep *him* alive, could she? And she couldn't justify hiding herself the way she wanted to, because she had to show her girls how to live. That was what Jace had asked her to do. That's what he would've wanted.

"Well, I'm glad to see that you're getting out and having so much fun." Even DeAnn's raised eyebrows conveyed her distaste for Tess's dancing antics. "It's hard to get over losing someone you love. But you seem to be moving forward."

"I don't have a choice." That was the truth.

"Right. Of course." She overexaggerated her smile. "I should get back to Steve. It was good to see you."

Tess didn't return the sentiment. In fact, she did an about-face, walked in the opposite direction, and kept going all the way out the doors and onto a patio where a huge firepit glowed. Late spring snow had started to softly fall on the stone benches, but the anger kept her toasty warm.

Out of habit, she opened her purse and pulled out her phone to call the ranch.

"Hi, Mommy!" Willow's little voice answered. "Are you having fun? You looked like a princess in that picture you sent." Her younger daughter was still very into princesses.

"Sure. It's great, honey." She'd had fun. Maybe for a half hour or so. She should be grateful for that. "What about you? Are you having fun with Grandma and Grandpa?"

"Yes! We're making chocolate chip cookies and then we're going to have a tea party."

"That sounds wonderful." She should've stayed home with the girls tonight. She could've been in her flannel pajamas by now, all snuggled up on the couch with them. "Can I say hi to Morgan?"

"Sure, Mommy! See you tomorrow." There was a shuffling as Willow handed the phone off.

"Hey, Mom. How's Uncle Aiden and Aunt Kyra's party?"

"It's good." She drew closer to the fire to warm her bare shoulders. "And how are things there?"

"We're having a great time," her daughter assured her. "I love it when Grandma and Grandpa come to visit." There was a pause. "Oh, we have to go, Mom! It's time to put the dough on the cookie sheet!"

"All right, sweets." She told them both she loved them and then hung up. Grandma probably made them get off the phone so Tess would be forced to go back to the party. But she couldn't go back. Not after that exchange with DeAnn...

Behind her, the door to the ballroom whooshed open.

"Tess?" Silas came charging at her. "I've been looking everywhere for you. It's freezing." He wriggled out of his suit coat and draped it over her shoulders. "What're you doing out here?"

To her utter horror, tears built in her eyes and spilled over.

"What?" His voice was panicked. "What is it? What happened? Did someone upset you? I'll go in there and find them and I'll—"

"No. It's fine." Her voice got all soggy and pathetic and she tried to turn away before he could see what a mess she was.

"Aw, come here, honey." He pulled her to him and wrapped his arms around her. "I can't stand to see you cry," he murmured against her hair.

She couldn't stand to cry either. And yet here she was, sniffling on his shoulder. "I'll be fine."

He said nothing more and simply stroked the hair at the back of her head while she shed a few more tears.

Okay. That was enough. She wouldn't continue to blubber all over him for the rest of the night.

Tess lifted her head and found herself peering up and into those baby blues that were usually so playful. Right now, however, they were filled with concern. For her. "Tess," he murmured in that intimate tone he so rarely used.

"Silas." It came out in a whisper. She'd looked into this man's eyes hundreds of times over the last few years, but this time something shifted. There was a hard tug at her heart and before she knew what was happening, her lips were touching his.

For the briefest second, Silas's arms tensed around her, as if the contact had shocked him, but then he seemed to recover and he tightened his hold on her with his hands strong on her lower back. Tess breathed him in, some masculine-scented cologne that reminded her of the woods right after a rainstorm. Their mouths fit together, exploring a rhythm she hadn't anticipated, powerful enough to grip her by the heart.

A moan resounded deep in his throat and then his tongue grazed hers and flung her body into delirium—blood racing through her, hot and fast, knees failing—and suddenly she was reminded that she was alive. She was still alive.

"Let's go upstairs," she murmured against his lips. They could go now and she'd still be in her own bed before the party ended and Lyric came back to their room.

Silas drew back a few inches, his breaths heaving, bewilderment in his eyes.

"You promised fun. With no judgment, no cares." She kissed him again, for herself, so the tingling in her body wouldn't stop.

"Take me upstairs, Silas. Please?"

CHAPTER TWO

Silas moved the cursor over the send button but couldn't seem to click.

In his previous line of employment, there'd been no room for hesitation. You take action or you risk losing a limb or your life. But he wasn't a SEAL anymore. And maybe that was the problem.

Without sending the email, he moved the mouse on his computer and clicked back to his latest game of Battleship with Thatch. Narrowing his eyes, he read the grid on the screen. As usual, Thatch thought he could outwit him by putting his destroyer in a diagonal formation.

"Nice try." He clicked the F8 square and blew up the ship, but Thatch wasn't around for him to gloat. His friend had taken the day off and headed to Jackson to run some errands. And God only knew where Aiden was. He'd been taking some extra-long lunch hours lately. Seeing how Aiden was engaged and had recently moved in with Kyra, Silas never asked questions.

And it wasn't like things were overly busy at Cowboy Construction right now. They were in between projects, and Silas knew where he'd want to be if he had a fiancée. Definitely not sitting in their office blowing up battleships.

When he, Thatch, and Aiden had first moved here to help Tess run Dry Creek Ranch after they lost their best friend Jace on their last mission, Silas had felt that same sense of duty, loyalty, and responsibility that had driven him when he'd served. But now... well, Tess didn't need them around as much. She'd gotten back on her feet and had hired some extra help. Meanwhile, his sense of purpose had been fading.

He'd never lived anywhere this long—not even as a kid. The confinement had started to mess with him. He had too much time to think. And he'd gotten too close to a certain woman. Sleeping with Tess two weeks ago—with his *dead best friend's wife*—had woken him up. He'd gotten too comfortable and let his guard down. He'd failed. He'd promised Jace he'd always protect Tess, and instead, he'd dishonored the man who had been a brother to him.

Yeah, it was time to skip town. He clicked back to the unsent email, scanning over his response again. When his old Navy buddy had contacted him about filling in on a government-contracted mission to locate and extract a missing US diplomat in Afghanistan, Silas had almost said no. Two years ago, he would've said no. Hell, six months ago, he would've declined. But he'd slept with Tess. And now, every time he saw her, the details came rushing back to him—how her lips had felt grazing his, how she had run her fingertips down his back...

He understood all too well now. The only emotion more powerful than guilt was desire. And he couldn't let his craving for her overcome his promise to his dead best friend.

Kneading his forehead, Silas scanned his response on the screen again.

I'm open to it. Let me know when we can discuss the details.

Before he lost the nerve, he clicked the send button and the email whooshed away. Accepting this offer would be for the best right now. This mission would give him some space, some distance so he didn't fool himself into wanting a life he could never have.

A life he didn't deserve.

And on that note...he stood up and strode across the office to the putting green. No thinking. No dwelling. He had to line up his next shot and move—

The door crashed open and Tess stomped in, her dark curly hair in disarray and her cheeks splotched with pink.

"Hey." The putter fell from his hands and he looked away from her before she could read the mess of want and guilt in his eyes. He wished he didn't know. How her lips tasted. How her silky curls felt beneath his fingertips. He wished he didn't know how soft her skin was or the sound of her low throaty laugh when he'd kissed her neck...

"Where's Aiden?" Tess demanded, looking around the room with her soft brown eyes ablaze.

"Uh. Don't know." Silas moved swiftly back to his desk and opened his laptop so he could focus on something other than the woman's face. He'd seen that face too often in dreams as of late. "He hasn't been around in the middle of the day this week. Probably working on wedding plans." Though Aiden and Kyra's big event wasn't until September.

"Well, that's just great." Tess uttered a groan of frustration. "Of course he's not here. Damn it. I need him right now."

Silas forced his gaze away from the Battleship grid and had to brace himself to look at her. He and Tess had seen each other since That Night but there'd always been other people around. "Uh. Well...what'd you need? Maybe I can help." As long as he could assist from a distance. He didn't trust himself around Tess anymore.

The woman eyed him doubtfully. "I just rode up to the high meadow and there was some jerk in a UTV shooting at—"

"What?" Silas lurched out of his chair so fast he knocked it over backward. "What the hell? They were shooting *at* you?"

"Not at *me*," Tess corrected. "I think they were shooting at the herd of wild horses."

Easing out a lengthy breath, he did his best to pick his heart up off the fucking floor. "You saw someone shooting at the horses?"

"I didn't see them." Her chin lifted stubbornly. "I heard them. And then the horses came tearing through the meadow. They were scared. I could tell."

Okay. Silas swallowed the fireball in his throat. She wasn't in danger. She hadn't almost gotten shot. Tess was fine. "You really think some of the horses got shot?" It was a federal crime to shoot a wild horse, but he guessed that didn't stop some people. Those horses stirred up quite the controversy with some of the local ranchers who thought they were destroying the cattle-grazing lands in the region. "Maybe the UTV only backfired or something."

"They were gunshots." Her glare dared him to disagree. "You know what? Never mind." She spun and headed for the door. "I have to get back up there and make sure none of those horses were shot."

Whoa. He met her in three quick steps. "Not by yourself."

"You don't have to come. I know you have stuff to do." There was a fair amount of guilt in her gaze too if he wasn't mistaken. And that was his fault. He'd messed everything up. He'd started this whole complication when he'd taken her up to his hotel room that night. Now they couldn't even look each other in the eyes without things getting weird.

"I'm coming with you." He turned and walked back to his desk where he slid open the bottom drawer to access the lockbox that held his pistol. "Can't be too careful if they're armed." He checked to make sure the safety was on and then shoved the gun into the waistband of his jeans and pulled his coat off the back of his chair.

Surprisingly, Tess didn't argue as he followed her out the door. He was likely the last person she wanted to spend the afternoon with, but he couldn't let her go back up that mountain alone. Not when people were randomly shooting firearms.

"We're taking my UTV," Tess announced, heading straight for the garage across the driveway. "I've already loaded up some gear. And I'm driving."

He didn't argue. He'd seen Tess handle those machines. She knew her way around the mountain trails. The woman happened to be fully capable, but he wasn't about to let her walk into a potentially dangerous confrontation without backup.

"We could call Chief Holbrook." He followed her into the garage and grabbed a helmet from a shelf nearby.

"We can call her when we get up there." Tess put on her helmet and adjusted the chinstrap. "We need to hurry."

"Right." Silas slid into the front seat next to her and clicked in his seat belt.

Tess started the engine. "I brought my bag just in case." She gestured to the back where her veterinarian supplies were stashed inside the small tailgate. Just before Jace died, Tess had finished her schooling to become a veterinarian so she could save them money by caring for the animals on the ranch. Little did they know at the time, she'd soon be too busy running the whole operation to open her own practice.

Silas kept his eyes straight ahead as she drove them out of the garage. What could he say to her? She'd clearly been avoiding him every bit as much as he'd been avoiding her these last few weeks. She couldn't seem to even glance at him for longer than two seconds without looking away.

Instead of trying to make conversation, he kept his eyes on the scenery. Tess had her eyes trained on the trail in front of them, steering around the barn and through the pasture behind the house and then finally into the trees where the grades started to get steeper.

"So...um...we haven't really talked about...well...you know," she half yelled over the growl of the UTV's engine.

"No, I guess we haven't." He had to raise his voice too. He'd made sure they hadn't had an opportunity to discuss what had happened between them. What good would come from talking about it? He wanted to forget. Holding her, kissing her, making love to her. He wanted all of those images to disappear. But they hadn't. They came back to him all the time—just as vivid and clear as if he were right back in that hotel room with her.

"We probably should talk about it." Tess's gaze darted to him but then quickly shifted back to the narrow well-traveled path ahead of them.

Did they have to go over the reasons that night shouldn't have happened? He already knew them all.

Tess didn't give him the chance to change the subject. "I mean, I think we both know what happened was a mistake."

Or, more accurately, *he* was a mistake. Always had been. His mom hadn't meant to get pregnant after a one-night stand at nineteen. Because of him, she couldn't finish school, she never had enough money, and they had to keep moving around to make ends meet. She didn't come out and tell him he was the biggest mistake of her life, but she might as well have, the way she always complained when he needed a new pair of shoes or money for a school field trip. And then there'd been all the ways she'd pretended she didn't have a kid, making him hide in his room when someone picked her up for a date...

Forget it.

That was all in the past. The day after he'd graduated from high school—with honors, thank you very much—he'd gone directly to the local recruitment office, and he'd never looked back.

Looking back did no good.

"Let's just forget about that night. Put it behind us." He didn't intend to be treated like the biggest mistake of anyone else's life ever again. "We can pretend it never happened. It didn't mean anything anyway."

It was past time to move on.

CHAPTER THREE

Lifting her eyes to the mountainous horizon ahead, Tess tightened her grip on the UTV's steering wheel. Up ahead, the crags in the peaks were still snow covered, and though the snowfields were shrinking with the changing of the season, the stark blotches of white dotting the mountainside still glared against the brilliant blue sky. But even with that beautiful view stretched out in front of her, the tension from her hands made its way through her arms and into her shoulders and neck.

She tried to focus on avoiding the ruts in the trail and the various rocks that had rolled into their path, but sitting next to Silas was jarring. Especially today of all days. May 12. Once, the date had marked one of the happiest days of her life, but now it had become just another day in her chaotic life.

Tess found her gaze wandering to the man next to her again. She was trying to pretend That Night had never happened. She was really trying. But it clearly hadn't been as easy for her as it had for him. She kept reliving every intimate moment of the few hours they'd spent together. How she'd lounged in his arms until she finally snuck back to her hotel room. How they'd ordered room service first, and he'd fed her strawberries and whipped cream while they stayed in bed together for as long as they could get away with. Like they'd be able to hide from reality...

"You missed the turn," Silas called, keeping his stony gaze forward.

Damn it. He had her all flustered and distracted. "Hold on." She cranked the wheel to turn around, then carefully steered up the switchbacks, irritation flaring. Why'd the man come up here with her anyway? Instead of rushing into their office, she should've *called* Aiden. Then she wouldn't be stuck with Silas alone out here all afternoon. Tess snuck another peek at him, noticing his rigid posture hadn't changed.

The UTV crested the final switchback and the view of the high meadow opened up before her—the threadbare grasses that had been laden by heavy winter snows were rising again, new and green. A thick stand of pine trees stood at the southern edge where their property—*her* property—bordered the public land. In the center of the meadow, the cluster of white tents they used when they moved the cattle twice a year were nestled next to the small glacial pond with depths that turned the water turquoise.

Parking the UTV at the edge of the woods, Tess cut the engine. "We'll have to go on foot. I don't want to risk spooking the horses again."

And if that other vehicle was still out here somewhere, they could sneak up on them and call the police.

Using the overhead bar, she pulled herself out of the driver's seat and took off her helmet while Silas did the same.

"You think the horses are still around?" he asked as they left the UTV behind.

"I can't say for sure." Tess marched through the pine trees, keeping a healthy distance between them. Distance and indifference would be key on this mission. "But they probably haven't gone too far." Jace had told her that this same herd had run this land for well over a hundred years. Her husband had loved these animals, and a few times they'd been lucky enough to catch sight of them when they'd been up here camping. "The herd came flooding out of the trees and then spooked back into the woods over there." She pointed to the southern border in front of them.

"What were you doing up here anyway?" Silas fell in stride with her and peered at her face.

Tess immediately ducked her head. "I went for a ride." Her stomach clenched. Down the hill to their left—at the edge of the glacial pond—the bronze memorial they'd constructed for Jace glinted in the sun. This was where they'd spread his ashes. When she hadn't even been able to stand up under her own power, her brother, Aiden, had stood on one side of her and Silas had stood on the other side, supporting her weight.

"It's been a while since I've been up here." A note of regret played in his voice.

"Yeah. Me too." She used to visit all the time because it made her feel closer to Jace. Before their daughters had come along, she and Jace used to ride up here for the day and have a picnic, camp overnight near the pond. They would lie on a blanket and gaze up at the clouds, and sometimes make love under the shade of the trees.

The memory put another crack in her armor. "It's our anniversary," she admitted. "I mean, it would have been."

Understanding dawned on his face. "That's right. I haven't been paying too much attention to dates lately."

"It would've been thirteen years, and I forgot." She wasn't sure why she confessed to Silas of all people. Maybe because she knew Silas well enough to know he didn't judge anyone. Regardless of what had happened between them, they'd still walked through the grief of the last two years together. He and Thatch and Aiden understood what she'd lost. And she understood what they'd lost in their unofficial brother. "I can't believe I forgot."

She'd woken up at the same time she always did, but Morgan and Willow had to be at school early. As usual, her eldest daughter couldn't decide what to wear and they'd ended up leaving five minutes late. After dropping them off, Tess had come back home and brewed herself a whole pot of coffee before starting on the books for the ranch—yet another thing she'd gotten behind on. She'd eaten two fried eggs for breakfast, worked her way through paying all of the bills, and then flicked on the noon news while doing the dishes, and that's when she'd heard the date.

The man stopped hiking and turned to her. "You didn't forget." The words seemed to disarm the shield that had been in his gaze earlier. "You rode up here, didn't you?"

"I forgot until I saw the date on the news." And then it had hit her as she was rinsing the skillet she'd made the eggs in earlier. She'd dropped the skillet into the sink with a loud clang before running out the door in a panic.

"You showed up, Tess." Silas stared right into her with those perceptive blue eyes, his voice gentle. "It doesn't matter what time. Or how. You honor Jace every day by keeping this place going, by being such a kick-ass mom. You're doing him proud."

She found herself unable to look away, pulled in by the mystery of his eyes. This was Silas. Jace's best friend. The life of every party. The man who always had a quip ready or a wild story that made everyone laugh. But she'd caught enough glimpses behind the curtain of his antics to know he was so much more. What exactly he was, she couldn't quite grasp. But there was more to him than he let most people see.

Her throat tightened and heat gathered underneath her breastbone. He made her heart beat faster; that was a truth she couldn't deny. But she didn't know if she reacted to him because she'd slept with him. Or because she was just so damn lonely most of the time. Or if maybe there were actual feelings there? God, that would be complicated. Nope. Real feelings were not an option here. He'd put That Night behind him and she had to as well.

"Um, yeah, thanks." She quickly turned away. "We should probably keep moving."

"Lead the way." His tone had gone back to normal—light and jovial, typical Silas.

She tromped on ahead of him, their boots crunching the dried-out pine needles. "So, what were you doing when I crashed your office?" Maybe going to mundane, normal lines of conversation would help her look at him as just Silas again. She used to roll her eyes at the man at least three times a day. "I hope I didn't take you away from anything too important."

"Only some putting practice," he said quickly. "Things on the construction front have been pretty slow lately."

Did she detect a hint of boredom in the words? "I thought you three put out a bunch of new bids last wee—"

A faint grunting sound cut her off. Tess halted her

steps and held up a hand to keep Silas from speaking. Her ears strained.

More grunting and snorting.

"That's a horse." She started to jog toward the noise, dodging around tree trunks and pausing to listen. "Over here!" She waved Silas past an outcropping of rocks and into a small clearing.

"Oh my God." Her stomach lurched. A palomino lay on the ground fifteen feet away, its muzzle, throat, and chest all covered in blood. "She's been shot." Tess eased closer, holding out her hands. "Easy. Easy now," she soothed.

The horse grunted and squealed, her front hooves fruitlessly scraping the ground in an effort to stand.

"All right," Tess whispered. "We're here to help you. It's all right." She knelt down next to the animal.

Silas was right beside her. "What'd you need?"

"I need to stop the bleeding, to see where it's coming from." Right now, sticky red blood seemed to cover everything, but the horse was conscious and alert. They could save her. They *had* to save her.

"Here." Silas shrugged out of his coat and then whipped off his shirt, shoving it into her hands. "I'll go get your bag." He lurched to his feet and disappeared into the trees.

Anger welled up as Tess mopped the blood from the animal's coat. She should've stayed and confronted the shooter—or shooters—earlier. She should've made sure they wouldn't get away with this. "You're going to be okay," she murmured. "We're going to make sure you're okay." She carefully moved Silas's shirt, checking for the source of the blood.

The horse still grunted and snorted but her hooves had settled.

Tess examined the throat and chest; no gunshot wound there. She moved to clean off the muzzle, but the horse jerked her head.

"That's it, isn't it?" She'd been hit somewhere on the face. "I need to take a look. I need to see." She managed to get in a few gentle swipes of the shirt while the poor animal tried to avoid her contact. "I know, sweetie. I know it hurts." Carefully, she sponged off the horse's nose and found a gunshot wound a few inches from the nostrils. Looked to be small caliber judging from the size. Tess rose to her knees, searching around the horse's ears. Yes, there was a clean exit wound about five inches below the left ear.

"Here's the bag." Silas sprinted into the clearing, sweat glistening on his muscled chest.

"I found the wound." Tess showed him where the bullet had gone in. "Looks like it narrowly missed her brain. But her sinus cavity has to be fractured. And she probably has a concussion too." She rifled through her supplies.

"Why would anyone shoot a helpless animal?" Silas petted the horse's mane. "I mean, I know some people around here think they eat up all the grasses, but still . . ."

"It's complicated." Tess found her med kit. "The wild herds are overpopulated. They don't have any predators, they live longer than most wild animals, and they each have to eat up to twenty to thirty pounds of plants a day to survive." Those were the arguments she'd heard some of the local ranchers make anyway. "None of that justifies trying to take them out though." She withdrew a syringe of flunixin. "I have to give her a shot for the pain and swelling."

Silas nodded, leaning his body over the horse to help hold her down.

"This is gonna make you feel better," Tess murmured, administering the drug as quickly as she could.

The horse strained against Silas, but he carefully held her in place, shushing and soothing her. When the horse calmed, he sat back. "What else can I do to help?"

"We need to clean the wounds and get them bandaged as best we can." She withdrew a bottle of antiseptic and gauze from her bag. "And then we'll try to get her up, see if we can get her to walk." She always kept an extra halter and lead rope in her supplies. "Here." She handed the bottle of antiseptic to Silas. "You can squirt to irrigate the wounds and I'll wipe away dirt and debris."

They worked together to clean up the damage the gunshot had left.

"I'm surprised she's not putting up more of a fight." Silas leaned over the horse while he worked, his movements and manner careful.

"I suspect the pain med is starting to kick in." Tess blotted more dried blood from the horse's nose. "That and a concussion would make her a little more subdued."

"She's beautiful." He set down the antiseptic bottle and ran his hand tenderly down her flank. "Aren't you? You're beautiful."

"They're all beautiful." Tears clouded her vision but she smiled. "We used to see them up here sometimes, Jace and I. He loved the wild horses ever since he was a little kid. His grandpa used to feed them in the winters."

"Then I'm glad we could help her." Silas picked up the bottle again and irrigated the wound below her ear. He always withdrew when any conversation turned to Jace. They all did—Thatch and Aiden too. Though her brother had made more of an effort after he'd met Kyra.

Tess couldn't imagine what it had been like for them to watch their best friend die. At least she'd been spared the trauma of seeing Jace get shot. At least her last memories of him were full of love and hugs and kisses. Tess wanted to press on, to talk more about Jace, to see Silas's smile lines erase the guilt that etched his forehead whenever Jace was mentioned.

But too much had happened between her and Silas. So she changed the subject. "There's no way to bandage her nose." The wound was in an awkward spot and a bandage could interfere with the horse eating or drinking. "So she'll need to be monitored for infection. I'll have to clean the wound regularly."

"How're we gonna get her back to the ranch?" Silas stood and surveyed the area with clear concern.

"We can't get the trailer all the way up here." The terrain was too rugged.

"If she can walk, I'll lead her back to the ranch," he offered, standing up to pull on his coat.

Tess stood too. "It's well over six miles." That'd be a long trek. "It'll probably take you a few hours."

"That's all right." He hoisted her emergency backpack onto his shoulders. "Then you can drive down and get a pen ready for her. There's no other way to get her someplace safe. And we can't leave her out here in this condition."

"If you're sure." Tess slowly slipped the halter onto the horse and attached a lead rope.

"Should we look for the bullet?" Silas scanned the ground around them.

"I don't think we'll find anything. The adrenaline likely kept her on the run for a while." And if she was going to walk, they needed to get going now, before the meds wore off. "Let's try to get her up."

Tess took ahold of the lead rope and instructed Silas to get on the opposite side of the horse. "Now just lightly nudge her a bit," she said, tugging.

With Silas's prodding, the horse shifted and staggered to her hooves, wobbling and grunting, but at least she stayed upright. "Try to stop and let her drink from the river every so often." She handed the rope over to Silas.

"Got it." He tugged on the rope, encouraging the horse to take a few steps. "That's it. You've got this."

Tess stood back and watched him work with the horse. "I think she likes you."

"I like her too." And there was the smile she'd been hoping to see, softening his mouth. Oh, that mouth. If only she didn't know how it felt to kiss him...

"In fact, I think she needs a name," Silas continued. "Then we don't have to keep calling her 'the horse.'"

"Sure." She knelt down to pack up her supplies because she shouldn't be noticing Silas's mouth. She shouldn't be feeling that tingling warmth spread through her at the memory of kissing him. Not today. Not ever. "You can choose a name."

"How about..." The man paused as though it were a big decision. "Legacy?" he finally said.

"I like it." Tess lifted her bag and they moved slowly in the direction of the UTV. "I'll meet you back at the ranch," she told him. "We can get her settled and then go to the police before I pick up Willow and Morgan from school."

"Sounds good." Silas turned Legacy to the right and started to walk away.

Another burst of longing left her breathless. "Silas,"

she called before she could stop herself. "Thanks for coming with me."

The man stopped and slowly turned, tilting his head slightly. "I'll always be there for you. I promised Jace."

"I know." And that was exactly why she couldn't have feelings for him.

CHAPTER FOUR

"Y ou're a champ, Legacy." Silas paused to offer the horse a handful of the grasses and clover he'd ripped out of the ground on their way down the mountain.

She sniffed them halfheartedly but didn't try to eat.

"Still hurting, aren't you?" He dropped the greens and started off again, continuing at the slow methodical pace they'd kept all the way down the trail. Up ahead, the ranch came into view—the three red barns and Tess's quaint log house, the miles of fencing and pens along the valley's floor where the cattle grazed on the swaying grasses.

Strange that this view gave him a sense of coming home. No place had ever felt like home to him. Not the apartments he and his mom had lived in back in California, always moving from one to the next when she couldn't pay the rent. Not the nondescript brick ranch house where he'd occasionally spent time with his grandparents when his mother wasn't fighting with them . . . which hadn't been very often.

He glanced at the horse's tired brown eyes, feeling a

weariness spread through him as well. "We're kind of the same, you and I." The ranch wasn't his home. This place could never be his home. Tess would build a new life with someone, eventually. She had this big, bold, beautiful heart that would change some guy's life. But it wouldn't be his. "We've always gotta be on the move, don't we? We can never settle down." Much like this wild horse, Silas didn't know a lot about relationships. He'd never known a father. And his mom hadn't loved him. That's why he could never love someone else. He didn't even know how.

Legacy lumbered along, her hooves dragging slightly as they descended the final hill.

"I got shot once too." He wasn't sure why he was telling a horse, other than sustaining a gunshot wound happened to be yet another thing they had in common. He'd never told anyone else, but now his whole life story was spilling out. "It happened on my first mission." Before he'd met Jace, Aiden, and Thatch. "The bullet went right through my shoulder." He'd fallen in a pool of blood and had thought he was going to die right there on the battlefield.

After saying his prayers, he'd briefly wondered if his mom would even care, and then waited for the light or whatever the hell was supposed to come for him. Next thing he knew, a medic was dragging him through the sand. "It hurts like a son of a bitch, I know." The blast through his flesh had seared his body with a burning pain he'd never forget. "But it'll heal. Over time. And you'll—"

"You made it!" Tess came charging over the crest of the hill on Dreamer's back, her hair flying in the wind. "How'd it go? How'd Legacy do?" She halted Dreamer and dismounted. "I mean, it's a good sign she was able to walk that distance. Has she seemed okay?"

"She's been a trooper." He ran his hand up and down Legacy's muzzle. The key to forgetting sex with Tess was to never look directly into the woman's eyes. Or to stand too close to her. Or to touch her in any way, shape, or form. One touch and he'd be a goner. "She even stopped to drink a few times. Though I haven't been able to get her to eat anything."

"We'll work on that." Tess slipped her hands beneath the horse's chin groove and slightly lifted Legacy's head to inspect the gunshot wound in her nose. "Still looks pretty clean. But we should flush it out a few times a day so there's no bacteria buildup."

"I can help out." He and Legacy did have a bond, after all. Now the horse knew his secret. And he knew how it felt to be displaced the way she would have to be for a while.

"That would be great. I could use the help with her." Tess took Dreamer by the bridle and they walked in the direction of the lower pastures. "I've got the large pen at the edge of the meadow all cleared out for her. I figure she needs some space. She's not too used to fences and I don't want her to feel too confined."

"Good." He tried to think of something else to say but being with Tess alone made it hard to think at all. "How long do you think we'll have to keep her penned up?" That wasn't a totally ridiculous question.

"It depends." Tess didn't seem to be her usual talkative self either.

"I guess until I'm confident there won't be an infection," she said after a pause. "When she's in the clear, we can transport her back to the high meadow." Her tone was all business, not soft and husky like it had been when she'd asked him to take her upstairs to his hotel room at the party. "Hopefully she'll be able to rejoin her herd."

They reached the fence and Tess pulled open the gate. "In you go."

Silas unhooked the lead rope and prodded the hesitant horse into the pen.

Legacy stood straighter, seeming to take in her surroundings. She ambled to the fence and then trotted the whole perimeter of the pen as though searching for a way out.

"It's only temporary." He caught up to the horse and patted her flank. "We need to watch out for you. This is the best way."

"I'm going to give her some more meds." Tess hurried to a UTV that was parked near the pen. "Hopefully we can keep her calm enough. I don't want her getting too agitated with a potential concussion."

Silas faced the horse and petted her muzzle while Tess administered a few more shots. "That's it. All done."

"Told you she's a trooper." The horse had hardly flinched, even with all of those needles.

The woman eyed him, her expression unreadable. "She seems to really respond to you."

"I have a way with women." He'd meant it as a joke but Tess instantly turned away from him and cleared her throat. "Um...I'm sure you're starving. I made some sandwiches. They're in the house."

Yeah, he couldn't go into her house. He couldn't seem to say the right things around her. The last thing he wanted was to make her uncomfortable.

He should've thought of that before he slept with her.

Tess glanced at him over her shoulder, waiting for an answer.

"That's all right. I'm not hungry," he lied. "I should get back to the office anyway, check in with Aiden." Thatch was probably back by now too. Maybe they actually had some work to do. "We had a bunch of bids we were supposed to hear back on today, so I'd better catch up and get some work done."

"Oh." Tess stopped to wait for him. "Okay. If you're sure." She opened the gate that led to the driveway. "But you're coming to the police station with me, right?"

"Yeah." He couldn't back out on his promise to help her now. "We can head over there after I stop by the office. Come and get me when you're ready to go."

"Sounds good." They parted ways and Tess veered off to jog up the steps to her porch.

Easing out a long sigh, Silas turned left and pushed through the Cowboy Construction doors. Both Aiden and Thatch were there but neither one of them appeared to be actually working.

"We were wondering where you were." Thatch aimed a dart at the board on the other side of the room. He was always working on his aim. Usually to no avail.

"Tess had a situation." Silas went directly to his desk and told them about what had happened in the high meadow.

"Why'd she ride up there today?" Aiden stood in front of the sink at the minibar washing out a mug. "She usually goes on the weekends."

Silas almost wished he hadn't known why she'd been to the high meadow this morning. His throat got all tight and achy. "She was up there visiting the memorial. It's May 12."

"Shit. I completely forgot." Aiden dried the mug and set it on the shelf above the coffeepot.

"Me too." Thatch tossed another dart, narrowly missing the board. And that was why he could never beat Silas.

Silas never missed.

"I didn't realize the date until she told me." All of the days had started to run together in his head ever since Tess had turned his world upside down. He found himself thinking about her when he was supposed to be working. He found himself thinking about her when he was trying to fall asleep. And, yes, he was thinking about her right now while he was talking to her brother.

"How'd she seem?" Aiden sat at his desk but didn't open his laptop.

Silas shrugged. "She felt bad because she forgot it was their anniversary until she heard the date on the news." Was that really why Tess had felt bad about spacing on the date, or did her guilt have more to do with what had happened between them?

"Man. I remember when she'd start shutting down weeks before her anniversary." Aiden balled up some of the papers that had been sitting on his desk for the better part of two weeks and tossed them into the trash can. "But it's good she forgot. That means she's moving on."

Thatch plucked the darts out of the board. "Yeah, she's seemed different these last few weeks."

"Different?" Silas's head shot up. "What'd you mean?" Were they messing with him? Did they know? Surely they didn't know about him and Tess.

"I don't know..." Thatch gave him a funny look. "She seems to be smiling more, I guess. I've even heard her humming a few times. I guess she seems a little happier than she used to be."

"Yeah," Aiden agreed. "It's like she's letting go a little bit."

In Silas's estimation, Tess didn't seem thrilled about letting go of Jace. She'd seemed sad. But he didn't want to talk about Tess anymore. He couldn't risk Aiden and

Thatch seeing through him. "So have we heard back on any of the bids we put out last week?"

"Not yet." Thatch had resumed his dart throwing, clearly not concerned about work at all.

"Well, why aren't you staying on top of them?" he demanded, looking back and forth between his friends. "Check in, see if we're getting the job. We can't just hang out playing darts all the time."

"I've checked in." Aiden looked up from cleaning out his desk drawer. "You know how our business works. Sometimes there're a ton of jobs and sometimes we're waiting on jobs. That's how it's always been. What's your problem anyway?"

"Nothing." Nothing they could help him with. He needed work to keep him busy, that was all. To keep his mind off Tess.

"You've been an ass for weeks now." Aiden pointed at him. "Come to think of it, you've been an ass ever since my engagement party."

"What're you talking about? No, I haven't." He looked to Thatch for backup, but their friend nodded along.

"Yeah. You have seemed a little distracted," Thatch said. "What happened that night? I know you hooked up with someone. What's the problem? Now she won't call you back or something?"

"No!" He shot to his feet. "Why would you think I'd hook up with someone?" How the hell did these two know?

"For one thing, you disappeared and no one saw you until noon the next day."

Yeah, Silas hadn't felt like going back to the party after Tess had left his room.

Aiden's eyes narrowed. "And for another...because you're *you* and you hook up with women all the time."

Right. But this time had been different. This time the woman had been Tess.

"Also, I heard you talking to someone in your hotel room after I got back to mine." Thatch shot him a triumphant grin. "So you can't deny it."

Silas shook his head and opened up his email before they could continue their interrogation. Aiden and Thatch knew him better than anyone else. Sometimes even better than himself.

"If it's not a woman, what the hell is wrong with you?" Aiden got out of his chair and stood directly in front of Silas's desk. "And don't bother saying 'nothing' again. You can't lie to us."

"You could try but we'd know," Thatch added.

They'd never leave him alone unless he gave them something. So he went with the decoy. "I guess I've been thinking a lot, that's all."

"Thinking." Thatch sent another dart flying, this time hitting the bull's-eye.

"Yeah." Silas came around and sat on the edge of his desk next to Aiden. He'd have to tread lightly here. He knew Aiden and Thatch as well as they knew him. They weren't going to like him going on a mission like this without them. "Don't you guys miss having a higher purpose? I mean, we hardly have anything to do around the ranch anymore and our construction business is in kind of a lull at the moment."

"You mean do I miss dodging bullets in deserts?" Aiden gave a disgusted shake of his head. "No. Actually, I'm pretty grateful to be here in one piece." His weighted tone reminded Silas that not all of them had come back.

As if he could ever forget they'd had to leave Jace behind.

"Is this about money?" Thatch sent another dart flying at the board, but this one missed the mark and put another hole in the drywall. "Because we can do some advertising to bring in more business. I have contacts in Jackson..."

"It's not about money." Silas paced to the putting green and ripped a putter out of the stand. They all got plenty in retirement and hardly spent anything living around here. His investments would be enough to keep him comfortable for the long term. "I'm talking about having a focus." A focus he hadn't seemed to get back since that night with Tess. He'd been restless, torn, guilt-ridden, but that hadn't stopped him from thinking about her... from *wanting* her.

"You want a focus?" Aiden walked back to his desk and sat in the chair. "Maybe you should try sticking with the same woman longer than one night. Trust me. Your whole perspective changes when you make a commitment."

Silas shared a look with Thatch. With his newfound happiness, Aiden had recently become a regular relationship guru.

"I'm serious, you two." He went on wisely. "Sharing your life with someone does give you a higher purpose."

"This from the man who once snuck out a woman's window while she was getting ice cream from the freezer." Silas couldn't resist. He was happy for Aiden and Kyra, but one successful relationship didn't mean the man suddenly knew everything.

"Hey, I'm the first one to admit I wasn't always into commitment. But everything changes when you meet the right person."

Thatch made a gagging noise.

His thoughts exactly.

Aiden ignored them. "Maybe this woman who has you

all messed up *is* the right person." He shot Silas a know-ing glare. "She obviously got to you."

Damn. And they were right back on the road to Tess.

"Who is she anyway?" Thatch pestered. "Someone you met at the party?"

"There's no woman." No woman he could tell them about anyway. Aiden would lose his shit if he realized Silas had been anywhere near Tess. Thatch would get all annoying and probably remind him he had no business hooking up with their dead best friend's wife. "I just... feel like I need more. More challenges. More opportuni-ties." More distractions.

"Why don't you go on vacation?" Aiden suggested. "Take a few weeks off in some exotic place. Go deep-sea diving, cliff jumping, whatever you need to do to get your adrenaline rush, and then come back?"

"Maybe," Silas mumbled. But unfortunately, he couldn't leave tomorrow. Not when Tess was counting on him to help with Legacy.

CHAPTER FIVE

Tess stood behind the curtain in the living room and peeked out the window. She wasn't spying, exactly. More like...watching the Cowboy Construction office door to see if Silas had changed his mind about the sandwiches. Seriously. She'd invited the man inside her house *for food* and he'd turned her down.

Ugh. Would things ever go back to normal between them? She moved the curtain into place again and walked into the kitchen where a platter of beautiful roast beef and Asiago sandwiches still sat, untouched. It used to be that she and Silas could joke around. Some might have even called the banter between them flirting, though it had always been harmless. But now...she kept overanalyzing everything. Was he upset with her? Annoyed? Did he feel like they'd betrayed Jace too?

The front door opened, and her heart stuttered to a stop.

Aiden cruised into her house with a breezy hello. "Oh, sandwiches. Yum." He sauntered to the kitchen island and helped himself to three. "I'm starving. Keep forgetting to stock the office refrigerator."

"Glad I could help." Tess pulled two glasses out of the cabinet and poured them each some iced tea. So, the cowboys didn't have any food in their fridge and yet Silas still wouldn't come in here and have a late lunch with her...

"Hey, I'm sorry I didn't come by this morning," Aiden said around a mouthful of sandwich. "I didn't realize today was the twelfth. I should've remembered."

With all he had going on—and a new engagement—it wasn't surprising he hadn't. "It's fine. I don't expect everyone to swarm over here the second they wake up in the morning." A year ago, Aiden had been on her doorstep first thing. He'd made her coffee and had seen her off on her ride. But this year...everything was so different. *He* was different. She was different too. And she wasn't sure what grief was supposed to look like two years out. After Jace had passed away, her heart had gone dark, along with all of her sensual desires. And then the wrong man had woken them both.

Her brother stopped eating and set his sandwich on the paper towel. "It's okay you forgot the date, Sis. You know that, don't you?"

It didn't feel okay. She didn't feel okay about forgetting at all. "What else am I going to forget?" That's what really haunted her. "Will I forget the sound of his laugh? Will I forget how he'd look at me first thing in the morning, when his eyes were all droopy and sleepy and he had a lazy smile on his lips?" Would the countless memories of the moments they'd shared all start to fade with time? She closed her eyes, trying to see her husband's face. "I don't want to forget."

When she opened her eyes, Aiden looked at her sadly, the corners of his mouth drooping with empathy. "You won't forget the best parts of Jace because those things are part of you. They're part of your story, Tess. And no one forgets the best parts of their story."

"Today, when I realized I'd forgotten our anniversary, I felt like I was losing him again." She put her hand over her mouth to hold in a sob. She'd just started to feel like she was making real progress—that she was not only living but also *enjoying* life again—and then this reality she'd never asked for came barreling into her again and knocked her backward.

"Maybe you shouldn't look at it like you forgot," her brother suggested. "Maybe you should think of this as a sign that you're ready to add a new chapter to your story. Jace would want you to add new chapters. You know that as well as I do."

"Wow." Tess raised her eyebrows at the sudden role reversal. What happened to her being the one who always got to impart the wisdom? "Kyra is really rubbing off on you, huh?"

"I just never knew." Her brother's eyes were positively shiny with the light of new love. "I never understood how someone—the *right* someone—could make me want to be better, to be healthier and stronger and more understanding and more perceptive so I can give her the best of myself. She's it for me."

Based on that speech, Tess would agree. "And you're it for her." And in the fall, they would get married and build a beautiful new life together. Tears built in her eyes. Happy tears, sad tears. Tears of longing. Tears of heartache over what she'd lost. Her emotions hadn't been cut and dry since Jace had died. They'd all blurred together. "You know when you've found the right person. That's for sure." She'd known with Jace even though she'd only been sixteen years old.

"That's exactly what I was trying to tell Silas." Aiden went back to eating his sandwich. "That being with the right person can give you a higher sense of purpose."

At the mention of Silas's name, Tess stood up. "Really?" She could feel her face flushing—the heat, the mad rush of blood—so she turned to the sink to wash the dishes. "You and Silas were talking about relationships?" Damn it, her voice went too high. She had to be cool.

"Yep. He's acting weird."

A glass bowl nearly slipped out of her hands. "Oh. Really?" She fumbled with the dish, finally setting it down on the drying rack.

"We know he hooked up with a woman at the party and now she won't call him back or something." Irritation flickered in his tone.

Tess eased out a slow, controlled breath before answering. Unfortunately, she was working on the last plate in the sink and then she'd have no reason to continue hiding her face from him. "Why, um ... why would you think that?"

"Thatch heard someone in Silas's hotel room."

She fumbled with the plate. Thatch had *heard* them? Oh God. She should've been quieter! "That's strange," she squeaked.

"Not really," her brother argued. "This is Silas we're talking about."

Right. It probably wasn't strange at all for Silas to hook up with a random woman he met at a party. But in those few hours it had felt like more than sex. At least to her.

"He's been moody as hell lately," Aiden went on. "And then just now in the office he was talking about needing to get away for a while."

She spun, still holding the dripping plate. "Silas is leaving?"

"I don't know." He sipped on iced tea, looking all calm and collected while her heart was doing triple flips.

"I told him to go on a vacation," her brother said. "Have a little fun, take a break, and get whatever this is out of his system."

Tess turned back around and dried the plate. Did Silas really want to leave Star Valley? Was it because of her? She found the courage to face her brother again. "So you really think he's upset over a woman?"

He shrugged. "It's only a theory. But he did get pretty defensive when we brought it up." His eyes widened. "Did you see him spending time with a woman that night?"

"No!" Oops. She tried to rein in her tone. "I mean, I had to step out early too." Pure panic flowed through her veins now. "I had to call the girls before they went to sleep."

"Ah." Her brother nodded as though that made sense. "Well, I don't know who this woman could be. Think it's any of your friends who were there?"

"Nope." The denial ended in a burning cough. Her throat might as well have been smoking. "Uh-uh. I haven't heard anything about anyone hooking up with Silas." She happened to be the worst liar on the planet. One direct look at her right now and Aiden would know.

"Maybe it's Lyric," her brother mused.

She almost agreed but she couldn't sell her friend out like that. "I know for a fact it's not Lyric. We talk. She would've mentioned something to me." The woman was one of her best friends in Star Valley Springs.

"Well..." Aiden stood and threw the paper towel in the trash. "Whoever she is, this woman has clearly messed with our boy's head."

Had she? Had That Night messed with Silas as much as it had messed with her? Because he seemed pretty unaffected, in her opinion. Tess rushed to the refrigerator and started to rearrange things so she could cool off her face. "He didn't say anything about hooking up with a woman. Or having feelings for someone. Right?" She had to make sure.

"No. He tried to deny hooking up with anyone but we know better." Aiden grinned. "Hey, speak of the devil. Silas is headed this way."

"What?" Tess dropped a can of pop, which split open and started to spray everywhere. "Oh no!"

"Here." Aiden came to the rescue with some paper towels and nudged her aside. "You okay, Sis? You seem a little off too."

"I'm great! I'm—"

The front door creaked open and Silas stepped inside, then hesitated at the threshold. "Hey. I was gonna head out soon. Wanted to see if you were still planning to go to the police station."

"Yep! Sure am!" Tess was all too aware that the words had come out overly loud, but she couldn't seem to regulate her volume or her tone today. "We should go right now, as a matter of fact. I'll drive."

The man studied her cautiously. "I could just meet you there..."

"It's no big deal! We can ride together." She swept past

Aiden and grabbed her purse off the kitchen table. They had to prove to her brother that things were completely normal between them, that they could ride in a car together with no problem so he didn't suspect that she was Silas's mystery woman.

Or maybe she wanted to prove things were normal to herself. "No use in both of us wasting gas." And they needed to discuss a diversion strategy so no one found out their secret. She traipsed past Silas and out the door, leaving him to follow behind.

He paused at her truck. "You sure you don't want me to drive too?"

"I'm sure." She watched Aiden walk down her porch steps and wave. "This way we can talk about our strategy . . . with the *police*," she said loud enough for her brother to hear.

"Ooookay." Silas got into her passenger seat.

Tess kept a smile pasted on her face until after they'd cleared the driveway and her brother could no longer see them. "Aiden thinks you hooked up with a woman at his engagement party," she blurted. Oh God. They were going to find out. Everyone was going to find out about her and Silas and then they would all judge her for sleeping with her husband's best friend. Tess peeled out onto the highway. "No one can know we were together that night." Then nothing would ever go back to normal.

"Yeah. I realize that." Silas continued to stare out the windshield and she couldn't see his eyes behind his aviator shades. "Your brother would probably shoot me. And like you said, it was a *mistake*."

His voice dulled on that last sentence, but his unreadable expression didn't change. His face might as well have been carved in stone.

"Maybe Thatch already knew it was me." She tried to focus on the road. "Maybe he recognized my voice and he'll slip and tell someone."

"Don't worry about it. I'll take care of Aiden and Thatch. They're not going to find out." How could he be so calm? Not one inflection in his voice. "So what're you gonna tell the police?"

Tess wanted to ask how he planned to keep Aiden from finding out about That Night, but he clearly wanted to change the subject, so she let it go. "I'm going to tell them someone shot a wild horse on my property and they'd better get their butts up there and figure out who before I do."

Silas finally turned to face her, his electrifying grin stretching across his lips.

Warmth crept up her neck. "What?"

"That's what I love about you, Tess." She could feel his stare, even through the dark lenses of his glasses. "You're not afraid to tell it like it is."

Loved. He could've said *like*. She told people things she *liked* about them all the time. But he'd said loved. And he was wrong about her. She *was* afraid. Especially when her heart beat in this dangerous rhythm whenever she was close to him.

"I'm not kidding. If the police won't do something about this, I will." She had to keep the conversation focused on the horses. Not on the things they loved about each other.

Wait. *Were* there things she loved about him? The answer hit her much too quickly. His unyielding loyalty. His dedication to the things he cared about most. His smile. Definitely his smile. *Oh God.*

"Easy there, Maverick." Silas faced forward again.

"You're not doing anything alone. I said I'll help and I will. So we'll take on those assholes together."

Tess reached forward to turn on the air conditioning. Sure, it was only fifty-five degrees outside, but her body temperature kept rising. "Aiden said you're thinking of going away? Taking a vacation?"

Silas didn't look at her, but she noticed a reaction in his posture, a straightening of his spine. "I don't know. Maybe. But I won't go anywhere until these horse bullies are brought to justice. I promise."

They rolled down Main Street and Tess slowed the truck, her gaze searching for an open parking spot in front of the police station. "Well, where do you think you'll go if you take a vacation?" And how long would he be gone? She shouldn't wonder. She shouldn't care...

"Don't know." His shoulders still seemed rigid. "I've never been good at taking vacations. I can spend about three hours on a beach before I start getting restless. I like to be busy, on the move. I like to work."

"I used to feel the same way." Tess parked along the curb. "But that was before my daily life felt like so much work." Before having kids. Before becoming a single mom. While it was her favorite job ever, raising kids was intense and exhausting sometimes. Full of blessings but also stress and fear. Especially doing it on her own. "Nowadays? I could use a week at the beach." She laughed... not that she'd been joking.

"Then you should go." Silas unclicked his seat belt and got out of the truck, waiting for her to join him on the sidewalk outside the police station. "Why not? You have a whole army of people who'd take the girls. Go do something for yourself."

Why? Did he want her to leave? He wasn't smiling as much as he used to in her presence. And he hadn't tried to make her laugh all day. Everything was different now. So messed up. "Yeah, maybe I will go away somewhere." She could use a vacation from him right about now. "Anyway, let me do the talking in here." She soldiered on to the door but Silas hurried to open it for her before she got there.

"I wouldn't dream of talking for you, Tess." He followed her inside. "I know better."

Before she could ask him what that was supposed to mean, Terry Gladstone, the receptionist, came around the desk to greet them. "Tess! I haven't seen you in forever. How are those girls of yours?"

She hugged the older woman. "They're doing really well, thanks." The blessing of being able to say that was never lost on her. For all the girls had been through, they were resilient and thriving. And much of their recovery after losing their dad had to do with this community they were a part of. "Is Chief Holbrook around by any chance?" While she loved Terry, she didn't want to get into one of their half hour–long chat sessions right now.

"Sure. You can go on back." The woman moved from her to Silas. "Do I get a hug from my favorite SEAL too?"

"Come on, Terry. We all know I'm not your favorite," the man teased. "I heard you made a batch of your oatmeal raisin cookies for Thatch last week."

"Yours are coming, sugar," Terry said with a wink. "And I'll add in some chocolate chips to *prove* you're my favorite."

Oh please. Tess openly rolled her eyes. Silas had all the older women in town eating out of the palm of his hand.

He was too much of a charmer for his own good. Or for her own good. She should remember that.

Leaving him behind, she walked down the short hallway to Natalie's office, shaking her head the whole time. Tess paused outside the half-open door and knocked.

Natalie lifted her gaze away from her laptop screen. She was young for a police chief—barely thirty—but Tess had always respected the woman. She had a unique blend of compassion and badassery. No one ever wanted to mess with Chief Holbrook, but people also often came to her for advice.

"Hey, come on in." She gestured for Tess to sit in the chair on the other side of the desk. "What can I do for you?"

"We've got a wild horse with a gunshot wound at the ranch right now." No point in beating around the bush. She was on a mission here. "I was out for a ride in the high meadow when I heard gunshots coming from the west." She sat on the edge of the chair while Silas came to stand behind her. "Then the horses flooded my property. Dreamer spooked so I had to ride home. When Silas and I went back up to check on the herd later, we found a young mare with a hole through her nose and head."

"But she survived?" Concern gathered at the corners of the chief's wide blue eyes.

"Yes. But the bullet narrowly missed her brain." And now the horse was suffering, scared, confused, and without her herd. And Tess had to foot the bill to take care of her.

"Did you see the perpetrators?" Natalie refocused on her computer screen, clicking around, likely starting a new report.

"No." If only Tess could've gotten a look at the UTV they were driving. Then they might have something to go on. "When we got back up there, whoever had been firing was gone."

Natalie nodded, her lips tight. "Well . . . I can take a ride up there later and alert the Bureau of Land Management."

"In other words, you can't do much." Tess had expected to hear that, but disappointment still weighted her heart. She knew Natalie didn't have the manpower or resources to patrol the public lands and open spaces around here. That wasn't even necessarily her job. "There has to be something we can do."

The woman sighed and smoothed some of her dark hair back toward the neat bun sitting on top of her head. "If you give me some coordinates, I'll look around for evidence, but you know as well as I do that an investigation isn't going to go anywhere. I mean, the shooters could've been from anywhere. People come all the way up from Jackson to ride the trails around here."

"All due respect, Chief . . ." Silas stepped forward. "Random tourists aren't going to shoot a horse for no reason."

Yes! Tess shot him a look of appreciation. "You've heard the talk around here lately, same as I have. Some of the ranchers are fed up with the wild herds. They think they're doing too much damage."

"Listen, I get it." Natalie leaned back in her chair. "This is awful. I hate it every bit as much as you do. Trust me." Tess knew the woman loved horses and had a whole stable full of her own. "But we don't have the manpower to spend time tracking these guys down. I can put out the word to the county and to the Bureau of Land Management and ask for more surveillance, more flyovers, maybe . . ."

Which they wouldn't do. The county was too cheap to follow up on one horse getting shot.

"And I can keep my ears and eyes open too. If someone around here did this, they'll talk to the wrong person eventually. And we'll find them."

But probably not before they injured or killed more of the horses. "Fine." Tess rose from the chair. "I understand." She understood she would have to take matters into her own hands, after all. "Thanks for your time."

"You bet." Natalie walked them to the door. "I really will look into this. I'll do my best."

"So will I," Tess assured her before saying goodbye.

After another quick exchange with Terry, she and Silas stepped out onto the sidewalk.

"So what's the plan?" He caught her in a knowing gaze.

"Well...first we need to go pick up the girls at school. They had a special art class but it'll be over soon. Do you mind?" Tess climbed into the driver's seat.

"Uh, I don't know." Silas slid into the passenger side. "Maybe that's not a good idea. Me going with you to pick up the girls."

No. Oh no. He was not going to do this—back out of their friendship now. A month ago, he wouldn't have thought twice about picking up the girls with her. "Why not?" She had an inkling about where his hesitation was coming from, but she wanted to hear him say it.

"Because." His shoulders slumped. "You said it yourself. People might start to speculate. We're not acting normal around each other. I'm trying but..."

"But what?" She started to lean toward him but that was as close as she dared get.

"I don't want things to get complicated, that's all."

No surprise there. This was Silas, after all. He liked his hookups quick and straightforward. No strings attached. He probably didn't have to see most of the women he slept with ever again. "Things don't have to be complicated." What, did he think she had some expectation that he'd actually settle down with her or something? That was laughable. "I still need my friends, Silas. That hasn't changed because I slept with you. We both want things to go back to normal." And that would only happen if they could power through this awkward phase and get to the point where they could hang out the way they used to.

"All right. I'll pick up the girls with you." He clicked in his seat belt. "Normal, here we come."

CHAPTER SIX

Tess started the engine of her truck wearing the same determined expression Silas had come to recognize over the last year whenever she'd faced an obstacle or a difficult client at the ranch. Yes, she wanted to take on whoever had shot Legacy, but she seemed just as driven to make everything go back to the way it had been before they'd ended up in bed together.

Only he didn't know if that was possible.

"We'll have a town meeting." She slipped on her sunglasses and gave him a no-nonsense glance.

In the two years he'd lived in Star Valley immediately following Jace's death, Tess's facial expressions and her mannerisms had embodied the marks of grief in between fleeting and rare smiles. But these days...he wasn't sure he'd ever seen such strength in her.

"Great idea." He would do his part. He would agree with her. He would support her cause. Outwardly, he would do everything he could to play the role she wanted him to

play. *Friend.* Even if he spent every minute in her presence internally tortured by desires he didn't want. "We
could call a meeting at the café," he suggested, trying to
distract himself from how her lips had pursed the way
they did when she was deep in thought. He shouldn't want
to kiss those lips. "Louie and Minnie would be happy to
help." The owners of the finest eatery in Star Valley would
be all over a cause like this.

"Yes! Good thinking." She pulled the truck out of the
parking spot and flipped a U-turn. "We'll talk with everyone in town about the wild horses, about how important it
is to protect them, and then we'll try to gauge who in the
crowd is opposed to having them around."

"Exactly." They could bait the people who had a vendetta against the wild herd into showing themselves. "And
at the very least, we can inform everyone about what happened to Legacy and maybe even start our own patrols."
Hell, he wouldn't mind riding up to the high meadow
a few times a week to watch out for the horses. Aiden
and Thatch would be on board too. "The police and the
Bureau might not have the time to keep an eye on things
but that doesn't mean we can't."

"I love that idea." Tess's dark eyes were alight with the
possibilities. "The more people we can get involved, the
better."

He couldn't agree more.

She paused at the stop sign a few blocks from the elementary school. "If you don't mind, I want to keep this
quiet in front of the girls. I mean, I don't want them to
know Legacy got shot. It would scare them."

Because of their dad. Because they knew Jace had been
shot. The realization delivered a blow to his chest. To his

heart. "No. I would never say anything." And that was why he had to be a part of this fight. He had to protect all of them—Tess and Morgan and Willow. As long as there were unknown assailants wielding guns around here, he wouldn't let them go near that high meadow alone.

"They'll obviously find out Legacy is injured." Tess's mouth pulled into a grim line. "But I don't want them to know there were people with guns up there. We can tell them she got hurt running away from someone who was trying to catch her."

He nodded, physically unable to say a damn word. As much as they'd all recovered, as tough and resilient as they'd all been, the trauma of their loss would always be hidden beneath the surface. For all of them. Him included.

Tess turned the truck into the elementary school pickup lane and wound around to the front of the school. The girls marched out, Willow skipping and Morgan trudging along behind her. The younger girl made it to the truck first and climbed into the back seat of the extended cab. "Hi, Mommy! And Silas. What're you doing here?"

"I was helping your mom with something," he said as Morgan climbed in through the other door. Keeping his tone light and "normal" proved to be a challenge. "How was your day?"

"My day was great! I drew a picture of a butterfly in art class." Willow proudly held up a colorful rendition of a butterfly sitting on a flower.

"Wow." Silas turned around fully and inspected the artwork. "I didn't know you were a professional artist."

The girl shot him a toothy grin.

"Well, I had a terrible day," Morgan announced, heaving a dramatic sigh as she slammed her backpack to the floor.

Uh-oh. That didn't sound good. He'd spent a lot of time with Morgan and Willow over the last three years but his specialty was spinning them around or playing tag or admiring their drawings or making them laugh with goofy faces. He wasn't exactly skilled at talking them through drama. So, he did an about-face and let Tess take that one.

"What happened?" The woman slipped the gear into park and looked at her daughter over the seat, giving Morgan her full attention.

"Callie Kline is what happened," Morgan mumbled. "I wanted to play four square with the other girls at recess and she wouldn't let me. She said I sucked at four square. Right in front of everyone!"

Sounded to Silas like Callie Kline sucked at four square and was trying to make herself feel better. But he'd best let Tess handle this.

"Did you tell the teacher?" she calmly asked.

"No." The girl crossed her arms over her chest stubbornly. "I spit on her shoes."

"What?" Tess raised her voice. "Morgan Joy Valdez, what on earth were you thinking? You actually *spit* on her shoes?"

"She was being mean to me!" The words dissolved into tears. "She humiliated me in front of everyone! They were all laughing at me."

Silas didn't blame the girl for spitting on the bully's shoes, but he kept his mouth shut.

"And that gives you the right to *retaliate*? To *spit* on her shoes?" Tess covered her face with her hands. "Oh my God. I have to go in and talk to the principal. Right now."

"She deserved it!" Morgan wailed. "It's not my fault!

I shouldn't be the one to get in trouble for the bad thing she did."

From his side mirror, Silas watched Willow stick her fingers in her ears like she couldn't stand the sound of her sister crying.

He would've liked to have joined her.

Tess sighed, her eyes suddenly appearing weary. "Do you mind sitting with them while I go in there?"

"Oh. Uh. Okay." Silas peeked over his shoulder. Morgan was all-out sobbing now. What the hell was he supposed to do? This went way above his pay grade.

"Thanks." Tess gathered up her purse and hopped out of the truck. "This shouldn't take too long."

"No worries." He briefly wondered if a goofy face would help to improve the situation. But Morgan was currently too busy crying to notice anything he might do.

Willow unfastened her seat belt and leaned her head over the seat to whisper in his ear. "You should say something to her. Make her feel better."

"Right." Yes. That is what any normal, good person would do. The problem was he had exactly zero experience in the nurturing category. He hadn't been around kids a whole lot. No siblings, no family gatherings with cousins. And he'd gone straight into the military after school. The Navy had trained him for many scenarios but comforting a preteen girl wasn't one of them.

The younger girl nudged his shoulder and stared at him with wide eyes.

Okay. He could do this. He tried to think what Jace might've said to his daughter in this moment but came up short. His late friend had always known what to say to his girls. He'd been the perfect father—involved, protective, wise, patient. In comparison, Silas didn't have any clue what these kids needed. "Hey. It'll be okay. You'll see." He angled his body so he could smile at Morgan. "It sounds like this girl is a real bully. You should ignore her."

"*Ignore* her?" Morgan shrieked.

"Uh-oh," Willow muttered under her breath right before she stuck her fingers back in her ears.

"How can I ignore her when she's like the most popular girl in our whole grade?" Morgan rubbed her eyes and started whimpering again. "Everyone thinks she's so great. They all do whatever she says. Now no one is ever going to play with me again!"

"That's not true." He rubbed his face. Where was Aiden when he needed him? Their uncle used to be as clueless as him when it came to kids but he'd made strides over the last few years. Silas had clearly not. "You're a great person, Morgan."

"Then why doesn't Callie like me?" the girl demanded. "If I'm so great, why won't she let me play four square?"

"Because she's jealous of you?" he suggested. "Maybe she's afraid you'll beat her."

"Yeah!" Willow agreed, giving him a nod of approval. "She's just jealous."

Phew. Silas refrained from wiping sweat off his brow.

"What would you have done if someone was mean to you like Callie was mean to me?" A stray tear rolled down Morgan's cheek.

Back when he'd been in school, Silas had gotten into plenty of fights defending himself against the bullies that made fun of his off-brand clothes and shoes. And he'd done way worse than spit on their shoes. But Tess would likely frown on him sharing those stories. "Um...well...

I probably would've been really mad too," he acknowledged. "And maybe I would've even spit on her shoes." Or more likely he would've pushed the kid and ended up in the principal's office. "But then I would've realized I don't want to be a bully like her so maybe I would've apologized." Not back then for sure. But he might now. Rising above seemed like the right thing to do.

"That's stupid." Morgan turned her head to stare out the window. "I don't know why I asked you anyway. You don't understand."

Ouch. "Maybe you're right." He turned around to look out the windshield. Oh thank God. Tess was hurrying out of the school building.

"Sorry that took so long." She broke the awkward silence when she slid into the driver's seat.

"No problem." He made sure not to look in Morgan's direction, lest he piss her off again.

But Tess had an uncanny intuition. She looked back at Morgan and then at him again, squinting slightly. "Everything okay in here?"

"Yep." He checked his phone as a means of avoiding her gaze.

Morgan only sighed.

"Ooookay." Tess started up the engine. "Principal Howell was very understanding, Morgan. But we agreed that you and Callie might benefit from spending some time together."

"No!" The girl started to cry again. "I am *not* going to spend time with her."

That was actually pretty brilliant. With the rest of the kids out of the equation, the girls might actually get along. But he'd best stay quiet. Silas continued scrolling aimlessly through his phone.

Tess didn't even flinch at her daughter's reaction. "Yes, you are going to spend time with her. In fact, we're going to invite her and her father over for a playdate soon. You know that Callie has been through a lot this year, don't you?"

"I know her mom left and got divorced from her dad," Morgan mumbled. "But that's not my fault."

"No. It's not your fault. But we can be compassionate and understanding regarding her situation. She's really struggling. Maybe she needs some kindness." Tess glanced at Silas and nodded as though asking him to agree with her.

Did he have to? He'd already gotten himself into enough trouble with Morgan. "Maybe she needs a friend," he said after hesitating.

The girl answered with a frustrated grunt and then she put on a pair of headphones.

"What happened while I was gone?" Tess whispered.

"Silas tried to talk to Morgan," Willow informed her. "It didn't go well."

"Yeah. Sorry." He shoved his phone back into his pocket. "I did my best but apparently I know nothing."

Tess laughed. "Welcome to parenting."

CHAPTER SEVEN

Silas steered his truck down the ranch's winding driveway and continued past the Cowboy Construction office, past Tess's house, and all the way to the large corral at the edge of the woods.

The early morning sun beat down, warm enough to heat the air, bringing clouds of steam effervescing off the frost-laden grasses. Beyond the trees, the mountains rose up with their sharp angles and snow-encrusted crevasses, appearing almost purple in the pastel hues of the morning light.

Even after he cut the engine, he sat there for a few minutes, sipping his coffee from a travel mug, taking the time to really see the vista he'd come to take for granted. He wouldn't get views like this every morning if he went back to the Middle East. That was for sure. There he would see dust and sand and the white-hot sun. Instead of teeming with color like the Wind River Range, the mountains over there were barren and brown. Desolate.

But what did views matter when he'd be doing something important with his life? The views had never bothered him before, and he wouldn't get all sentimental now. Silas climbed out of his truck and pulled on a sweatshirt.

Inside the corral a few feet away, Legacy paced restlessly along the perimeter of the fence that ran closest to the woods. So close to what she wanted—freedom and the companionship of her herd—yet she was stuck. He could relate to seeing what you wanted—what you craved—right in front of you and not being able to do a damn thing about it.

After grabbing the bag of carrots off the front seat, he slammed the door shut and approached the gate, giving the horse a few extra seconds to size him up before he went into the pen. "Hey, Legacy." He kept his distance, giving her space but held a few of the carrots out flat on his palm. "You hungry?" Tess had texted him last night to tell him that the painkillers seemed to be working because the horse had managed to eat some hay, even with the wound in her nose. "I bet you'd like a carrot."

From the other side of the pen, the horse stared at him, those glassy, wise dark eyes astute and all-seeing.

"I won't hurt you." He tried to speak the way he'd seen Tess talk to the horses—with quiet, calming murmurs. "The more you can eat, the better off you'll be. The faster you'll heal." He took one step in Legacy's direction, holding out his hand even farther.

The horse raised her head, her nose lifting higher into the air as though she was trying to sniff out his offering.

"They're organic carrots," he informed her. "The best I could find at the grocery store this morning." He took another step.

Legacy turned and trotted in the opposite direction,

moving around the perimeter of the pen to get closer to him without approaching him directly. He supposed she wasn't too used to people bringing her treats, seeing as how she was a wild animal and everything. Like Tess had said, when he'd led Legacy down the mountain the concussion had probably subdued the horse, but today she seemed to have a different, wary energy.

"That's okay. I can leave them here." He set the carrots on the ground and then backed away, letting himself out of the gate. "So you can try them if you want. *When* you want."

Now that he had removed himself, Legacy ambled to where the carrots sat and sniffed them before gobbling them up.

"See? I told you they were the good stuff." He folded his arms over the fence, watching the horse search the ground for more. She really was a beautiful animal—light brown with a silverish tail and mane. He'd never had a horse of his own. He'd never even ridden until he'd met Jace in the service and had visited the ranch those few times they'd all had leave.

He and Aiden and Thatch would find a rental in the area and spend some time with Jace and his family at the ranch—in between hitting the nightlife scene in Jackson and fishing and climbing mountains, of course. During those brief reprieves from fighting, they searched out ways to feel human again. For Jace that had meant spending every moment he could with Tess and his girls. They had been Jace's entire world, his motivation, his joy. And Silas had envied him; that was the painful truth.

Though his friend had always welcomed Silas into his home, he now felt like an intruder at the ranch. He'd slept with Tess. And, worse than that, he felt something for her. Something real and deep. Something that was not just going to go away by pretending.

With her search for more carrots proving fruitless, Legacy trotted along the fence again until she made it to where he stood at the gate. She pushed her muzzle into his shoulder, nearly knocking him over.

Despite the weight sitting in his gut, Silas laughed. "Liked those carrots, did you?" He pulled three more out of the bag and held them flat on his palm.

The horse took them, leaving behind a mess of slobber.

"Thanks for that." Silas wiped his hand on his jeans and then took a chance petting the horse's forehead. "See? I'm not so scary."

Legacy stood there for another minute, letting him pet her but then she tossed her head and went back to her fruitless pacing along the inside of the fence.

"Looks like she made a friend," Tess said behind him.

As usual, the woman's voice brought two powerful emotions clashing inside of him. Want and guilt. "Hey." He watched her walk to the fence. How long had she been standing there? "I thought I'd check up on the patient before I head to the jobsite today." Amazing they actually had some real work to do. Their next project was only building a new barn for Kyra—which she insisted on paying for even though her fiancé was part owner of the company—but at least the project would distract him and keep him busy.

"She seems pretty happy to see you." Tess slipped inside the gate. "It took me an hour last night to get close to her so I could administer her meds. But she came right up to you."

"It took a while." Patience and giving her space. "And honestly the carrots are what won her over." He held up the bag, which only had a few left now. "I basically bribed her to like me."

Tess shook her head, a small smile gracing her lips. "I tried carrots last night and she wanted nothing to do with them." Sure enough, the closer Tess got to the horse, the farther Legacy paced away.

"Would you mind offering her another carrot?" the woman asked, giving the horse some space.

"Sure." Silas rustled through the bag and held one out on his palm again. It took a few minutes, but Legacy eventually sidled up to him to eat while Tess sneakily approached and inspected her wound.

"No signs of infection so far. But we have to stay on top of it." She let herself out of the gate and came to stand by Silas. "Hey, about yesterday when we picked up the girls...I hope Morgan didn't make you feel too bad."

"Nah," he lied. He'd only thought about their conversation all night—about the things he should've said, the many ways he'd failed in trying to make the girl feel better. Everything he'd said only seemed to make her feel worse.

"She would've reacted that way with anyone, Silas." Tess faced him, those brown eyes of hers unfathomably deep. "She was upset. Preteen girls come with a fair amount of emotions."

"And I didn't help the situation." That had been clear even to Willow.

"You're wrong." Tess laid her hand on his shoulder.

Silas closed his eyes for the briefest second trying to steady himself against the temptation her touch brought. He could turn to her fully right now, take her in his arms and hold her close and kiss her. But he wouldn't.

"She told me last night before bed that she felt bad

about the way she'd treated you." The woman dropped her hand back to her side. "She actually mentioned something about calling you stupid while I was in the school?"

"She didn't call *me* stupid. She called *what I said* stupid." And she'd been right anyway. Instead of offering dumb solutions, he should've simply listened to her. He could've offered her some sympathy. Maybe he should've hugged her. That's probably what a father would've done.

"Well, she'd like to apologize to you sometime." Tess grinned at him. "I told her you were pretty tough and could handle a few rude comments."

He could handle the rude comments. But he'd made it clear he couldn't handle children. "I didn't know what to say. I panicked." He'd never panicked before. When Morgan or Willow cried, he'd always been ready with a goofy face or a funny dance, but this time he'd wanted to offer more. Because as much as he tried to ignore it, this stubborn hope still hid underneath all of his doubts. Maybe someday he could be the kind of man who was worthy of a family. So he'd tried to help, to make things better... and he'd failed.

"I really appreciate you trying," Tess said, seeming oblivious to his inner turmoil. "That's what my girls need. People who try. People who will be there. I can't do this on my own. All of you are an important part of their lives. Especially since Jace is gone."

"I'm happy to try." Even though he'd likely always fail. "But you should know you really are doing an amazing job with them." He saw how she loved her daughters, how she always knew what they needed, how she'd given up on anything she wanted for herself to be who they needed her to be. If he'd had a mother like Tess, he might be a different man. He might not be so useless when it came to relationships. He might know something about how to love someone else.

"Some days I feel like I'm an okay mom." Her smile weakened. "And some days I feel . . . well, to put it in Morgan's terms, stupid. I just hope you won't be afraid to try again. If you have wisdom to share with her."

"I won't be afraid." But he wouldn't be around to share much with Morgan and Willow soon anyway. Last night, he'd talked to his buddy more about the contract gig. They wouldn't be ready to move on this thing for a month. That should give him plenty of time to fulfill his promise to Tess. After that, he'd be on his way to Afghanistan. The mission would give him the time and space to get his head back on straight. He wasn't sure how to tell Tess that though. He'd have to find a better time. Right now he had to get to work. "I'd better head over to Kyra's. Get started on that outbuilding she wants done. I'll see you around." He turned to walk away.

Within a few steps, Tess caught up to him. "Before you go, I wanted to let you know I asked Louie and Minnie if we could hold the town meeting about the shooting situation at the café tomorrow night. They're happy to host."

"Great. I'll be there." He parted ways with her and when he glanced back over his shoulder, he caught Tess watching him walk away. Could she tell something was off? Could she tell he had a hard time standing next to her, looking into her eyes? Probably. He'd never been good at pretending. That's why he'd go back to avoiding her, only spending time with her when other people were around to provide a distraction.

Silas climbed into his truck and drove away, trying to figure out how to tell Thatch and Aiden about his intention to work for Fletch. It was time.

When he reached Kyra's property, Aiden and Thatch were already setting up the tools. The outbuilding's foundation had been laid by the concrete guys two weeks ago and now they could start the framing. Not his favorite part of the job, but at least they'd be busy when he told them he was leaving.

"There you are." Aiden fiddled with an extension cord attached to their generator and plugged in the table saw. "I thought you'd beat us out here this morning since you've been so bored and everything."

Silas pulled his tool belt out of his truck. "I stopped to see Legacy on my way." And Tess too. He might not be able to spend time with her, but that didn't stop him from thinking about her. How beautiful she'd looked in her bright blue coat with the morning sun beaming on her face and making her eyes shine...

"Or were you having some secret rendezvous with your mystery woman?" Aiden crossed his arms and leaned against his tailgate. "Did she finally call you back or what?"

Well, hell. And he thought they'd let this go. He should've known better. These two loved to give him shit.

"It was Kyra's friend from nursing school, wasn't it?" His friend wore a cocky smirk. "Eliana?"

"It had to be," Thatch agreed, walking over to join them. "Come on, bro. Spill it. Did you hook up with her again last night?"

"It doesn't matter who I hooked up with at the party." He'd promised Tess no one would ever find out about them, and there was only one way to get them off the trail. "Because I won't be sticking around here long enough to start a relationship with any mystery woman."

Aiden bolted upright. "I'm sorry. What?"

There was no easy way to tell them, so he simply put it out there. "Conrad Fletcher got in touch and asked if I could help out on a recon mission next month."

Thatch let out a low whistle and Aiden seemed too shocked to speak. They knew Fletch. The ex-SEAL was a legend. Right after an early retirement, he'd started a clandestine freelance business that took on overseas operations that the military couldn't officially sanction for one diplomatic reason or another.

"I told him I'm open to it," he went on when neither of them said anything. "If we can get everything squared away, I'll be headed to Afghanistan in a month."

Thatch exhaled loudly and Aiden marched up to him with a dark scowl. "You mean to tell me you're going back to that hellhole?"

He shrugged, downplaying the significance. "I'll go wherever I can make a difference." He knew the dangers over there. He also knew he couldn't stay here.

"That's it?" his friend demanded, getting in his face. "You're just going to up and leave when you have commitments here? What about our company? What about the ranch?"

Silas crossed his arms, not backing down. "You know as well as I do, Tess doesn't need us as much anymore. She doesn't *want* to need us." She'd made her quest for independence clear when she'd hired three other ranch hands this spring. "In case you haven't noticed, she's hired enough staff now to take on most of the work. And

Cowboy Construction isn't exactly busy either. You two can keep up with the current project load without me."

"So you're saying you want out of the company?" Thatch's tone struck a calmer note. He seemed surprised, but he wasn't speaking with the same edge as Aiden.

"I'm saying that this is what I need to do right now. I won't be gone for more than a couple of months." At least that's what Fletch had thought. "I can remain on here as a silent partner, take a lower percentage. Or you two can decide to continue on without me." He wouldn't blame them if they did.

"I don't understand." Aiden threw up his hands. "We fucking lost Jace over there. And now you want to go back? You know how selfish you're being? I shouldn't be surprised."

Silas withstood his friend's fury without retreating. If anything, Aiden's reaction stirred up anger. He'd expected his friends wouldn't be thrilled, but this was over the top. "Why shouldn't you be surprised?"

"Because this is what you do." His friend glared at him. "You make decisions without even thinking about how they're going to affect other people. You do whatever the hell you want and don't consider the consequences."

Silas didn't argue. That's what had made him so good at his job. He acted. None of them had ever had the luxury of considering consequences in their line of work. "I'm not asking for your permission. I've already started the process." He'd pass the background check no problem. The paperwork was only a formality. "I'll come back." But this would get him away for a while. Away from the monotony.

Away from Tess.

"I can't believe this." Aiden ripped off his tool belt and chucked it into the bed of his truck. "You know what, Silas? Screw you." He stomped past him and headed into Kyra's house, giving Silas's shoulder a hard bump on the way.

At least he hadn't sucker punched him.

Silas watched him go and then turned back to Thatch. "That went well."

His other friend seemed to size him up. "We're both surprised. You have to understand that. Maybe you've been thinking about this for a while, but this is the first we're hearing of it."

"Yeah. I get it. Maybe this wasn't the best way to bring it up." He'd been trying to get them to lay off on the whole mystery woman thing, but sitting at the café with a couple of beers might've been a better venue to broach this subject.

Thatch came to sit with him on the truck's tailgate. "You sure you really want to go back to that life?"

He didn't know what other life he could ever have. "Not full-time. But I go on one mission. Help out the bigger cause. I have nothing keeping me here." Except for a woman who considered him a mistake. "I miss having a purpose."

Thatch nodded as though he could relate. "You know why Aiden is so pissed off, right?"

Silas had thought he'd known their friend pretty well, but in his opinion, that reaction had been overkill. Aiden was downright angry with him. Did he really think the three of them would live the rest of their lives in Star Valley Springs working construction jobs? Aiden was moving forward—getting married. Shouldn't they all be free to live their lives the way they saw fit? "Maybe you should enlighten me."

"Because we won't be there to protect you," Thatch

said, staring out at the mountains. "We were always in it together, Si. The four of us. We always had each other's backs."

"And still we lost Jace," Silas pointed out. "If something's gonna happen to me, it'll happen whether or not you guys are there."

"Still...he's worried about you." Thatch pushed off the tailgate. "And quite honestly, I am too. This all seems like kind of a rash decision. Does your rush to leave have anything to do with the woman from the party?"

Silas avoided eye contact. "Stupid question." He couldn't get those images of Tess out of his head. He couldn't live day in, day out, pretending he didn't want his dead best friend's wife. "I need to do this. I need more in my life. Come on. You can't pretend you don't understand."

"No, I do." Thatch hesitated. "I understand a lot more than Aiden. Kyra changed his whole perspective. Funny how fast you forget what life was like before a woman changed everything."

"I wouldn't know." But Thatch had had a girl back home when Silas first met him. They'd been pretty serious from what Silas could tell. And then a year later, he quit talking about her altogether. Thatch hadn't said a word about how the relationship unraveled though. And Silas hadn't asked. It used to be that they didn't get too far into each other's personal business. Until now apparently.

"Listen, I'm not gonna lecture you." His friend walked back to the outbuilding's foundation and started to measure out the chalk lines for the frame. "I've actually taken up a new venture myself recently."

"Seriously?" *Huh.* So he wasn't the only one with a secret. Silas pulled out his tape measure and got to work drawing the lines on the other side of the foundation. "What kind of venture?"

Thatch paused his work and glanced toward the house like he wanted to make sure no one else would hear. "I've been trying my hand at bronc riding. I'm thinking I can compete at the amateur rodeos around the country."

Now it was Silas's turn to be shocked. "Bronc riding." And Thatch was giving him shit about the dangers of *his* potential new job?

"Yeah. I met up with an old bronc-riding legend in Jackson. He's giving me some training in exchange for work on his house."

"So that's where you've been sneaking off to every weekend." He knew his friend had been busier lately, but he hadn't gone snooping around to find out what he was up to.

Thatch hauled over a 2x8 and lined it up. "Like you said, we're not exactly busy here. I figured it's time to take up a new hobby."

Silas laughed. "A hobby, sure. But I've been to those rodeos. Man, you can get busted up pretty good." He went over to hold the post in place while his friend used the nail gun to secure it.

Thatch shot him a look. "And you can't get busted up going back to the Middle East?"

"Good point." He dragged another 2x8 into place. It seemed they'd be framing the outbuilding without Aiden's help today.

Thatch nailed the board in place. "I want a new challenge too. But I wasn't gonna say anything until I can actually stay on the bronc's back for more than a few seconds at a time."

Thatch on the back of a bucking bronc? That'd be something to see. "I'll have to come and watch you sometime."

"Not for a while, man. Trust me." He set the nail gun down on their worktable. "I've got a ways to go. But I'm with you. We should all be free to keep moving forward with our lives. Especially now that Tess insists on hiring hands to do most of the work around the ranch."

"My thoughts exactly." It didn't matter where they went or what they did, the three of them would stay close. They had a bond. If Aiden would forgive him, that was.

"Aiden'll come around. Give him some time." Thatch clapped his shoulder. "We're great at giving each other shit but not so good at talking about how we really feel."

"Yeah." Feelings had never mattered much to him. He'd kept himself too busy to pay much attention to them. But now . . . well, ignoring them was difficult to do.

Thatch picked up the nail gun again and they got back to work. "Hey, I'd appreciate it if you kept my bronc riding on the down-low for the time being," his friend said.

"You got it." Silas held the next board in place.

"And just make sure you're doing this for the right reasons." Thatch shot in a few more nails. "You know? Not because you're running away from something. Make sure this is what you really want."

Silas nodded, but he already knew. He couldn't have what he really wanted.

CHAPTER EIGHT

W hy am I nervous?"

Tess let out an exasperated sigh and gave Kyra and Lyric a desperate look. "I mean, it's not like I don't know everyone in this town." But for some reason the thought of getting up to speak in front of them all had her stomach tied in knots. She'd thought having a happy hour margarita with her friends before the meeting would settle her nerves, but seeing everyone start to congregate around them made her want to get up and walk out of there.

"You'll be great." Lyric popped a nacho into her mouth, smiling as she chewed. "Trust me. There's nothing to worry about."

Easy for her to say. Lyric was a natural public speaker. Her friend did everything with an air of both confidence and elegance.

"Just pretend we're all hanging out for a normal night at the café," Kyra suggested.

"These are the same people we see every Friday night when we come. You don't have to impress them. They already think you're amazing."

"But some of them don't think the wild horses are amazing." That's what really had her nervous. She wanted to share what had happened to Legacy, to get everyone riled up about the injustice of an innocent animal being shot, but what if no one cared as much as she did?

"The people who are against the wild horses don't matter." Lyric sipped from her margarita. "We'll focus on the people who'll support you and this cause."

"Exactly." Kyra dipped a chip into the salsa. "Stay focused and make sure you include a call to action in your speech."

A call to action...

Tess's stomach tightened even more. "I hadn't really thought of a call to action." What exactly did she hope to accomplish here tonight? "I guess I'd like everyone to be on the lookout. Maybe we could even set up some citizen patrols to monitor the herd so we can prevent this from happening to another horse." Silas had mentioned a patrol after they'd visited the police station.

"That's a great idea." Kyra's enthusiastic expression beamed encouragement. "I'm sure plenty of people would love to pitch in and help."

Tess nodded while she watched Thatch and Silas file in through the door. When Silas made eye contact, she immediately looked at the table and picked up her margarita. "Where's Aiden?" she asked Kyra.

Directing her gaze across the room to where Silas and Thatch were ordering a beer, her friend leaned in. "Something happened between him and Silas. I'm not sure what, but yesterday he came storming back into the house when he was supposed to be helping those two frame my new barn."

Panic gripped Tess by the throat. "What happened?" He hadn't found out she'd spent the night with Silas, had he? Oh dear God. That would be so bad. What would her brother think if he knew she'd fallen into bed with Jace's best friend? "Why were they fighting?"

"I have no idea." Her friend's mouth pinched in frustration. "He wouldn't tell me. He only said he didn't want to be anywhere near Silas right now."

That didn't sound good. Tess unzipped her sweatshirt and slipped it off her shoulders, letting it hang on the seat behind her. She opened her mouth to ask more questions but thought better of it when she saw Thatch and Silas walking toward their table.

"Evening, ladies." Thatch tipped his cowboy hat. Not surprisingly, his gaze lingered on Lyric much longer than it did on her and Kyra.

"Ready for the meeting?" Silas had focused on her.

Every time their eyes connected, heat clouded her face. "Um. Yeah. Sure." She darted her gaze back to her margarita and took a sip. Was she looking at him too much? Not enough? Would others notice something awkward between them?

"Why isn't Aiden with you?" Tess asked, pretending to study her phone.

"He'll be here," Thatch said quickly. "I think he was finishing up some paperwork at the office."

Silas remained quiet but she noticed his frown. Another jolt of panic shot through her. He knew. Her brother knew. What else would get between those two? They were best friends. Always giving each other a hard time but only because they loved each other like brothers.

More people had started to arrive, some ordering drinks at the bar, others chatting at tables. But she couldn't focus on the meeting until she knew what was up with her brother.

Tess stood up fast, the back of her knees hitting her chair. "Hey, Silas. Would you be able to help me out with something real quick?" She waved him away from the table to a quiet corner.

"You have nothing to worry about," Silas assured her before she could say anything. "I know Kyra probably mentioned that your brother and I got into it yesterday, but the issue has nothing to do with us. Not that there is an us." He exhaled as though frustrated. "Just don't worry. He doesn't know we spent the night together. I promise. He won't ever know."

"Okay. Good." She breathed easier. "But then what's going on? Why is he so mad at you?"

The cowboy's expression tensed. "It's not important. We can talk about it later. You should focus on the meeting, get everyone organized."

"Right." By now the restaurant was full. Almost every table had been occupied with familiar faces. What had she planned to say again?

"Tess, are you ready?" Minnie waved her to the front of the bar. "You can get started while we serve the drinks."

"You're coming with me, right?" She glanced at Silas. "I mean, you were there too. You saw what I saw. You helped get Legacy back to the ranch."

"Sure. I can come with you. Lead the way." He gestured for her to go first.

As they took their places in front of the bar, Aiden rushed into the café wearing a scowl. Though his expression seemed to soften when he sat down next to Kyra.

"You have the floor, my dear." Minnie nudged her shoulder and the room quieted.

Inhaling deeply, Tess pictured Legacy, the beautiful horse that had been all bloodied and suffering when they'd found her. That was all it took to help her focus. "Okay. So. Um..." She clasped her hands in front of her waist. "Thank you all for being here tonight." Too quiet. She was speaking too quietly. "We wanted to alert you all to the fact that the wild horses who've inhabited this land for generations are in danger," she said louder. "When I was out riding the other morning, I heard gunshots and the herd came charging onto my land." *Take a breath. Let them process the information.*

After a few beats of silence, she continued. "Later, Silas and I rode back up the mountain and discovered a mare with a gunshot wound to the head." She paused again, taking in the concerned expressions around the room. "We were able to save her and she's now recovering at the ranch, but we should all be concerned about someone targeting these beautiful animals. It's our duty to protect them."

"Yeah it is," Aiden called out, giving her a supportive thumbs-up from the front row of tables.

Tess stood a little taller seeing all of the nods and smiles around the room.

But then Ford Leach stood up. The old rancher had grown up on the south side of town and always looked like someone peed in his morning coffee. "We all know the wild horses are overpopulated around here," he grouched. "And as a rancher, Tess, you know how much we rely on those grasslands for our cattle. Hell, what's one less wild horse if it means our cattle can eat?"

A few murmurs of agreement went around the room. They weren't as loud as the supporters though.

"I know the issues surrounding the wild horses are complex. But the fact is, they were here long before we were." She struggled to maintain a diplomatic tone. "And they shouldn't be shot through the nose and then left to suffer and die. Need I remind you that shooting a wild horse is a federal offense, thanks to the Horses and Burros Act of 1971? These animals are federally protected, and they shouldn't be targeted for sport."

"Hear, hear." Minnie started to clap, and the majority of the room joined in with the applause.

Tess used the momentum to keep going. "Now, it's all of our responsibility to coexist with the wild animals who call Star Valley home. And I'm hoping we can band together to make sure no more horses suffer the way Legacy has. If Silas and I hadn't found her, she likely would've contracted an infection and died a slow, very painful death."

"It's only a useless horse," Darrell Braxton called from a table near the window. "And they're everywhere now. They'll take over this whole valley if we let 'em."

"They're not taking over," Minnie yelled back. "And they deserve to live in peace without being hunted."

Sounds of agreement bounded around. It appeared the majority in attendance wanted to help protect the wild horses, but those other few could prove to be a problem.

More arguments started—with Ford and Darrell the main instigators.

When the volume in the room started to rise, Tess clapped her hands. This was no longer a productive meeting. It wouldn't help anyone to sit here and go back and forth with men who had no regard for the animals' welfare.

"Thank you all for your input," she said above the noise. "My intention was to make this an informational meeting, a reminder for all of us to keep our ears and eyes open. For those who are *interested* in staying involved in the conversation and actually doing something to help, I've left a notebook at the bar. You can sign your name and email address so I can be in touch."

It wouldn't help to set up a patrol schedule now, with all of the naysayers listening in. "I appreciate everyone being here. If you have any questions, please come and find me." She turned her back on the room and picked up the water glass Minnie had left for her while people started to stand and chat.

"Nice job." Silas gently elbowed her arm. "You gave exactly the right amount of information without—"

"This is a whole lotta trouble you're goin' through for one damn horse, Tess." Darrell butted in between them. "Most of us don't have time for this. We're all barely keeping up as it is. I'll tell you right now if it comes down to the survival of those horses or the survival of my own cattle, it's not gonna be a hard decision."

Tess studied the man's grizzled face. He was only in his fifties, but the years of sun exposure had aged him. "It sounds to me like you wouldn't mind shooting a wild horse yourself, Mr. Braxton." She gave the statement a few seconds to sink in. "Is there something you'd like to confess?" He could've easily ridden his UTV up there and shot Legacy. Maybe he was on a one-man crusade to rid the valley of wild horses.

The man's ruddy eyes steeled. "Don't you go making

accusations you can't back up," he spat. "You're supposed to be one of us. Jace would've—"

Silas thrust his hand onto the man's shoulder. "That's enough. I think you need help finding the door, Braxton." He roughly directed the man toward the exit while Tess turned back to the bar, bracing her hands against the surface, trying to breathe.

Jace would've what? What would Jace have done? He wouldn't have stood for the brazen and illegal killing of a wild animal. She knew that much.

Once again, she felt the acute awareness of her husband's absence. She was still getting used to standing on her own, confronting the challenges of life as a single woman instead of as a couple. The truth was, Jace had done most of this. The confronting. The standing up. The challenging. He would've led the charge and she would've been happy to support him. But now she was learning how to follow her convictions—how to *act* on them.

"You okay?" Silas approached her with the same concern that had been in his eyes when he'd found her crying That Night.

"I'm fine." She stuffed those memories down deep where they belonged. She needed all of her energy focused on Legacy and the wilds right now. "I'm encouraged, actually. It seems most people aren't going to stand for this in Star Valley."

In fact, much of the crowd was still gathered in groups around their tables discussing the situation. "Thanks for getting him out of here though." She tucked her hair behind her ear and peered up at Silas. "It's nice to know someone has my back."

She only wished this someone didn't make her heart

spiral out of control every time he got close. She wished she didn't want to pull that someone close and push him away at the same time.

"You were great, Tess." His eyes lingered on hers for another few seconds before he looked away. "Uh, I should go help Minnie and Louie clean up in the kitchen. I'm sure they have a lot to do." He moved around the bar and walked away.

Tess watched him, her heart still thumping. Silas was always doing things to help people out. Sometimes, on a particularly busy Friday night, she'd heard he'd stay after closing at the café to do the dishes and make sure Minnie and Louie were able to get home by a reasonable hour.

"Tess? Excuse me." A man tapped her on the shoulder.

She whirled around, lest anyone notice that she'd been staring after Silas like an enamored puppy.

The man standing in front of her smiled. "I don't know if you remember me from the PTA meeting but I'm—"

"Brad Kline." She blinked a few times so her brain could catch up. "Callie's dad." She shook his hand. "Of course I remember. I was hoping to talk to you about the girls." She hadn't even noticed him sitting in the crowd. During her speech, all of the faces had blurred together. It was surprising he hadn't stood out more because she'd been meaning to talk to him.

"Yeah, I listened to your phone message earlier today, figured we could talk tonight since Callie is home with my parents." He exhaled that tired-parent sigh she recognized all too well. "I'm sorry about what happened at school. Trust me, I talked with Callie about the situation, and she'd like the chance to apologize to Morgan."

"I can't say Morgan handled things well either." Had

her daughter really spat on someone's shoes? "In fact, the reason I called is because I'd like to invite you and Callie over for an afternoon this weekend. If the girls spend some time together, I have a feeling they'd quickly get past their differences."

"That would be great, actually." The man appeared pleasantly surprised. "We haven't gotten out much lately. There's a lot to do at the ranch. And I'd be lying if I said I didn't tend to avoid the gossip in town."

"I get it. Trust me." This was a small community—and a beautiful community in many ways. But everyone did know everyone else's business. She'd hardly been acquainted with Brad and his ex-wife, and yet even she'd heard about their ugly divorce. "How about Sunday afternoon, around two?"

"We'll make it happen." His smile evened out. "Thank you again for being so understanding. Callie's changed a lot this year, I'm afraid. She could use a good friend right now."

Good friends were the only way Tess made it through the last two years. Her people had picked her up and carried her along until she was able to walk on her own two feet again. Now she was in a place where she could do the same for someone else who needed support. "We all can use good friends."

"Isn't that the truth?" The man's pocket started to buzz. "I'd better take this call. I'll see you this weekend."

Not even one second after Brad walked away, Kyra was by her side. "Who was *that*?"

Tess ignored her friend's exaggerated eyebrow raise. "That was Brad Kline. He's the father of a girl from Morgan's class."

Kyra watched the man walk along the storefront windows all the way to his truck. "Is he single?"

Here we go. "Yes. Recently." She glared, daring Kyra to make any inferences. "Why do you ask?"

"I don't know." Her friend popped her shoulders into an overly dramatic shrug. "Just wondering, I guess."

Uh-huh. "Well, don't get any fancy ideas in your head." Seriously. That was the problem with people who were in love. They wanted everyone else to fall in love too. "Morgan and his daughter have had some issues at school so we're going to get them together to try and work through things."

"I think that's great." Her friend linked their arms together. "There's nothing wrong with hanging out with an attractive cowboy once in a while."

Brad had a nice face—receptive hazel eyes complete with smile lines, a nicely angled jaw, and an easy demeanor. The man had a certain charm. But there was only one cowboy occupying her thoughts lately.

"There wouldn't be anything wrong with it if I actually felt something for said attractive cowboy." Brad was good-looking. He seemed nice. And that was it. Nothing extra happened inside of her when she looked at him or talked to him. No sparks. No distinctive urges or anticipation. Not like when she looked at—

She had to stop thinking about Silas. But she couldn't deny that in the last two years, he was the only one who had managed to light a spark.

"Oh, there's Lynn." Her friend waved at the woman across the room. "I need to go ask her how her oven burn is healing." Kyra hurried away. As the only nurse practitioner in town, she was always on call.

"Nice job up there tonight, Sis." Aiden joined her,

a beer glass in his hand. "I know you don't like public speaking, but I was impressed."

"Thanks." Now that she had her brother alone, she didn't want to make small talk about her speech. "What's going on between you and Silas?"

"Oh, he didn't tell you?" Aiden rolled his eyes and gave his head a good shake. "I don't know why I'm surprised. Of course he didn't tell you."

Unease spilled through her stomach. Silas had something to tell her? "What'd you mean?"

"He didn't tell you about his plans?" Her brother scanned the room with annoyance. "Looks like he's already gone home. He's probably avoiding everything like he always does."

"He's in the kitchen helping Minnie and Louie." She wasn't sure why she felt the need to defend Silas. Why was her brother being such a jerk? "What was he supposed to tell me?" She thought through their conversations that week. "Oh wait. You mean that he plans to take some time off, go on a vacation?"

"He's hardly going on a vacation," Aiden muttered. "Look, it's not my place to say. But he's being typical Silas. Acting with no thought for anyone but himself."

In truth, she happened to think Silas always thought about everyone else. He'd certainly shown her a lot of consideration—taking all of that time to help her with Legacy. And he didn't have to be standing in Minnie and Louie's kitchen right now doing the dishes. "I don't understand." She tried to read her brother's eyes. Maybe it wasn't anger she saw there. Maybe it was hurt. *Plans.* Aiden had said something about Silas's plans...

A different kind of panic set in. "Is he leaving Star

Valley? Did he take another job or something?" He couldn't be leaving. He wouldn't make plans to leave without telling her, would he?

Her brother's jaw tightened. "You'll have to ask him that."

"Okay. I will." Her voice got too high and shaky, but she didn't even care. Right now, she didn't care if her brother caught on to her emotions because she couldn't control them—not the ache in her heart or the apprehension simmering in her stomach. "I'll ask him what's going on the next time I see him."

But she wasn't sure she wanted to hear the answer.

CHAPTER NINE

Silas drove into the café's cramped parking lot and squeezed his vintage Bronco in between two massive trucks.

It was early as hell—barely seven o'clock—but when your friend texted you, *Need to talk. Meet me at the café ASAP*, you hauled your ass out of bed and showed up. Where was Thatch anyway? He didn't see him sitting in any of their usual booths by the windows. He must've had to settle for a table in the back.

Still groggy, Silas climbed out of his car and cruised in through the café's squeaky door.

Minnie nearly bumped into him, armed with a coffee-pot in hand. "Mornin', sweetie." She sidestepped him. "It's awful early to be laying eyes on your gorgeous face."

"Tell me about it," he grumbled. Especially since he'd been here until ten last night. Then when he'd gone home, he hadn't been able to shut off his mind. Even playing a round of solitaire hadn't gotten his thoughts off of Tess. "I'm supposed to meet—"

"Silas!" Kyra waved at him from the table in the back corner. Aw, hell. What were she and Aiden doing sitting with Thatch? He wasn't in the mood for Aiden's bullshit at this hour of the morning.

When Silas approached the table, Aiden stood abruptly. "What're you doing here?"

Silas shot their guilty-looking buddy, Thatch, a hearty glare. This was clearly a setup. "I got a text."

"So did I." Aiden directed a not-so-friendly look in Thatch's direction too.

But their friend pointed at Kyra, deferring the blame. "Don't look at me like that. It was all her. I swear. She made me text both of you, even though I told her this wasn't going to be pretty."

"Don't be ridiculous." Kyra signaled to a passing waiter and quickly ordered a round of cinnamon rolls because she knew full well none of them could resist Minnie's cinnamon rolls. That was the only reason Silas would stay.

"It's time to get over whatever is going on between you two." She tugged on her fiancé's hand. "Now sit."

Aiden dropped back to his chair, glowering at Silas. As if this little meeting had been his idea. He could've still been in bed dreaming about Tess right now.

"And you can sit right there," Kyra told him cheerfully, pointing to the seat across the table that already had a steaming mug of coffee sitting in place waiting for him.

It didn't appear as though he had a choice. Silas had to hand it to Kyra, she knew how to get her way. He took a seat and got started on the coffee. He was going to need all the caffeine he could get for this discussion.

"I'm sorry I had to resort to extreme measures to get you two in the same room, but this had to be done." Kyra's bright smile turned stern. "You guys are like brothers. And you're always there for each other no matter what. So we're going to sit here and talk about what's upsetting you both."

"Can't we just go outside and punch each other instead?" Silas asked. "That's typically how we like to handle things."

The woman gaped at him with a mixture of bewilderment and horror.

Yeah, she didn't get his sense of humor. "I'm kidding." Sort of. He and Aiden had decked each other a few times over the years. And the physical altercations always solved things much faster than using a bunch of words. Silas had never been good with words.

"Now, it's important that we all get on the same page," Kyra went on with an overly calm tone that she likely used on her pediatric patients. "We're supposed to be making wedding plans right now and Aiden has a question he needs to ask you."

This ought to be good. Silas set down his mug and sat back, watching his friend with a smirk.

"I was going to ask you to be one of the best men in my wedding. But you probably won't even be around next fall anyway." Aiden crossed his arms. "So Thatch will have to run the mission solo."

Was he serious right now? "I'll be around for your wedding." Silas had always shown up for these guys when they needed him. "I wouldn't miss that day for anything."

"You don't know that," Aiden argued. "You might be off on some contract mission. Or you might get yourself killed over there."

"Ah. Okay." Kyra's head bobbed in a perceptive nod. "This is good. Silas, I think Aiden is trying to express that he would be very concerned for your safety if you take that contract job."

"No," Aiden countered. "I'm telling him only a dumbass would walk back into the fight that we were all fortunate enough to survive."

"He's *worried*," Kyra rephrased.

Then he could get over it. "First of all, there is no *if*. I *am* taking the job." He'd already told Fletch he'd help and he never went back on his word, so his friends had better get used to the idea. "Would you rather have me stick around here if I'm not happy?" He didn't dare mention the real source of his unhappiness.

"No," his friend grouched. "Yes. I don't know."

"No one wants you to be unhappy." Oh, look who decided to join the conversation. Those were the first words Thatch had spoken in this showdown that he'd helped facilitate.

A waitress interrupted and delivered their cinnamon rolls but Silas couldn't eat his. He didn't even pick up his fork. "I'm going on one mission. Because you, Thatch, and Jace made me a good soldier. I can help out there. I can make a difference." He wasn't making a difference here. "This is important to me. It's something I feel like I need to do." And he needed his friend to support that.

"Good, Silas. Thanks for sharing how you feel." Kyra turned to her soon-to-be husband. "How does his point of view make *you* feel?"

Aiden focused on carving up his cinnamon roll with a fork. "Does it matter how I feel? You'll go anyway."

Silas waited until his friend looked at him across the table. "I'll go because you wouldn't want to hold me back. Even if you're pissed as hell right now." His friend was already relenting. Aiden's glares had cooled off about twenty degrees. "As my friend, you would want me to do something that makes me feel useful and fulfilled."

Aiden didn't answer, but Kyra nudged her fiancé and cleared her throat.

"Fine," he said around a mouthful of cinnamon roll. "I want you to do something that makes you feel useful and fulfilled."

"I knew we could resolve our differences." Kyra poured them all another round of coffee from the carafe on the table. "Now, honey...did you want to ask your friends something?"

"You two are gonna be co–best men in our wedding. Capeesh?" Aiden didn't even look up from eating. "I'm not choosing between you two."

"Sounds good to me." Silas finally took his first bite of cinnamon roll. He had to admit...using words wasn't all that bad. Now things were back to normal and neither one of them even had a bloody nose or a shiner.

"I'm in," Thatch added. "As long as I get to walk Lyric down the aisle."

"Why don't you just ask her out already?" Kyra demanded.

Silas had been wondering the same thing. Their friend had had his eyes on Lyric for months.

"I'm considering my options," Thatch said mysteriously.

"Oh please." Silas took another swig of coffee. "Everyone knows you—"

"Hey, Aiden." Brad Kline and his daughter, Callie, approached the table. Silas didn't know the man—he'd never even had a conversation with him, but his family had a good reputation in town.

"Hey. Nice to see you." Aiden stood and shook the

guy's hand. "What're you two up to today? Got any more fences that need fixing?"

"Nope. We finally finished up all the repairs." Brad slipped on the cowboy hat he held in his hands. "Later today, Callie and I are actually headed to your sister's house. The girls know each other from school, so Tess invited us over."

Silas choked on a piece of cinnamon roll and had to cough it out. Thankfully no one else seemed to notice. Brad Kline was going to see Tess? To spend time with her?

"You enjoy yourself," Aiden was saying. "Tell her Kyra and I are planning to stop by tonight."

"Will do." The man said goodbye and led his daughter to a nearby table.

"Why do you think he's going to Tess's house?" Silas's throat was still scratchy. And now his heart was beating faster too, damn it.

"You heard him." Aiden added some sugar to his coffee. "Their girls are getting together."

"But he made it sound like he was staying there too." He replayed the conversation in his head. Yes, he'd said Tess invited *us* over. "Why wouldn't he just drop off his daughter and leave?"

Aiden gave him a funny look. "No clue."

"Do they hang out a lot?" Silas pushed. "I mean, how well does Tess know him?"

"I don't think they're good friends or anything. Why do you care?" A look of suspicion narrowed his friend's eyes. "If Tess wants to date someone, that would be a good thing. She *should* start dating again if that'll make her happy."

Silas avoided his stare. All of their stares, actually.

Thatch and Kyra were gazing at him with open curiosity too.

"This is Tess," he said, struggling to mask the red-hot jealousy. "I mean, we promised Jace we'd protect her." That was all. That was the only reason his gut had tightened at the thought of cowboy Brad paying her a visit at home. "I'm only trying to watch out for her."

"That's good news." Aiden chuckled. "For a second I thought you were jealous or something. Then we'd have real problems."

Right, because he wasn't good enough for Tess. There wasn't one person in this pseudo-family who thought he could ever be good enough.

Including him.

CHAPTER TEN

Whoa." Tess slowly approached Legacy, holding out a few carrots on the palm of her hand.

"I need to check on your wound," she murmured. When she'd come out to the corral earlier this morning, the horse had refused to let her get too close, so she'd come back with bribes. "You like carrots. Remember?" At least the horse seemed to like them when Silas was the one offering them.

Tess had actually hoped she might run into Silas out here. He'd been checking on Legacy a couple of times a day—talking to the horse like he would a friend, from what she could tell. She wondered if he'd talked to the horse about whatever it was that had Aiden so upset. Had Silas confided in Legacy about his plans?

"He's not moving, right?" She might as well talk to the horse too. "He's been part of my support system since Jace died." And sure, nowadays she needed less support, but he was still a part of their family. It startled her to realize how much she'd miss him if he was gone.

"I'm not supposed to have feelings for him." At least not these kinds of feelings—the ones that made her heart throb with pain and anticipation and desire and fear and hope all at once. Maybe there'd been inklings before That Night in the banter between them, the friendly flirting. But ever since they'd kissed, those emotions had gained strength and momentum, threatening to carry her places she couldn't go.

Legacy shuffled closer, stretching her neck to sniff toward the carrots.

"That's it." Focus. She had to *focus*. Tess leaned in to get a better look at the horse's nose. "I'd say you're healing very well." No redness or drainage coming from the gunshot wound was a good sign. "Go ahead," she coaxed. "Eat the carrots."

The horse finally gave in to temptation and scarfed them both out of her hand at the same time.

"Hey, Mom." Morgan wandered to the fence and climbed up onto the first rail. "Whatcha doin'?"

"I was checking on Legacy before Callie and her dad come over." That's all she was doing. She hadn't been out here hoping to run into a certain cowboy so she could figure out what secret future plans he'd made. What would she do if he told her he was leaving anyway? Beg him to stay? She couldn't. Tess let out a controlled sigh. "Hey, hon, can you please refill Legacy's water trough for me?"

Morgan hopped off the fence and dragged over the hose that was attached to a nearby water spigot. "Someone shot her. Didn't they?" She slung the hose over the side of the watering tank and then went back to turn on the water.

"What makes you think someone shot her?" Tess let herself out of the gate and joined her daughter by the fence.

She'd never lied to Morgan. She simply hadn't given her all of the information regarding the horse's injury. As a mom, she wanted to protect her daughters from the ugliness in the world as long as possible. But she knew she couldn't protect them forever. Her daughter was observant and smart.

"You said someone hurt her." A look of grave concern fell over her daughter's features. "And she's got that hole on her nose."

"Yes, honey." She put her arm around Morgan's shoulders. "Silas and I found her with a gunshot wound." She decided not to tell her daughter that she had been close enough to hear the gunshots. "But please don't tell Willow, okay? I don't want her to be scared."

Thankfully, Aiden and Kyra had volunteered to take Willow out to lunch and over to their house for the afternoon so Morgan and Callie would have some space to make amends without the little sister interfering.

"I won't tell Willow," she promised. "Why would someone do that, Mom? Why would someone hurt Legacy so bad?"

There were so many moments as a parent that she didn't have an explanation to offer. And in this case, she couldn't even make one up. "I don't know. It's nothing I can understand."

"They're bullies, aren't they?" Morgan frowned up at her. "Anyone who picks on someone else who's not as strong as them is a bully."

"That's true." Tess prodded her daughter to move toward the house since Brad and Callie would arrive any moment. "And it's important to stand up to bullies. But standing up to them is not about getting revenge." If nothing else, she could at least turn this into a teachable moment.

"You mean like when I spit on Callie's shoes." Her daughter didn't phrase the words as a question. She'd gotten old enough to recognize a parallel when she saw one.

"Right." She paused and faced her daughter. "Can you think of something else you could've done instead?"

Morgan seemed to give the question some thought. "I guess I could've started a new game," she finally said. "With some of the other kids she's mean to. She's mean to a lot of people."

"That's too bad." Tess hoped she didn't regret inviting Callie over for the afternoon. But it was too late now. Brad's truck turned onto their driveway. "Maybe you'll have the chance to see a different side of her today." Unless she missed her guess, the girl was hurting. She was probably feeling insecure. Her mother had *chosen* to leave. While Morgan and Willow both understood that the choice hadn't belonged to Jace. He would still be here with them if he could've been.

"I'll be nice to her today." Morgan started to trudge toward the house. "But if she's mean to me, we don't have to invite her over again, right?"

"No. We don't have to invite her over again if she's not kind to you today." As much as she wanted Morgan to learn to do the right thing, she also wanted to teach her daughter healthy boundaries. "If someone treats you poorly even when you're kind to them, then it's time to walk away." Being kind and letting someone walk all over you were two very different things.

"Okay, Mom." Her daughter gave her a smile as they waited for Brad and Callie to meet them in front of the porch.

"We're so glad you could come." Tess shook Brad's hand again.

"Hi, Callie. I'm really sorry I spit on your shoes," Morgan added with her eyes downcast.

"That's okay." The girl tossed her long red hair over her shoulder. "I guess I was being kind of a jerk. At least that's what my dad said."

Brad held up his hands in protest. "I did *not* call you a jerk."

"I know." The girl smiled sweetly. "You said I had been very mean to Morgan and I should be ashamed of my behavior. So I'm sorry too."

Morgan's small smile widened into a grin. "Hey, that sounds a lot like what my mom said."

Both girls snickered and Tess couldn't help but smile herself. At least they were finding some common ground to stand on.

"You wanna go see the wild horse we have staying here right now?" Morgan asked, waving her new friend away.

"Sure." Callie caught up to her. "I heard about how she got hurt. Is she getting better?"

"She's doing great. Wait until you see her. She's beautiful." The two hurried past the house toward the back pasture.

When they were out of earshot, Brad sighed. "Well, at least they can bond over how annoying their parents are."

Tess laughed. "I guess I could think of worse starting points." At least both the girls had seemed good-natured about the situation. She'd been worried that Callie was going to be difficult and angry.

"I want to thank you again for inviting us over. I know you've been through a lot." Brad shoved his hands into his pockets, his eyes not quite meeting hers. "I have so much respect for Jace. Always have. And his sacrifice isn't lost on me."

"Thank you." Not long after the funeral, the Klines had sent her a heartfelt card and the most beautiful tribute flowers. "I know your family's going through a hard time too. And, from someone who's walking the single parenting road, I'm truly sorry."

"That means more coming from you than it does coming from the people who randomly say it at the grocery store." The brief spark of humor in his eyes cooled. "No one else has really bothered to reach out to us. I think Callie's friends' families feel a little awkward ever since Hannah left."

"I can relate." No one had seemed to know quite what to do with her after Jace had died either. Many of the families they'd once gotten together with had seemed to think she'd feel uncomfortable going to a party without a husband. "We're glad you could come." She swept an arm toward the porch where she'd set out a pitcher of lemonade and cookies earlier. "I thought we could sit on the porch. That way we can keep an eye on them while they're running around outside."

"Perfect." He waited for her to lead the way up the steps and then they both sat in the Adirondack chairs Jace had built.

"That was an interesting meeting last night." Brad poured her a glass of lemonade.

"I should've known it would get contentious." Tess took the wrapping off the plate of cookies. "I probably should've asked around to see who the supporters were and then had the meeting here instead of at the café. That pretty much opened up the floor to everyone who had an opinion."

"I think it's good information for everyone to hear."

Brad picked up his glass and leaned back in the chair. "Unfortunately, my father seems to agree with Darrell and Ford. He grew up protecting his cattle at all costs. They almost lost the ranch a few times when he was a boy. So he can be pretty stubborn."

Tess wasn't surprised. The elder Kline spent a lot of time with Darrell and Ford. "I understand people are concerned about their cattle being able to graze, but shooting the wild horses isn't the answer."

"What is the answer?" Brad angled his body toward hers as though truly interested.

Tess waited for a flicker of appreciation that should've come with an attractive man looking at her so intently, but she felt nothing. "We need to find a way to manage the horses so they're not staying in one spot long enough to decimate the land." Herd management was the only solution that made sense. "I know the Bureau is trying. I'm thinking about partnering with them, actually. To take in some of the wild horses and care for them on my property."

She hadn't told anyone else that yet, but using her land for the cause would help protect them from being hunted. "Becoming a sanctuary for wild horses is a lengthy process but I feel like that's how I can keep them safe and also help the public lands regenerate so there's plenty of grazing to go around."

"That's an interesting prospect." He set down his half-full glass. "And it sounds like a lot to take on."

"It will be. But I have help." She had her brother and Kyra. Thatch and Lyric. Her heart slumped at the thought of Silas potentially leaving. She might not have as much help as she'd counted on in the past. "Between my family and friends, we should be able to handle it."

"That's great that you have so much support." Brad helped himself to a cookie. "I feel pretty maxed out since Hannah left. Even with my dad and mom helping out. They can't take on too much anymore." The words didn't have a ring of self-pity. They were simply honest. "I took it for granted. Having a partner. And then when that partner was gone, I realized how much she was a part of me. It's almost like that part of me is gone too."

Tess could've said those same exact words. She knew the truth behind them all too well. "Yes. You have to discover a new part of you. A part you didn't know was there." And that kind of self-discovery was still an ongoing process for her.

"That's where I'm at now." The man finished the cookie and dusted the crumbs off his hands. "I suppose I'll get through the tough part eventually."

"I'm not sure you're ever fully through it." Tess winced at her boldness in making that statement. "Sorry. That doesn't sound very hopeful."

He grinned and waved off the apology. "At least you're honest. I appreciate the honesty. I appreciate being able to talk about how hard it is without having to pretend I'm sailing right through."

"There's no sailing, that's for sure." She found a smile. "It's more like just trying to keep your head above water most days."

"And going under sometimes," he added. "But you also start to find yourself. The old you, I mean. The one you were before you became part of an *us*."

Tess let his words sit. "I agree. Jace was selfless and giving. And I let him take on too much, I think." Not because he took over but because she got comfortable and sat back.

"I never would have started this wild horse fight while we were married." She laughed a little. "But he would have. And I probably would've made him do most of the work."

When he'd been home, she knew Jace felt this pressure to get things off her plate—to give her a break since she dealt with so much in his absence. So he'd handled almost everything. But this cause with the horses...this was hers alone. And just the thought of that energized her. "I think part of finding a new normal is taking on new challenges."

"I get it." Brad's expressive eyes widened into a look of mock horror. "I've recently learned the skill of braiding hair. Thank God for YouTube."

Tess's heart warmed for him. She let herself stare at his face a few extra seconds but still felt nothing deeper than a certain camaraderie with him.

"I never did those things when Hannah was around," he went on. "I never took an interest in Callie's hair. Or her clothes. And now I'm learning. Not only to braid but how to help her see herself as the beautiful person she is."

And Tess knew firsthand that could be quite a challenge these days, with all of the pressures of social media. "Raising girls isn't easy," she lamented. "Especially on your own."

"No, it's not," he agreed emphatically. "But it's good to have friends to talk you through it. Speaking of...would you want to go to dinner next weekend?"

The question sat her up a little straighter. "Oh. Um... probably not." *Shoot!* That sounded so rude. "I mean, I'm not looking for anything in the relationship department quite yet." Good lord. She should stop talking now. Maybe he wasn't even asking her out on a date! That

Night had made her hypersensitive. Sheesh. Clearly, she wasn't ready for dating.

"I'm not looking for a relationship either." Her sudden panic seemed to amuse the man. "But that's the beauty of friendship. We go out and enjoy dinner. No pressure. No awkwardness. Just an easygoing evening spent with another grown-up who can relate to braiding hair and managing meltdowns."

Huh. That seemed simple enough. "I probably do need to get out more." If her mother's opinion was any indication.

"Great." He poured himself more lemonade. "We can reacquaint ourselves with what it's like to go out. As friends. No expectations. No wondering where the boundaries are. Just good food and good conversation. You're pretty easy to talk to."

"So are you." She relaxed back into her chair. "That does sound kind of nice." She went out with Lyric and Kyra all the time, but neither one of them had a tween girl to deal with at home. They couldn't exactly commiserate with her or celebrate the small successes.

"Besides, I'd like to learn more about the wild horses and stay involved." The man made it difficult to turn him down. "I have to admit, I don't know much about the herds. But I'm happy to help your cause."

"Yes. Let's do it." She needed all of the support she could get in this quest. "We can meet for dinner at the café next weekend." Getting together with him would be a nice departure from her usual routine.

And besides that, maybe a night out would help her finally get her mind off Silas.

CHAPTER ELEVEN

T ess? Hello?" Lyric came into view, standing above her. "I said you can move into your bridge pose now."

"Sorry." Tess quickly lifted her hips away from the floor, tensing her hamstrings to hold herself in the pose. "I can't focus today." Lyric did a yoga session with her and Kyra every Wednesday morning after Tess dropped off the girls at school, and usually it was a time to concentrate on her mind-body connection, but ever since the meeting at the café, she'd been off-center.

"What's up?" Lyric killed the music on her phone and lay down on her mat between Tess and Kyra, finding her own bridge position.

"You have seemed a little distracted this week," Kyra commented, wincing. "Can we go back to happy baby pose now? My butt is killing me."

"Sure." Lyric turned her head back to Tess. "So spill it. What's going on?"

She couldn't tell them how much she'd been agonizing

over the possibility that Silas might leave Star Valley. Or
how she'd been hoping to see him the last few days, but
he'd made himself scarce. So instead she said, "The other
night at the meeting, Aiden made it sound like Silas is
planning to leave Star Valley and I'm worried the girls
are going to be upset." There. That didn't sound overly
invested. She glanced sideways at her friends and Kyra
immediately looked at the opposite wall.

Aha! She knew something. Aiden must've told her
about Silas's plans. "What is it? What's going on?"

"Um. Well..." Kyra rocked slightly side to side in her
happy baby pose. "I think you should probably talk to Silas
about it. I mean, it's not my place to be sharing his news
all over town."

"So he has news." Tess let her feet come back to the
floor. "Of course he has news." She pushed into a seated
position. Normally, she loved Lyric's small studio in the
holistic clinic she and Kyra ran. It used to be the large
master bedroom in the old Victorian house they'd converted. With light bamboo floors and the walls painted
robin's-egg blue and the row of leaded glass windows
along the opposite wall, it was a bright and airy space.
But now she felt too smothered and confined.

"It seems I'm the last to know that Silas has been making plans. Isn't that nice? You'd think someone who'd
been spending a ton of time with my children would give
me a heads-up that he planned to take off, but no." She'd
slept with him only a month ago. It wasn't like he'd mentioned anything about skipping town that night.

"Whoa." Lyric sat up too. "You're not the last to know.
I didn't know either. Sheesh. What's got you all fired up?"

"Nothing." She was careful to lighten her tone so they

wouldn't suspect there was something more behind her anger. "It's just...the girls have gotten used to him being here and now he's going God knows where. I don't want them to experience more loss."

Kyra was the only one who remained in the happy baby pose, relaxing away. "If the prospect of him leaving is bothering you this much, why haven't you asked him about it?"

"I haven't seen him since the meeting. I think he's avoiding me." She'd found evidence that he'd been to visit Legacy. Yesterday the water tank was mysteriously full, and the day before that the hay supply had been replenished. But she hadn't actually *seen* Silas. And she hadn't wanted to try too hard to track him down or her feelings about his departure would be way too obvious.

"Why would he be avoiding you?" Now Kyra sat up too. "What on earth is going on with you two? Both of you have been acting very weird lately."

"I agree." Lyric pulled her legs into a perfect butterfly pose. "You two sure seemed intense when you rushed off to have that private discussion before the meeting at the café. You hadn't even finished your margarita yet."

Kyra's mouth popped open. "That's right! And I'll tell you another thing...when Brad Kline stopped by our table at the café the other morning and mentioned he was on his way to Tess's house, Silas got all agitated."

Hold on just one second. Tess scooted closer to Kyra. "When were you at the café with Silas?" How was it that he could manage to find time to spend with everyone else but then hide from her?

"It was no big deal," Kyra said. "I just wanted to get Aiden and Silas together to talk about their issues. And it worked. They're besties again and Aiden finally asked those two to be in our wedding."

"Just now?" Lyric stretched her long legs out in front of her. The woman could never sit still. Tess had always envied her flexibility. "You asked us like two months ago."

"What did Silas say?" Tess's heart had started to hum. "What do you mean he acted agitated?"

"I don't know." Kyra's eyes narrowed as she studied Tess's face. "His cheeks got a little red—kind of like yours are now. And he asked a lot of questions."

"Interesting." Now Lyric studied Tess too.

In fact, both of her friends stared at her as though trying to read her innermost thoughts.

"What are you looking at me like that for?" she squawked. "I don't know why Silas would've gotten all upset about Brad coming over to see me." He couldn't be jealous. Because in order to be jealous he would have to have real feelings for her. And he didn't. Did he?

"How was the visit with Brad anyway?" Lyric asked in a singsong tone.

"It was good." That was the best way to describe their time together. Good. Nice. Amiable. And a whole host of other mild adjectives. "He's a really nice guy."

"A nice guy you'd like to spend more time with?" Kyra asked.

"How do you feel about starting to date again?" Lyric added.

That was the best thing about her friends. They didn't have any preconceived notions about how she should be living or when she should be dating. They didn't judge or project. They asked questions that helped her explore her own feelings.

Tess lay back down on her mat and stared up at the swirled clouds painted on the ceiling. "I think I could be ready to date." For so long she'd been hollow and numb, but now she'd started to feel things again. Deep things. Powerful things. The problem was, she felt them for the wrong man.

"So you *are* attracted to Brad?" Lyric lay down next to her. "He's so handsome. And he does appear to be a good person."

"He seems like a good option if you're ready," Kyra added, crawling past her to lie on her other side.

"I'm not attracted to Brad. At all," she admitted. "But he asked me to go out for dinner. As friends. Kind of a parent hangout night so we can talk about the girls."

"Sounds pretty boring if you ask me," Lyric muttered, pulling her leg into a hamstring stretch.

"I think it will be refreshing." At least she wouldn't have to worry about what he was thinking or feeling or not thinking or not feeling, the way she constantly did with a certain cowboy. "Dating again feels like a big step." More like a big, terrifying leap. "But dinner with a friend is the perfect way for me to get back out there with no pressure." Spending time with Brad felt easy because she wasn't interested in anything more than a friendship with him. "Not every encounter with a man has to be passionate and high velocity and fiery and intense." Memories of the night with Silas stirred up her pulse.

"No, but some encounters are definitely that way." Kyra's stare turned thoughtful. "Your face got pretty red earlier when we were talking about Silas. And you seemed flustered."

"That's true," Lyric mused.

"No, it's not," Tess said quickly. "My face didn't get red."

Her cheeks turned molten right then. Geez, why didn't Lyric have the air conditioner on in this place? It was an exercise studio for crying out loud.

"Oh, you definitely blushed all right." Kyra shared a perceptive look with Lyric. "I'd say your face got fiery even. Kind of like it is right now."

"Mmm. Good description." Lyric elbowed her in the ribs. "Tess...are you holding out on us? Is there something going on between you and Silas?"

These two! They were like high school girls with all their snickering and wide eyes and questions. They were never going to let this go. "It was one night," she blurted. "Only one night."

"I knew it!" Kyra sat up and raised her arms in victory. "That's why he acted so weird with the Brad Kline thing. Because he totally has the hots for you."

"No." Tess hugged her knees into her chest. "He doesn't have feelings for me. We don't have feelings for each other. Not real feelings." That she would admit to anyway. "It was only sex."

"*Only sex* has led to many life-changing relationships," Kyra said knowingly.

"It's not like that for us. It *can't* be." She had the girls to think about. How confusing all of this would be for them. And complicated for her. All everyone in town would think about was how she was dating her husband's best friend.

"When did it happen?" Lyric had abandoned her yoga routine and gave Tess her full attention. "Where?"

Tess didn't want to talk about this. She didn't want to remember every tantalizing detail. But it was too late to go back now. "During your engagement party. At the hotel."

"Of course!" Kyra popped up and went to the refrigerator

in the corner of the room. "I should've known. Aiden mentioned something about a mystery woman who hooked up with Silas. But the answer is so obvious. You *both* disappeared that night." She brought back three water bottles and reclaimed her spot in their circle.

"You told me you'd met up with an old friend and spent most of the party catching up in a quiet corner of the lobby!" Lyric shook her head with a laugh. "I can't believe I fell for that. Your hair was a mess when you came back to the room."

"I'm sorry." She sipped water to squelch the fire in her throat. "Jace's cousin DeAnn said some things that got to me."

"I should've been there." Remorse clouded Lyric's expression.

"It's not your fault." Tess sighed. "She caught me off guard, that's all." Because Tess had been having so much fun with Silas. "I walked out to that patio where the fire-pit was. And then Silas came looking for me." Her whole body shivered thinking about how he'd wrapped her up in his arms, how he'd stroked her hair. "I still don't know what happened. I was lonely, I guess."

"You're sure you only spent the night with him because you were lonely?" Lyric asked quietly. She liked the hard questions.

And right now, Tess had no answers. She only knew the thought of him leaving made her ache with emptiness again. "Maybe it wasn't only the loneliness. Maybe there is something more there. For me, at least. But he was Jace's best friend."

"Whew." Kyra blew out a weighted breath. "I know this feels complicated, Tess. It *is* complicated. But you don't have to carry any guilt about feeling something for him. He's a single man. You're a single woman. And you two have gotten close. You share a bond with him. It's natural that you would develop feelings for someone under those circumstances."

"Exactly." Lyric leaned closer. "Did that night with Silas happen to be passionate and high velocity and fiery and intense by any chance?"

The blush flashing across her face was likely all the answer they needed. "You can't say a word about this to my brother," she told Kyra.

"I would never," her friend assured her. "You know that. You can tell me anything and I won't tell another soul." Kyra seemed to hesitate but then continued. "I will say though...that morning in the café...it was pretty clear to me that Silas does have some feelings for you too. He tried to hide them, but he didn't do a great job."

For a split second, Tess's heart hung suspended in hopefulness. But logic is what was needed here. "Pursuing a relationship with Silas would be too complicated. Especially for the girls." And for her. "We have too much history. All of us together." And she couldn't trust her heart. Maybe she was simply trying to maintain a connection with Jace through Silas. Rather than examining that possibility, she jumped up and rolled her mat. "I should get going. I've got a ton of work to do at the ranch today."

Kyra stood too. "And I've got patients coming soon."

Lyric handed both of them their waters. "Don't forget to hydrate." She focused on Tess. "And we're always here if you want to talk about anything."

"Thanks." Unfortunately, talking wouldn't change any of her circumstances.

She said goodbye to her friends and walked out into the

bright spring sunshine with Kyra's words lingering at the edges of her thoughts. *Silas does have feelings.* There'd been times in the last month when she'd wondered if he experienced the same stirring of hope and fascination she felt when she saw him—a kind of lifting in her heart. But she hadn't been around him enough to tell much. He'd helped her with the horse situation, but other than that, he stayed away.

Tess climbed into her truck and pulled away from the curb, rolling down the windows so she could breathe in the scent of the blooming lilacs in various yards throughout town. If Silas did have feelings for her—if she acknowledged her feelings for him—too much would change. *Everything* would change. And she and the girls had only just found their solid footing. They'd already created their new normal and she couldn't upset their rhythm now.

She turned into her driveway and headed for the garage but hit the brakes when she saw Silas's truck parked past the house near Legacy's corral. Right on cue, her heart dropped, prompting a distinct change in her pulse. Instead of turning into the garage, she cut the engine and got out to make the long trek to the corral, already knowing she would find him there.

Silas's back was to her when she quietly approached Legacy's pen. She wasn't sneaking up on him, per se... actually, she totally wanted to eavesdrop.

"I know how you feel, Pal," he was saying to the horse. "It sucks to be stuck right in front of the thing you want most, all the while knowing you can't have it."

Tess's hand went straight to her mouth, stifling a gasp.

But Silas must've heard anyway because he whirled around.

"Hey." She let her hand drop back to her side, heart beating so fast she was sure he could see her ribs buckling.

"Hi." He did that evasive maneuver with his eyes again. "I didn't hear you coming."

No, she'd made sure to shuffle her feet lightly over the grass, avoiding any sticks or crunching gravel. "Um, sorry." She eased out a slow exhale. "What were you saying to Legacy?" What did he want most but couldn't have?

"Oh..." He turned back to the horse, petting her mane. "I just think she hates being confined in this pen. Haven't you seen how she paces along the fence all the time? She clearly wants her freedom."

So freedom was what he wanted too? To leave Star Valley?

"She's in a good place." A tremble worked through her voice. "I'm taking care of her—feeding her, keeping an eye on her wound. What's wrong with being confined if you're with people who care about you?" What was freedom when you were alone? she wanted to ask. Is that what Silas wanted? To be alone for the rest of his life?

"It's time for her to rejoin the herd," he said firmly. "Look at her. Her nose is healing up good. And she's clearly miserable here."

Miserable? Was he miserable in Star Valley? Had she made his life miserable by relying on his help and his friendship? Tears stung her eyes but she held them back. "It's not time. It's too soon. And besides that, there's no guarantee the herd will accept her back now. And she won't make it out there alone." No one could thrive when they were alone. "Isn't it okay to be stuck if you're in a good place, surrounded by good people?"

The man slowly turned to her and regarded her with an unyielding stare. "She is in a good place. But maybe it's not the best place for her." He seemed to have picked up on the fact that they weren't discussing Legacy anymore.

Well, good. Because she'd never excelled at speaking in code. "Are you leaving Star Valley?" she asked directly.

Instead of avoiding her gaze this time, Silas's intensity seemed to lock their eyes together. "Not permanently, no. But I'm joining Conrad Fletcher's group for a recon mission next month."

Tess recoiled. He might as well have punched her in the gut. "You're going back over there?" To the same place where Jace had been killed? "How *could* you?" The words came out breathless and seething. "How could you do this to the people who care about you?" To her?

"Being a soldier is what I know, Tess," he said quietly. "It's *all* I know. It's who I am."

No. She wanted to shake her head at him. Maybe that's all he had been before he'd come here but over the last two years he'd become more. He'd been her helper and her protector and her friend. Along with Thatch and Aiden, he'd lifted her up and carried her along until she'd regained her strength. He'd become a part of her life.

But she couldn't say those things to him. They'd spent one night together. With no strings attached. He didn't owe her anything. Not even an explanation. But fury rose up inside of her anyway.

"What about Willow and Morgan? You can't leave them." She let herself into the pen through the gate. "They love you." And her. What about her? Tess held on to her anger so she could withstand the wave of sadness that threatened to come crashing over her. "Aiden is right. You do whatever the hell you want without thinking about how it's going to affect anyone else."

"Maybe I *am* thinking about you." Silas's tortured gaze bore into hers. "Maybe that's why I have to go."

The quiet admission immediately disarmed her. She stood there in front of him feeling as naked as she had been That Night.

"You know all the reasons I can't stay here, Tess. You know why I can't be this close to you. Not anymore."

Who cared what she knew in her head? In the last two years, her heart had only beat like this for him. And if he spent months away from her—if he left and something happened to him—her heart might never beat like this again.

"I have to go. I have to get away, or..." He shut his mouth and shook his head.

"Or what?" Tess stepped toe to toe with him. "Or *what*?" she asked more forcefully.

A decisive smolder took over his eyes. He reached for her, sliding his hands around her waist, pulling her close to him, making her heart sigh with pure relief.

"Or I'll do something reckless," he murmured, dropping his hungry gaze to her lips. "Something I haven't been able to stop thinking about doing for one damn long month."

Then just do it already, she tried to tell him with her eyes. But he was taking too long. Way too long. So Tess touched her lips to his, ending the anticipation and welcoming the rush of desire. God, his lips were even better than she remembered, firm and demanding and teasing too. And that scruff on his jaw lightly scraped the edge of her cheek, sending a ripple of goose bumps down her right side, tingling on the surface of her skin.

Tess pushed her hands into his chest and backed him up against the fence post, fitting their bodies together the way they'd been That Night. The night she'd finally felt something again. When the sparks had consumed her for the first time in forever.

A groan hummed from Silas's throat, and he brought his hands to her low back, urging her in closer. "Yes." She needed more. Tess ground her hips against his, feeling him against her—all of him—and she lost her breath in a sharp intake of air.

Silas skimmed his lips across her cheek and then pressed them to the edge of her jaw, working his way down her neck, his breath hot against her skin, while she clutched his shirt in her fists and whimpered.

She couldn't tell him she didn't want him to go. She couldn't ask him to stay, but she could kiss him. She could show him how she felt. Placing a shaking hand behind his neck, Tess brought his face back in line with hers, looking into his darkened eyes, letting him see her. He had feelings too. They were there. Right there trapped in his eyes, as powerful and vivid as her own. But he couldn't seem to speak either.

So Tess kissed him again, willing him to understand—how she wanted him, why she couldn't have him... though she seemed to be forgetting all that stood between them herself.

She seemed to be forgetting everything but the faint minty taste of his mouth, the way his tongue grazed hers, igniting a fire that burned low and deep—that burned for *him*.

A kiss could say so much. More than words. More than—

Noise. Engine noise. Tess separated from Silas, gasping for air, lifting her eyes in the direction of the truck barreling down the driveway.

"Shit. Your brother's here." Silas strutted away from her and leaned over the fence with his head down.

"I don't think he saw," she squeaked. Aiden probably couldn't have seen them kissing from all the way down the driveway. But he'd see now. He'd see her face red, her lungs gasping, her hair all over the place from when Silas had roved his hands through it.

Her brother parked near the corral and got out of the truck, giving her no time to even panic before he called, "Hey, you two okay? Is something wrong?"

Silas finally straightened but he stayed near the fence. "We were . . . arguing."

"Yes, arguing." Tess smoothed her hands over her hair. Brilliant. Silas was brilliant. Aiden knew firsthand how fired up she could get during an argument.

"Arguing?" Aiden let himself into the pen with them. "About what?"

She took a hard swallow before attempting to speak. "Silas thinks we should let the horse run free again. And I think she should stay a few more days. So we can be sure she's fully healed before she tries to rejoin her herd."

"You know what?" Silas snuck out of the pen, not even glancing back at her. "You're right. She should stay a few more days. I don't know what I was thinking."

"Okay. Well, good. Yes. Thanks." Tess tried to sound stern but she still seemed to be hyperventilating.

"I should get to the office." The man was already ten feet outside the pen and moving swiftly away. "I'll see you two around."

"Yeah, I'll be there soon," Aiden called to Silas's retreating back. Then he turned to Tess. "Did he tell you about his contract job?"

She tore her eyes away from Silas's amazing cowboy butt and tried to concentrate. "Um, a little. We didn't really have too much time to talk about the details." They hadn't really had much time to talk at all before she'd mauled him with a kiss.

"He's so damn stubborn," her brother grumbled. "I don't understand why he'd want to go back over there."

"I guess it's what he feels he needs to do," she said weakly. So *this* wouldn't keep happening. The kissing and the wanting and the acceleration from zero to sixty in the span of ten seconds.

"We should try to stop him," Aiden said.

A shudder ran through her thinking about Silas walking back into danger.

"This assignment he's going on won't be the same as the ones we went on as a team." Concern hollowed her brother's voice. "He won't have the same level of protection going in."

"I know." Nausea churned in her gut. She couldn't do this. She couldn't love another man who was willing to give up his life in a fight for someone else. That conviction and dedication was one of the things she'd loved the most about her husband. But she'd feared it too. She feared it more now that she'd lost him. "I'll talk to Silas."

But she already knew she couldn't force him to stay.

CHAPTER TWELVE

Silas trudged across the meadow, dragging along a whole new set of regrets behind him.

As a solider, he'd been taught to never let down his guard because that was when you always got into trouble. But when it came to Tess, he didn't seem to have a guard. He couldn't guard himself against touching her or kissing her or letting himself tell her how he felt about her. He should've told her he was leaving because he needed a new challenge, a change of scenery. Instead, he'd let her see his inner conflict—that he wanted her, that he was running from his own desires. What good would sharing that with her do either of them?

If he needed any more confirmation that he was doing the right thing by getting the heck outta Dodge, that kiss was it.

He banged through the door of Cowboy Construction and slammed it hard behind him.

"Easy, man," Thatch said from his desk. "We don't

need to waste money and supplies fixing something you break around here."

Silas marched straight to the punching bag they'd hung in the back corner of the office without acknowledging his friend. Nothing like a few hook shots and uppercuts to work out some tension. He slipped on a pair of gloves and went to work punishing the bag.

"What is wrong with you?" Thatch had abandoned whatever building plans he'd been going over and joined him at the bag. "Watch it or you're gonna break your hand."

"I'm fine." This wasn't his first rodeo. He took a few more good shots, already breaking a sweat.

"Does this knock-down, drag-out session have anything to do with Brad coming over to Tess's house?"

The question stopped him cold. "What're you talking about?"

"Okay, I'm just gonna say it." Thatch backed up a step first, wise man that he was. "You got all weird at breakfast that morning. When Brad said he was going to Tess's house later. Something's up with you. It's like you're secretly in love with her or something."

Well, shit. Silas held his expression neutral but it wouldn't do him any good. He and Thatch and Aiden had learned to communicate without words when their lives had been on the line.

The longer he remained silent, the wider his friend's eyes got. "You and Tess? Holy smokes, man. What're you thinking?"

"There wasn't a whole lot of thinking involved," he admitted. "Neither of us meant to end up in my hotel room together but—"

"At the party?" Thatch slapped his forehead. "Are you

fucking kidding me, Beck? Right under Aiden's nose? He's going to kill you. He's literally going to use his bare hands to kill you."

"He's not gonna find out." They'd had a close call a few minutes ago, and he wouldn't make that mistake again. He'd promised Tess no one would ever know their secret. Silas pulled off the gloves and tossed them onto the weight bench that completed their small workout area. "This is why I'm taking this assignment. I can't even be around her anymore without giving myself away." He couldn't stand alone with her for five minutes without giving in to the craving to taste her lips again. Instead of his feelings going away like he thought they would if he kept denying them, the urge to be with her only got stronger.

"You've gotta tell Aiden. He's gonna find out." His friend kneaded his temples the way he always did when he got stressed. "Jesus. I can't believe you slept with Tess, of all people. You know everyone'll find out. Hell, Lyric and Kyra both probably already know everything."

Silas sank to the bench. He hadn't thought about that. "You really think she told them?"

"Hell yes." Thatch sat beside him. "If *I* figured it out, then they know for sure. They're her best friends."

But if they were Tess's best friends, they weren't going to go giving up her secrets to everyone. "I'm not telling Aiden." He and Aiden had already had enough trouble between them this month. "First of all, it's none of his damn business. He's not in charge of Tess." She could sleep with whoever she wanted to sleep with. Even Brad if she chose. Just the thought of that made him want to put those boxing gloves back on and spend another hour hitting the bag. "And second of all, Tess and I spent one night together. That's it. End of story." He wouldn't tell Thatch about the kiss he and Tess had just shared outside.

"Do you care about her?" Thatch asked the question as though he already knew the answer.

"Of course I care about her." He couldn't say for sure when his feelings had crossed over the boundaries of their friendship. He'd be lying through his teeth if he said That Night was the first time he'd felt attracted to her. There had been other moments that had caught him off guard during the last year. And now that he'd acted on that attraction, things were only getting worse.

"It doesn't matter." He pushed off the bench and went to his desk where he'd left the mountain of paperwork he had to turn in for his new endeavor. "I have no idea how to be a dad. I'm not sure I ever want to be a dad." And Morgan and Willow had to be the most important thing in Tess's life. In her life and in the life of whoever she fell in love with. He wouldn't want anything less for them.

Thatch wandered back to his desk. "I have no idea how to be a dad either. But that won't stop me from trying someday."

Yeah, well, he didn't want to try and fail. The stakes were too high. "I didn't have a father. I don't even know what it means to be a father." Thatch had one of those idyllic childhoods—all warm chocolate chip cookies from his mom after school and tossing the football with his dad in the yard and taking fun family vacations to the beach. He was still close to both of his parents.

"Seems to me that being a father is something you figure out as you go along." His friend sent a folded paper airplane flying at him. "Knowing everything up front isn't a requirement. You didn't know everything before you became a SEAL, did you?"

"I didn't know *anything* before I became a SEAL." Those experiences had taught him about life, about dedication, about perseverance, about pain, about sacrifice. And maybe he could learn how to be a dad eventually. Maybe he could be good at parenting if he tried. But there was another reason he couldn't be with Tess. "I could never be good enough. Jace was the best."

Thatch froze. Yeah, it was pretty rare that any of them mentioned Jace. They didn't like to talk about him.

"He's gone, Silas," his friend finally said. "I hate it too, but the fact is, Jace isn't coming back."

"But Tess and the girls have already had the best there is." Silas flipped through the paperwork he'd filled out earlier and signed his name on the line, indicating that all of the information he'd included in his background check and application was accurate. He didn't have to sign it now, but that was easier than watching his friend's reaction. "I could never live up to the man that he was. And I already know I wouldn't be the one he chose for them."

"You *can't* know that," Thatch countered, his glare intensifying. "Jace would want Tess to be happy, bottom line. That's all he would want. He'd want her to be happy and taken care of."

"I can't make her happy." He'd never even had a relationship last for more than a few weeks. "You know me. I don't do relationships. I'll find a way to screw it all up. I've only lived one kind of life—moving around, finding the next mission, the next excitement, the next challenge."

"That's a cop-out." Thatch stood and walked to Silas's desk, standing across from him. "You can't say you'll screw it up before you even try." His friend planted his palms on the surface of Silas's desk and leaned in. "You're afraid. That's what this is. You can go hunt down terrorists in the Middle East but you won't even take a risk on a woman you care about."

Silas lurched to his feet, hands tightening into fists. "She's too good. You got that? I won't risk hurting her. I won't risk her heart." As promised, he'd help her find Legacy's assailant and then he would give her space.

He would always protect Tess. Even from himself.

*   *   *

It had been much too long since Tess enjoyed a whole evening alone with Morgan. But with Willow spending the night at a friend's house, she'd found the perfect opportunity to reconnect with her eldest.

Loosening her hold on Dreamer's reins, Tess followed her daughter up the switchbacks leading to the high meadow, marveling at how far Morgan's riding skills had come over the last year.

"Bravo really responds to you," she said, steering Dreamer alongside her daughter's horse. "You two are so in tune with each other."

"He's the best horse in the whole world." Her daughter patted his rump. "I don't know what I'd do without him."

A brief pain twinged through Tess's heart. Bravo had been Jace's gift to Morgan not long before he'd passed away, and now her daughter and the horse had a special bond. Jace had spent hours with the two of them, teaching Morgan how to ride, how to connect with the horse. Little had he known at the time, he was giving his family yet another beacon of light to lead them forward after his death.

"Your dad would be so proud of you, honey girl." Her tears made the landscape glimmer. She didn't remind

Morgan of that fact enough. "He *is* proud of you." She could feel him still, his heart beating through hers, swelling with the same pride she had for her daughters.

"I really miss him." Morgan stopped Bravo and peered at Tess, her eyes bright with tears too. "Every time I come up here, I remember how much I miss him. But it doesn't hurt like it used to."

"I understand." Instead of despair, these days Jace's absence in her life brought on more of a yearning, a longing for the kind of love they'd shared. It was only because of him that she'd known what true sacrificial love meant. While it was hard to let go and she hated that she'd forgotten their anniversary, it was freeing to not obsess so much about every date that passed without him there. Moving forward was part of the process too. "We've come a long way together, haven't we?"

Nodding, Morgan jiggled the reins and got her horse moving again, into the meadow, in the direction of Jace's memorial plaque. "It's gotten easier. That's what I told Callie too," her daughter said wisely. "It's super hard for the first few years one of your parents is gone but missing someone gets easier."

"So how are things with Callie?" Tess had to push Dreamer into a trot to keep up with Morgan. "It seemed like you two had a great time together at our house."

"We did!" Morgan's thick red curls trailed behind her in the wind. "She's my really good friend now. I kind of understand what she's going through. We've both lost a parent."

"That's true." Tess smiled to herself, remembering that day in the truck when Morgan had been so upset with Callie. But look what happened when you offered someone a little compassion. "I'm really glad you two have become friends."

"Me too." Her daughter slowed the pace as they approached the pond. "She asked me if I could come over to her house and have a sleepover soon."

"Sure. I think we can arrange that." Tess stopped Dreamer and dismounted a few steps away from the memorial.

Morgan followed her, leading Bravo along by the bridle. "Callie also told me her dad asked you out," her daughter said tentatively.

"Oh." The word came out in a gasp. She hadn't planned on telling the girls about their dinner. "He kind of asked me out, I guess. But it's not like a date or anything. We're just two friends going out to dinner." Even with the cool evening air, her cheeks fired up. She wasn't sure she was ready to discuss men or dating with her daughters. It would likely be difficult for them to picture her with anyone besides Jace...

"But maybe you two could date eventually and then Callie and I could be sisters!" A look of hope widened her daughter's eyes and crushed Tess's soul.

"Sweetie, I'm not sure I'm open to getting married again." Six months ago, opening her heart that way again had seemed like an eternal impossibility. Now her heart had opened, only to let in the wrong man.

"I know you're not. *Right now*." Morgan let go of Bravo's bridle and the horse started to graze on the green grass. "But maybe someday, right?" She touched the bronzed plaque that bore her father's name. "I mean, Daddy would want you to be happy. I know he would. He would want us all to be happy. That's what you always say."

"I believe that with all of my heart." She patted her

pocket, where she always carried the folded-up letter that Jace had written to her *just in case*. In his final goodbye, he'd told her to let herself find happiness with someone again. He'd told her that, even if he was gone, she had to show the girls how to love someone so they would know what a healthy relationship looked like.

But she didn't know how to love someone else when she'd loved Jace so much. "I am already unbelievably happy. With you and Willow." She smoothed her daughter's hair away from her cheek. "You girls are everything good in my life. I don't need a husband to make me happy."

"But you're not too old yet," her daughter argued. "Maybe you'll want a husband someday. And Brad seems really nice."

"Well, thanks for saying I'm not too old." Tess had to laugh. Some days she did indeed feel too old to fall in love again. It almost felt like she'd lived a lifetime with Jace. "Brad does seem nice. But we've decided we're only going to be friends."

"Fine," Morgan said. "But if you do want to get married, keep Brad in mind."

"Will do." Tess laughed again and ruffled her daughter's hair. "I can't believe how much you're growing—"

Pop! Pop! Pop!

Tess whirled around. The sounds were faint, but they were definitely gunshots.

Bravo and Dreamer both lifted their heads, ears perked and twitching.

"Mom, what was that?" Morgan's face had paled.

"Come on." Tess nudged her daughter toward Bravo. "We need to get out of here, okay? We need to ride home fast."

Morgan quickly stuck her boot into the stirrup and pulled herself onto Bravo's back while Tess got situated on Dreamer.

"They're gunshots, aren't they?" Her daughter's voice trembled. "The bad guys are shooting at the wild horses again!"

"It's all right, honey girl." Tess's heart raced. "We're fine. But we need to get home as quickly as possible." Before they got caught in the cross fire. "Come on. This way." An engine noise sounded somewhere nearby. More pops cut into the air. "Go, Morgan! Faster!" Tess slowed her horse, letting her daughter get out in front. She turned the horse around, squinting into the woods. *There.* Across the meadow, barely into the trees, a flash of the UTV caught her eye. White with a purple stripe.

"Come on, Mom!" her daughter screeched. "We have to get out of here!"

"I'm right behind you, honey!" She paused and pulled out her phone, turning on the camera and zooming in to snap a picture. Maybe it would be enough for the police to go on.

"Mom!" Morgan was already halfway across the meadow.

"I'm coming." She crouched low and nudged the horse into a gallop. Side by side, she and Morgan tore across the meadow and slowed on the switchbacks heading back down into the valley. "Keep going but take it easier," Tess called, out of breath.

"I'm scared," Morgan whispered, whimpering.

"Everything's all right." Anger burned through her. "I won't let anything happen to you. We just need to get home as quickly as possible." She'd never been afraid to ride up to the high meadow. It had never occurred to her that she had to fear people with guns roaming around the woods. This had to stop.

They navigated the trail all the way back to the ranch and once she saw the barn, Morgan gave her horse its head. Tess struggled to keep up with her daughter and they both came to an abrupt stop outside the stables.

On the other side of the driveway, Silas stood stock-still halfway between the door to the Cowboy Construction office and his truck, watching them intently. "Morgan, what's wrong?"

Her daughter started to cry again. "We were riding in the high meadow and the bad guys were up there . . . shooting at the horses!"

Tess watched the man's entire countenance change. A darkness fell over his expression and his body recoiled as if he'd been hit.

"They were on the southern border again—in the woods," she told him, still rattled to her bones. "Not on our land, but close." Very close. *Too close.*

"You two go into the house." The man lurched toward his truck and pulled out a rifle.

"Wait." Tess rushed to him and caught his free hand in hers, towing him back to her. "Don't go alone. Please." The people who were shooting wouldn't be able to see him any better through the trees than they would've been able to see her and Morgan.

"Thatch is in the office. He'll go with me." He squeezed her hand before letting go. "Call the chief and tell her what's going on. Maybe she can get up there in time to catch these guys."

Tess nodded and forced herself to step back. She stood with Morgan as Silas ran back into the office. He and

Thatch quickly emerged and bolted to the outbuilding where she kept the UTV.

While they peeled out and drove away, Tess led her daughter into the house.

"What're we gonna do, Mom?" Morgan asked, still sniffling.

They were going to do what she'd been trying to do for days. Mobilize. She'd sent out an email to everyone who'd signed up at the town meeting, but she was done waiting to get responses. "We're going to get on the phone right now and invite everyone in our community to gather here. And all of us are going to put a stop to this together."

CHAPTER THIRTEEN

Silas topped out the UTV's odometer at sixty miles per hour, launching them down the dirt road that ran through the back pasture behind the ranch.

"You better slow it down before we hit the trees," Thatch called, gripping the roll bar above their heads. "If you really want to bust these guys, we've got to make it up to the high meadow first."

"We're gonna find them." His helmet muffled the words. "I don't care if I have to get out and run all the way up there." For the second time, Tess had been out there exposed when those assholes were randomly shooting in a heavily wooded area. And now Morgan too. Bile rose up in the back of his throat. Anything could've happened up there.

"What's the plan when we find them?" Thatch raised his voice over the engine noise. "We gonna go all SEAL on them or what?"

Silas knew what Thatch was asking. Was this situation going to put them in a fight that would inevitably get messy? "We're gonna talk to them," Silas decided. He'd thrown the rifle in for protection—but he had no intention of using it unless someone else fired on them first. "And then we'll hope to God the chief gets there before the confrontation has the chance to escalate into something ugly."

He slowed their speed and steered over the ruts and into the first patch of forest they would have to travel through. There was no way they could maintain sixty miles per hour the whole way up.

In the seat next to him, Thatch adjusted his helmet. "I assumed the fuckers who'd shot Legacy were from out of town but that happened more than a week ago. Would outsiders really stick around that long?"

"I'd guess we're dealing with locals." That was the only thing that made sense. It wasn't hunting season. And there weren't many campers around this time of year. But in the end, it didn't matter who they were—he'd find them. "I can't imagine someone would target wild horses if they didn't have an agenda." And he wasn't going to let them carry out their vendetta anywhere near Tess and her daughters.

"You have any ideas on who they are?" his friend asked.

Silas cranked the wheel to get them around a fallen tree across the road. "I have some suspicions." Mainly the men who'd publicly challenged Tess at the café. Those guys were old-school. They'd made it clear that they saw the wild horses as a threat to their land. And they'd also made it clear they didn't care who knew exactly how they felt.

"Let me guess. Ford and Darrell?"

"They'd be my top suspects if I were the chief." It was

one thing to disagree with Tess, but to actually take it a step further and publicly challenge her meant they felt passionate about their cause.

Thatch braced his hand against the dash while they flew over a series of deep potholes in the road. "Doesn't seem like the chief is too concerned about what happened to Legacy."

"She doesn't have the manpower to deal with this situation." He jerked the wheel back and forth, doing his best to stay on what was now two barely visible ruts in the forest floor. He continued to push the UTV as fast as he dared, but the elevation gain was slowing them down.

"Any more making out with Tess lately?" Even with the roar of the engine, Silas could hear the humor in his friend's voice.

"No." He didn't smile back. He never should've told him about Tess. Now his friend seemed to be on a mission to convince him they had a shot at a future. "We haven't even talked." And things were better that way. It didn't matter how many pep talks he gave himself about being smart and keeping his hands off of her, Tess always seemed to bring his resolve to its knees.

"I overheard her talking with Lyric at the café yesterday," his friend pushed. "She's going out to dinner with that Brad guy this weekend." He seemed to watch for a reaction.

Silas did his best to shrug lightly, but his shoulders stayed tense. "Good." Like Aiden had pointed out the morning they'd seen Cowboy Brad, Tess *should* be dating. She *should* do what makes her happy. "Brad has a daughter. He knows the ropes." He was probably great dad material.

Silas guided the UTV around a series of boulders, gunning the engine enough to make it too loud to talk.

"Yeah, I've been thinking about what you said about not knowing how to be a dad," Thatch yelled. He clearly didn't want to let this conversation die. "This right here is something a dad would do—chase down the guys who'd put his kid in danger." He paused while Silas gunned the engine again but then went right back to the lecture. "You obviously love Morgan and Willow. We all do. And it seems to me that love is all you need to be a dad."

He did love those girls. As much as he knew how anyway.

Facing another steep incline, Silas had no choice but to slow them down to a crawl. It was time to end this little chat for good. "Every time something happens between Tess and me, she treats me like a mistake." That was all the reality he needed. "When her brother drove up while we were kissing the other day, she freaked out. Because she doesn't want me. Not really."

Maybe he made her feel good for those few minutes they kissed or for that night they'd spent together. But her actions spoke volumes; she didn't want anyone to know about them. "I don't want to be some dirty little secret Tess has to keep."

"Yeah, I don't blame you." Thatch finally seemed to give up on the conversation, turning his attention instead to the landscape in front of them.

They rode in silence the rest of the way and then came over the top of the last rise before the land evened out into the meadow. Silas punched the gas again. "She said the shots came from the public lands." Yet another confirmation that these guys were locals. They clearly knew where

Tess's land boundary ran, and it sounded like they hadn't crossed over. At least from what she'd seen.

At the edge of the woods, he stopped the UTV and cut the engine so they could listen. He and Thatch took off their helmets, sitting in silence for a few minutes. Sure enough, the buzz of a UTV finally whirred faintly in the distance.

"Sounds like we should head north," Thatch said. "Let's try that trail." He pointed to a narrow path that disappeared into a grove of aspens.

"On it." Silas plunked the helmet back onto his head and fired up the UTV before slipping it into gear. He drove fast, cranking the wheel to follow the faint path, turning to wind in between trees, gaining more elevation. At a fork in the trail, he stopped again but didn't have to turn off the engine to hear that the other UTV was somewhere close by.

"We're getting there." At least the culprits were still out in the woods. Now they had a chance of finding out who they were—and turning them in.

"They're gonna hear us coming." Thatch had his game face on—mouth tense, jaw tight. It was the same expression he'd worn into every mission.

"There's no stopping that." Silas only hoped they could get to them before they took off. After a few more sharp bends, the trees opened up and he caught a glimpse of another machine about a quarter of a mile up the trail. "Hold on." He hit the gas pedal, thankful that the trail had flattened out some, but the white side-by-side UTV in front of him must've seen them coming. There were three figures inside—two of them holding what appeared to be small-caliber rifles. They made a hard right turn, going off the trail.

"They're definitely armed," Thatch yelled, reaching back to grab the rifle Silas had thrown in.

"They won't shoot at us." They knew they were caught and now they were trying to get away. "We've gotta keep up with them, see if we can get a look at their faces." As it was, all three of them were wearing hunting hats— bright orange beanies that pretty much every man in town owned. "I don't recognize the UTV." He'd seen a few of them around Star Valley—but no white ones with a purple stripe. That had to be a unique color choice.

"They're headed back toward the trees," Thatch warned, setting the rifle on the floor at his feet.

"I see that." Silas cranked the wheel and sped up, trying to cut them off before they could get out of sight. "We'll follow their sorry asses all the way back to town if we have to." He could still see them, though he was losing ground. "We've gotta go faster or they'll get away." He tightened his grip on the wheel, increasing their speed. He really should've spent more time playing Mario Kart with Morgan and Willow.

"Left," Thatch yelled. "Get to the left!"

"I'm trying," Silas growled back. "It's not like this thing has awesome power steering."

"Right!" Thatch leaned in that direction as if he could control the UTV with his body movements. "Hard right!"

"Yeah, I've got—" The left wheels lifted off the ground and their momentum pitched them sideways. Silas braced his body while the UTV rolled down an embankment. Slivers of sky and trees and earth flashed in front of him as the impact jarred his body until they came to rest on the right side of the vehicle.

The second they stopped, he turned his head to check on Thatch.

"Well, shit," his friend said mildly. "That was fun."

Silas let out a breath, grateful they both seemed to be in one piece.

"You okay?" Thatch pulled off his helmet, undid his seat belt, and crawled out of the vehicle onto the ground.

"I'm fine." Thanks to the roll cage. Silas wrestled out of his seat belt too and then pulled himself out of the driver's seat before ripping off his helmet and letting it fall to the ground in frustration. The left front end of the UTV was crunched into the ground. Steam rose from the mangled metal. "Looks like we're out of commission though." Damn it. And they'd been so close to catching those guys.

"I'll call the chief." Thatch stood and dug out his phone. "Hey, Natalie." He paused. "Oh. Yeah. Great. Glad to hear you're on your way up here. We were following the UTV with the shooters in it but we wrecked and lost them." Another long pause. "Right. But we're fine. No injuries," his friend finally said. "No, I'm sure they're long gone, but we could use a lift back down to the ranch."

While his friend finished up on the phone, Silas walked around, looking for any evidence of casings on the ground. Not that he'd be able to see much in the high grasses.

"Chief'll be here in a few," Thatch called. "I gave her our coordinates."

Silas walked back to meet him. "I should've slowed down on that turn."

His friend waved off the comment. "We would've lost them either way. They had the jump on us from the beginning. They didn't want to get caught, that's for sure."

"I just hope they didn't shoot any horses today." Silas walked the area, doing his best to scan the woods, but the wild horses were nowhere to be seen. "They must've scared them all away with the gunshots." He couldn't help but wonder what that meant for Legacy. Would the horse be able to find her herd again when they finally turned her loose?

"It's pretty reckless to be out shooting when you have no idea who's nearby," Thatch said, doing his own visual scan.

When Natalie rolled in a few minutes later, she cut the engine on her side-by-side vehicle and jumped out. "You two sure you're okay?"

"We're fine." Silas picked up his helmet. "Any sign of the white UTV?" He'd heard Thatch giving her a description over the phone.

"Nope. Didn't even hear them." She walked around Tess's UTV checking out the damage. "You can ride back with me. I'm sure whoever those guys are, they're headed home now. They're not gonna stick around after this."

Silas would've liked them to stick around so he could have a word with them, but he would find them. He wouldn't give up until he knew for damn certain that Tess and Morgan and Willow could ride up to the meadow without worrying about being shot. Hell, he'd delay leaving for his new assignment until this was settled.

They all climbed into the police UTV with Silas in the front seat while Thatch sat in the back. "You ever seen a white UTV with a purple stripe around town?" Silas asked the chief.

"Never." Natalie slipped on her helmet. "That's not the typical color choice for most people around here." She started the engine and drove back through the high meadow at a much slower pace than he'd maintained during the chase.

"But they have to be locals if they're back at it just over a week after shooting Legacy." Thatch leaned forward over the seat. "It's got to be the same guys."

"I would agree." The police chief maneuvered them through the trees with a methodical deliberation.

"So what's the plan then?" Silas asked, checking his phone.

Natalie shrugged. "At this point there's not much we can do but watch and wait."

Perfect. The two things he sucked at the most.

"Tess or Morgan could've been hit by a stray bullet," Silas reminded her. And if that had happened... well, he couldn't even go there.

"I know." The woman shifted into a lower gear. "Trust me. I'm every bit as pissed off as you are about this. But it's not like I can go searching garages and barns all over the valley to find the UTV. Without a warrant, I can't do anything."

"I get it." But that wouldn't stop him from doing his own investigating and stopping them before someone got killed.

Rather than continue talking over the engine noise, Silas sent Tess a text to fill her in on what had happened and the state of her UTV.

She texted him back immediately.

So glad you're okay! Don't worry about the UTV. That's what insurance is for.

Nice of her to say, but he still couldn't help but feel like he'd let her down.

By the time they arrived back at the ranch, the sun had

started to set. Silas climbed out of the UTV. "I'll go talk to Tess," he said, already heading for the house. He had to get a look at her, to make sure she was okay. He had to check on Morgan too.

Thatch simply smiled and saluted him before getting into his truck.

"Thanks," Natalie called. "I'll add everything into the report you two filed the other day. We'll do our best to stay on top of this," she promised before driving off.

So would he. Silas climbed the steps to Tess's porch, his heart bouncing around in his chest.

She threw open the door mid-knock. "Are you sure you're okay?" She stepped outside and closed the door behind her. "God, I was so worried. You should get checked out at the hospital or something. You never know about a head injury or internal bleeding or—"

"I'm fine," he assured her. "Thatch and I both walked away without a scratch." Only his pride was hurt. "How's Morgan?" He'd likely never get the terror in the girl's eyes out of his head.

"She's better now." Tess glanced in through the living room window. "She fell asleep on the couch watching a movie." She leaned against the house with a sigh. "The thought of people shooting a gun up there really terrorized her."

"I can imagine." The thought of her and Tess being so close to the gunfire terrorized him. "I won't let this go. I promise. I'm going to take a daily ride up there from now on, keep an eye on things until Natalie finds the people responsible." They'd talked about the possibility of starting a patrol at the meeting, but they hadn't had a chance to coordinate yet. That would change today.

The glow from the setting sun lit her eyes. "Will Natalie find the people responsible?"

He had to believe she would. Or he wouldn't be going anywhere for a while. "It's not every day you see an older model white UTV with a purple stripe." Hell, he knew he'd be watching the trails and roads. "If they live around here, they shouldn't be too hard to find."

Tess sat down on the top step. "I set up a community meeting here for Sunday night. I invited everyone who wrote their email address down at the café."

Though he thought better of it, he sat next to her. "That's a good idea. Now that we have a description of the vehicle, everyone should be on the lookout. I'm guessing other people will help with patrols too."

"I think so." Tess crossed her arms tightly over her chest as if she was chilled. "Hey, Silas...um...about our... *conversation* the other day. In Legacy's pen..."

Without warning, he was hit with a memory of the second she pressed her lips to his and rendered him helpless. "That wasn't much of a conversation."

A pinkish hue bloomed on her cheeks. "Um, right. I suppose there wasn't much talking." She cleared her throat. "The thing is...you can't go back to that place, to that life. It's too dangerous and I...I don't want you to leave. I don't want you to be gone for however many months the mission will take."

"Why not?" Damn, there was nothing more dangerous than looking into Tess's eyes. He could lose himself there real easily.

"Because the girls will miss you," she half whispered. "You're a part of our family. You and Thatch. You're important to them. I don't want them to lose someone else they care about that way."

Right. She wanted him to stay for the girls. He beat back disappointment and stood so he could escape this conversation. "I'm careful, Tess. I'm very good at what I do. And I'll still be a part of their family. Even when I'm gone. I'll be there for them however I can." *Walk away now.* Before it was too late. "It's been a long day. I should get home. I'll see you at the meeting—"

"*I'll* miss you," Tess cut him off and leapt to her feet. "Damn it, Silas. Don't you understand? I don't want you to go because *I'll* miss you. *I* can't lose you."

He stopped moving but didn't turn around. He couldn't. Once again, his resolve to keep space and distance between them had started to quake dangerously. But he couldn't give in this time. He couldn't touch her. He couldn't kiss her.

Tess came down the rest of the steps and moved into his line of vision. "I try to picture my life without you in it... and I can't."

Damn that hope. It kept rising up in him, especially when she looked at him with her eyes ablaze.

"I have feelings for you, Silas." She was almost whispering now. "But everything would be so complicated. With the girls and with all of our friends and with everyone who knew Jace." She rested both of her hands on his chest.

No. He couldn't feel her touch right now. He couldn't act on impulses that were firing in his body. Silas stepped back. "What do you want, Tess?" And suddenly he knew he would give it to her. Anything she wanted. Whatever she asked for. This woman held all of his strength in her hands.

"I don't know." She ran her hand through her hair. "I

don't know. We could see each other secretly. We could be careful and no one would ever have to know. Not the girls or Aiden or our friends..."

The words stung worse than a slap. That was the one thing he couldn't give her. "We won't be able to hide. I mean, sure we would be careful around the girls to protect them. But we'd be lying to everyone else." Star Valley was a small town. They were around their friends all the time. He'd already proven he couldn't be near her without giving himself away. "We'll never be free to be together." He had to accept that.

"We could be." She was getting frantic now, gesturing with her hands as she spoke. "We could sneak off for weekends together—"

"No." That hope that had built him up only minutes before crashed. "I won't do that."

"So I'm not enough to keep you here. Is that it?" she demanded with a fire in those vivid brown eyes.

"You don't want *me*." That was the plain truth. "You'd want to keep our relationship a secret. You'd want to hide me from everyone." Didn't she understand? That meant she didn't think he was good enough for her either. "I can't be with someone who's ashamed of me." And he understood. He already knew he wasn't worthy of her. Why would she want him when she'd already had someone like Jace? "I can't do what you're asking me to do. I've lived that life before. My own mother was ashamed of me. And I won't do it again."

Tess stared at him, wide-eyed, tears rolling down her cheeks. "I'm sure that's not true."

She only said that because she didn't know. No one knew. He'd never told anyone much about his childhood.

Not even Thatch and Aiden. But despite all of that, he found himself telling her now. "My mom used to make me hide in my room when she had a man over. She'd get all my stuff out of the living room of our apartment so there was no evidence she had a kid. She didn't put up any pictures of me on the walls." He'd thought that was normal until he'd visited one of his friend's houses once and saw pictures hanging everywhere.

"She told me if I made any noise at all she'd leave me with her parents forever. And believe it or not, my grandparents treated me worse than she did." His grandpa had a temper and had taken his belt to Silas on more than one occasion. "When I was old enough, I found my way out. Through my career in the Navy, through my training. I built myself a better life. And now I won't go back to being someone's dirty secret. I can't."

Leaving it at that, he walked away.

CHAPTER FOURTEEN

Why had she ever agreed to go out to dinner with Brad? With so much on her mind, even hanging out with a friend seemed like a painful prospect right now.

Tess gave herself a once-over in her bathroom mirror. She should probably put a little more effort into her appearance besides pulling her hair into a ponytail and throwing on one of her softest worn flannel shirts, but right now she couldn't bring herself to care how she looked.

I won't go back to being someone's dirty secret.

Those words Silas had spoken last night were seared into her heart. She teared up again, picturing him as a little boy, sitting alone in his room, afraid to make any noise, fearing his mother would abandon him. Nausea swelled in her stomach. She'd never intended to make Silas feel like she was ashamed of him, but she had... sneaking around, coming unglued when Aiden almost caught them kissing in Legacy's pen—

"Mom?" Morgan poked her head into the bathroom.

"Are you ready yet? We're supposed to be at Auntie Kyra and Uncle Aiden's in a few minutes."

Tess sighed and spritzed her hair with some spray to tame the frizz. "I suppose I'm as ready as I'll ever be."

"Really?" Her daughter wrinkled her freckled nose. "I thought you were supposed to dress nice for a date."

"I already told you; this is not a date." Tess prodded Morgan out of her bathroom. And she couldn't stomach the thought of trying to put on a front with Brad when she'd left things so badly with Silas last night. Jeez. She wasn't being honest with anyone right now—not her brother, not Silas, and definitely not herself. The hurt that she felt for Silas right now—the unrelenting desire to soothe his pains from the past—only proved she had real feelings for him. Deeper feelings than she cared to admit.

Tess followed Morgan to the living room and found Willow jumping on the couch. "Auntie Kyra said she was going to get us ice cream and we could watch *The Princess Diaries*."

"Again?" Tess teased as she caught her younger daughter in her arms.

"It's the best movie in the whole world." Morgan impatiently pulled on her coat near the front door.

"We love it!" Willow wriggled out of Tess's grasp and found her coat hanging on the hook.

"Yes, I know. I have the entire movie memorized, remember?" Tess directed the girls outside to the truck and helped her younger daughter climb into her seat.

All the way to her brother and Kyra's ranch the girls sang "Stupid Cupid"—one of their favorites from the movie—at the tops of their lungs.

The second the truck stopped, both girls were out the doors and racing for the front porch.

Kyra must've seen them coming because she opened the door and greeted them with hugs. "Girls' night! I can't wait! I've got chocolate fudge brownies and birthday cake ice cream."

"Our favorite," Willow squealed.

"Maybe we'll have time to watch *The Princess Diaries 2* too," Morgan said hopefully.

"I doubt that." Tess climbed the steps behind her. "Dinner won't be more than an hour or so." Especially with her mood tonight. "You girls be respectful and polite." She bent to kiss their sweet faces.

"They always are." Kyra ruffled their hair as they hurried past her into the house.

"Bye, Mommy!" Willow called without looking back. Morgan was in too much of a hurry to say a thing.

"Thanks again for hanging out with them tonight." Tess lingered on her friend's porch. She was in no hurry to get her evening started.

"I've been looking forward to it." Kyra stepped out and shut the door as though she knew they had a few things to discuss. "Are you looking forward to having dinner with Brad?"

She couldn't even muster a smile. "It'll be nice, I guess." But there were so many other things she should be doing right now. Things she couldn't take care of while she sat across the table from Brad.

"You're not excited." Kyra tugged on her arm and led her to the two chairs in front of the living room window.

"No. I'm not." Tess sat down and told Kyra about the exchange with Silas the night before. "I had no idea what his childhood had been like. I didn't know he grew up that way . . . feeling unwanted and unloved." But then she'd tossed and turned all night thinking about him. Wondering about him. Why had she never asked any questions about his life before coming to Star Valley? How could she not have known he'd dealt with so much pain?

"That's heartbreaking." Kyra looked thoughtful. "It's huge that he told you about his childhood though. I'd be surprised if he's ever shared those things with anyone else."

"I know Jace had never mentioned anything. In fact, he always said Silas was very evasive about his life growing up."

"I can understand why," Kyra said sadly. "It sounds so painful. My mom had her problems but she never made me feel unloved or unwanted."

Tess could say the same. She and Aiden had the most wonderful childhood, with their parents both being jovial, loving, doting kind of people. "You should've seen his face when he told me." She'd always thought of Silas as the most upbeat and laid-back out of the whole group, but now she suspected that his humor and cheerfulness covered up his past hurts. "His eyes were so empty." She couldn't get that expression out of her head.

"You haven't heard from him since he walked away?" Kyra asked.

"No." She hadn't tried to get in touch with him either. Maybe she should've called him, but she hadn't even known what to say. "I feel awful. I never meant to make him feel like I was embarrassed of him." But of course he would feel that way when people had been doing that to him his whole life.

"Then why are you so afraid about people finding out there's something between you two?" At least her friend asked the question gently.

"I'm not sure." Another lie. Tess shook her head at herself. She had to stop. She had to be honest for once. "I guess . . . I'm more afraid that being with Silas will be too hard for everyone to accept." What if it was hard for her to accept too? "And I'll have to make decisions if we decide to be together. Decisions about him, about my future. Decisions that could change everything." Yes. That was exactly why she'd rather hide. That was why she'd lost her mind and suggested they keep their relationship a secret. "After losing Jace, decisions like that are a scary prospect." She alone bore the weight of how her choices would affect Morgan and Willow.

"That makes perfect sense." Kyra laid a hand on her shoulder in a show of solidarity. "But all of those future decisions don't have to happen right away, you know. Sometimes it's best to take things one day at a time so you can figure things out little by little. Silas knows better than most people what you've been through. He's walked the road with you. If you two were together, you could take it slow. But you couldn't keep it a secret. That would never work."

"I know. I can't even believe I suggested that." She'd felt desperate to keep him in Star Valley. With her. But she would hate lying. Tess rose from the chair, suddenly anxious to get through this dinner with Brad. "Maybe I can find some time to talk with Silas later."

Kyra walked her to the steps. "Thatch told me earlier that Silas is in Jackson tonight. He told Thatch he had some errands to run and was going to stay overnight. But Thatch thinks he left because he knew you were going out to dinner with Brad."

Tess's shoulders slumped. "So I can't talk to him tonight."

"I'm afraid not—"

The door flew open behind them, and Willow ran out. "Come on, Auntie Kyra! We've been waiting forever! It's time to stop talking! We need to start the movie."

"Yes, we do." Kyra took Willow's hand. "Have fun tonight." She waved to Tess. "You know we're happy to have the girls here as long as you can spare them."

"I won't be long." She already knew she'd run out of the energy to pretend everything in her world was fine by seven o'clock. "Thanks again," she called, walking to her truck.

A myriad of emotions clashed within her as she drove back across town. Sadness. Some fear. Maybe even a little hope. And gratitude. She didn't know how she would get along without Aiden and Kyra. Their fun nights with the girls had given her many moments of reprieve.

Going out with Brad might not be the way she truly wanted to spend the evening but it would be nice to sit and eat a meal and drink a glass of wine without having to get up and down five times for various things and then do the dishes after. An evening off from parenting might be exactly the breath she needed to get herself together.

When she pulled up in front of the café, Brad was waiting by the door. He looked nice in dark jeans and a freshly pressed plaid shirt but he hadn't gotten himself all fancied up either. Tess relaxed a little as she climbed out of the truck.

"Hey," she called. "Sorry I'm a few minutes late."

"Not a problem." He opened the door for her and ushered her into the restaurant. "No pressure here. Remember? This is an easy dinner."

Before she could respond, Minnie scurried up to the hostess desk. "Well, hello there." Tess could see the wheels in Minnie's head spinning out of control. "Just the *two of you* dining together tonight, hmm?"

"Yes, ma'am." Brad winked at her. "Table for two."

"My, my, my," the woman murmured, selecting two laminated menus and the wine list from the stand. "Isn't this fun? Follow me. You'll have the best table in the house." She led them to a quiet booth near the window that showcased a picturesque view of the mountains. "Are we celebrating any *special occasions* this evening?"

Tess gave her a deadpan look. "Nope." Maybe she and Brad should've driven to a different town for dinner. Minnie was going to take this casual dinner with Brad and run with it. Tomorrow she'd be offering Tess the café for a wedding reception.

The woman positively beamed as she went over the specials and Tess listened patiently before ordering a glass of wine.

"Not champagne?" Minnie asked, withdrawing her pencil from behind her ear.

"Just the chardonnay for me," Tess said firmly.

Brad ordered a beer and the appetizer sampler for them to snack on while they decided what they wanted for dinner.

After Minnie walked away, they settled into an easy conversation about the girls.

"I've got to say, I'm impressed with your handling of the whole situation between them." Brad unrolled his silverware and laid his napkin across his lap. "Callie has been a different kid since she and Morgan became friends. So thank you. It's been good for her."

Tess could relate. "I remember how angry Morgan was after Jace passed away. Willow was too young to understand fully, but Morgan was downright mad." Oh, the struggles they'd had. Her daughter had acted out at home and at school and it had taken a good year of counseling for Morgan to start to deal with her emotions in healthier ways. "That year was very challenging behavior-wise, I can tell you that."

"This year has been for Callie too." He reached for the pitcher sitting at the edge of the table and filled their water glasses. "But it's good to see that she's healing a little bit now."

Healing was a long process; Tess knew that from personal experience. "Does she ever see her mom?"

"Only when she has a break from school." His easy expression tightened. "She'll spend part of the summer out in Denver. Her mother isn't quite established with a steady job yet. And I'm not too sure about the man she's dating. So we'll see what happens." He shrugged as though there wasn't much he could do about it. "Right now my parents are helping me give Callie as much stability as we can. That seems to be what she needs more than anything."

A server swooped in and delivered their drinks and the appetizer and then rushed away. As per usual, the café was packed for the dinner hour.

"Family support is very important." Tess sipped her wine. "The girls and I wouldn't have survived without Aiden, Thatch, and . . . Silas." Her heart seemed to sigh. If only she could be sitting across the table from him instead tonight.

She let herself picture it for a few seconds—what it would be like if they could simply go out on a date together, no hiding, no worrying, no baggage between them. It was a nice picture but seemed so far out of reach. Sighing, Tess tuned in to what Brad was saying again.

"I understand why everyone says raising kids takes a village." He set one of the appetizer plates in front of her. "Oh, by the way, Callie was hoping Morgan could come over and spend the night. I know you're having that meeting at your house on Sunday. I was thinking the girls could stay over at our house with my parents if you think that would be helpful."

"That would work out great, actually. The girls would love it." Brad's mother had worked at the county library and had always been very sweet to them. "Morgan has been pretty upset about what's going on with the wild horses, so I'd rather not have her and Willow within earshot when we discuss what to do." She told him about the gunshots during their ride earlier that week.

Brad shook his head. "Shooting that close to private property is just plain irresponsible. I can't even fathom being that careless with a gun."

Tess helped herself to some of the chips and salsa from the appetizer platter. "We're finally getting that citizen patrol schedule finalized so we can keep a better eye on things." What choice did they have? Natalie had gone up to the high meadow a few times but still hadn't seen anything.

"Well, like I said, I'd be happy to help out," Brad replied. "I've got a UTV that I can take up there."

They talked a little more about the wild horses, with Tess filling him in on some of the history of the herd, and when Minnie came back, they ordered their entrees.

"Would you like more wine?" the woman asked, bouncing her eyebrows a few times.

"I'm good," Tess told her, trying to send her a look that told her to take her hopes down a few notches. Sheesh. Tess hadn't even finished her first glass of wine and Minnie was trying to get her all liquored up.

When they were alone again, Brad shot her a smile.

"I know we said this was a casual dinner, but I'm really enjoying spending time with you."

"It's been nice," Tess agreed. Only nice though. She enjoyed talking to him, and she could relate to him struggling through the single parenting thing, but both her mind and heart were somewhere else right now.

"Would you want to do it again sometime?" He hesitated before continuing. "And maybe make it a real date?"

The question caught her off guard, but she should've seen it coming. Conversation came comfortably between them, and they laughed easily together. But she couldn't keep hiding from the truth. She had to start speaking up, right now. "Actually...I have to be honest." She held his gaze. "There is someone in my life right now. Sort of." *Ugh.* Why was this so hard for her to say? Why did admitting her feelings out loud make her heart break and beat faster at the same time?

"I mean, I don't know if anything will come of it, but I don't want you to get the wrong idea. I don't want to lead you on." She grasped at courage. "Silas and I have a history together. It's complicated. But there are definitely feelings there." Now she knew for sure. "On both sides."

Brad nodded with a good-natured smile. "I'm pretty sure there's no such thing as an *un*complicated relationship. People are messy. That's just part of it."

She could not have said that better. "I appreciate you being so understanding." Again, she felt her shoulders relaxing, the tension leaving her neck. Maybe telling the truth really did set a person free.

Brad sipped his beer. "I'm happy to hang out as friends too. Right now I'm mainly interested in friends, in building community for Callie. My ex and I rushed through our relationship and probably got married long before either of us was ready to. I don't intend to make that mistake again."

"I'm always looking for friends too." And she had a feeling Brad would become a good one. "You're sure it's okay if the girls come over on Sunday night?"

"More than okay." Either the man had an incredible poker face or her rejection really hadn't stung him. "Mom'll love it. She'll probably plan all kinds of crafts and activities for them."

The server arrived, carting along their entrees—the steak for Brad and the trout for her. The rest of the meal passed comfortably while they discussed the girls' school—with Tess trying to explain how the PTA worked.

"Thanks for solving that mystery for me." Brad tossed his napkin onto his mostly empty plate. "I didn't even know what the acronym stood for."

Tess laughed and put down her fork. She was stuffed. "Call me anytime you have questions about the mysteries of elementary school. I've become something of an expert."

"Thanks. I suppose I should be at the next PTA meeting," Brad said, a tad unenthusiastically.

"Don't feel like you have to do everything." She wished someone would've told her that once. "There's a really great volunteer base at the school. So pitch in where you want to and let other people pick up the slack when you can't." That's how a community was supposed to work.

"Good advice." The man finished off his beer. "I'll remember that."

Right as he set down his empty glass, Minnie appeared. "Can I get you a dessert? Maybe the chocolate cake for *two*?"

"Sorry, no." Tess almost hated to bust the woman's romantic bubble. "We were just getting ready to head out."

"We're full," Brad confirmed.

Though she tried to split the bill with him, he paid for everything, leaving a generous tip, and then they walked out of the restaurant with Minnie shaking her head sadly on the sidelines.

Tess thanked him for a nice evening and made plans to drop Morgan and Willow off at his house an hour before the meeting. When she climbed into her truck, her soul felt lighter somehow. Maybe acknowledging her true feelings would get easier each time she did it.

Starting the engine, she briefly thought about driving to Jackson to try and track Silas down, but the logistics seemed overwhelming. And after their exchange last night, he likely didn't want to see her. So she would wait and talk to him tomorrow. After the meeting. Right now she needed to speak to her brother.

Minutes later, Tess knocked on Aiden and Kyra's front door.

Her friend answered and quickly glanced at her watch. "Hey. What're you doing back here so early?"

Morgan appeared behind Kyra. "Aw, Mom. We're not even done with the movie yet."

"You can keep watching until it's over." She focused on her soon-to-be sister-in-law. "I need to talk to Aiden anyway. Is he around?"

Kyra nodded, a knowing smile in place. "He's cleaning the garage."

"For some reason he didn't want to watch *The Princess Diaries* with us," Morgan called, already making her way back into the house.

"I don't blame him," Tess whispered.

Her friend laughed. "For some reason that movie never gets old to me. Lyric and I watched it together all the time when we were kids."

Tess always marveled at how Lyric and Kyra had been best friends as young girls and then were reunited less than a year ago when Kyra's dad passed away. "Well, I'm glad *you* enjoy that movie." She was going to enjoy not having to watch it a fourth time this month. "I'll come back and hang out with you once Aiden and I have had a little chat."

Kyra nodded. "I'll be anxious to hear how it goes. He might be surprised but he does want you to be happy, Tess. That's the most important thing to Aiden."

"I know." But telling him that she was falling in love with Jace's best friend wasn't going to be easy. Tess jogged down the porch steps and crossed the driveway to let herself into the property's main outbuilding. For two years, Aiden had made it his job to protect her, to counsel her, to help her, to make her life easier. And he had in many ways. But now she needed to stand on her own and tell him the truth.

She found her brother standing among piles of horse supplies and feed and snow removal equipment. "Hey," he said, setting down a crate of tools. "I thought you had a date with Brad tonight."

"It *wasn't* a date." Tess let out an exasperated sigh. She should've worn a sign. Instead, she pulled out a stool from his workbench and took a seat. "This conversation cut our dinner short though."

Aiden pulled a handkerchief out of his back pocket and wiped his face. "You didn't have fun?"

"It was fine." She picked up a rope scrap and started

to unravel the edge, needing something to keep her hands busy. "He's a nice guy. Only he's not the guy I'm interested in right now."

Aiden came to stand in front of her, looking at her intently as if for the first time. "But you *are* interested in someone?"

"Kind of." She focused on the rope, her fingers fraying all of those little strands at the end. "Er, I mean, yes. *Yes*. I think I may be interested in someone." The erratic beating of her heart only proved how interested she was in Silas. Onward. She must press onward. "I know this might come as a surprise. Or maybe it won't. I don't know. I mean, I know *I* was pretty surprised—"

"What're you talking about?" Her brother shoved another crate of junk out of the way so he could pull out the stool next to hers. "I've already told you I'll be fully supportive when you decide to date again. We all know you loved Jace, Sis. Dating again won't take away from that."

"Thanks." Tess lifted her head and dropped the rope on the workbench. "It's Silas."

"*Silas* Silas?" Aiden shot off the stool. "As in *my* friend Silas?" His voice rose three octaves higher. "As in *Jace's* friend Silas?"

"Is that so surprising?" Tess stood too, facing off with him. "I've spent a lot of time with the man in the last two years. He's become a big part of my life."

Her brother turned away from her and exhaled loudly. "He's nothing like Jace, Tess. *Nothing*."

"You really think I would only be attracted to someone like Jace?" She nudged Aiden's shoulder to turn him around. "Jace is dead. I know he's dead. I know he's not coming back. I'm not trying to replace Jace." She never could. What they'd had was different than what she would have with someone else. She didn't expect a new relationship to be the same as her marriage. "Hell, I don't even want to have feelings for anyone. But you don't always get to decide what your heart wants, now, do you?"

"Okay." Aiden leaned against his workbench and kneaded his temples. "Okay...Silas isn't a good idea. I love him like a brother, but he's taking off on a mission, Tess. He's not permanent. He was the only one out of all of us who actually enjoyed being on the move all the time. Can you really see him settling in to be Morgan and Willow's *father* someday?"

Aiden didn't know. He didn't get why Silas had never put down roots anywhere. He didn't understand what Silas had run from. And she wouldn't tell him. It wasn't her place. "I didn't say I wanted to *marry* Silas." She let her irritation burn through the words. "I said I have *feelings* for him."

She wasn't about to share that she'd acted on those feelings a few times. Her brother didn't need to know anything about her sex life, thank you very much. "I'm not asking for your permission, by the way. I just thought you should know." She went to make a dramatic exit, but Aiden caught her arm.

"Wait. I don't want you to get hurt, that's all. Not after what you've been through." He sat back down on the stool. "Jesus, Tess. You know what could happen to him over there."

"Yes. I know." And her stomach hurt every time she thought about it. Underneath all of her fears, she had to hope that he would choose to stay. And if he'd already committed to this one mission, maybe he'd agree it would be his last. She slumped on her stool next to her brother. "Like I said, I wasn't planning for this to happen."

"Happen? What do you mean *happen*? Has something *happened*?" There he went, lurching to his feet again. "Please tell me nothing has *happened* between you two."

Forget this. Tess stood and calmly pushed the stool back under the workbench. "I don't know why I came to talk to you in the first place."

"Don't be like that." Aiden followed her outside. "It's a bad idea, that's all. You and Silas...what would that be like for the girls? Having you be with one of their father's best friends?"

"I don't know." She threw up her hands. "I don't know what any of it would look like or where these feelings might go. I don't know how Morgan and Willow would feel or how they would handle him becoming a bigger part of our lives." She only knew that her heart seemed to grow about three times bigger when she laid eyes on the man. She knew that Silas was the one she thought about in the lonely late night hours. She knew that she wondered about him all of the time and she wanted to make his life better.

And maybe that was all she needed to know.

CHAPTER FIFTEEN

Tess cut the brownies she'd made earlier and neatly arranged them on a platter.

Next to her, Kyra was setting out the plates and silverware on the kitchen island while Lyric made a pitcher of iced tea. Everything was just about set. Nearly twenty people milled around her living room, catching up on all the latest news in town. But one very important person remained missing.

Tess looked for him again. It felt like a year since Silas had walked away from her front porch. She hadn't heard from him, and now he was late to the meeting.

Sighing, she dumped some popcorn into a bowl. "How's my brother doing?" she asked Kyra. Tess hadn't talked to Aiden since she'd dropped the Silas bombshell last night. Currently, her brother stood across the room in front of the fireplace, deeply engrossed in a conversation with Louie and Thatch. But he hadn't said a word to her when he'd come in.

"He'll be fine." Kyra rearranged the napkins into a fancy flower-like formation. "He needs some time to process the thought of you and Silas, that's all. He was surprised."

"He wasn't the only one," she muttered, glancing out the window for the fifteenth time. Where was Silas anyway?

"I'm sure he's on his way." Lyric poured them each a glass of iced tea and handed them around. "Silas wouldn't miss the meeting. He knows how important this is to you."

"I have a lot to discuss with him. After everyone leaves." She wasn't as concerned with him missing the meeting as she was with him sticking around to talk to her after the meeting. Silas would support the cause of the wild horses. He'd already made that clear. He'd gone on a wild chase when he'd thought she and Morgan were in danger, risking his own safety to bring the shooters to justice.

So why wasn't he here?

On the other side of the living room, her front door creaked open, lifting her hopes. But it was only Brad.

"Hey." He greeted a few people on his way into the kitchen. "Sorry I'm a little late. I was making sure the girls were all set."

"Are they having fun?" Tess gasped. Oh shoot! She'd forgotten all about the buffalo chicken dip she put in the oven a half hour ago. She shoved on her oven mitts and spun.

"They're having a blast." Brad closed the oven door for her after she extracted her slightly overdone dip. "Mom was teaching them to paint with watercolors when I left. She's really enjoying entertaining them."

"I'm sure they're enjoying being there." Tess sprinkled on the green onions she'd cut up. "Thanks for including Willow too. She was so excited to have a sleepover with the big girls."

"The three of them get along great." The man started

talking about some other things Callie had planned for the evening, but Tess felt something over her shoulder. She turned in that direction and her heart dove for the floor.

Silas. At some point he had come into her house and was standing only a few feet away, watching her talk with Brad. How long had he been there?

Tess refocused on Brad, realizing he was waiting for her to say something. "Uh, that's great. They're going to have a blast. Thanks again for letting them come over."

"Anytime. I have a feeling this will be the first of many sleepovers."

Tess tried to smile at him, but she kept glancing at Silas, who had now moved to the other side of the kitchen island. He was scrolling through his phone, but he was clearly within earshot of their conversation. From the outside looking in, it probably seemed like she and Brad were awfully close. Especially standing there alone together talking about the girls. While Tess had been occupied with managing the dip, Lyric and Kyra had moved over to join Thatch, Louie, and Aiden by the fireplace.

Once again, Brad was waiting for her to say something.

"Yes, we'll have to have Callie over here for the sleepover next time. In fact, I'm having a little gathering for Willow's birthday on Wednesday night. It'll be really simple. Dinner with a few friends and family." That's all her younger daughter wanted—to have her favorite people in one room together. This might not be the best time to ask him, but she'd promised Willow before she'd dropped her off at the Klines' house. Since Callie had invited her to spend the night, Willow wanted to invite Callie to her birthday. Tess set a basket of crackers next to the dip. "You and Callie would be more than welcome."

"That sounds great. Callie will love it."

"Wonderful. We'll get together after school. About four o'clock." She sidestepped him. "Um, I should get ready to start the meeting." After she had a chance to talk to Silas, that was. "But I've put out some snacks and drinks. Help yourself."

"Sounds great." Brad grabbed a plate.

Silas had wandered to the row of chairs Aiden had set up in front of the television set. He clearly wanted to avoid her, but she cornered him anyway. "Hi. I didn't know if you were coming."

"I told you I'd be here." He gave her a cool look. "The girls are at Brad's house, huh?"

So he had heard her entire conversation. She knew she didn't owe him an explanation, but she offered one anyway. "Yes. Because Callie and Morgan are friends. And I didn't want them overhearing anything upsetting at this meeting, given what happened on our ride." Morgan was still having a hard time falling asleep at night.

"Yeah, that's a good idea." He smiled a little, but his eyes held distance between them.

"How was Jackson?" Tess wasn't going to give up that easily. She got that he had a default self-protection mode, but he didn't have to protect himself from her.

"Fine." He seemed hell-bent on keeping that detached expression on his face. "I had to pick up groceries and supplies for a job."

And get away from her. Tess didn't respond. There was so much to say to him but twenty people were waiting for her to get this meeting started. "Can we talk later? After everyone else leaves?"

"Sure." His jaw went slack. "But you don't owe me any

explanations, Tess. I don't know why I said all of those things the other night."

Because he'd been hurting. And for once he'd let some-one see his real feelings. "You have nothing to apologize for," she told him. Glancing around, she realized that most everyone had taken their seats. "We'll talk later. Promise me you'll stay after the meeting."

"I promise." He took a seat near the corner, and she turned to make her way through the crowd.

Inhaling deeply, Tess moved in front of the window with all eyes on her. "Thank you all for coming tonight. I'm going to get started, but feel free to go help yourselves to snacks and drinks in the kitchen if you haven't already."

Her front door opened, causing a brief interruption. Natalie hurried inside. "Sorry I'm late." She slid into a chair in the back row. "Don't mind me. Carry on."

"Thanks for coming." Tess appreciated the chief's sup-port. "Okay, as I said in the email, there's been another incident with the horses." As quickly and efficiently as possible, Tess detailed what had happened when she and Morgan had been up riding in the high meadow.

"You two could've been hit," Minnie called out in horror.

"It's time to find these jerks," Louie added. "We can't have them terrorizing people like that. Hell, I'll go up there and find them myself."

Murmurs of agreement made the rounds.

Tess waited for the noise to settle. "We do have a little more information than we did before. There appeared to be three men riding in a white UTV with a purple stripe. We don't have much to go on at this point, but we have to assume they're familiar with the area. Because, from what we've observed, they're not crossing the border onto our property." And there were no fences up there. If they were hunters or campers from out of town, they wouldn't know where the public land stopped and hers started.

"It has to be Darrell," Thatch said. "Or Ford." The man turned around in his chair to look at Natalie. "Can't you go question them or something?"

"Yeah. Go see if one o' them are hidin' that UTV on their property," Louie added.

"I can't do that." The chief stood to address the whole room. "I know everyone suspects Darrell and Ford, but there's no evidence. I can't show up at their properties and start interrogating them. Things don't work like that."

"Well, what if we question them?" Silas asked.

"I can't tell you not to." The chief sat back down. "But nobody do anything stupid. If you see something—if you find something—you call me right away."

"Besides, we don't even know if Ford and Darrell are responsible." Tess took the floor back. While those two men were exactly where her suspicions rested too, there wasn't much point in public accusations without evidence. "We can all keep our eyes open. Watch for a vehicle of that description when you're out on the trails."

"We'll watch for it, all right," Doris Gatlin called. Doris was one of Minnie's best friends and a part of the Ladies Aid Society that fed and took care of pretty much everyone in town. "We'll find these dirtbags together."

"Hear! Hear!" Minnie cheered.

"Yes. We'll all pitch in to find them together." Tess grinned at the older ladies in the group. They'd always been fearless, thanks to growing up in the backwoods of Wyoming. "And I do think we're close. And we're thankful for Chief Holbrook here who's doing her best to get someone up there a few times a week. And our citizen patrols can help to fill in the gaps."

"How often do you want the patrols to run?" Minnie asked.

"Good question." They couldn't have eyes on the meadow 24-7. "If we have enough people sign up, we'd like to see someone ride up in the morning and late afternoon." If everyone sitting in the room signed up, they'd have no problem watching out for the horses for the next few weeks.

"I have a sign-up sheet with the days and times set out by the snacks in the kitchen. Feel free to put yourself down for as many shifts as you'd like to take." She glanced in Silas's direction and resisted the temptation to let her gaze linger. "And if you do happen to see the UTV while out on patrol, don't approach them on your own." They didn't need anyone else getting into a wreck or taking a stray bullet.

"Yes. Please call me before trying to engage the suspects at all." Natalie fired a pointed look in both Thatch's and Silas's directions.

They grinned and saluted her.

"All right." Tess hurried to end the meeting. The quicker people left, the faster she'd be able to talk to Silas. "I think that's about it, everyone. Thanks for coming. Meeting dismissed." The chatter rose around the room again while people got up and folded their chairs. Tess showed Thatch where to stack them and then nearly ran into Brad, who was making a beeline for the front door.

"Leaving already?"

"Yeah." He slipped on his cowboy hat. "I should get home and help out my parents with dinner for the girls. Thanks though. This was great." He sidestepped her and rushed away. "Oh, and just let me know what spots are left over on the sign-up sheet. I can take a few," he called.

"Okay. Sure. Thanks." Her words were met with the closing of her front door. Tess shook off the man's hasty retreat and started to collect discarded paper cups.

"It was so fun to see you and Brad at the café last night." Minnie gave her a hug. "Did you two have a good time?"

Tess spotted Silas standing a few feet away. Why did he always have to be within earshot when she was talking to or about Brad? "We had a nice time as *friends*," Tess said pointedly. "But, as I'm sure you saw, it wasn't a romantic date."

"Well, of course not." Minnie's head bobbed with understanding. "You don't want to move things too fast. I understand that."

Did she though? "We're not moving things at all. We've talked about how we would make much better friends than anything else." Of course, now that she was offering a full explanation, Silas had moved across the great room to join Aiden and Thatch in the kitchen. God, she hoped her brother didn't say anything to him about their conversation last night before she could.

"Well, you never know what could happen, my dear," Minnie insisted.

Tess gave up on convincing the woman there was nothing between her and Brad, saying a polite goodbye so she could make the rounds, thanking everyone for coming and walking them to the door one by one.

"Thanks for coming." She stepped out onto the porch with Natalie. "I know your hands are tied right now but I really appreciate the support."

"I'll do what I can," she promised. "Keep me posted on everything."

"Will do." Tess stepped back into the house, ready to collapse on the couch. But laughter drew her to the kitchen where Aiden, Kyra, Lyric, Thatch, and Silas were all sitting around the table.

Would it be rude for her to kick out everyone except for a certain cowboy?

"Saved you a seat." Lyric patted the chair next to her.

"And here's a drink." Kyra handed her a margarita.

"I don't know who made these, but I'm very grateful." A margarita was her go-to cocktail of choice, especially after such a hectic day.

"Silas made them," Lyric murmured, and a collective hush seemed to fall over the group.

"Yeah, and now I should probably clean up." The man pushed away from the table and walked around collecting dishes and trash before going to the sink, keeping his back to them while he washed everything up.

"Maybe we should all get going." Kyra's yawn could not have been more fake. "I don't know about you guys, but I'm pretty tired."

"It's only eight o'clock," Aiden argued. "It's been a long time since we've all hung out together. Maybe we should play some cards." He reached for the shelf behind him and pulled down a stack of playing cards.

"I'm down for cards." Thatch poured himself another margarita from the pitcher at the center of the table.

"We are not playing cards." Kyra swiped the deck out of Aiden's hands. "I'd like you to take me home now," she said sweetly.

"I'm going too." Lyric brought her empty margarita glass to the sink where Silas was still doing the dishes.

"Guess that means I'm bailing. I've got the early patrol

shift in the morning anyway." Thatch dumped his margarita back into the pitcher and Tess tried not to grimace. Now she'd be dumping the rest of that pitcher down the drain.

Everyone started moving through the living room, with Thatch and Lyric getting out the door first. But Aiden stopped. "Aren't you leaving too?" he called to Silas.

Tess felt her face flush. "He's going to stay for a few minutes."

"Yeah, I want to take out the trash." Silas shut off the kitchen sink and bagged up the overflowing kitchen trash can.

"Come on, cowboy." Kyra linked her arm through Aiden's and dragged him out the door. "Good night," her friend called cheerfully.

She walked them to the door and then returned to the kitchen just as Silas was coming in from the garage.

"You didn't have to take out my garbage." But man, it was sexy when he did things like that—took the trash out, rolled up his sleeves to wash the dishes so she didn't have to do them later. A dizzying attraction overtook her equilibrium.

"I know I didn't have to take out the trash." But that right there was the kind of thing Silas was always doing. Picking up the slack wherever he saw a need.

"Can we sit down for a minute?" She beckoned him to the living room couch. "I've been wanting to talk to you." And now that they were finally alone, she had no idea where to start. She dropped to the couch, almost too tired to stand anymore.

Silas sat, leaving a healthy distance between them. "Before you say anything, I'm sorry about how I left things the other night. I shouldn't have unloaded on you like that. And I shouldn't have walked away."

"You didn't unload on me. You shared something. And I'm glad you did." Now she saw more of him—the whole picture—his pain, his resilience. "You'd never mentioned your childhood before."

"It's not something I talk about much." He leaned back into the cushions, sighing. "I don't exactly have great memories of growing up. Thinking about the past always puts me in a mood. But I shouldn't have said what I did about deserving better." His expression softened. "There is no one better than you, Tess."

And there went her heart again, doubling, tripling, quadrupling, in both size and tenderness for him. "You *do* deserve better than to be hidden away like you don't matter." She inched closer to him. As close as she could without touching him. She would touch him eventually—she had to. But first there were a few more things she had to tell him. "I need you to know that I'm not keeping what happened between us a secret only because I'm afraid of what other people will think." She closed her eyes to concentrate on stabilizing her breathing. When she opened them again, Silas had straightened, leaning in toward her slightly, waiting, hoping.

"I understand how it may have seemed that way," she continued. "But I realized that I'm keeping the secret because I don't know what to do with my feelings for you." She dropped her gaze to her hands so she could get through this.

"I never planned to feel this way again. I know Jace's letter told me I should, but I didn't want to. And then something happened. I started to think about you. Long before we spent the night together." She peeked into his eyes again. "I noticed I always looked forward to seeing you. And when we were all together in a group, sometimes I could only focus on you." And yet she kept downplaying all of those things as if she could simply will the yearnings of her heart to go away.

"I love how you always make me laugh." Confidence bolstered her words. He needed to know this. He needed to know how much she valued him, how much she cared for him. "I love how you're always quietly stepping in to help people—like Minnie and Louie at the café. And you spent this whole evening in my kitchen." Making her margaritas because he knew she loved them and then taking care of all the cleanup himself. "I love that you're loyal and dedicated and that you want to make the world a better place." She could keep going on, but his stare into her eyes was growing stronger and bolder and her breath failed her. "Silas, I feel this intensely strong connection with you." She couldn't hold back the tears any longer. "I don't know what it means . . . or if I will ever be able to fully love someone again. I don't know a lot of things. But I can't bear for you to think that I'm hiding because I'm ashamed of you. I'm hiding because I'm afraid."

He didn't say anything. He simply moved closer to her and wrapped her up in his arms.

Tess let her cheek rest against his chest and let go of a sigh she hadn't realized she'd been holding back. A few more tears slipped out, sprinkling his shirt. But she didn't move. She closed her eyes and focused on the rhythm of his breathing, the sound of his heart beating quickly but steadily in time with her own.

"I don't know a lot of things either," he murmured into

her hair. "But I feel that connection too. And the harder I try to deny it, the stronger it gets." He leaned back, looking at her with a new vulnerability.

"Then maybe we should stop denying it." She rose to her knees on the couch in front of him, bringing her face level with his. "And let ourselves see where this connection leads us." She kissed him, just a slow, small brush of her lips over his, but that simple touch ignited her body.

"I can't wait to see where it leads us," Silas whispered against her lips. He pressed into the kiss again, luring her into a dream, guiding her mouth to open to his. Tess inched forward, straddling his waist, settling into his lap while she clasped her hands at the base of his neck. This time the kiss was different. Slow and savoring, as if they had all the time in the world to explore each other. Tess relaxed into him, her senses consumed with Silas, the minty-ness of his mouth, the scent of his woodsy cologne.

But she wanted more. Not only a kiss. Not only sex. She wanted *him*.

Tess eased herself off of his lap and somehow stood with her knees quaking in the best possible way. "Come on." She tugged on his hand, pulling him up with her. "Let's let this connection lead us to my room."

Silas broke out laughing. "Now that was cheesy." He slid his hands down to her hips, holding her close.

"No, it wasn't." Her laugh betrayed the feeble argument. It had been a while since she'd engaged in any sexy talk. So, yes, maybe she was out of practice.

"Trust me, Tess. That was a cheesy line." He kissed her jaw. "But I liked it." His lips moved down to her neck. "I like *you*."

"I like you too." She whispered the words in his ear, all

breathy and hot. "Let me show you how much I like you." Pressing her hands to his muscled chest, she nudged him toward the hallway that led to her bedroom. With each step they took, another article of clothing dropped to the floor between kisses—his shirt, her shirt. His belt. Her bra.

Outside of her bedroom door, Tess kicked off her shoes. Silas followed suit and by the time they made it to the bed, only their jeans were left.

"You're sure about this?" He caressed her shoulders. "It's not too late to turn back."

Tess held her hands on either side of his face. "I'm sure." She was done hiding. "I'm *very* sure." She kissed him with a greater urgency, her breath hitching when he unbuttoned her jeans and slid them down her hips.

Tess stepped out of the pants and kicked them aside. "Sit." She pushed on Silas's shoulders until he sat on the bed in front of her.

She straddled his lap and reached around into his back jean pocket, pulling out his wallet to find a condom and then placing it next to him on the bed.

Silas touched his lips to the center of her collarbone, kissing and caressing his way across her chest while her head tipped back.

"You're the best thing I've ever tasted," he murmured against her skin.

"Mm-hmm," was all she could manage in response. His tongue skimmed her skin, reaching all of her hyper-sensitive spots.

Tess slid off his lap so she could open the button fly of his jeans and Silas got to his feet, helping her push them down.

Good lord, the man knew how to wear a pair of boxer

briefs. Last time they'd been together, she'd hardly noticed his body in her haste to get into bed, but now she looked him over, seeing the scars, the definition, the SEAL trident tattoo on his left pec. "You're beautiful," she told him. Battered but also beautiful.

Silas grabbed her hand and towed her to him, holding their bodies together. "And you, Tess, are exquisite." Kissing his way down her abdomen, he hooked his fingers through her underwear and lowered them to the floor. As he stood back up, his hands roved, fingers grazing her inner thigh before stroking between her legs.

Her knees faltered, but she managed to stay standing and push his boxer briefs off his hips. Silas slipped on the condom and kissed her harder, filling her with more strength, more passion, as he backed her up against the wall. His hand trailed down her thigh again, and then his fingers found the spot that made her gasp and whimper.

He lifted her right knee, bringing her up against his hip and she looked into his eyes while she guided him into her, bringing their bodies fully together.

He closed his eyes, his chest rising and falling, and Tess kissed him, her lips pressing into his. With her hands on his low back, she urged him to move, to push deeper, to let himself get as lost as she was. Holding her tightly against him, Silas moved inside of her while she murmured how good it was, *finally* to be with him again. Why had she waited? Why had she been hiding when he made her feel so good?

Everything in her lower abdomen tensed with unreleased pleasure and pressure. She moved her hips faster, finding the rhythm that would surely shatter all of her control.

Tess went over the edge first—she couldn't stop herself, couldn't hold back the flood any longer. The blinding sensations took her fully, quaking through her, and then Silas cried her name, tightening his hold on her while his body shuddered.

With a few stumbling steps, they both fell back to the bed out of breath, arms and legs entwined. Even with her body now a boneless heap, Tess managed to prop her head up so she could see into his eyes. Silas kissed her lips again, uttering a long, lazy sigh while his fingertips traced her arm. "I don't deserve you," he whispered.

Tess threaded their fingers together and held on to him. "You do. You deserve everything."

CHAPTER SIXTEEN

Silas dragged the hose to Legacy's trough and turned on the water.

On the other side of the fence, the horse paced and whinnied, already restless even though the sun had only just come up.

"I know." He withdrew a carrot from the bag he'd brought outside with him and held it on his hand. For a few seconds the horse stopped her frantic footsteps, but after she'd eaten the carrot, she went right back to the pacing.

He hated to see her like that. All desperate and trapped. "We're gonna get you home soon. I promise." Now that another few days had passed, her wound was hardly visible. Tess had taken good care of the horse, but it was time to let Legacy go back to her herd. He shut off the water and then pounded the loose fence post he'd found earlier back into place.

Glancing around, he tried to gauge whether there was

any more work to be done. He'd already opened the pasture fences for the cattle, checked all of the troughs, gone through the stable to feed the horses...damn, he was efficient this morning.

Normally he woke up and dragged himself out of bed, puttering in the kitchen of his small cabin while he made coffee and scrounged up something for breakfast. But he'd woken up this morning with Tess in his arms and energy he hadn't felt in a long time. After quietly getting out of bed to let her sleep, he'd decided to take on all of her chores and check on Legacy.

And now he couldn't wait to get back to the bedroom to surprise her.

Silas let himself into the pen once more and waited until the horse approached him. Legacy had gotten friendlier, and it didn't take her long to come and nudge his shoulder. "All right. One more carrot. Then I have to go wake up Tess." Hopefully she hadn't gotten out of bed yet, because he had plans for the woman this morning.

He held out the carrot and the horse ate it eagerly. "Everything'll be all right." He ran his hand up and down her long nose. "A few more days and you'll be running free again." He and Tess could take Legacy back up to the high pasture together. Even though they'd all miss the horse, she wanted to go back to her life.

Not wanting to keep Tess waiting, he let himself out the gate and hoofed it back to the house, kicking off his boots inside the kitchen door. After a quick washup in the sink, he moved down the hall, pausing outside of Tess's bedroom door to listen. Still pretty quiet in there. He inched it open slowly so the hinges wouldn't creak and then walked to the bed.

The woman was gorgeous. Lying on her side with her curls draping over her lovely face.

Silas stripped off his dirty jeans and sweatshirt and climbed back into bed with her, slipping his arm around her.

She smiled before her body even stirred and then her eyelids fluttered open. "You," she murmured with a teasing frown, "did not let me get much sleep last night."

"Sorry about that." He brought her knuckles to his lips. "You make it very difficult for a man to want to go to sleep."

"Oh, I'm not complaining." She yawned, stretching her bare arms up and over her head. "What time is it?" Her gaze landed on the clock on the bedside table. "Oh no!" The woman sat up straight. "It's almost eight o'clock! I have to feed the horses!"

"Already done." Silas pulled her back down to lie with him and smoothed his hand over her silky hair.

"I have to open the pasture gates and check the water troughs and make sure Legacy has enough food," she said, making no attempt to move.

"Done, done, and done." He kissed her lips. "You don't have to worry about anything. This is one morning that you can relax in bed. I'll take a shower and then I'm going to make you breakfast."

Her smile brightened his whole world. "You make breakfast too?"

"I most certainly do. You've never had the chance to witness my culinary skills. Prepare to be amazed."

"I can't wait." Tess wrapped her leg over his. "Thank you for taking care of all my chores. I honestly can't remember the last time I slept in."

And he couldn't remember the last time he'd enjoyed

a morning this much. Seriously. He could live to make this woman smile at him every morning exactly like she was now—sleepy and happy. Silas kissed her once more. "Keep resting and your breakfast will be done soon."

But first, he needed to wash the scent of hay off his body. Tess was watching him walk away from the bed so he gave her a little show—losing his boxers on his way into her bathroom. He flicked on the water in the walk-in shower and waited for the steam before stepping in.

"Room for me in there?" Tess placed her hand up the wall on the outside of the shower, kicking out her hip and giving him a full view of her naked body. Did she really have to ask? Shaking the water off his head, he grabbed her hand and invited her inside. "I thought you were going to take advantage of lounging in bed."

"You didn't really think I was going to let you shower alone, did you?" She stepped into the line of spray, her body glistening in the water.

"I'm really glad you decided to get up." Silas snuck his hands round her waist and held her warm, wet body against his. "Remember how you said you could use a week on a beach somewhere?" He swayed their hips, dancing with her while the water rained down on them. "I'd like to take you someday." He could see it—the two of them walking hand in hand while the sun set over the water. Maybe it was only a fantasy that they'd be together in the future. Maybe this was all a fantasy. But he couldn't wake himself up.

Tess moved with him, caressing his shoulders. "I thought you said beach vacations made you restless."

"There's no way I would be bored on a beach if I was with you." Did the what-ifs about the future even matter? Not when he touched her. Not when she kissed him.

Right now mattered. Silas let his hands and mouth wander, exploring her body, kissing and tasting her soft skin, touching her until she was moaning and restless. She took ahold of him then too, her hand moving in long strokes that brought him outside of himself.

"Yes . . . let's . . . go to the . . . beach sometime," she whispered, gasping between the words.

"Yes," he repeated, fighting his body's rush to give in. "I'd go anywhere with you, Tess." He danced his fingers into her, needing to hear those sounds she made—the cries and the moaning sigh when she couldn't hold on anymore. Tess slumped against him, her head on his shoulder and only then did he relent, letting her long, stroking caress set him free. He murmured her name, holding on to her while the release rocked his body. And then he kissed her neck and earlobe, his legs still trembling. "Sharing the shower is fun."

Tess laughed, her arms coming around him. "Yes, it is." She swayed them fully back into the spraying water. "Wait until you try my sugar scrub."

He never dreamed he'd use sugar scrub, but the fruity scent did have a certain draw. They scrubbed up, kissing and laughing about how slippery the scrub made the floor.

"About that breakfast you promised me." Tess shut off the water and then handed him a towel.

"Coming right up." Silas got dressed and beat her out to the kitchen. He opened cabinets until he found the ingredients he'd need and then he whipped up the fluffiest cinnamon vanilla pancakes he'd ever seen, plating the last one when Tess walked into the kitchen with her hair dried and loosely pulled back. She'd put on a pair of dark form-hugging jeans and a thin mossy-green sweater.

"Hey, good-lookin'." Instead of sitting at the table, she came for him. "What's cookin'?"

He laughed at her cheesy line and then led her to the plate and coffee he'd set out. "Only the best pancakes you'll ever taste." He sat down with her and it felt like the most natural thing in the world to share breakfast together.

Tess sipped her coffee and oohed and aahed over his pancakes. "So how did Legacy seem this morning?" she asked after a couple of bites.

"She looks good." He thought about changing the topic, but they needed to have this conversation. "I think it's time to get her back up there. With the others."

"I know it is." She took another bite of her breakfast, chewing slowly while she seemed to think it over. "How about we make a plan to take her back up to the high meadow on Saturday? Aiden and Kyra are taking the girls to Jackson for a show over the weekend. We can bring Legacy up there and wait around to see if the herd makes an appearance." A slow smile took over her face. "And then maybe you can spend the night."

"I like that plan." Silas found himself smiling too. He'd probably smiled more this morning than he had in his previous lifetime.

"Hey, I also wanted to tell you..." Her expression turned serious. "I talked to my brother. About you and me."

Silas dropped his fork and it clattered onto the plate. "You did?" So this wasn't some fantasy he'd have to wake up from later today?

"I told him I have feelings for you." She covered his hand with hers. "He knows. And so do Kyra and Lyric."

Silas laughed. "And Thatch."

"That's good." She scooted out of her chair and came

to sit on his lap. "So we don't have to keep this a secret. But I still want to be careful with the girls."

"Yes." He brushed a kiss over her lips. "I want to be careful with them too. They miss their dad. We all do."

"We do." Tess rested her forehead against his, and her eyes were beautiful and open and bright. "I'd like to give us some time before we tell them anything. Or let them see us like this."

"We'll wait as long as you think we need to." And in the meantime, he'd earn their love and their trust. He'd do everything he could to become the man those girls deserved.

"There's one more thing." She hesitated and glanced away.

"What is it?" He smoothed a curl from her forehead.

"This mission you're supposed to go on." Fear clouded her eyes. Real fear. He could see it there, rising up, taking over.

"I've already committed." No matter how much he regretted telling Fletch he'd go, he couldn't back out. "I gave him my word." Damn his sense of duty. It had been ingrained in him since he was eighteen years old.

"I know," she said softly.

What could he say? How could he take the fear away? "You know I'm really good at what I do over there, right?" He took her cheeks in his hands. "This isn't as dangerous as the assignments we used to go on." But he'd still have to say goodbye to her. He'd still have to leave her behind. He'd still be going into some sketchy situations.

"I love your loyalty and dedication," Tess told him firmly, as though she was trying to be brave.

He would always offer her both of those things. "I promised you I'd help you find whoever hurt Legacy, and I will. Even if it means I have to delay leaving and meet up with the team somewhere."

"I know you're a man of your word." She kissed him once more and then went back to her own chair. "And I know how good you were at your job. I just can't lose you."

"You won't." He wouldn't put her through any more pain. There was always a chance he wouldn't have to go. It was possible the diplomat would surface before they left. He could always hope. "Now back to the mission I've taken on here...maybe we should go check out Darrell's and Ford's places."

Tess set down her fork. "You mean like break into their garages?"

"That's not quite what I had in mind." Though he had plenty of experience breaking into places he wasn't supposed to be on his missions. "I can't get busted by the cops for anything right now or Fletch would lose it. The powers that be frown on legal trouble for their contractors."

"Right." She carted her plate to the sink. "No, we can't break any laws to catch these guys."

Silas met her at the kitchen island. "But we can go talk to Darrell and Ford directly. At least take a look around their properties without committing any misdemeanors." If nothing else, they could search for the white UTV.

"That's the perfect plan." Tess took his hand and pulled him to the front door, swiping her purse off a hook on the wall. "I'll drive."

Fifteen minutes later, they were slowly making their way up Darrell's private driveway. Silas read the many No Trespassing signs on the way.

No trespassing. Due to the increased price of ammo, do not expect a warning shot.

No trespassing. This property is protected by the second amendment.

No trespassing. If you can read this sign, you're in range.

That sign depicted a rifle and a target.

"Wow. Darrell seems like a stand-up guy, huh?" He never would've called the man friendly, but seeing his opinions posted around his property drove his attitudes home.

"It would appear the man is obsessed with guns, that's for sure." Tess eyed the signs with disdain as they passed. "But he's been around forever and he's harmless. A few signs won't scare me off."

"I'm not worried either." Silas wouldn't let anyone hurt Tess. He'd take down anyone who tried.

They drove past a few weathered outbuildings—all closed up tight—and then Tess parked in front of a simple cabin. Smoke curled from the brick chimney.

They both climbed out of the vehicle, but Silas made sure he approached the front door of the cabin first. He knocked and then stepped back, keeping himself between Tess and the door.

Darrell appeared behind the battered screen. "What'd you two want?" He hiked up his sagging jeans over his belly even though they were held up by a pair of red suspenders.

"Hi there," Silas said politely. "We were just out and about. Thought we'd stop in to see how you're doing today."

The man lumbered out to the concrete pad where they stood, his eyes squinting against the bright sunlight. "You never come up here to see how I'm doing."

Tess took a step toward the man. "We were actually wondering...do you happen to have a white UTV by any chance?"

"Why the hell are you asking me that?" he growled.

"Because we have evidence that links a white UTV

with a purple stripe to the horse shooting," she said sweetly. "And we thought we'd take a look around."

Silas almost laughed. The woman was fearless.

"You get off my property." Darrell reached for the door handle, but Silas kept the door closed with his foot.

"You sure you don't know anyone with a white UTV? Because those shooters are gonna get caught eventually. We'll make sure of that. And it'd probably be better to share what you know with law enforcement on the front end."

The man's laugh came out more as a snarl. "You think I'm afraid of the consequences for shooting a wild horse? It's a misdemeanor, son. A little slap on the hand and a fine. Hell, they rarely even hand out any jail time in those cases." Darrell ripped open the door and went inside. "Now, I'm not gonna warn you again to get off my property. You read the signs. I'm not afraid to protect what's mine."

"We can take a hint." Silas slipped his arm around Tess's waist and guided her back to the car, where he opened the driver's side door for her.

"He's right, you know," Tess said when he climbed in next to her. "Even when we catch the person who shot Legacy, they'll get off pretty easy."

"Maybe by the law's standards." He settled his hand on her thigh as she started up the engine. "But more importantly, we'll be exposing them for who they are. Most of the people in town aren't going to put up with men who'll target innocent animals. If Darrell is involved, you know he won't survive without his daily morning coffee and cinnamon rolls at the café. But if Minnie finds out he shot the horse, she won't be serving him anymore."

"That's true." Tess was smiling again as she slipped the truck into gear and started down the driveway. "I also think we need to do more to protect the horses. I'm considering applying with the Bureau of Land Management to become a contracted wild horse sanctuary."

"That's a great idea." If they could keep the horses on Tess's land, people won't target them.

She stopped the truck and looked both ways before turning out onto the highway. "It would be a lot of work though. I'd need some serious help to run that kind of operation."

"You'll have all the help you need," he assured her. This would be a whole new mission for him and Thatch and Aiden. And probably the fifteen or so others who came to the meeting at Tess's house. "I'll bet the majority of the town will get involved."

"I know. And there'll be plenty of work to go around." Instead of turning south at the fork in the road, Tess continued west.

"Aren't we heading to Ford's house?" As far as Silas knew, their other suspect lived south of town.

"He's not going to offer up any more information than Darrell did," she said with a sigh. "I really do think those two are involved somehow, but they're not going to rat themselves out. So I thought we'd head over to pick up the girls." She slid him a glance. "If you don't mind."

"Oh." Why did picking up the girls together make him nervous? "You sure that's a good idea?" He'd seen how Brad had looked at Tess at the meeting last night. Even though she insisted they were friends, the man was clearly interested in her. And wouldn't the girls wonder why Silas and Tess had been together so much more lately?

"I told Brad you and I had feelings for each other. When we had dinner. I told him I wasn't interested in dating because I was interested in you." Now Tess put her hand on his thigh. High on his thigh. High enough to make him whimper.

"See?" The woman had one hell of a smirk. "I'm not hiding you away."

"I do have feelings for you." He put his hand over hers. He hadn't prepared for his feelings to run so deep...to make him question everything about his future. But he needed to. He needed to consider the kind of future he wanted in light of his feelings.

Tess turned off the highway and into a gravel driveway. Two log houses were separated by a meadow with a few barns and outbuildings clustered between.

"This is quite the place." Kline clearly had money.

"Brad lives here with his parents." She slipped the gear into park and left the keys in the ignition.

"I'll wait in the truck." He didn't want to make things awkward for Brad or for the girls by going inside.

While Tess was gone, Silas checked his phone. He'd missed a text from Aiden this morning.

Are you still at my sister's house?

Yeah, he wouldn't be answering that. But eventually he and Aiden would have to hash out his friend's obvious disapproval of Silas being with Tess. It likely didn't help matters that he was getting ready to go back to Afghanistan. He scrolled through a few new emails, including one from Fletch.

Hey, man. Still waiting on some intel. Should be ready to shove off in three weeks. I'll keep you posted.

Silas wouldn't be ready to shove off in three weeks. He'd never be ready.

The doors started to open and Morgan climbed in first.

"What're you doing here?" she asked as she settled into her seat.

"We were doing some investigating this morning," Tess said quickly while she helped Willow buckle up.

"Did you find the people that hurt Legacy?" the youngest girl asked.

"Not yet. But I think we're getting closer." Silas buried his phone back in his pocket. He didn't want to think about going on a mission right now. Not with Tess sitting beside him and two pretty awesome girls sitting behind him. How would he prove himself to them if he was gone for a month or two? How would he earn a place in their lives?

"Did you two have fun with Callie?" Tess asked as she drove back out onto the highway.

"So much fun!" the girls said in unison.

"We rode bikes this morning," Willow told them.

"And Mr. Brad built an obstacle course for us!" Morgan added. "He's soooo much fun."

Silas tried not to take the comment personally, but they likely didn't talk about him that way. Of course, he'd never made them an obstacle course either. Maybe he could get an epic tree house built before he went overseas . . .

"I fell off my bike and hurt my elbow." Willow stuck her arm over the seat to show them the scrape. "And Mr. Brad made me feel all better."

"Oh, and he made us the most *amazing* breakfast this morning." Morgan took over again. "Yummy waffles with *real* strawberry syrup that he made all by himself."

"While we ate, he sang the silliest songs." Willow started to giggle. "We were laughing so hard."

"Sounds like fun." Silas smiled at Tess, but pressure was building in his chest. Brad Kline really did seem like the perfect father.

"He's *so* great, Mom." Morgan leaned as close to the front seat as her seat belt would allow. "You should *totally* marry him."

"Morgan!" The truck swerved the slightest bit as Tess took her eyes off the road. "I've already told you; Brad and I are only friends."

"You're gonna get married?" Willow exclaimed.

"No!" The woman shot Silas an apologetic look. "Sheesh, girls. I am not going to marry Brad Kline, so you can get that idea out of your heads right now."

"You never know," Morgan said in a singsong tone.

Silas continued to stare out the windshield, careful to hold his expression neutral. He knew they didn't mean anything by what they said. There was no way they could know what had changed between him and Tess. They *shouldn't* know. Not right now. But his heart bled a little bit hearing them talk about the man they hoped might someday be their father.

When they made it back to the ranch, he climbed out of the truck and gave both Morgan and Willow high fives and played a quick game of tag before Tess sent them into the house to wash their hands for lunch.

Before going inside, Willow paused on the porch. "You're coming to my birthday party, right?"

"Wouldn't miss it," he called. The invitation for Willow's birthday dinner had come a month ago and he'd put the date on his calendar right away.

"It's going to be the best day ever!" the girl declared, and then she ran inside.

"I was thinking I would get her an art set." He never knew what to get the girls for their birthdays, but Willow seemed to love painting and drawing.

"That would be perfect." Tess walked around the truck, following him to his vehicle with a slump in her shoulders. "I'm sorry for all of that silliness on the way home."

"You don't have to be sorry." He didn't touch her in case Morgan and Willow were looking out the window. "They had fun with Brad. In a kid's estimation, that makes him perfect marriage material."

She laughed a little. "True. Life is so simple to them." Tess rubbed her hands up and down her arms as if she were nervous. "I wish we could tell them how we feel about each other. But they get their hopes up so easily. And given the history with Jace, knowing about you and me might be confusing. I'd rather ease them into this. Maybe we'll tell them after you get back."

"For sure. I don't want to confuse them." He didn't want to worry them either. He needed more time to try—to build them obstacle courses and kiss their owies and make them his special pancakes for breakfast. He needed more time to show them that, even though he wasn't as good of a dad as Jace, he would give the job everything he had if that's where things went between him and Tess. Given what Morgan and Willow had been through, Silas would only get one chance to earn their acceptance and approval.

And he could never be with Tess if he blew his shot.

CHAPTER SEVENTEEN

Silas lifted his rifle case out of his extended cab and brought it around to lay it on the hood, opening the latch to inspect the contents. Two years. It had been two years since he'd held this gun in his hands. Two years since he'd lugged it out into the field with him before laying down his weapon to fulfill a promise to Jace.

He hoped he'd honored his friend's memory. He hoped Jace knew that Silas had done his best to take care of Tess, to watch out for Morgan and Willow. He hoped he'd done his friend proud during his time in Star Valley.

When he'd first walked away from his career in the Navy, Silas had never thought about going back. The first time he'd joined up, he'd been confident that was the best path for him to take, but now...he'd be lying if he said he wasn't having second thoughts about going back into a fight. He'd never had to leave someone he cared about before.

"Hey!" Thatch yelled from the window of his truck as he pulled up and parked next to him. "What's up? When I got your text, I wasn't expecting you to say you wanted to meet at the shooting range." His friend hopped out. "It's been a while since we've shot up a couple of targets together."

Silas closed his gun case again. "I need to brush up on my skills. It's been way too long." From what Fletch had told him, they suspected the diplomat had been kidnapped for ransom. His friend was currently pinning down the holding location and then they'd have to go in. So Silas figured he'd better make sure he could still aim.

"Come on. You were the best marksman out of all of us back in the day." Thatch hoisted his rifle case out of his truck. "You'll be fine."

Then why had the thought of going back into the field been keeping him up every night this week? He shook off the concerns. He'd trained for years, and all of his skills and instincts would come right back to him. They would have to come right back.

They walked side by side to the range's entrance—a small trailer set up by the gate—and paid the attendant before selecting the first station to set up.

Thatch laid his rifle case on the edge of the picnic table and went about assembling the pieces. "How does Tess feel about you going?"

"I know it scares her." And that made him feel like crap. "We haven't talked about it too much." And he hadn't even given her any real details. For one thing, he couldn't say too much. This assignment was supposed to be off the books. And for another, he hadn't seen her in a few days—not since they'd visited Darrell's house and had picked up the girls. They'd texted constantly and FaceTimed after the girls went to bed, but that wasn't exactly the best way to have a conversation. But tonight he'd see her at Willow's party, and the anticipation was already humming through him.

"What's up with you two anyway?" Thatch loaded a round. "I mean, I figured when Kyra kicked us all out of Tess's house the night of the meeting you two would finally get over yourselves and get together."

"It's not that simple." Silas concentrated on getting himself set up. Though he'd put this gun together so many times, he didn't have to think much about what he was doing.

"Seems pretty simple to me." Thatch slipped a pair of noise-canceling headphones around his neck. "You have feelings for her. She has feelings for you. What more do you need?"

He needed Morgan and Willow to accept him too. That would have to happen in order for him and Tess to have a clear path to move forward. But Thatch wouldn't understand that. "You have feelings for Lyric. What's happening on that front?" When all else failed, he always deflected.

"Things are moving along." Thatch lifted the rifle to his shoulder and lined up his vision with the scope, aiming at the target.

"Moving along how?" He could be every bit as nosey as his friend.

"Okay, fine." Thatch lowered the rifle. "I've got nothing. None of my usual tactics are working. Lyric hasn't given me the time of day."

"You mean asking her about yoga pointers for your sciatic problem didn't interest her?" Sarcasm had always been one of their favorite forms of communication.

His friend shot him a glare. "I have some other ideas. But I don't have a lot of time right now anyway. I've been in Jackson a lot."

Silas put his headphones around his neck and slipped on his safety goggles. "How's the bronc riding going?" He joined his friend at the barrier, waiting for an answer before they shot.

"It's painful, I'll tell you that." Thatch winced. "You should see all the bruises I've accumulated."

Keeping the safety on his rifle, Silas raised it to his shoulder, finding the target through his scope. "But you're sticking with it."

"Hell yeah." Thatch was busy aiming at the farthest target. "You can't bail when things get painful, we both know that. You have to stick it out—work through the pain to see the rewards."

Silas lowered his gun. His friend may have been talking about physical pain, but the same could be said for relationships. Could he stick it out with Tess even with the potential pain of having things not work out? He didn't know the answer, so he put on his headphones. "Worst out of one clip buys the beer later," he yelled.

"You're on." Thatch moved his safety gear into place and then they took turns shooting at the farthest targets with Silas coming out on top.

"Lucky shots," Thatch grumbled when they'd taken down their headphones.

"I guess you were right earlier." He couldn't resist rubbing in the victory. "I still am the best marksman out of all of us."

"You're still the most humble too," his friend said.

While they were packing up their rifles, another pair of patrons came lumbering down the path. "Gentlemen." Silas tipped his hat to the two men, getting a better look at their faces. *Interesting.* He waited until they'd walked on past and then turned to Thatch. "You know who that is with Ford, don't you?"

Thatch took another look at the man who'd set up shop in the station next to theirs. "Looks like the older Kline. Brad's dad. What's his name again?"

"Paul, I think." At least that's what he'd heard around town. He'd never spoken to the man personally. "There were three men in that UTV when we chased them down."

Thatch closed up his rifle case. "You're thinking Darrell, Ford, and Paul are in on it together?"

"It would make sense, right?" Silas stashed his headphones and goggles into his bag and disassembled his rifle. "When Tess and I confronted Darrell, he didn't deny anything." In fact, the man had displayed a kind of weird pride about the whole thing. "And if Ford and Paul are palling around together, I wouldn't be surprised if they're in agreement about the horses being a nuisance."

Thatch gave the men to their left another surreptitious look. "We can't go over there and accuse them of anything. You said yourself Darrell wouldn't give you any information."

"No. We can't accuse them." Silas packed up his rifle case and they walked out of the station. "But now would be the perfect time to take a drive over to Ford's property and take a look around." The man had lived alone since his wife had passed away two years ago. "We could at least try to look in the windows of his garage or something, see if he has a white UTV."

"I guess." Thatch followed him past the trailer at the entrance. "I mean, I was going to spend my afternoon getting thrown off a bronc. But whatever."

"Come on." Silas unlocked his truck. "I need to figure

out who's behind these shootings before I head out of town. So Tess and the girls don't have to worry when they want to go out for a ride on their property."

"Fine." His friend opened the driver's side door of his truck. "But you know you won't be going out of town to work for Fletch if you get us arrested, right?"

"We're not gonna get arrested." Silas secured the gun case into the back seat. "We'll be quick. Those two will probably be here for at least an hour. Trust me. They need the practice. They're terrible shots." Legacy was living proof of their inabilities. He climbed in behind the wheel. "I'll meet you at Ford's place."

"Yep." His friend pulled himself into the driver's seat. "But if Natalie finds us snooping around up there, I'm blaming you."

"I'm good with that," Silas told him through the window. "With any luck, we'll find that UTV and she'll be able to bust them instead." He peeled out with his friend close on his tail, both sets of wheels skidding on the gravel road. Silas slowed down through town—it wouldn't do for Natalie to catch them speeding before they even got to Ford's place.

Silas pulled over to the side of the road before he reached the man's driveway and eased his truck into a stand of trees out of sight.

Thatch parked behind him. "You do realize that Ford will be coming back with his gun from the shooting range, right?"

"He's not going to shoot at us." And if he did, it wouldn't be their first time dodging bullets together. "We'll make this quick." Silas led the way across the street, and they moved swiftly down Ford's dirt driveway. There was one barn and two smaller shed-type outbuildings behind the log house. "You take the north; I'll take the south."

"Ten-four." Thatch gave him a smart-ass salute before trotting to the smaller of the two buildings.

Silas walked the perimeter of the larger shed before finding a high window in the back. He dragged over a trash can and climbed on top to see in. A John Deere tractor was parked in the middle of a mess of lawn equipment—leaf blowers and rakes and shovels. Most of the stuff looked like it hadn't been touched in a few years.

"See anything?" Thatch called from the other shed.

"Nah." Silas climbed back down. "What about you?"

His friend crossed the grass. "There are two UTVs in there, but neither one of them is white. So maybe the white UTV belongs to the Klines."

"I can't imagine." Silas scanned the driveway to make sure they were clear before they walked out into the open. "Brad was at Tess's house for the meeting. She asked if anyone had seen a white UTV. Surely he would've said something if he owned one."

"I don't know. Maybe he doesn't want to get in trouble with the law." Thatch turned his gaze to the road. "Shit, isn't that Ford's truck coming?"

"It would appear so." Silas shared a pained look with Thatch and then they both took off running through the field, ducking down in the tall grasses so they wouldn't be seen.

"You might be a better shot but I'm a faster runner," his friend yelled.

"Yeah, yeah, yeah." Silas let him win the race back to their trucks. They leaned against Thatch's tailgate, both out of breath. "You think he saw us?" his friend asked.

"Let's hope not." Or they'd be asking for trouble.

*   *   *

Silas climbed out of the truck and took Willow's gift from the back seat, inspecting his wrapping job yet again.

The technique was a little rough around the edges but after four attempts, nearly a whole roll of tape, and two YouTube videos, he'd managed to at least get most of the wrinkles out of the brightly colored butterfly wrapping paper. At least he wouldn't be embarrassed to give it to her now. He couldn't wait to see her face when she opened it.

He'd bought the best art set he could find—with all of the supplies stored in a nice wooden case. Hopefully she'd love it.

Before he started up the porch steps, the front door swung open. "Silas!" Willow bounded to him. "You're the first one here for my party!"

"I am?" He pretended to be surprised, but his early arrival had been by design. He wanted to make sure he was around to help Tess with any setup or prep she needed to do.

"Ohhhh." The girl inspected the gift he was carrying. "Is this for me?"

"It sure is." Silas held out the package. "Do you want to carry it inside?"

"Yes!" She snatched the offering out of his hands. "Mom," she yelled, running back into the house ahead of him. "Silas brought me a present!"

"Isn't that nice?" Tess met them inside the door, and Silas stepped toward her, ready to pull her into his arms before he remembered he couldn't. Not in front of Willow.

"Uh. Hi." He stepped back again. He'd have to admire her from afar. She always looked gorgeous but he loved her hair like this, pulled back loosely. And her eyes were as bright and happy as they had been when they'd spent the night together. He wasn't sure how tonight should look with this new thing between them, but it would be a challenge for him to keep his distance.

"Hi." She drew the word out, almost teasing him with her playful tone and smile.

"I'm going to put my first present by the fireplace," Willow announced.

"Mom, I'm done tossing the salad," Morgan called from the kitchen.

"Great, honey. Thanks for all of your help." Tess's eyes never left his.

"I could help too," Silas offered. "Since I'm so early. You can put me to work."

"Actually, there is something you can help me with in the garage." Tess beckoned him through the kitchen and headed toward the laundry room.

"Hey, Morgan." He gave her a high five as he passed.

"Hi, Silas. Look." She pointed at the birthday cake on the counter. "I helped Mom make that."

"Wow." He admired the pink frosting and the white flowers. "It's a work of art. And I bet it's delicious too."

"It is," she confirmed with a grin. "I taste-tested the frosting."

"Can't wait to try it." He followed Tess through the laundry room and they stepped into the garage, the door shutting behind them.

"What'd you need me to do?" He turned to her, and she pulled him close.

"Kiss me."

"Sneaky." Silas slid his hands around her waist. "You

sure?" Like he'd be able to resist her. Once he started kissing her, it would be hard to stop.

"Please." She pressed her body to his. "There's so much going on with school winding down for the year. My calendar is filling up and all I can think about is when we can steal some time together alone before you leave."

Every time he had to face the prospect of leaving her behind, he got this gut-wrenching pang. "We'll find time," he promised. "This weekend'll be perfect." With Aiden and Kyra taking the girls for a special overnight in Jackson, he and Tess would have a lot of time to just be together without any worries.

"I can't wait." She moved to her tiptoes but Silas took his time moving in for the kiss. He studied her eyes first, her lovely luminous eyes that were so open he could read her emotion. Then he looked down at her lips, which now smirked at him.

"I hate to be impatient," she murmured. "But we'll have a whole houseful of people here soon."

"Right." He slowly drew in a breath, committing the details of her face to memory. "I love you, Tess." He needed her to know that. Even with everything that could stand in their way, even if she didn't love him back. He loved her.

"I think I might love you too." Tears made her eyes even brighter. "I think I might've loved you for a while."

Silas touched her cheek, drawing her face to his. Something happened whenever his lips touched hers; a new energy took over. He willed her to sense everything that changed inside of him while their mouths found this perfect cadence, moving together, exploring, tasting. She had to feel the physical hunger she generated in him, but there was also this fierce yearning to give her everything, all of him, not holding back.

Tess kissed him with the same urgency, her chest sighing against his.

"We should probably get back inside," he finally murmured when they both took a breath. As much as he'd like to believe they existed outside of time and reality right now, people would be waiting for them.

"Yes." She kissed him once more and then took a second to smooth her hair back toward her ponytail before leading him into the house.

Aiden and Kyra were in the kitchen with Morgan and Willow, also admiring the cake.

"How's everything in the garage?" Aiden directed the question at Silas with a deadpan stare.

"Good. We got everything all fixed up." He breezed past them to answer the doorbell before anyone could ask what, exactly, they were fixing.

When Silas opened the door, he found Brad and Callie standing on the porch with a massive box that had been wrapped with perfect creases in the corners.

"That's a pretty big present." Silas should've kept the opinion to himself, but wow. It was twice Willow's size.

"It's an art easel," Brad whispered. "Willow loved the one that Callie has when she came over. It comes with all kinds of markers and paints and drawing lessons."

"That sounds like an epic gift." Ten times better than the one Silas had gotten her. Was it too late for him to swipe his present off the pile and disappear for a while?

"Callie!" Willow pushed past him. "Whoa, Nelly! That's the biggest present I've ever seen! That's for me?"

"It sure is." Brad started to lift the box, and Silas

jumped in to help. Taking one side, he maneuvered the thing inside the door.

"We can put it near the fireplace." Or *in* the fireplace . . .

Yes, that was a petty thought. He shouldn't begrudge the man for getting Willow such a nice gift.

The three girls ran in behind them, still oohing and aahing over the sheer size of the box.

"Maybe it's a new obstacle course!" Willow squealed.

"Nope," Callie told her. "But you're going to love it."

"We're going to love it," Morgan said, putting her arm around her sister's shoulders.

"This is good right here." Silas set his side of the box down on the floor next to the hearth.

"My goodness." Tess joined them. "I hope you didn't spend too much," she said to Brad. "I should've told you a gift wasn't required."

"It's not as expensive as it looks," he assured her. "We wanted to get her something she'd love."

So had Silas. He'd made a special trip to Jackson and looked at every art set he could find. Where had the easels been hiding?

The doorbell rang again and he quietly stepped away from the chaos in the living room to answer. Lyric stood on the porch and Thatch was just walking up.

It made him feel better that their gifts were both small too.

"So have you tried those stretches I recommended?" Lyric asked Thatch as they all stepped inside.

Silas snorted but then covered by loudly clearing his throat.

"Uh, yeah. I gave them a go." Thatch was totally trying to play it cool.

"Any improvements?" Lyric seemed to visually assess his friend's gait.

Before Thatch could answer, Willow and Morgan ambushed them with hugs.

"Thank you for coming to my party," the younger girl blurted. "I'll take those presents."

The doorbell rang a few more times and Silas let in three of Willow's friends from school. Everything ramped up after that—the volume, the chaos, the work. He spent most of his time in the kitchen helping Tess set out the food and serve the lasagna and refill the drinks cooler. How had he missed the amount of work that went into these gatherings?

After the cake was served, the unthinkable happened— the volume increased even more, with the girls turning up music and dancing and singing while they worked off their sugar buzz.

Tess caught him alone in the kitchen. "It would be understandable if you were rethinking a potential relationship right now," she whispered. Not that anyone would be able to hear them over the noise.

"I'm actually thinking how happy people are in your home." The adults were on the couches and chairs discussing summer plans and the kids were all dancing around and everyone felt comfortable and content. "And how lucky I am to be part of this."

She exhaled slowly and tilted her head to gaze at him. "Maybe we could go back to the garage real quick."

He would've, but Willow started chanting, "Present time! Present time!"

So instead he followed Tess to the living room.

The girl ripped through her presents in no time, jumping up in between to hug whoever had brought the gift.

"An art set!" she cried when she opened his. "Thanks, Uncle Silas! I love it!"

"I'm glad." He'd done his best and that was all he could offer.

"I wonder what this one is." Willow circled the big box, which she'd saved for last. In no time she'd ripped the paper off and started to jump up and down. "It's the easel! I love it! This is the best gift ever! Thank you! Thank you! Thank you!" She hugged Brad and then Callie.

All of the kids closed in to examine the pictures on the box.

"How about I set it up for everyone?" Brad pushed off the couch. "Then you can all make a picture to take home."

Cheers went around the room.

Silas got up to start cleaning the torn wrapping paper off the floor. In his head he knew he shouldn't feel like he was involved in some kind of popularity contest but disappointment still crept in. He'd wanted to get Willow a gift that meant something and now she probably wouldn't even remember. He stuffed the paper into a trash bag and walked out into the garage. "Oh." He stopped on the step.

Aiden was putting a box into Tess's truck. "Hey," his friend said coolly. "Kyra and I brought some canned food for the drive at the school."

"Ah." Silas stuffed the trash bag into the bin. He almost went back inside but he paused first. "Do we need to talk about Tess and me?" They might as well have this out now so he could gauge exactly where his friend stood on the issue.

"As far as I'm concerned, there is no you and Tess." Aiden crossed his arms and leaned against the truck's tailgate. "Not yet. Because you're taking off. And that's not fair to her."

"Yeah. The timing's not great." He should've told Fletch

no. But he never dreamed Tess would want him. He'd never dreamed he could have a future with her.

"If you want to be with her, then you're gonna have a responsibility to her." Aiden stepped up to him. "You'll have responsibility for those girls. Your life won't be your own anymore. Everything you do will affect them." His friend's tone got heated. "There is no you and Tess, Silas. Not until you choose her. And if you choose her, you're choosing Morgan and Willow too."

"I know." He already bore the weight of that truth. And he didn't want to let any of them down.

CHAPTER EIGHTEEN

Tess tightened Dreamer's saddle into place and added a water bottle to the satchel, still smiling about the text she'd gotten from Silas. He'd suggested they camp up in the high meadow when they brought Legacy back this weekend. The two of them, sleeping under the stars. She couldn't imagine anything better.

"There you are." Aiden sauntered into the stable all decked out in his cowboy boots and hat. "You ready to head up for the afternoon patrol?"

"I'm ready." Tess led Dreamer past her brother and out into the sunlight. "Not that I think we'll see anything up there. Based on the email reports I've received, the high meadow has been pretty quiet the last few days." Word must've gotten out about their citizen patrols. So far, the shooters hadn't made another appearance.

"You sure you want to go up on horseback?" Aiden checked his watch. "We'll be cutting it a little close to when the girls get home from school. We could always take the UTV that Silas didn't wreck."

She shot her brother a warning glare. "We have plenty of time." Tess pulled herself into the saddle. "I haven't been out riding at all this week. Dreamer needs some exercise."

"Sounds good." Aiden unlatched his trailer and led his horse Recon out. "This guy could use a little exercise too." He mounted and sidled up next to her.

"Come on, Dreamer, let's show them how it's done." Tess nudged her heels in and set off across the driveway and into the pasture, the horse quickening her pace as they approached the edge of the woods.

"I was surprised that you signed up to ride patrol with me." She shot her brother a sideways glance. "Since you've seemed a little bent out of shape about Silas and me." Her brother and Silas had disappeared from Willow's party just long enough to make her nervous.

"I'm not bent out of shape," he protested. "I know I didn't handle the news all that well—"

"All that well?" Tess laughed. "You lost your shit, Aiden. And I have no idea what you said to him at Willow's party, but I'll bet it wasn't encouraging."

"Yeah, I guess I've made my feelings obvious," he admitted.

They rode in silence, both horses intent and focused. Dreamer and Recon knew this route, so Tess let the reins go slack, trusting her horse. This part of the ride was warm and peaceful, crossing through the patches of sunlight that filtered through the tree branches. A few wildflowers had already started to pop up—white rock jasmine, yellow milk vetch, and even some red windflower.

She enjoyed the scenery until they started climbing in

elevation and then she decided Aiden's time was up. "The thing I can't figure out is what you have against Silas when he's done so much for you. And for me. And for the girls." That's what really bugged her. "He didn't have to move here after Jace died. He didn't have to follow through on the promise he made, but he did." He'd spent the last two years here looking out for her and her girls. Didn't that mean anything to her brother?

"Silas is one of my best friends." Aiden slowed Recon and let her go ahead as the trail narrowed into switchbacks. "I know he's a helluva guy."

"Then what's the problem?" she demanded, letting her frustration show.

"I was there, Tess." The words came so quietly she almost didn't hear them. "I sat with you and I told you about Jace and I watched you fall apart. I watched your heart break right in front of me and there was nothing I could do to stop it." An uncharacteristic emotion strangled her brother's usually deep tone. "There was nothing I could do to help. Nothing I could do to change that nightmare for you."

Tess pushed Dreamer up the last switchback and then pulled her to a stop when the ground evened out so she could look at her brother.

He exhaled as though pushing out the emotion and went on. "And then I was there when you told the girls. And I watched their worlds shatter. I couldn't stop their suffering. I couldn't make things better for them. I wanted to. I was desperate to. But I was helpless." He moved his horse past her, leaving her to catch up.

"You were suffering too," she reminded him. Aiden had watched his best friend die and then he'd struggled with survivor's guilt. "And we got through the suffering together. You got us through it, Aiden. You and Silas and Thatch. Somehow, we got through that pain together." And look where they were now. Aiden was getting married to the love of his life. Morgan and Willow were thriving.

And Tess's heart was opening again.

A breeze whooshed around them, swaying the grasses and the flowers dotting the high meadow.

"He's leaving. And I don't want you to have to live through that kind of pain again," her brother said. "I don't want the girls to ever experience anything like that again. I know that doesn't give me the right to choose for you, but the truth is I'm afraid for you."

The sincerity in his expression drained all of her frustrations away. Yes, Aiden could be clueless sometimes, but her brother had a huge heart. "None of us know when we'll have to face losing someone we love. But now I also know there's healing on the other side. And I know love is worth whatever it costs. Loving Jace was worth everything I lost, everything I went through."

She spotted her husband's memorial glistening in the sun down by the pond and turned Dreamer in that direction. "I would marry Jace all over again, even knowing I would lose him. Because he gave me so much." They'd shared more than she ever dreamed they could've even though they weren't given a whole lifetime together. And now she was ready to share her heart with someone else. "I think I could love Silas someday too." She hadn't dared to think these feelings would be possible for her again.

"Okay then," her brother said, trailing behind her. "Just know that Silas has always found his purpose in serving the greater good. That's why he signed up for this mission. Fighting for good is what drives him."

"And I love that about him." He didn't fight for himself. He fought for other people. He believed in the greater good, even after the way he'd grown up being cast aside. When it came to hard times, she knew he'd fight for her and the girls too.

Dreamer stopped to munch on some clover near the sandy edge of the pond, so Tess dismounted and walked to the bronze marker.

"So you're fine with him going on this assignment with Fletch?" Aiden joined her there and used his shirt to wipe smudges off the surface.

Tess let the question sit for a few seconds. "I can't say I'm *fine* with it. No." Even though Silas had told her it wasn't as dangerous as his other missions, she knew what could happen. "But I won't ask him to give up that part of himself either. Not if that's what he feels he needs to do." She cared for him. She wanted him to be fulfilled and passionate about what he did with his life.

"And what about the girls?" he asked carefully, as though he knew he was overstepping again. "How are they going to handle all of this?"

"I don't know." Like she'd told him before, she didn't have all of the answers. "But I do know I don't want to hide my feelings for much longer." She didn't want to waste too much time. "I'm ready. I'm ready to open my heart and live again. And that will be good for them to see."

Tess carefully withdrew the letter she always kept in her pocket, unfolding it slowly, smoothing out the creases. These were the most precious words she'd ever received— her husband's last words to her, especially the part about Morgan and Willow.

My beautiful Tess,

Hopefully you'll never have to read these words, but I had to write them just in case. There is nothing I want more than to spend my entire life with you— loving you, raising our babies with you, growing old with you. But if you're reading this, that means I'm gone and our life together was cut too short....

You have to live for both of us now, babe, and that means you'll have to live big. That means you have to make the most of every opportunity, especially when it comes to love. Love is the only thing in this world worth living and dying for. You and Morgan and Willow taught me that....

Our girls are watching you, babe. They need to see that love is worth whatever it costs—that it's worth fighting for over and over and over again, even if you lose it. So I'm telling you to embrace those feelings when they come again. I know they'll come again because you are brave and passionate and you deserve to be loved....

Your best days are still ahead of you, my love. Live them to the fullest.

All my love, Jace

"I know Jace wanted you to find someone." Aiden peered at her over the top of the paper. She'd made him read the letter back when he'd been going through his own struggles with PTSD. "I hate that he's going back overseas. That won't change. But if you really feel like Silas is the one, you know I'll support you. I'll support you both. I only want you and the girls to be happy."

She hated that he was leaving too but she wouldn't ask him to stay. "I am happy." And she fully believed that Morgan and Willow would be happy to have Silas become a bigger part of their lives eventually too. She couldn't hide her heart away and she couldn't hide the happiness she'd found with Silas from her girls. "It's terrifying but I think I'm ready."

He shot her a grin. "Then I promise to get out of the way and stop interfering."

"Thank you." Now that they'd settled that, Tess pulled herself back into the saddle and prodded Dreamer to get moving again. "You should tell Silas that too," she said when Aiden steered Recon alongside her. "I know there's been some distance between you two lately." And she didn't like being the cause of any rifts in their friendship.

"I'll talk to him again after Kyra and I take the girls to Jackson," he promised.

And she would hold him to it. Tess kept quiet while they rode along the woods, looking and listening for anything out of the ordinary. But after a good half hour, it was clear their perpetrators had taken another day off. There was no sign of the wild horses either.

"Maybe this is over," Aiden suggested as they rode back down through the woods. "Maybe they'll leave the herd alone."

"This isn't over." Tess couldn't give up and forget about what happened to Legacy. She'd started this fight and she'd finish it. "This won't be over until we get justice for Legacy. Until we make sure they get caught."

The rest of the way back to the ranch she told Aiden about her plans to set apart a section of her land to become a wild horse sanctuary. "I'll need a lot of help. We'll have to add new fencing and section off the property so we can move the herd periodically to revegetate."

"I'm happy to help." Aiden took the lead through the pasture. "And I know Kyra will help out as much as she can when she's not busy at the clinic."

"Thanks." She slowed Dreamer on the driveway and watched the school bus turn off the highway. Perfect timing.

Morgan and Willow bounded off the bus. "Uncle Aiden!"

Her younger daughter made it to them first. "I can't wait to go to the ballet show in Jackson!"

"Me neither." Her brother dismounted. "I've been practicing my ballet." He put his arms overhead and twirled around in a circle.

"Uncle Aiden, you're such a goofball!" Morgan shook her head, but she was laughing.

"*And* you're the worst ballet dancer I've ever seen," Willow added.

He totally was. But he was also the best brother in the entire world. "So you'll pick them up tomorrow after school?"

"Yep." Aiden led Recon into the trailer and closed it up. "We'll go have a fancy dinner and see the show and maybe even swim in the hotel pool."

The girls both cheered and launched themselves at him for hugs.

After Aiden left, Tess walked them inside. "How about some cookies for a snack?" She went right into the kitchen and set the chocolate chip cookies they'd made last night onto a plate.

"Look, Mom." Morgan walked in carrying a bunch of photos. "Callie brought me pictures from our sleepover. Isn't this the coolest bike I was riding? She has three bikes. Can you believe that?"

Tess studied the picture. Callie and Morgan and Willow were posing on bikes in front of Brad's open garage. "Wow."

Wait a minute... She looked closer. The very corner of a white UTV was visible in the background. But she couldn't see enough to tell if there was a purple stripe. "Morgan, do you remember what that UTV behind you looked like?" She pointed to the grainy image. "Did it have a purple stripe running around it?"

Her daughter looked at the picture again. "I dunno. Why?"

"No reason." She set the plate of cookies on the table, keeping her voice light. "Just wondering." Oh, she was wondering all right.

She was wondering if Brad had been lying to her all along.

CHAPTER NINETEEN

S o let me get this straight." Lyric crouched on her knees and started to fold up her yoga mat. "You think Brad Kline owns the white UTV with the purple stripe?"

"Yes." Still sitting on her mat, Tess took a long sip of water. Her yoga session had ended but she was no more relaxed than she'd been when she'd arrived at the studio an hour ago. Since Aiden and Kyra had picked up the girls from school to head to Jackson, Tess figured she would get Lyric's opinion on the whole situation while she got in a good workout.

"But you haven't talked to Brad about your suspicions?" Her friend grabbed a broom from the corner of the room and started to sweep the floor around her.

"No. I haven't spoken with him yet." Brad had the opportunity to tell her the UTV belonged to him after the meeting at her house, but instead he'd rushed out like he was nervous. Or maybe she'd been imagining his haste. And anyhow, she hadn't had time to do much since she'd been on the phone all day with various beef customers. Even with everything else going on, she still had a ranch to run.

"Brad knows we're looking for a white UTV. You were at the meeting. No one spoke up and said they'd seen one. If he lied then, he's not going to tell me the truth now." She went back through their conversations in her head. None of this made sense. Brad had seemed just as disturbed as she had been about the shootings in the high meadow.

Tess rolled up her mat and began packing her bag. "I guess I could try talking to him. Or maybe I shouldn't handle this at all. Maybe I should tell Natalie." The police could confront Brad. They were supposed to be the ones solving crimes, after all. Surely the man wouldn't lie to a police chief. If Natalie could stop by his house, maybe she'd see the UTV for herself.

"Have you talked to Silas about your suspicions?" Lyric swept the dust she'd collected into a dustpan and emptied it in the trash.

Ah, Silas. Her heart turned all warm and gooey at the mention of his name. "Not yet. But we're hanging out Saturday night and all day Sunday." Tess figured there would be plenty of time to discuss the latest developments with him while they were up in the high meadow waiting to see if Legacy's herd accepted her back in. Yes, they'd have plenty of time to talk...and time to do other things too, hopefully. Tess stood on wobbling legs. Thoughts of that man never failed to mess with her equilibrium.

"You mean you're hanging out Saturday night *into* Sunday?" Lyric grinned at her as she turned off the music and the lights. "I take it things are going well with you two then."

"Yes." Tess slung her bag over her shoulder and followed

her friend out the door and through the clinic's main waiting area. "Things are going well."

"Is he still going to Afghanistan?" Lyric held the front door open for her and then locked up.

Tess had to pause and steady her voice before she spoke. "I think so." She lingered on the porch, not quite ready to walk away from her friend. "He already committed to the job and I know how he feels when he makes a commitment." It was how Jace had felt too. And Thatch and Aiden. They never broke their word. "I'm trying to tell myself he'll be okay over there. He had the best possible training and years of experience and he's strong and smart and capable."

"But logic doesn't always soothe the heart, does it?" Lyric linked their arms together and drew her down the stairs to where their cars were parked along the curb.

"No. It doesn't." Her heart had been shut down for so long that she'd almost forgotten how deeply she could feel everything—joy and anticipation and apprehension too. That's what currently weighted her down.

"Have you asked him to stay?" Lyric slipped on her sunglasses and dug out her keys.

"No. I don't want to take him away from something he feels he needs to do." But she didn't want to tell the girls about them until he came back so they wouldn't worry as much either. "Willow's class is doing an end of the year choir concert for parents and I keep thinking about how nice it would be if we could go together. Sit together. Cheer her on together." She'd pictured sitting there in the audience with him, holding his hand, smiling at each other when Willow did something adorable. But Silas would be gone.

"It's okay for you to ask for what you need in a relationship," her friend said quietly. "Trust me, that's important. If you need him to stay, then ask."

Tess studied the serious expression on her friend's face. For once, Lyric wasn't smiling. She'd been married once, right out of college, but she didn't talk about that time in her life much. Tess only knew the relationship had ended badly.

"I have to get going, but we can talk more anytime." Lyric unlocked her Jeep.

"Sounds good. And thanks. I'll talk to Silas tomorrow." She gave her friend a hug. "Is it just me or do you have a hot date waiting for you somewhere?" She couldn't resist teasing her. As long as Tess had known her, Lyric hadn't dated much.

"It's not a date." Her friend waved her off. "I'm just going to help Thatch with some stretching. His back has been bothering him."

"Reeaaallly?" Tess couldn't stop the smirk. "Thatch wants to do yoga?" She didn't mean to laugh but the visual was too funny.

"He wants to stretch," Lyric corrected. "And you can't tell him I told you. This is supposed to be top secret."

"Mmm-hmm." She made sure her tone was as teasing as possible. "I think he might want more than a good stretch, my dear."

"What?" Her friend looked genuinely surprised. "What'd you mean?"

"Seriously?" Tess slipped her arm around Lyric's shoulders. "That man has been pining for you for a while now. In case you didn't know."

"Thatch?" Now Lyric was laughing. "No. Those guys are flirts, that's all. You know that."

"Okay." She infused the word with her disbelief. Had Lyric truly not noticed Thatch's long enamored glances at her? Or the way he always sat by her and singled her out to chat with when they were together?

"I'm serious." Lyric opened the Jeep's door. "This is nothing more than a stretching consult."

How adorable. "Have fun." She waved goodbye to her friend and got into her truck. On her way down Main Street, she slowly rolled past Natalie's patrol car, conveniently parked in front of the station. Right now seemed like the perfect time for a chat with her favorite police chief, given the new information she'd found.

She swung the truck into a parking space and hopped out. With any luck she could hand her concerns about Brad off to Natalie and then the police could handle this investigation. One less issue to deal with right now would be nice.

Inside the station, she found Terry at the receptionist desk, but the woman was on the phone. Tess pointed down the hallway and Terry nodded, waving her by.

The chief's door stood wide open, but Tess still paused and knocked.

Natalie looked up from her computer. "Hey, Tess. Come on in." She shut her laptop while Tess settled herself in the chair across from the desk.

"I think I've found something." She pulled the picture Morgan had given her out of her purse and slid it across the desk. "Look right there." She pointed. "There's a white UTV in the Klines' garage."

Natalie leaned over the picture, squinting. "I guess so, but you can hardly see it."

"True," she said patiently. "But that vehicle is clearly

white." And white wasn't a common color for a UTV. "This could be the one the shooters used."

"It *could* be. But I can't just show up on the Klines' property making accusations and searching their garage." Natalie slid the picture back to her. "I'm sorry, but this doesn't prove anything."

"I know the picture can't *prove* anything." Proving the facts was what the investigation was supposed to do. Frustration steamed Tess's face. "This is the best lead we've had to go on. I know you're low on resources right now, but we can't let these people get away with shooting horses."

"We haven't had another incident in a while, Tess. Maybe this is over." Natalie opened her laptop back up. "Maybe whoever is responsible now knows that everyone's watching so they'll find something else to do."

Tess shot to her feet. That was it? The woman was just going to let this go? "They should still be held accountable for what they did to Legacy." And what if she and Morgan were out riding again in a few weeks? Would she always have to worry about getting caught in the crosshairs of someone's vendetta against the wild horses on her own land?

Natalie dismissed her concerns with a shrug. "I'm sorry. Without real evidence or proof that the UTV in Kline's garage has the purple stripe, there's nothing I can do."

"All right then." Real evidence. The woman needed real evidence... and Tess knew exactly where she would find it.

*   *   *

Breaking and entering had never been a skill Tess wanted to master, but Natalie had given her no other choice.

She parked the truck down the hill from the Klines' property and cut the engine, her nerves prickling. When her alarm had gone off at two o'clock in the morning, she'd briefly considered abandoning her mission, but she had to know if that UTV was sitting in Brad's garage. If Natalie wasn't going to check, she had to. She had to get a peek in that garage for her own peace of mind. It wasn't breaking the law if you were just planning to look in a friend's garage in the middle of the night, right? She wasn't going to take anything, after all.

Before she lost the nerve, Tess put up the hood of her dark sweatshirt, grabbed her flashlight and backpack, and then slid out of the driver's seat into the cold. Everything seemed so much quieter at night. Even her footsteps in the grass sounded deafening as she crept away from the truck, though it was hard to hear much over the thundering beat of her heart.

Keeping a low profile, Tess made her way through the woods, aiming the flashlight at the ground in front of her boots. She'd considered bringing Silas in with her but she couldn't ask him to risk getting caught. She would ask him not to go on this upcoming mission but she didn't want to force him to stay because she'd gotten him into trouble.

So she was on her own out here. In the middle of the night. Just her and the coyotes and the bears.

At the edge of the woods, Tess paused, gauging the best route through the pasture. The waning gibbous moon gave off enough light that she could see out in the open, so she tucked her flashlight in her backpack and decided to move along the fence all the way up to the property. Judging from the picture Morgan had shared with her, it appeared the UTV had been stored in the main garage, which would prove tricky given its close proximity to both Brad's house and his parents' place.

She would have to move quietly and not get caught. There was no other option.

With that in mind, she moved slowly along the fence line, watching the houses to make sure all stayed dark. Now all she needed to do was get close enough to peek in the windows of the garage so she could snap a picture on her phone and then she'd be out of there.

Tess swiftly crossed the driveway, doing her best to stay out of the floodlights coming from the houses, and walked the perimeter of the garage in the shadows.

Damn. Curtains covered every window. She tried the door handle on the back side but it was locked. Okay, new plan. She'd climb in through one of those windows and take a quick look around.

Tess walked back along the right side, away from both houses—which still sat dark and quiet, thank God—and pushed against the glass pane. It slid open a crack, enough that she could get her fingers inside to open it the rest of the way. Standing on her tiptoes, she moved the curtain aside, but couldn't see much past Brad's huge diesel truck. Great. Now all she had to do was figure out a way to climb inside without killing herself.

Channeling her inner gymnast, Tess pulled herself up into the window frame, leaned her upper body through first, but then momentum took over and pitched her all the way over, feet flying up as she flipped and landed on the floor on her back.

Crash!

Her flailing boot hit the glass on the way down, shattering it all over the floor around her.

No! Inching herself away from the mess, she quickly scrambled to her feet. Amazingly, she wasn't bleeding at all but the whole window had broken.

And that had been one loud crash.

She didn't have much time. Tess flicked on her flashlight and maneuvered around the truck to the back of the garage but there was no UTV. Just a big empty space where you might park one and muddy tire tracks. They must've moved it—

A buzzing noise sounded and the lights flicked on. The garage door started to slowly roll up.

"Hey! Who's in there?" That sounded like Brad's father...

"I'm calling the cops," the man yelled.

Tess made a run for it—unlocking and bolting out the back door and across the pasture, then down through the trees, not stopping until she made it back to her truck. She threw herself into the driver's seat and gunned the engine before peeling out onto the road. All the way back to the ranch, she watched for a patrol car, but it never passed by.

When she finally turned into her driveway and pulled into her garage, she cut the engine and let her head fall back. So much for finding real evidence. All she'd done was break a window—and she'd nearly gotten caught by Mr. Kline.

She clearly didn't have what it took to be a criminal.

CHAPTER TWENTY

I s it really almost time to let her go?" Silas steered his horse up the last switchback behind Tess and Dreamer, still guiding Legacy with the lead rope they'd rigged up before they'd left the ranch. "I'm not sure I'm ready to send her back out into the world."

He was the one who'd pushed to set her free again but he hadn't expected the sadness that had accompanied him on the ride. Legacy had become his pal while she'd been staying at the ranch. He'd gotten used to greeting her first thing in the morning, offering her carrots in exchange for a chat. Now he might never see her again.

"You were right. It's definitely time." Tess pulled Dreamer to a stop at the top of the ridge and waited for him to catch up. "She's ready. Look at her."

Yes, ever since they'd left the ranch, Legacy had moved with a different energy—fluid and purposeful instead of frantic and rigid like she was when she paced inside the fences back at the ranch. He knew the horse belonged out here—in the wide-open spaces, free to roam. But his gut still clenched. What if the herd had traveled too far away? What if they rejected her?

"We'll have to take her back to the ranch if they don't accept her in again, right?" He wasn't hoping, exactly. But he and Legacy had developed a bond. Somehow the horse seemed to understand him . . . or at least sense his feelings. And she trusted him. Even though she clearly yearned for her freedom, she hadn't fought his lead on the entire trek back up to the high meadow this morning.

"Yes, if the herd rejects her, we'll take her back to the ranch." Judging from Tess's empathetic smile, she could sense his feelings too. "But I don't think that's going to happen."

"Yeah. You're probably right." Silas scanned the meadow, his eyes searching for the other horses. "So how does this work exactly?" They were supposed to simply let go of the lead rope and she'd run away from them? *Great.* Now his heart clenched as much as his stomach. He wasn't used to feeling this kind of emotion.

"I thought we'd set up camp near the pond for the day." Tess nudged Dreamer to move again. "We'll say goodbye and let Legacy run and then we'll wait to see what happens. When it comes to wild animals, you can't have too much of an agenda."

"I've never liked waiting." Silas held his horse back, trailing behind at a much slower pace again. He'd never minded goodbyes, until now apparently. "How are we gonna know she's okay?" With anyone else, he might've been embarrassed to ask but Tess had his number. She clearly already knew he'd gotten attached to this horse.

"I'm hoping we'll see the herd." She slowed Dreamer up again, patiently waiting for his horse and Legacy to trudge in line with her. "We'll give her a while and then maybe we'll ride around a bit. I know the herd tends to spend a lot of time right here in the meadow too, and according to our patrols, there haven't been any gunshots to scare them off."

"Right. Sounds good." Silas watched the pond as they approached. In reality this sounded awful. He was just supposed to let go of that rope and be done with Legacy?

"This is a good spot." Tess pulled Dreamer to a stop and dismounted near the water's edge. Not far from Jace's memorial, he couldn't help but notice.

Silas hadn't visited the memorial much. He'd never been one for monuments. He saw Jace everywhere else—in Morgan's and Willow's smiles and laughter, in the banter between him and Thatch and Aiden. Those are the places his friend still lived.

Keeping ahold of Legacy's lead rope, Silas slid off the saddle and onto the ground.

"That's amazing." Tess watched him from a few feet away. "Legacy totally trusts you. She's not pulling or fighting the lead rope even though she wants to."

"Maybe she doesn't want to." Silas ran his hand down the horse's flank as he'd done every morning. "Maybe she liked life at the ranch better. Maybe she liked being in a place where she's fed and taken care of and she doesn't have to worry about getting hit by bullets." Without knowing who had shot her, they couldn't ensure it wouldn't happen again.

Tess walked closer, the sway in her hips almost enough to distract him from the sadness dragging him down. "You were the one who said Legacy needed her freedom." The woman stood toe to toe with him. "Remember? You said she shouldn't be confined by fences. She should be free."

Yes, he had said all of those things. Maybe because he had wanted freedom for himself. Freedom to go. Freedom not to care so much for someone who might not end up loving him. "Maybe there *is* freedom in having one true home." He looked into Tess's eyes as he said the words, his chest lifting.

Before either of them could speak, Legacy whinnied and tossed her head, shaking out her mane.

"She wants to go." Silas turned back to the horse. And he had to let her be free. "Here." He dug a few carrots out of the saddle bag attached to his horse and held them out. "You be careful out there," he murmured, fully aware of how silly he sounded talking this way to a horse. But Legacy wasn't just any horse. She was a miracle horse. She'd survived a gunshot wound. And even though she'd been hurt by a man, she'd trusted Silas. She'd shown a resilience he envied.

The horse's whiskers brushed against his hand as she gobbled the carrots he offered. "You can always come back to the ranch," he told her. Like she could really understand him. "You come back if you need anything."

Tess moved to his side and snuck an arm around his waist. "I have a feeling she'll never go too far from here," she murmured, leaning her head on his shoulder. "I don't think we've seen the last of Legacy."

"I hope not." He gave the horse one more good scrubbing along her neck and then carefully removed the halter and lead rope. "Bye, Legacy." He stepped back, giving the horse permission to go.

Tess stayed by his side, squeezing his hand. "She'll be fine. I know she will. I've never seen a stronger horse."

Silas nodded but he kept his jaw clenched so no rogue

tears would slip out. He'd never gotten attached to an animal. He'd never been allowed to have pets. But this horse had changed his life. She'd brought him and Tess together. She'd shown him that he could open up and feel something.

Legacy took a few steps, as though tentatively testing out her freedom. And then, he could've sworn she gazed directly at him before bolting in the opposite direction, her mane and tail flying in the wind behind her. At the edge of the woods, the horse stopped again, turning as if offering him one last goodbye. Then she trotted into the trees and out of sight.

"So what now?" He turned back to Tess, looking for a distraction from the small empty space that had opened up inside of him.

"Now we set up camp." She unclipped one of the saddle bags. "I came prepared. I have plenty of food for lunch and dinner, everything we need to start a fire, and sleeping bags in case we have to spend all day tomorrow out here too."

Silas stole the bag out of her hands and tossed it on the ground. "I want to spend as much time as possible with you." He took her hands and pulled her to him. "I can't wait to sleep under the stars with you." This woman. Good God. He was always afraid to let himself look at her too long— because it was so hard to believe that she could be his and he could be hers. That maybe…just maybe there was a true home for him in this world. With Tess. With Morgan and Willow. Aiden was right. They had to be his priority. "I'm going to tell Fletch I can't go to Afghanistan."

"Really?" Tess rested her hands on his shoulders, gazing up at him with tears gathering in her eyes.

"I can't go." Not with this whole new part of his life starting. "There's nothing more important to me than being here for you and the girls. Nothing." Being a soldier used to be the most meaningful thing in his life, but that had changed. "If I go, I'll lose time with all of you. And I want to show the girls how much I care about them. I want to bond with them so they'll accept me."

Tess's tears spilled over. "I was going to ask you to stay." She kissed him with a sniffle. "But I was afraid to because I don't want you to give up anything you truly want to do."

"I would give everything up." He took her hands in his. "You've changed everything for me."

"You've changed everything for me too." She inhaled deeply. "I want to tell the girls we're seeing each other. When they get back from Jackson. I want them to know. I need them to know."

Silas let go of her hands. "I'm not sure that's a good idea." He glanced to where his horse was grazing with Dreamer. He wasn't ready. There'd been a time when the only thing he'd feared was dying, but now his biggest worry was that Morgan and Willow would reject him, that they wouldn't want to give him a place in their lives. "Maybe they need more time." Maybe he needed more time to prove himself to them.

"I don't like having to hide." Tess moved into his line of vision. "I don't like sneaking you out into the garage when I want to kiss you. You are the best thing that has happened to me in two years, Silas." Her hands moved to his face and held him there. "And I want to share this with them."

He stepped away, his heart pounding. "I'm afraid," he admitted. He didn't think he'd ever spoken those words out loud. Never. But Tess was safe. "I don't know anything about being a father. Especially compared to Jace." His friend would've wanted only the best for Tess and his girls. "There's no way I can fill his shoes. And I'm afraid they won't want me."

"You don't have to fill his shoes." Tess held his hand again, tighter than she had before. "Jace was a good man. But he wasn't a perfect man. He didn't do everything right. He made mistakes. He said things he didn't mean, just like we all do." She stood on her tiptoes and brushed her lips over his. "I'm not looking for perfect, Si. I'm looking for someone who'll love my girls. Someone who'll love me. Someone I can love." Her hands found his. "I'm not looking for perfection. Or extravagance. Just something real. And that will be enough for the girls too."

He wanted to believe her. He'd never wanted to believe someone so much...

"I have faith in you," Tess whispered close to his lips. "Do you hear me, Silas Beck? You are loyal and protective and strong and selfless." Her smile brought him hope. "And you know—maybe better than most people—how important it is to show someone you love them. Because you didn't have that as a child—someone to show you love." She kissed him again, her lips clinging to his longer, softer. And when she pulled away, a light glowed in her eyes.

"But you have someone to show you love now. And we'll figure this out together."

CHAPTER TWENTY-ONE

When Silas opened his eyes, the first thing he saw were the pink swirls of dawn churning in the sky above him.

The cold air chilled his face, but warmth simmered inside. He held Tess in his arms, both of them smothered in the nest of sleeping bags and blankets she'd brought along.

After waiting and seeing no sign of Legacy throughout the evening, they'd spent the night under the stars, nestled together, talking about their lives, their heartbreaks, their hopes for the future. They'd decided that Tess would tell Morgan and Willow alone, and then they would give them some time and space to get used to the idea. The fear of their rejection still lived in him, but it was losing power.

At some point they'd fallen asleep together in this warm haven, Tess on her side with her body facing his and her head resting in the crook of his arm. And now he didn't want to move.

Before last night, he'd always found hope difficult to grasp. But spending time with Tess put his hopes in reach. Now, if he could only hold on to them.

Without moving his body, Silas turned his head so he could peek at her face. This woman who'd changed his life by opening her heart. If she'd opened her heart to him after all she'd lost, how could he keep his heart closed?

Tess still slept peacefully, her breathing rhythmic and calm, her body relaxed against his. Before her, he hadn't known how it felt to have someone's love fill the hollow deep places, the ones that even his service and dedication had never touched. *I have faith in you.* Tess would never know what those words meant to him, how—

A dull rumbling seemed to echo all around him. It sounded like...thunder. But only wispy clouds billowed in early morning pastels above.

Silas lifted his head, scanning the woods to their west. The horses. They were flooding into the far edges of the high meadow.

"Hey." He gently nudged Tess. "Wake up, beautiful!"

Her eyes fluttered open. "What time is it?"

"I don't know but the horses are coming." He pushed to a sitting position, easing her along with him. This is what they'd been waiting for. Though he wouldn't complain about the delay. He'd enjoyed every minute of being wrapped up with Tess.

"Oh wow," she breathed. "They're all together. Where's Legacy?"

"I don't see her yet." But they were an amazing sight. All of those powerful animals running together like a wave in the direct rays of the rising sun.

"There she is!" Tess pointed to the end of the herd.

"Yes, that's her." He let go of a sigh. "She made it. She's back."

"She's back!" Tess threw her arms around him and planted a kiss on his lips. "They're so gorgeous." She leaned her head on his shoulder and said nothing more while the herd moved past them, grazing their way back into the trees and out of sight.

When they'd disappeared, Tess peered up at him. "Are you okay?"

"Yeah." He wrapped his arms around her even tighter. "She's where she belongs. And so am I."

The woman turned to face him fully, still bundled in the sleeping bag, and inched forward until she straddled his lap. "Yes, you're where you belong too." She touched her lips to his, shutting out the rest of the world. "Want to go back to my house for a shower and breakfast?"

"Nothing has ever sounded better." He could do this every morning—look into Tess's eyes first thing, kiss her lips, secure in the fact that he'd held her all night long.

"Then let's get a move on." Tess scrambled out of the sleeping bag and got to her feet.

Silas pulled on his shirt and then quickly followed suit, helping her pack up.

They rode down the mountain in about half the time it had taken them to ride up to the meadow the day before. Back at the ranch, they led the horses into the stables and swiftly unloaded everything, making sure the horses had plenty of hay and water before finally stepping inside the house.

"Now I *really* need a shower." Tess tugged on his shirt, pulling him down the hall with her.

"Yes." That was all he could say. Yes, to everything.

He kissed her while he fumbled with the hem of her sweatshirt, only pulling back to yank it off over her head and discover a thermal shirt underneath. "You're wearing layers," he whined.

Tess laughed. "Come here." She tugged on the waist-band of his jeans, guiding him into the bathroom before shoving his pants down his hips. Moving his lips down her neck, Silas managed to get the extra shirt and her bra off. She took over then, gasping as she wrestled out of her leggings and underwear.

"Too many clothes," she complained, tossing them aside.

"Way too many." He turned on the shower and then hastily put on a condom before going back to Tess and dancing her into the shower.

"I like showering with you." She faced him and wrapped her arms around him, the warm water and the feel of her glistening silky skin making him moan.

"I could make you *love* showering with me." Silas kissed his way down her neck, moving his lips over her perfect breasts while he trailed his fingers across her hip and along the front of her thigh before touching her with teasing strokes.

Tess's breathing grew rapid with little whimpers sneaking out. "Don't make me wait," she whispered. "I *can't* wait. I need you right now."

"I need you too." Silas lifted her knee level with his hip and worked his way inside of her, taking his time to kiss her again, to feel their connection.

"More. Give me more. Everything. All of you." Her breaths were as ragged as his were.

"Yes." He was done holding back. Silas urged her to

move with him, feeling her all around him, bringing him deeper before he backed out in a long, fluid motion.

"Yes, like that," Tess panted. "Oh, Silas. Yes, Silas."

Hearing the sound of his name on her lips loosened his control. He moved deeper, pulling her to him while his hand caressed her butt. The rhythm of their bodies together drove him closer to losing control, but he tensed against the pull.

"I can't...I can't..." Tess didn't finish her sentence before crying out and clinging to him. God. One more push and his body let go, riding wave after wave of pleasure until he was spent.

Trying to slow his breathing, he let his head tip forward onto Tess's shoulder.

"Okay. I *love* showering with you," she said breathlessly.

"Not as much as I love showering with you." He held her while they rinsed off together, trailing kisses along her neck, her shoulders, her lips. "How about I go make us some breakfast?"

"Yes, please." Tess sent him out of the shower with a slap on his butt.

After hastily drying off, Silas pulled on his underwear and headed for the kitchen. Wait...was he humming? He couldn't remember the last time he'd hummed. Had he ever hummed? He wasn't sure but he kind of liked it, so he kept up the humming while he mixed the pancake batter and heated a griddle over the stove.

"I'm starving." Tess appeared, dressed only in a short robe, perfect for showing off her toned legs. "Nice of you to leave most of your clothes in the bedroom so I can have a good view while I eat."

"I live to serve." He poured the first batch of batter onto the griddle while Tess watched over his shoulder.

"Those smell amazing—"

The front door flew open and cut her off.

"Mom, we're home!" Morgan bounded inside, followed by Aiden, Kyra, and Willow.

Silas froze next to Tess.

"What're you doing here, Silas?" Morgan stopped cold, halfway to the kitchen. Her eyes went wide. "Are those your *underwear*? And, Mom, why are you wearing your robe?"

Behind the girls, Kyra and Aiden shared a panicked look. "We're so, so sorry," Kyra called. "I know we weren't supposed to be home until this afternoon but Willow got a bad stomachache before dawn and nothing worked to calm her down. She wanted you, Tess."

"We left you messages," Aiden added, avoiding Silas's gaze altogether.

Yeah, his friend was surely going to try to kick his ass later.

Morgan posted her hands on her hips and glared at Silas. "Did you spend the night here with my mom? Is that why we had to go away to Jackson? So you could be alone?"

He didn't know what to do. What to say. He couldn't do or say anything in his underwear. So, he bolted, down the hallway and into the bedroom where he found the rest of his clothes.

"Calm down," Tess was saying when he made it back to the kitchen. "This is good, actually. I'm glad you're here. I was going to talk to you anyway. Silas and I have been spending some extra time together lately and—"

"You're dating him?" the girl shrieked. "You can't date! He was my dad's best friend!"

Silas flinched at the hostility in her tone. He quickly turned back to the stovetop, bracing both hands against the counter.

"How could you do this to me?" Morgan wailed.

He didn't have an answer for her. Yes, how could he have done this to any of them? To Tess, to Morgan, to Willow? They shouldn't have found out like this. He shouldn't have put them in this position. Jace never would've done something like this. His friend had been wise and careful and self-controlled.

"I hate you!" Morgan yelled. "You'll never be my dad, do you hear me? Never!" Judging from the sound of pounding footsteps, she took off running down the hall.

"Wait." Tess must've gone after her, but he couldn't turn around. He couldn't look. He couldn't face Morgan and Willow.

"We should probably get going," Kyra said awkwardly from the other side of the room.

That got him to turn around. "Don't go. Please don't go," Silas begged. He had no idea what to say to these girls right now. Aiden knew. He was their uncle. And Kyra...she was their favorite aunt. They would know what to say, how to help.

Kyra looked at Aiden and they both sat gingerly on the couch.

Willow walked into the kitchen, dragging along a scraggly teddy bear, and looked up at him with those big blue eyes. "Did you have a sleepover with my mommy and now you're gonna be my daddy?"

"Uh. Um. We. Well..." He swallowed the rest of the fumbling explanation and changed the subject. "Do you want some pancakes?"

"Sure." The girl grinned and went to sit down at the kitchen table. "I'm hungry now that my tummy feels better."

"Good." *Whew.* "Great!" He scraped the burnt batch that he'd forgotten all about off the griddle and quickly poured more batter, watching the circles rise and bubble before flipping them. When they were perfectly browned, he plated two. "Want some syrup?" he asked, bringing them to the table.

Willow scrunched up her nose. "I don't like syrup."

"Right." He probably should've known that. "You two want pancakes?" he called to Aiden and Kyra, who were having a quiet discussion on the couch.

"No thanks," they said in unison.

"Why is Morgan so mad?" Willow asked, cutting the pancakes with the edge of her fork.

"I guess she doesn't like that I'm here." He looked to Kyra for some backup.

"I think Morgan is feeling extra tired from our late night." The woman stood and joined them at the table, calming Silas with her warm smile. "She didn't fall asleep during the ballet like someone else did." Kyra winked at Willow.

"It was kind of boring," the girl whispered to him. She took a bite of the pancakes and made a face. "*Ew.* These are *gross.*"

Gross? Silas inspected the pancake on her plate. They looked good to him. In fact, they seemed extra fluffy.

Kyra knelt next to the girl. "Willow, that's not very nice."

"Well, they are. They're too chewy." She pushed the plate away. "I don't like them. My daddy made *much* better pancakes."

Of course Jace had made better pancakes. Jace knew

what the girls liked. He knew how to take care of them. He knew how to comfort them when they were upset. And Silas had no clue. He took the plate from her and dumped them into the trash. "Sorry."

Tess emerged from Morgan's room. "She'll be fine. She just needs a minute."

Willow hopped up from her chair. "Mom, I'm hungry and I *hate* Silas's pancakes."

"Willow!" Tess squeezed her eyes shut and sighed before looking at her daughter again. "That's not a very kind thing to say," she said more gently.

"Well, it's true." Her daughter marched past Silas and then Tess en route to her room. "I don't like them and I'm *not* eating them."

Silas shut off the burner and stashed the few dishes he'd used into the dishwasher before walking out of the kitchen. "I should go." This morning had turned into a complete disaster. Being with Tess had been a fantasy. He didn't know what he'd been thinking. He couldn't do this. He sure as hell wasn't qualified to play house.

He'd made it two steps out the front door when Tess caught him.

"Wait."

"This'll never work." He was supposed to make her life better, not harder. Not more complicated. "I'll never be what your girls need. I'll never be the kind of father they deserve."

Anger stirred in her eyes. "Because Willow didn't like your pancakes? Because Morgan got upset?"

"No." Those weren't the only reasons. "This is too... hard." Morgan had said she hated him. They didn't want him. They knew he wasn't as good as Jace. "I'm sorry—"

A police car turned onto Tess's driveway.

Silas watched over his shoulder as it pulled up to the porch and stopped. "Is that Natalie?"

Tess's face had paled. "Uh-oh."

"What'd you mean 'uh-oh'?" That protective instinct kicked in, pushing him to stand by her side. "What happened?"

"I broke into the Kline's garage two nights ago," she hissed. "I only wanted to see if I could find that white UTV, but everything went wrong. I broke the window and I had to run away. But they must've known it was—"

"Hey, Tess." Natalie got out of the cruiser. "We need to talk."

Silas moved closer to Tess.

"Paul Kline called me early yesterday morning to report a break-in." Natalie stood a few feet away from the porch and shaded her eyes from the sun. "He said he thought he saw you, Tess. And the thing is, they have surveillance cameras all over their property."

That wasn't good. *Damn.* Had she come to arrest Tess? He couldn't let her. He couldn't let Natalie make a scene in front of the girls. "It was me," Silas interrupted. "I broke into the Klines' garage."

The woman ripped off her sunglasses and glared at him. "*You?*"

"Yeah." He held his gaze steady and dared the police officer to disagree. "I wanted to see if that white UTV was parked inside."

Tess gazed at him, wide-eyed, and shook her head and he snuck a quick squeeze of her hand to reassure her. He could handle this. She should've left the breaking and entering to him in the first place. She had the girls to think about. Morgan and Willow were already upset enough. They didn't need to watch their mother get hauled away in the back of a police cruiser.

"So you engaged in both criminal trespassing and vandalism to see if a white UTV was parked in the Kline family's garage." Natalie's deadpan tone made it clear she didn't believe him.

"Yes. That's exactly what happened." He didn't much care if she believed him or not. That was his story and he'd stick to it all the way to a holding cell if he had to.

"No, Silas," Tess whispered. "I can't let you—"

"They're pressing charges." Natalie approached the steps, a warning in her tone. "These are misdemeanor crimes, but I have to arrest someone if we find the person responsible."

"So, arrest me." He stepped in front of Tess and held out his hands. "Like I said, I'm the one who broke into the Klines' garage." He wondered if Tess had found the UTV, but she must not have or they wouldn't be having this conversation. Natalie would be going after them for shooting a horse instead. "Do you need a written confession or something?" he asked when the woman didn't move.

"I don't want you to do this," Tess murmured behind him.

"Come on, Chief." He ambled down the porch steps before the woman incriminated herself. "You have a full confession. You want me to put the cuffs on myself?"

The chief still didn't move. "The person on the surveillance video appears to be a lot smaller than you, Silas."

Appears to be but the woman couldn't say for sure. "You don't have a good look at the face though, do you?" *Good job, Tess.* Grainy surveillance images weren't enough to provide proof.

"No." The woman exaggerated a frown. "The images are too dark. All we can see is a hoodie."

"So, what evidence will hold up better? A full confession or a grainy image?" Silas walked to meet her.

Natalie's glower made it clear she already knew he wasn't going to give in.

"Let's go down to the station and—"

The front door banged open and Morgan stalked out onto the porch. "I'm going horseback ri—" She halted when she saw Natalie. "What're you doing here?" She turned to her mom. "Why are the police here?"

Tess opened her mouth to speak but Natalie stepped in. "I'm investigating a break-in, honey. That's all. Nothing to worry about."

"Right." Silas drew all of the attention back to him before this got out of hand. "I broke into the Klines' garage and Chief Natalie here was just about to arrest me."

Morgan gasped. "You're getting *arrested*?" She spun to Tess. "You're dating a *criminal*?"

"Yep." He held out his hands in Natalie's direction again, but the woman rolled her eyes. "For the love of God, Silas. Get in the car. We'll talk about this at the station."

CHAPTER TWENTY-TWO

I don't believe this," Morgan huffed. "You'd rather date a criminal than Callie's dad? That makes no sense!"

Her daughter marched back inside the house, but Tess could only stare at Natalie's police cruiser while the taillights disappeared down the highway. Why had she let Silas take the fall for her stupid decision? She'd panicked. She'd never been in trouble with the law before . . .

"Silas is in big trouble," Morgan was announcing on the other side of the door. "The police came and took him away!"

"He didn't do anything." Tess stepped inside and knelt so that she was eye level with her daughter.

Aiden and Kyra both still sat on the couch, and now Willow sat between them, but nobody said a word.

"*I* was the one who broke into the Klines'," Tess told her daughter. Why hadn't she told Natalie the truth when she'd had the chance? "Silas is trying to protect me." But she couldn't let him shield her from this fiasco.

"*You* broke into Callie's house?" Morgan shook her

head, her mouth gaping. "How could you do that, Mom? How could you break into my best friend's house?"

"It wasn't the *house*. It was the *garage*." Tess stood back up, torn between staying to offer an explanation and getting in her truck to follow Natalie to the station.

"Are you going to jail, Mommy?" Willow started to cry. "What's gonna happen to us? Please don't go away."

"I'm not going away." Tess opened her arms so her youngest could run into them. "Shh. Everything's all right," she soothed as Willow rested her head on Tess's shoulder. "I need you to go to the station," she said to Aiden. "Please. Go make sure you can get Silas out of this mess before it's too late."

"Sure thing." Aiden stood.

Kyra jumped up too. "Do you want me to stay for moral support? Or Aiden can drop me off at home on the way."

"You can go home." She needed to handle this with Morgan and Willow alone.

Her friend passed by, giving her shoulder a squeeze. "Let me know if you need anything. I'm there whenever you need to talk."

"Thank you." Tess set Willow's feet back on the floor. She actually needed to quickly chat with her friend right now. "Can you girls please go sit on the couch and wait for me? I need to talk to Kyra for a second."

Morgan hesitated but then did as she was told with Willow following behind.

"I'll be right back," she said to the girls before following Aiden and Kyra onto the porch.

"What a disaster we caused." Kyra winced. "I'm so sorry. We thought it would be safe to bring them back at noon."

"This is not your fault." The blame rested solely on her

shoulders. "We spent the night up in the high meadow until we knew Legacy was reunited with the herd and we got back late this morning." She should've been watching her phone just in case the girls needed her.

"You really broke into the Klines' garage?" Her brother kept his voice down. "What the hell were you thinking, Tess?"

"I got a little carried away." *Ugh.* Her head hurt almost as bad as her heart right now. "I didn't mean to cause any damage. And I didn't mean for Silas to get involved."

"Silas can handle himself," her brother insisted.

"He'll be fine," Kyra added. Then she tugged on Aiden's arm. "I'm sure everything'll work out, but you'd better head over there right now to see if you can help."

Tess caught her brother's arm as he walked away. "I love him." She did. Somewhere in the heartbreak and restoration that had taken place in the last two years, she'd fallen in love with Silas and she needed Aiden to know. "He said things could never work out between us. And maybe he's right. You saw what happened with Morgan and Willow in there." Talk about an unmitigated disaster. Maybe she should raise the white flag and give up...

"Any man who is willing to go to jail for you clearly loves you too," her brother said. "Maybe it'll be difficult for the girls at first, but the journey would be worth the work."

"Yes." Tess threw her arms around her brother's neck. "Thank you." That was exactly what she needed to hear right now. "Now go." She waved him away. "Make sure Natalie doesn't really arrest him. I can come down to the station to talk to her after I settle things with the girls."

"You got it." Aiden grinned at her. "I do have plenty of recon experience. I'll break him out of there if I have to."

"Don't get him into any more trouble," she told him

sternly. After a wave at Kyra, Tess slipped back inside the house. Morgan and Willow sat side by side on the couch watching a television show.

Tess picked up the remote and clicked the TV off. "We need to chat, girls." She wedged herself between them and put her arms around her babies—who weren't really babies anymore. "I love you both so much," she started. "You two are the most important part of my life. And that will never change, no matter what." She would remind them that as often as she had to so they would always believe.

"We love you too, Mommy." Willow got up on her knees and kissed Tess's cheek. "Are you sure you're not going away?"

"I'm sure." Natalie had mentioned that the infractions were misdemeanors. So, when she took responsibility, she wouldn't have to serve jail time. She'd most likely end up with community service and a hefty fine. Which she deserved.

"Why'd you break into Callie's garage?" By all appearances, Morgan hadn't forgiven her yet.

Tess released a weary sigh. She wanted to protect her daughters from everything ugly in the world, but she also wanted them to understand fighting for a cause. "What I did was wrong. I shouldn't have tried to break in. I was only trying to look in the window to see what they had parked inside." She explained to the girls about how the people who shot Legacy were driving a white UTV. "I think maybe that UTV belongs to the Klines."

"That's really scary." Willow crawled into her lap. "I didn't know Legacy got shot. Are the bad guys going to shoot us?"

"No, honey." She cradled Willow in her arms. "We're safe. But I want the horses to be safe too."

"The Klines shot at the horses?" Morgan's mouth

twisted in anger. "Why would they do that? Why would anyone shoot at animals?"

"We don't have any evidence yet. So, I can't say they were involved for sure." But seeing that UTV in the picture had been a mighty big coincidence. "Sometimes people do things we don't understand."

She still couldn't figure out why Brad had acted so interested in protecting the horses when he might have the UTV at his house. Was it his father's? Maybe. He could've been trying to protect his dad when he didn't say anything at the meeting. There were still so many unanswered questions. "But when someone is mistreating any living thing, it's important to hold them accountable. I didn't go about this the right way. I should've let the police handle things." She couldn't have her girls thinking they could ever justify breaking the law. "It was all a mistake and I'm very sorry for what happened." Especially since Silas was now dealing with the consequences of something she'd done.

"Why did Silas tell the police he broke in if he didn't do it?" Morgan asked.

"He wanted to protect me." That was Silas. The protector. "Because he cares for me very much. And he cares about you girls too." He may not have thought he knew how to be a father, but he knew how to protect and defend and sacrifice and love. "Silas is very important to me," Tess went on, with tears heating her eyes. "He has always been there for the three of us when we needed anything." Often behind the scenes, taking care of things around the ranch, doing the grunt work he never got any credit for.

"It was really nice of him to get arrested for you," Willow murmured.

"Yes. It was." Though Natalie likely wouldn't officially

arrest him when she clearly knew the truth about what had happened. "He might not make the best pancakes. And he might not have any kids of his own or know how to do everything the way your dad did. But I really believe he would do anything for us. And I know it might take time, but I'd like him to become a more important part of our lives."

She had to hope that they could make a space for him in their little family, that they could give him the kind of love and acceptance he'd been denied for most of his life.

"I'm sorry I yelled at him." Morgan looked down at her hands. "I thought I wanted you to get married again, but seeing you with Silas made me sad. I wish Dad were still here, that's all. I miss him so much. I wish he wasn't gone."

"He's still here." Tess pressed a kiss to the top of her daughter's head. "Your dad will always be here. In you." She brushed her fingers over Morgan's cheek. "And in you." She feathered Willow's wispy curls. "And in me. Because he's forever in our hearts. And that won't change. Even if we let ourselves love someone else."

*   *   *

Silas kicked back in the chair across from Natalie's desk with his hands behind his head.

Maybe he should be worried about the scowl currently gracing the chief's face, but right now, he couldn't bring himself to care. All that mattered was that Tess didn't have to be the one sitting in this chair. He might not be able to do much for her, Morgan, and Willow, but he could take the punishment off of her and make her life easier.

"Let's go over this again." Natalie delivered the words with an irritated edge. "You drove to the woods near the

Klines' property and walked across the pasture before breaking a window and entering the garage."

"That pretty much sums it up." He didn't want to offer any additional details because . . . well, he didn't know the details.

"What'd you use to break the window?" The chief leaned back in her chair and crossed her arms. She was trying to trip him up.

"Can't remember exactly." He shrugged, eyes widened with innocence.

Natalie's glare intensified. "So, you remember breaking the window. You just don't remember how you broke it."

"Must've been the adrenaline." He shot her a grin that hadn't failed him once. "It all happened fast."

"One more time," Natalie said tightly. "You *intentionally* broke the window?"

"Sure." He made another noncommittal shrug. He'd keep his answers as generic as possible so she couldn't prove anything.

"Then how come the surveillance video shows the person simply opening the window and then falling inside the garage, *accidentally* breaking the window with their boot?" A victorious glint sparked in her green eyes.

Silas almost laughed. The chief was stubborn, he'd give her that. But his bullheadedness had gotten him through SEAL training. "That might've looked like an accident," he said, enjoying the challenge she'd presented. "But I assure you, that was an intentional stunt. I kicked out the window on purpose."

"Come on, Silas." Natalie threw up her hands. "I know you didn't break into the Klines' garage, so you can give up the act."

"All due respect, Chief, you—"

The door creaked open and Brad Kline poked his head inside the room. "Hey, Natalie, can I have a word with you please?"

Well, this was an interesting development. Either Brad was here to confront someone about breaking into his garage or he'd come to confess he had a white UTV with a purple stripe.

Sighing, the chief pushed up from her chair and pointed at Silas. "This is not over. I'll be right back."

He nodded emphatically while she stepped past him and disappeared into the hall.

Whew. He let his head rest against the chair back. With all of the distractions momentarily gone, he remembered the look on Morgan's face when she'd seen him standing in the kitchen. Shock. Contempt. Disdain. She'd been mad enough then, but now she likely thought he was some kind of criminal getting hauled away to the police station. That was okay though. He could handle her judgment if it meant taking Tess's place in this predicament. He'd blown his chance with the girl anyway. She hated him. And Silas couldn't see any path forward for him to step into their home and their lives when neither Morgan nor Willow wanted him to be there. He'd ruined things.

The door opened and Silas sat up straight again.

Natalie reappeared, along with Brad Kline. "You're free to leave." She waved him out of her office. "It looks like you're done wasting my time today, thank the good lord."

Silas stayed where he was. She was just going to let him walk out? So she could go after Tess instead? "I'm sorry?"

"Brad has dropped the charges." Natalie crossed the room and sat back down at her desk.

"You're dropping the charges?" He turned his attention to Brad.

"I didn't realize Tess was the one who'd broken into the garage until my dad told me." He still hung out by the door. "In fact, I didn't realize there'd been a break-in at all until an hour ago. My father called it in without telling me. I know what Tess was looking for. And if I would've just come to Natalie earlier, none of us would be here right now."

"Ah." Silas stood and faced the man. So, Tess had been right about the white UTV in Brad's garage.

"Obviously we're not pressing charges." The man replaced him in the chair across from Natalie's desk. "My father, Ford, and Darrell were the ones shooting at the wild horses. I didn't know until the meeting at Tess's house." He removed his cowboy hat. "I didn't want to turn them in, so I confronted them instead and told them to knock it off or I'd have to tell the police. Obviously, with everything that's happened, I won't have a choice now."

"We'll have to start a report. I'll have to alert the Bureau too." Natalie was already typing away on her laptop.

"Sorry about all of this, Silas," Brad said. "Please offer my apologies to Tess too. I should've just turned them in when I first realized what was going on."

"I get it." He knew a thing or two about loyalty. "I'll let you handle things from here, then, Chief." He gave Natalie a salute.

She gestured for him to leave her office, but she was smiling too.

After a brief hug and promise of cookies from Terry,

Silas left the station and nearly ran into Aiden, who was on his way in.

"Whoa." His friend moved aside so Silas could step out onto the sidewalk. "Tess sent me down here to bail you out. But I can see you don't need my help."

"I don't need a bailout but I could use a ride." He tried to gauge Aiden's mood. After the morning he'd had, Silas wasn't exactly up for a fight. "I appreciate you coming down here."

"I've always got your back." Aiden whacked his shoulder like old times. So, it seemed he'd forgiven him for making a scene in front of Morgan and Willow. Or maybe he'd only assumed Aiden had been angry. Silas wouldn't blame him. He was angry at himself. "You know that."

Did he know Aiden would have his back? "Actually, I'm surprised you came." Silas started to walk toward Aiden's truck. "I know you weren't sure about me and Tess. But you don't have to worry about it now anyway." He couldn't continue to make things difficult between her and her girls.

"And why is that?" Aiden asked when they'd both climbed in.

"I'm stepping back. I won't come between Tess and Morgan and Willow." And now that he didn't have to deal with a misdemeanor, he'd be free and clear to take off for a while. With him gone, they could get back to normal. The girls would forget all about that awkward moment in the kitchen. Tess would miss him...maybe as much as he would miss her, but what other choice was there? He couldn't stay here so close and avoid them. He didn't want to cause Morgan and Willow more pain. And that was exactly what he'd seen on Morgan's face earlier. Heartbreak.

Aiden started the engine but didn't back out of the parking spot. "So, you're going to walk away from her? From the girls? From the chance to be a part of their lives?"

What choice did he have? "Morgan hates me."

"No, she doesn't," Aiden shot back. "She was upset. Kids say all kinds of things when they're upset. Trust me. I'm sure she's said she hated me a time or two."

"I wanted everything to go differently." He'd had a plan. He was going to build them a tree house and spend time with them. He was going to take them riding up in the high meadow and let them get to know him in a different way. "I feel like I already messed up." And he feared he wouldn't get another chance.

"So, you messed up." Aiden released the emergency brake and backed out of the spot. "I've watched you take care of my sister and Morgan and Willow for two years now. They might not even realize everything you've done for them, but I've seen it. You gave up everything to move here so you could fulfill a promise. And today you stepped up to protect them."

"I didn't plan to fall in love with her." In fact, that was the last thing he'd imagined when he'd come to Star Valley. He assumed he'd stay long enough to help the woman stand on her own like he'd promised Jace and then he'd be off again, moving on to the next place, like he always did.

"I know you didn't plan this." Aiden's expression was uncharacteristically solemn. The two of them hadn't exactly had a lot of heart-to-hearts over the years. "But Tess fell in love with you too. And I may have given you a hard time at the beginning, but she deserves this chance to love someone again. I think Jace would approve of you and Tess, if you want the truth. He had a lot of respect for you. For your work ethic and your loyalty and your commitment. And so do I." He paused at the stop sign in front of the café. "I know you'd do everything you can to make them happy."

"I would." Silas had a lot to learn about love, about being a father. And apparently about making pancakes. But he couldn't deny the truth. "I would do *anything* to make them happy." If he was given the chance. "But I won't force my way into their lives."

CHAPTER TWENTY-THREE

Tess turned into the school's carpool lane, moving the wheel with one hand while she sipped coffee from the travel mug she held in the other.

Hello, Monday morning. With two weeks left of school, they were literally limping to the finish line. Morgan had changed clothes three times that morning, lamenting that she had nothing cool to wear.

When had she started to care so much about being cool?

And Willow had done her stomachache bit—saying she couldn't possibly go to school when she felt like she was going to barf. For some reason, her younger daughter only felt like she was going to barf on Monday mornings.

"I don't want to go to school," Willow complained, kicking her feet into the back of the front seat.

Tess took another sip of coffee and inched forward in line. Seriously. Was there any greater torture than the elementary carpool line?

"I understand." She tried to sound sympathetic, but she

wasn't exactly chipper this morning either. She'd been hoping to talk with Silas after Aiden had picked him up at the station yesterday, but instead the man had her brother drop him off at the ranch and then he took off in his truck before she had the chance to go out and see him. And she hadn't heard from him either, which of course had kept her up all night wallowing in questions. Had he written her off? Did he still think nothing would ever work between them?

"I should've worn my red shirt." Morgan sighed loudly. "There's Mia and she's wearing red. She looks so good."

"So do you." Tess glanced in the rearview mirror. "You are beautiful, Morgan Valdez. Whether you're wearing pink or purple or brown."

"*Brown?*" her daughter asked in a horrified manner. "Mom, I will *never* wear brown."

"Oh, would you look at that. We made it to the front." Tess stepped on the brake. "Bye, girls. Have a great day, love you."

Their parting words came out in unintelligible mumbles as they climbed out of the car and joined their classmates walking into the building. *Whew.* Tess eased forward, moving slowly around the circle in front of the school before coming to a stop again. The carpool line at the elementary school happened to be the only place in town where there were traffic jams.

"Hey, Tess," Brad called through her open window. He approached the passenger side of her truck.

"Brad. Hi." She would've rather crawled into her glove compartment than face him right now, but she literally had nowhere else to go. At least he'd convinced his father to drop the charges. Natalie had called to tell her yesterday afternoon. She'd also learned that Brad's father had been responsible for harassing the horses, along with Darrell and Ford, though they swore they never meant to hurt one.

"I've been meaning to call you," Tess said. "I'm so sorry about the broken window. And for trespassing." She still didn't know what she'd been thinking. "I should've come to talk to you instead." But she'd learned her lesson. Committing misdemeanors wasn't her strong suit.

"Don't worry about it. I made plenty of mistakes in this whole situation myself." He leaned his forearms on the window frame, good-natured smile intact. "You didn't hurt yourself, did you? That fall through the window looked painful on the surveillance video."

Tess's cheeks heated. He must've gotten a few good laughs watching the video. She was lucky he hadn't posted it on social media. "No. I didn't get hurt. Just a few bruises." And a wound to her pride. "I'll pay you for the window though." Traffic started to move again, but the cars behind her easily got around her.

"No need to pay. My father is the one who started this whole mess anyway." The man's smile faded. "I should've told you at the meeting, so technically it's my fault too. When you described the UTV, I knew who it was right away. But I was trying to keep him out of trouble."

"I understand why you didn't say anything." Talk about an uncomfortable position, deciding whether or not to turn in your parent. "What's Natalie going to do to them?"

"They'll have to pay a steep fine and do community service." Irritation flared through the words. "Honestly, she let them off easy. I'm disgusted by the whole thing. I mean, growing up on a ranch, my parents taught me to respect animals, and then my father goes and does something stupid like shoot at a herd of wild horses."

"That doesn't make a lot of sense." At least Brad wasn't involved. She was glad they could still be friends. "Did he say why they did it?"

The man shrugged. "The three of them feel like the herd is threatening the cattle. They're worried there won't be enough food to go around, I guess." He straightened, taking a step back from her truck. "Dad said they were only trying to scare the herd off the land." His expression remained skeptical. "Either way, they needed to be held accountable. And I'm sorry I made trouble for you by keeping quiet."

"Well, I didn't exactly handle the whole situation well either." That was clear. "I could've simply asked you about the UTV instead of proving what a terrible criminal I am." Breaking into his garage hadn't been one of her finest moments.

"We'll put the whole thing behind us." His smile returned. "And just so you know, I suggested that their community service should revolve around helping you turn the ranch into a wild horse sanctuary like you were talking about. And I'm more than happy to help too."

"That would be great." She was going to need all the help she could get installing the fences.

A car honked behind her.

"I'd better get going," she told Brad. "But bring Callie by this weekend. The girls would love to hang out with her."

"Will do. Thanks." He gave her a wave and then Tess drove off.

Instead of going home, she found herself driving to

Silas's small craftsman only a few blocks from Main Street. Seeing his truck in the driveway brought on a rush of adrenaline.

She parked along the curb, hesitating only for a moment before she turned off the engine and climbed out of her truck. The few times she'd been to Silas's house, she'd been struck by how bare the place was. He had nothing out on his front porch—unlike most people in town who at least had a few chairs or a bench to sit on. And the lack of comfortable personal touches continued to the inside too.

Silas had never put down roots. But he'd never had a reason to. She had no idea what he was thinking after the scene at her house. She had no idea how he felt right now, or what he planned to do. She only knew she had to see him. She had to kiss him. And she had to tell him that she didn't care how long it took Morgan and Willow to come around. The waiting would be worth it.

Footsteps sounded behind the door and either the porch shifted or her equilibrium did. He answered within a few seconds, before she could brace herself, before she could right her balance.

"Hey."

How could he speak? Didn't he feel the same chaos she did when he looked at her? Words were swirling in her brain, tangling and rebounding off each other, but none of them seemed right for this moment. She wanted to tell him she was sorry for what Morgan had said, and she wanted to tell him he was wrong, they could make anything work. But instead she stared at him.

"You want to come in?" He stepped aside, making room for her to move past.

She walked through the door, holding her breath when

she caught sight of the boxes stacked on the outskirts of his living room. "Are you packing?"

He shoved a large box away from the front of the couch. "Just going through things and getting rid of a bunch of stuff."

Tess's heart deflated. "Are you leaving?"

"I haven't talked to Fletch yet." He hadn't made direct eye contact with her since she'd walked in. "I just don't know what else to do, Tess. If I go, it'll give the girls some space. I don't want our relationship to make things so hard for you."

A sudden desperation pushed her to him. Things should not have gone this way. They'd been so close to having something. So close. And now he was giving up. "I'm sorry for how the girls acted toward you yesterday."

"I'm not upset with them." His gaze finally held hers and his jaw softened. "Not at all. They were surprised and they had every right to react." His voice quieted. "And I'm not upset with you either. I couldn't be."

Then why hadn't he come to see her? Why hadn't he called or texted? "I thought you would stop in at the house. When Aiden brought you to pick up your truck."

Silas took her hand and prodded her to sit with him on the couch. "I don't want to force anything on Morgan and Willow." He let go of her. "They're not ready to let someone else in. And that's okay. It just means I have to take a step back right now."

But it wasn't okay. This was frustrating and difficult. All she wanted to do was sink into his arms, but he didn't open them for her.

"They don't want me to be a part of your life." Silas stood. "And I can't go back to being your friend. Not after knowing what it's like to be with you. I can't go back, and I don't think we can move forward together right now."

He'd made up his mind. She saw the resolve. But she couldn't leave things this way between them. The girls might not be so sure about Silas becoming part of their lives yet. But they would come around. She had to believe. He may have given up, but she wouldn't.

Tess pushed off the couch and marched to him, moving to her tiptoes to touch her lips to his. She kissed him for all she was worth, holding back nothing, her hands cupping his jaw, her tongue finding his, their connection sending electrical currents all through her. Silas melted into her, his arms holding her tight, his body fitted together with hers. And surely, he couldn't deny this. That they were meant to be just like this together. That their time would come, no matter how far he tried to run.

When she could no longer breathe, Tess pulled away and walked out of his house.

Hopefully that kiss had given him enough to hold on to.

CHAPTER TWENTY-FOUR

"Mom, my science fair project is due next week."

"Really?" Was it that time of the year already? "Maybe we should talk about it tomorrow."

Why ruin a perfectly beautiful Saturday morning with talk of a project that inevitably brought out the worst in both her and Morgan every year? The problem wasn't that she disliked helping Morgan with the project. The problem was simply that her daughter tended to have expectations that far exceeded the final product. Even with their best work, her daughter was never satisfied. She'd inherited her father's perfectionist tendencies. And science had never been Tess's strong suit.

She sipped her coffee and gazed out at the morning sun that had only just started to peek over the mountaintops in the distance. Morgan and Willow both sat at the table with her, drinking hot chocolate with extra whipped cream and sprinkles. A hot chocolate bribe always gave her a few extra minutes to sit and relax before having to make them breakfast, and she was dragging this morning. In fact, this whole week had left her weary.

She'd kept busy with beef orders, holding meetings with her buyers, and planning for the horse sanctuary, but none of those things had soothed the aching hollowness that seemed to spread with each passing day. Silas was supposed to leave in less than a week, and she hadn't seen him since she'd kissed him and walked out of his house.

"This year I want to build a life-size model of a wild horse," her daughter announced.

Tess choked on a mouthful of coffee, spraying some out of her nose. She coughed and sputtered, cleaning her face and table with a napkin. "I'm sorry...what?" she asked when she could finally speak.

"I'm going to build a life-size model of a wild horse," Morgan repeated impatiently. "And I'm going to show everyone in my school what happened to Legacy. Where she got shot and how she survived and then everyone will know more about wild horses and no one will want to hurt them anymore."

Her heart melted at the same time dread crept in. "I think that's a very important project." She had to tread carefully here. "But do we have to *build* a life-size model? Maybe you could *draw* a life-size picture. Remember the bridge we made last year? That didn't go very smoothly." Had her daughter already forgotten about the Popsicle stick fiasco when they tried to build a model of a bridge? The entire structure kept falling apart and Morgan had at least four meltdowns in the process. "You know I'm not very good at building things."

"*I* remember the Popsicle stick bridge," Willow said

helpfully, licking a dollop of whipped cream from her upper lip. "You cried like every day, Morgan."

"I did not." Her eldest daughter pushed her iPad across the table. "This is what I want to do. We have to make the horse really big so I can write all of the information and make sure people can see the details. Oh! I can use yarn for the mane."

Yep, her daughter was getting carried away again. Tess studied the picture that depicted wood-working plans for a 3D seven-foot-tall horse. *Oh boy.* "Honey..." She didn't even know what to say here. "That's a really cool idea. But I can't help you build that." She couldn't build a horse out of wood. "And Uncle Aiden and Kyra are gone this weekend, remember?" Her brother had chosen the perfect weekend to whisk his fiancée away for an impromptu camping trip to Yellowstone. "Besides, that's quite a big project. We would've had to start something like that a month ago."

She should've known this project would come up soon, but she'd had a few other things on her mind as of late. And she couldn't have imagined that Morgan would want to build a life-size horse. "I love that you want to educate people about the wild horses. I think a drawing or a painting would—"

"It *has* to be a model." Morgan studied the picture again. "Then everyone will want to know what it is. Everyone'll notice it. The horse will stand out from all the other projects and people can learn about what happened to Legacy."

How was she supposed to say no to that?

"I'll help you build it," Willow told her sister. "There's some wood out in the barn. I saw it. And I know where Mom keeps the hammer."

"Thanks, Willow. But I don't think we can build it our-selves." Her eldest daughter's eyes widened. "But Silas will help us! I know he will."

"Yes! Silas!" Willow popped up from her chair.

Tess's heart clutched. "Oh...girls...I don't know. I'm sure he's busy." She hadn't mentioned anything about him to them. She'd been waiting for Willow and Morgan to talk to her about him. But she probably needed to start preparing them for what was coming. "He's getting ready to leave for that new job he has overseas."

"Well, he can't leave." Morgan stood up, obviously unde-terred. "He can't leave because I need his help. I need him here." Her smile was full of promise. "I know he won't leave if I ask him for help, Mom. He's always been there for us when we needed him."

"Yes. He certainly has." Tess blinked away tears. She understood why Silas had taken a step back. He hadn't wanted to push the girls. So, she hadn't pushed them either. He'd wanted them to accept him on their own. When the time was right. And maybe...just maybe the time was right now.

"Come on, Mom!" Willow tugged on her hand, urging her out of the chair. "Go get dressed so we can ask for Silas's help. He's super good at building stuff."

"Yes!" Morgan gathered up her iPad. "We can go over to his house and ask right now! It's been forever since we've seen him anyway. Aren't you two supposed to be dating?"

"I'm not really sure." Tess scrambled out of her chair, leaving the rest of her coffee unfinished. "But I suppose we'd better go over there and find out."

*   *   *

Silas loaded the last of the boxes into the basement storage room and locked up.

His house was nearly empty now...not that it had been all that full before. This stint in Star Valley Springs was supposed to only be a stopover. He'd never planned to stick around forever. He hadn't *wanted* to stick around forever.

But now he didn't want to leave. Even for a month or two, or however long this assignment with Fletch would take. He didn't want to go. That was the bottom line.

He walked up the narrow staircase and found himself standing in the austere kitchen. The man who'd sold him the house had updated everything with a clean, plain modern style, all whites and grays, and he'd never thought about making any changes. Mostly because he'd never thought of making any place a home. He'd never needed a home. He'd never longed for a home because he'd never known one.

Until Tess.

Yet again, he fought against his instinct to pick up his phone and call her. At least twice a day this entire week he'd had to force himself to set down his phone. As much as he'd wanted to see her, to spend time with her, he couldn't sneak around, hiding everything behind Morgan's and Willow's backs. They deserved better than that and so did their mom. Maybe Morgan and Willow would come around, like Tess had said when she'd stopped by his house. And what if he was gone when they did? Would they feel abandoned?

Silas pulled his phone out of his pocket. He'd never been good at waiting. He liked action. But if he wanted to be with Tess, he couldn't keep doing things the way he'd always done them. He didn't have to go all the way across the world to give them space. He'd given them space this whole week. And if he told Fletch he wasn't coming, he'd be here if Morgan and Willow ever came looking for him.

Before he could call Fletch, the doorbell rang.

Silas stuffed his phone into his pocket and opened the door. "Morgan?" The girl stood on his stoop holding a tablet.

"Hi, Silas! I was wondering if you could help me with my science project for school." She marched into his house. "It's due next week."

"Uh." She wanted *him* to help her? He glanced past her to where Tess's truck was parked in his driveway.

"Mom is helping Willow out of the truck but I would like to get started as soon as possible." She held out her iPad so he could see the screen. "I need to build a 3D horse exactly like this, and my mom said she has no idea how to do that, and I said, 'I know! We'll ask Silas.' Because you always help us with stuff."

Some internal dead bolt in his chest unlatched, allowing him to breathe easier. "You're sure you want *me* to help you?" The last time he'd seen her, she pretty much hadn't wanted anything from him.

Morgan grinned at him. "I couldn't think of anyone better to help. Mom said you might be too busy because you're getting ready to leave for your new job but you're not really going to go, are you?" This girl gave new meaning to the term puppy-dog eyes. "We need you here. Me and Willow and Mom. We don't want you to go. *I* don't want you to go away."

A sense of purpose swelled through him, far more powerful than any he'd experienced before. To be there for these girls, for Tess...that was all he would need for the rest of his life.

One sentence. That was all it took to change his entire life.

"Hi, Silas!" Willow skipped in through his front door, followed by Tess.

Tess was here. She'd pulled her hair up with just a few strands curling down along her neck. She wore no makeup and had on a tattered sweatshirt and leggings. And she was the most beautiful thing he had ever seen.

"Hey. Sorry to stop by unannounced like this." The woman nervously touched her hair, eyes shifting uncertainly. Because she didn't know yet. She didn't know that Morgan had laid a claim on his heart. If these girls had truly let him in, he would never let them down.

"Are you kidding? You have no idea how happy I am to see you."

"Can you make me some pancakes, pretty please?" Willow gazed up at him with her round, innocent blue eyes.

Silas lowered so that he was eye level with the girl. "I thought you didn't like my pancakes too much."

"I don't," she said simply. "But I really like you." The girl threw her arms around his neck and instant warmth filled his eyes.

"I like you too." He could hardly speak.

"Before you make pancakes, I need to know if you can help me build the horse." Morgan showed him the picture again. "I want it to look exactly like this."

Still kneeling, Silas studied the screen. The woodworking plans depicted pieces all cut out of oak plywood and put together like a 3D puzzle. "Sure, we can do that.

We have plenty of scrap wood at the office. And I'm sure we have all of the tools we'll need."

"Yes! Thank you!" Morgan hugged him too and then the two girls started to dance around him, making up a song about building a wild horse.

"This was all Morgan's idea," Tess told him. What was she doing still standing so far away?

Silas closed the distance between them. "I know." He had seen the authenticity in both girls' simple requests. "I will help them with anything," he murmured. "I will do anything for them and I'll do anything for you."

"Stay." Tess clasped her hands in his.

"I'm not going anywhere." Not now. "In fact, there's something I need to do." He pulled his phone out of his pocket with the three of them standing there watching him.

Fletch answered on the third ring. "Yo, Beck, I was just getting ready to call you."

"I can't go," he said before his friend could continue. He'd never done this. He'd never gone back on a commitment. But he wanted to make a more important pledge to these three special girls. "I have to back out because I fell in love. With Tess and Morgan and Willow. I can't leave them..."

"Whoa." Fletch paused for a moment of stunned silence. "Well, hey," his friend finally said. "I think that's great, man. I'm happy for you guys."

"Really?" Silas breathed out in relief.

"Hell yeah. Couldn't be happier for you. And there's not gonna be a mission anyway. The government's decided to go another way. Apparently, they want to work with the local authorities instead of ambushing the kidnappers. So, we're off the hook for this one."

"Good. That's great." He told his friend goodbye and tossed his phone down on the table. "I'm officially sticking around this summer."

The girls cheered and Tess opened her arms for a hug, but Silas hesitated. What would the girls think? Yes, they had invited him in, but he still didn't want to rush things for them.

Morgan stopped dancing and regarded him with an astute stare, one side of her mouth lifting in a lopsided grin. "You can hug her. Just don't kiss in front of us. That's disgusting."

"Yeah! That's disgusting," Willow chimed in.

"Got it." They would have to save the kissing for later.

Right now, he caught Tess in his arms and held on tight.

CHAPTER TWENTY-FIVE

Tess rode Dreamer along the newly installed welded-wire fence that segmented the lower meadow behind the ranch into two hundred–acre pastures. Up ahead, her hero volunteer crew was finishing stretching the last panels of fencing into place.

Well...some of the crew was putting the fence into place while the rest of them were setting up for the big celebration to commemorate the completion of the Dry Creek Ranch Horse Sanctuary.

"Looking good, guys." She rode to Darrell and Ford and Paul Kline, who were stapling the wire panels into the posts. "Almost done now." She had to give these men credit...though they might not have been exactly thrilled with their community service assignment to assist with setting up the pastures for the wild horse sanctuary at first, they had really stepped up—joining the volunteer crew every weekend for the last four months to complete the requirements outlined by the Bureau of Land

Management. After Tess had turned in the application to manage the herd of horses on her property, the real work had started. "You're all going to stick around for the festivities after the work is done, right?"

"Only if you're sure we're welcome." Paul pressed the staple gun to the post and secured a few more rungs into place. "We don't want to impose."

"It's no imposition at all." Each of these gentlemen had made a formal apology to both her and Morgan for scaring them the way they had when they'd been riding in the meadow. And now the three of them were the first patrons of the Adopt a Horse program she was starting for the sanctuary. They would be personally paying a monthly stipend for Legacy's care. She and Silas had kept an eye on the horse from afar, catching glimpses of her with the herd every so often. And with the Bureau rounding up the herd and delivering them today, Tess couldn't wait to see Legacy again. "You *should* be a part of the celebration." The more they'd learned about the wild horses, the more enthusiastic they'd become about helping out.

"Then we'll stay." Ford tipped his hat to her. "Thanks for the invite."

"You're more than welcome." She clicked her tongue, giving Dreamer the signal to keep moving down the fence line. They were so close! Only three more panels to secure into place and the last section would be ready for their new friends.

Tess rode to where Silas, Thatch, and Aiden were holding the panels taut and in place to make sure they wouldn't have any gaps while Ford, Paul, and Darrell stapled them to the posts.

"I can't believe we're this close." She pulled her horse

to a stop next to Silas and slid off Dreamer and into his arms—a move she'd perfected over the summer months.

"I can believe it." He held her close, letting her brother and Thatch steady the panel on their own. "You've worked hard for this. And you've inspired a whole town to take action." He brushed a kiss across her lips, something he did often now, even though her daughters were only fifty feet away helping Minnie, Lyric, and Kyra set the tables for the picnic they'd planned.

It had taken all of her close friends to load up their trucks to get enough supplies out here to feed the crowd that would be coming to get a look at the majestic creatures that almost everyone in town had come together to protect. "We did cut it close," Tess reminded him.

In preparation for the sanctuary's opening, the Bureau should be arriving to deliver them to the ranch any time now. "We have to have the fence finished before they show up."

In order to help preserve the delicate environment, they'd sectioned off the two hundred–acre pastures the horses could graze on so they would still have plenty of room to roam. Every few months they would move the herd to a different pasture so they could experience new territory while lightening the impact on the grasses and foliage.

"We'll make the deadline." Thatch moved aside so Ford could staple in the last of the fencing. "This is it. The final post."

"And then it's time to party," Aiden added, wiping the sweat off his face with a handkerchief.

"Mommy!" Willow waved her arms from one of the tables. "Miss Minnie made chocolate chip cookies!"

"And cupcakes too!" Morgan added. "Come see!"

"I like cupcakes." Silas took Tess's hand and they walked toward the girls together. When they'd made it halfway, Willow raced to meet them and Silas caught her youngest daughter in his arms, swinging her up into the air and then settling her onto his shoulders.

"I love being this tall." Willow giggled, stealing Silas's cowboy hat and putting it on her own head.

Tess's heart swelled about three times bigger, making her chest full and warm. She and Silas had taken things slow over the last few months, being careful to include the girls in their growing relationship, easing all of them into it, and now Morgan and Willow had developed such a bond with this man.

"I want a piggyback!" Morgan rushed over when she saw her sister on Silas's shoulders.

"Climb on." Silas lifted Willow over his head and held her while he knelt down so her older daughter could climb onto his back. Somehow the man managed to stand up with both girls clinging to him.

"Look at them," Lyric commented while Tess helped her set out plates. "Those two girls are absolutely smitten with Silas."

"They're not the only ones." She watched the man dote on her daughters, the three of them laughing together.

"I think Aiden is a little jealous," Kyra murmured, stirring a pitcher of iced tea. "In a good way, of course. The girls hardly acknowledge him when Silas is around. But that's how it should be."

"Have you two talked about the future?" Lyric asked, pausing from her work.

"Some." Truthfully, they'd been so busy enjoying the

present moments together they hadn't dwelled on what would happen next. "Silas has said he wants the girls to decide what his place in their lives will be." She knew he would love to officially adopt them eventually. But he'd made it clear to her that he wanted them to decide. "We're not in a hurry. These last four months have been beautiful." A slow sort of progression as they all navigated new relationships. During their times together, the four of them had talked about Jace a lot. No matter what, both she and Silas were adamant that Jace would still be a part of their family.

"Maybe there will be another wedding soon," Kyra mused, almost to herself.

"We won't overshadow your wedding." Her brother and Kyra were set to be married in a few weeks, and Tess couldn't wait to celebrate with them.

Lyric grinned, her eyes sparkling with playfulness. "Since you're the maid of honor and Silas is the best man, it'll be good practice for walking down the aisle."

"You know what they say," Tess teased back. "Weddings usually happen in threes." She gave her friend a meaningful look.

"Not this time," Lyric insisted. "I'm not—"

A loud engine noise grumbled in the distance and a line of semitrucks turned onto the ranch's long driveway towing livestock trailers.

"They're here, they're here!" Morgan hopped down from Silas's back.

"Stay close," Tess reminded her. Both the drivers and the horses would need room.

With the fences completed, everyone clustered around the tables, watching as the trailers backed up one by one and unloaded the wild horses from the trailers into the pasture.

"Look, there's Legacy!" Willow pointed to the horse Tess and Silas had rescued. The horse that had brought them together.

"There she is." Silas slipped his arm around Tess's shoulders, gathering her to his side.

While many of the horses seemed slightly disoriented, scattering to the edges of the fences, Legacy ambled to the gate closest to where they stood and gazed at them with her ears perked.

"I think she'd like to say hello to you." Tess nudged Silas forward. The horse seemed to watch him intently.

"Hey, Legacy, old friend." He approached the fence slowly with Tess holding the girls back. "Give them a minute," she said quietly.

The horse stayed still while Silas reached his hand to her snout. And then, after a few seconds, she nosed his shoulder, sniffing and snorting and grunting.

"She remembers him," Morgan marveled.

"Can I give her a carrot?" Willow called to Silas.

He nodded and waved the girls forward. They ran to the table where Tess had left a bag of carrots and then approached Legacy with caution, the way Tess had taught them to do with any animal who wasn't familiar with them. The horse gobbled the carrots out of their hands. Silas lifted both girls up—one in each arm—so they could pet her mane and Tess took out her phone to snap a picture.

Hopefully their future would be full of beautiful moments just like this one.

CHAPTER TWENTY-SIX

Silas loosened his tie as much as he could get away with and sipped the whiskey that was supposed to be calming his prewedding jitters.

Thank goodness Kyra had let them go with a casual sport coat and tie for this shindig instead of tuxes. Damn. This wasn't even his wedding and yet he couldn't remember the last time he'd been this nervous. Not for the wedding part—that was all Aiden and Kyra—but for the part that would come later when he could get Tess and the girls alone for a few special moments to propose.

"You okay, man?" Thatch asked, giving him a careful appraisal. "You seem nervous. Normally you love being the center of attention."

"I'm fine. This day isn't about me." He did a visual check on Aiden, who sat between him and Thatch at one of the reception tables in the barn Kyra had had renovated for this day. "You good, man? Anything you need?" He and Thatch had flipped a coin to determine who would

run point on this co—best man thing, but right about now
Silas was sure Thatch would've been a better fit.

"I'm good." Aiden didn't seem to be sweating nearly
as much as Silas.

"Good. That's great." He stood, too antsy to stay still
anymore. "I'll go check on...stuff." There had to be
something he could do to keep busy until the ceremony
was supposed to start. Other than thinking about pop-
ping the biggest question he would ever ask anyone in his
whole life. He swore that Tess's ring and the girls' necklaces were burning holes right through his pockets.

He stepped outside and walked to where the ceremony was set to take place. Rows of fancy white folding
chairs faced a wooden arbor in front of a breathtaking
view of the mountains. Everything looked ready. Many
of the guests had already arrived and taken their seats.
Was he supposed to do anything else before the ceremony? He couldn't seem to think as clearly as he usually
did.

"Silas!" Morgan called his name and he spun, searching for her. *Thank God.* There she was, with Willow
and Tess on the front porch of Aiden and Kyra's house.
He really needed to see his girls right now. Leaving his
nerves behind, he hurried to where they stood.

They looked beautiful. All three of them. Morgan and
Willow in their fluffy pale pink flower girl dresses and
Tess in a long light green dress that hugged her silhouette
perfectly. "You three are the loveliest ladies I have ever
seen," he said as a greeting.

"And you're the handsomest." Willow held on to his
hand. He still wasn't used to the feeling that came over
him when one of the girls reached out to him. A mixture

of gratitude and resolve and hope and purpose so over-whelming his eyes stung.

"You really are the handsomest." Tess reached forward to straighten his tie. "Is everything okay? You look a little nervous."

She knew him so well.

"I'm good." And he'd be even better when he could sneak these three away from the reception for a few minutes to make their little family official.

"It's almost time." Tess's lips touched his cheek in a lingering kiss. "I'd better go see if Kyra needs anything before we walk out there. Can you hang out with the girls for a second?"

"I would love to." This was exactly the opportunity he needed to go over their plan once again.

Tess disappeared inside the house and then Silas knelt so he was eye level with the girls. "Remember the plan?" he whispered.

Excitement gleamed in both Morgan's and Willow's eyes.

"Of course we remember." Morgan let out a squeal. "I've been waiting for today forever and now it's finally here!"

"Why do you have to wait until the reception to ask Mommy to marry you?" Willow asked. "Why can't you do it right now? Keeping secrets is *hard*."

"I know." He quickly checked the inside pocket of his suit coat to make sure their necklaces were still safely stashed inside. Between that surprise for them, Tess's engagement ring, and Kyra's wedding band he had to keep for Aiden during the ceremony, he was holding on to a lot of precious cargo today. "We don't want to distract everyone from Kyra and Aiden though, right?"

Both girls shook their heads.

"Good. Now let's go over the plan again." So he could be sure everything would go smoothly.

"At the reception, you're going to request that one song." Morgan squeezed her eyes shut as though trying to remember.

" 'Lucky,' " he filled in. Tess loved that song by Jason Mraz and Colbie Caillat.

"Yes! The song 'Lucky.' " Willow hummed a few bars. "And then you're going to dance with Mommy and when the song ends—"

"We'll all step outside the barn together so you can tell Mom you love her and want to marry her," Morgan finished triumphantly.

"Exactly." And then he would also give them their necklaces and tell them how honored he was to join their family. But they didn't know about that part of the plan yet.

"This is gonna be *so* much fun." Willow danced around him. "We're gonna get married too someday and then we'll all get really dressed up and you'll become our daddy."

Silas's heart stopped beating. In all the time they'd spent together, he hadn't talked with them directly about his role in their lives, other than telling them that he loved them and wanted to be there for them. He hadn't wanted to push or displace Jace as their father...

"Are you going to be our dad?" Morgan asked quietly.

He took his time answering so he could choose his words carefully. "I would love nothing more than to be your dad." He gathered them both in closer. "But you girls can choose. Jace will always be your first dad, and an important part of our family. Even after I marry your mom. No matter what you decide, that won't change."

Both girls nodded but didn't have the chance to say anything before the door opened and Tess rushed out. "Time to get a move on, girls." She playfully shooed Silas away. "Go make sure my brother is ready for this."

"I'm on it." He couldn't resist kissing her lips before he walked back to the barn where his friends were waiting. "It's time," he announced. "Your bride is on her way."

"Let's do this." Aiden led their processional out of the barn and over to the ceremony site where Lyric met them under the arbor. It seemed in addition to teaching yoga and running her holistic store, the woman was also ordained to perform weddings.

When he looked out and saw the crowd, Silas's heart started to thump again. Tess would say yes. He was *almost* positive. The girls didn't seem nervous. And maybe he wasn't as nervous as he was anticipating that moment.

The small string quartet set up to the right of the wooden stage started to play and Morgan and Willow led the way down the aisle, walking slowly and waving and blowing kisses to everyone seated around them while the audience rewarded them with a collective *aww*.

Tess walked down the aisle next, all grace and beauty. He loved her in that pale green curve-hugging dress with her hair pulled loosely back every bit as much as he loved her when she was in her ripped jeans or her ratty old pajamas. It never mattered what Tess wore, Silas couldn't take his eyes off her.

About halfway to him, her gaze shifted to his, and he felt his knees buckle. Would she say yes to him today? Would she make his life complete? Hope had become his constant companion. She and her girls were everything.

Before taking her place on the other side of the stage,

Tess winked at him and then everyone there turned to look for Kyra.

Silas watched Aiden's face when his bride appeared from behind the barn on Louie's arm. His friend's expression was all bewilderment and longing. He imagined he wore a similar expression every time he looked at Tess.

When Kyra had made it all the way down the aisle, the bride and groom embraced and Louie sat down with Minnie.

Lyric greeted everyone and started the ceremony by encouraging Kyra and Aiden to recite their vows. But Silas had a hard time paying attention. His gaze kept wandering to Tess, and his mind to the future. *Their* future together. The future he'd never imagined he could have.

"Now we will exchange the rings as a symbol of these vows," Lyric said, giving Silas a look.

Was he missing something? Why was she looking at him like that?

"The ring?" Aiden whispered.

Oh, right. Yes. The ring. He'd almost forgotten. Silas reached into his pocket and took out the ring, holding it flat on his palm.

His friend narrowed his eyes as he studied it. "Uh, that's not the ring *I* bought."

"Huh?" He looked down at his open hand. "Oh no." How could he have mixed up Tess's ring with Kyra's wedding band? He fumbled with the ring in his hand, nearly dropping it on the ground.

Tess gasped.

She'd seen it. Damn it. He'd ruined the surprise. "I have the right ring. I promise." Heat crept up his neck. He held Tess's diamond in a tight fist and patted another pocket, his heart racing, the stares of all one hundred people boring into his back. There! He'd stashed the one Aiden had given him earlier in the other pocket. He withdrew the wedding band carefully and held it out. "Sorry. Here it is."

But Aiden and Kyra only shared a smile. "You can't put that beautiful diamond back in your pocket now," Kyra said, nodding toward Tess as she bounced her eyebrows.

He couldn't propose *here*! This was *their* wedding ceremony...

"We'll give you a minute." Aiden took the wedding band out of his hand like he didn't trust him with it anymore and stepped back, his arm around Kyra's waist.

Now all eyes were on him.

This wasn't what he'd planned—crashing his best friend's wedding with a proposal of his own. It was not supposed to happen this way. But when he caught sight of Tess, her eyes so big and bright with anticipation and her chest rising and falling with carefully controlled breaths, he couldn't put the ring back in his pocket. He couldn't hold on to it for another second. He had to put that ring on her finger.

"You're sure?" He addressed the question to Kyra. This was her wedding, after all. She'd planned out every detail over the last several months. Every detail except for this one.

"This will be one of my absolute favorite memories when I look back on this day," she assured him.

Well, in that case...

"You're right. I can't put this ring back in my pocket." He stepped closer to Tess, but paused there, searching for two very special girls in their chairs in the front row. "Hey, Morgan and Willow." He waved them up to join them at the front. "It's time."

"Now?" Morgan popped out of her seat.

"Yes!" Willow dragged her sister up the step to where he and Tess stood on the simple wooden stage. "I can't wait anymore!"

Neither could he. Under the watchful eyes of all of their closest friends, he lowered himself to one knee. "Tess and Morgan and Willow..." A few sniffles sounded from the crowd. "You three beautiful girls have changed my life. You all have my heart forever." He stopped there and stashed Tess's ring in his pocket—only for a second— so he could find the necklaces he'd bought for the girls. Delicate gold hearts with a diamond in the middle.

Morgan gasped and Willow covered her mouth with both hands as he put them around their necks. "I love you both like you were my daughters."

"We love you too," they said together, and then hugged him tight.

He gazed up at Tess, at the tears streaming down her cheeks. "You saved me," he said. "With your big heart and your courage and your faith in the future." This woman had lost everything and yet she had still offered him so much. "You showed me what love is, that it's worth fighting for. Marry me, Tess. I just want to be with you. All the time. Forever."

"Yes." She yanked on his arms to get him to stand up. "Oh my God, I love you. Yes!"

Silas slipped the ring onto her finger and the four of them fell into a group hug.

Applause broke out then, complete with whoops and hollers and a yeehaw from Minnie. When the noise died down, Aiden and Kyra took center stage again.

"Are we good to continue?" Lyric asked with amusement dancing in her eyes.

"By all means." Silas stepped to the side while the girls hurried back to their seats. He had more to share with Tess, but the words could wait. Now they would have a whole lifetime together.

*   *   *

Tess couldn't stop glancing down at the sparkling stone on her left hand.

There'd been a time not long ago when she'd believed that her ring finger would stay bare forever. But her heart had proven to be more resilient than she ever could've imagined. They had all been through some very dark days, but, as she stood on the outskirts of the cake cutting ceremony, watching Aiden and Kyra smoosh the cake lovingly into each other's mouths, she marveled at how far they had all come.

Thank you, Jace.

More than ever, she felt him with her tonight. His presence, his love, his sacrifice. She was here right now, able to love Silas and to take care of her girls because of all Jace had given to her. As usual, she carried his letter, neatly folded and tucked into her purse.

You can't hide your beautiful heart away. No matter how much you might want to. You have to continue opening your heart so our girls know they can open theirs too. I want you to embrace life, embrace love, embrace anything and everything that brings you joy no matter what anyone else says or thinks.

Those words. She hadn't accepted them for a long time. She hadn't been able to face what he was asking her to do.

But now...embracing was all she wanted to do. She had to believe Jace would be proud of her. She had to believe she was honoring his love and his life by living hers.

While Aiden kissed the frosting off of Kyra's lips, Tess grabbed Silas's hand and led him away from the crowd.

"Can we go home now?" he asked the second they stepped outside onto the beautiful stone patio Cowboy Construction Inc. had built for the occasion. "I want to take you home. Put the girls to bed." His eyebrows peaked. "Put *you* to bed..."

"Soon," she promised, feeling that same impatience simmering in her. But it wouldn't do to leave the party before the bride and groom. "I just needed you alone for a minute." She tugged on his loosened tie. "I needed to do this." Her lips found his and her body melted against him, heart sighing, knees loosening. "I can't wait—"

"There you are." Morgan bounded out the door to where they stood, with Willow on her heels.

"Were we lost?" Silas stepped away from Tess, making room for the girls to join them.

"Yes." Willow posted her hands on her hips. "We were looking all over the place for you. We need to ask you a very important question."

Tess tried to hide her smile. In Willow's estimation, every question was a very important question and she asked about a hundred of them a day.

"Sure." Silas sat on a bench near the firepit and patted the space next to him. "Ask away."

Morgan looked at Willow and the girls seemed to communicate silently before she spoke. "Can you become our daddy for real?"

A tremor worked through Tess's heart, exposing a fault

line of emotion. She sat on the other side of Silas, keeping quiet, letting him take the lead on how he wanted to handle this conversation.

At the moment, the man seemed too choked up to speak. Tears glistened in his eyes.

"Can't we go to a judge and tell them we want you to be our dad?" Morgan asked. "That's what happens in the movies and on TV."

He turned his head to look at Tess, his eyes questioning her. They had talked through the possibility of an official adoption but neither one of them had thought the girls would ask for this so quickly. Tess squeezed his hand in hers and nodded. She had hoped the girls would choose him, that they would want to bestow that very important title on him when they were ready.

"Yes. I would love to adopt you." He seemed too afraid to believe that's what they were asking. But Tess saw the hope blooming in their smiles. "If you're sure that's what you want."

"We want everyone to know," Willow said. "We want the judge to say it's real. We want everyone to know you're our real dad forever."

"Then we'll make that happen." He pulled them both in close for a hug. "As soon as we can."

Willow climbed onto Tess's lap and Morgan sat between her and Silas all nestled in.

"We're going to be a real family," her youngest daughter murmured.

"I never thought we'd be lucky enough to have the two best dads in the whole world," Morgan added.

"I'm going to be a dad." His bewildered expression made Tess smile.

"I'm going to be a dad." He jumped up and swept both girls into his arms, dancing around with them while he sang, "I'm going to be a dad," and the girls sang, "You're going to be *our* dad!"

Laughing, Tess joined in and then Silas pulled her close, somehow managing to get his arms around all three of them.

"I already know that this is going to be the best job I've ever had."

EPILOGUE

G ood morning, beautiful." Silas greeted her at the entrance to the kitchen with her cup of coffee in his hand.

"Morning." Tess slid her arms around him and gave him a kiss, completing her new favorite early morning ritual.

"Pancakes are on." He handed her the mug and then hurried back to the stove and picked up a spatula.

Tess sat on a stool at the island, watching him work while she drank her coffee. She loved watching Silas in the kitchen. He took his new job as breakfast chef quite seriously. Every morning she admired this view—her husband in his joggers and a thermal shirt, his hair still spikey and mussed from sleep, his tanned skin still sun kissed from their destination Hawaiian wedding.

They'd spent a whole week in Maui with only their closest family members and friends. Her parents had kept the girls in their condo and she and Silas had luxuriated during lazy mornings in bed and early nights in their own private spa tub. They indulged in sleep and food and sex and some fun island excursions. But it turned out he was pretty good at lying on a beach when he was with her too.

Since arriving home, they'd settled into a routine that she loved too. Mornings where they woke in each other's arms and worked together to get the girls off to school before they each went about their work for the day.

"Mom, can you check my math?" Morgan shuffled into the kitchen first, maneuvering her folder out of her backpack.

"Sure." Time to stop admiring the view and jump into action. Tess filled the girls' glasses with orange juice first and then joined her daughter at the table.

"I smell pancakes!" Willow bounded into the kitchen next and went directly to the stove to stand next to Silas. "And they have chocolate chips!"

Every once in a while, Silas snuck a little extra treat into the pancakes.

"Can I flip puhleeeaasse?" her younger daughter begged.

"Right after I flip you." Silas captured her in his arms and turned her upside down while she giggled.

"Your math is perfect." Tess handed Morgan's workbook back to her. "You're doing so well in school, honey."

"Thanks, Mom." She shoved the workbook back into her bag and then Silas and Willow served the pancakes.

They all ate together while the girls told them some of the details about their upcoming school day, and then there was a mad rush to pack them up so they wouldn't miss the bus.

"Lunches." Silas got their insulated bags out of the refrigerator and the girls stuffed them into their backpacks.

Together, they walked out the front door and down the driveway, with Tess and Silas hand in hand.

As per usual, the bus got to the end of the drive before they did.

"Love you, girls." It didn't matter how late they were running, Silas always gathered them in for a hug and kissed their foreheads.

"Love you too, Daddy," they called in unison.

Tess snuck in her hugs and kisses too and then Morgan and Willow disappeared onto the bus.

"Whew. That never gets old." Silas slipped his arm around her. "Time for a shower?"

Their morning shower was another of her favorite rituals, but today she had something planned. "Actually, can we go for a ride first? We don't have to be out too long but I'd love to get some fresh air right now."

"Sounds good to me." He steered her toward the horse stables. "We haven't visited Legacy in a few days anyway."

They saddled up Dreamer with the tandem and then trotted out of the barn. Tess leaned against Silas's chest while he wielded the reins, steering the horse past the house and into the trees so they could get to the south pasture.

"Have I told you I love you yet today?" Silas murmured in her ear.

"I don't think so." But she could feel his love. And she saw it in the way he cared for her and the girls.

"I love you." He kissed her neck.

"And I love you." She peered over her shoulder and into his eyes and almost said more, but she couldn't ruin the surprise.

Dreamer navigated the woods like a champ—she knew where they were headed. And Tess was content to settle in and enjoy the view. The leaves overhead were already starting to fall, and snow would start flying soon.

"What'd you have planned for today?" Silas asked, taking the reins in one hand and securing his other arm around her waist.

"I have a doctor appointment." *Don't say more.* She couldn't say more yet.

"You have to go to the doctor?" He snuck a peek at her face. "Everything okay?"

"It's only a checkup." Of sorts. "What about you? What's your day look like?"

She'd best change the subject before she blurted everything out.

"Thatch and Aiden and I are starting work on the new rec center."

"Oh, that's right." The town council had finally approved funds to build an indoor swimming pool. The project would keep Cowboy Construction busy for the next eight months.

"There's Legacy." Silas pointed to their left where the trees opened into the south meadow.

The horse stood by the fence as though expecting them while the rest of the herd grazed.

Silas pulled Dreamer to a stop and dismounted before helping Tess down. "Why don't you get the carrots out?" She pointed to the saddle bag. "I packed them last night."

"Sure. You want some carrots, Legacy?" he called, digging around.

The horse whinnied in response.

Tess watched him, her heart suspended in anticipation.

"What're these?" Finally, Silas pulled out the newborn-size cowboy boots she'd planted in the saddle bag after he'd fallen asleep last night.

"They're cowboy boots." She kept her tone neutral and waited for his reaction.

"Wow. They're tiny." He held them up and inspected them. "What are they? Christmas ornaments?"

Tess laughed. "No, silly. They're for our new little buckaroo."

"Oh." It took a second but he finally jerked his head to stare at her, his eyes slowly widening. "Our new...*our* new buckaroo? *We're* having a buckaroo?"

"We are." She stepped to him, her hand on her belly. "Probably sometime next May, but I can't be sure yet."

Silas blinked. And breathed. She could see his chest rising and falling.

"A baby?" He rested his hand on her stomach too, and she felt him trembling. "We're having a baby?"

She nodded, tears running freely. "I thought Legacy should know too. Since she's kind of the one who brought us together."

"A baby!" Silas laughed, wrapping her up in his arms and spinning her around.

"Oh!" He set her feet back on the grass. "Oh no. Sorry. Are you okay? Is the baby okay?"

"We're fine. You can pick me up anytime you want. Although that'll likely get a lot harder in a few months." She pulled his face to hers for a kiss. "You're going to be a daddy again, Silas Beck. That's three kids in less than a year."

He let out a whoop and laughed again with tears running down his cheeks too. "I can't believe this. This is the best news ever. We have to put an addition on the house. And buy a crib. And—"

"Whoa, cowboy." Tess brought him back to her. "There'll be time. We probably have at least eight months, but we'll know more when we go to the doctor today."

"Eight months. Okay. Eight months. We're having a baby in eight months!" He swept her up into his arms again. "This is everything. You, our girls, our baby...this family is everything."

ACKNOWLEDGMENTS

I would like to thank Jess Oldham from the Wind River Wild Horse Sanctuary for not only educating me about their operation and the wild horses, but also for helping me understand the issues at play. Drawing from his knowledge and experience, I did my best to write an accurate portrayal of the wild horses, and any mistakes or misrepresentations are all mine. The Oldham family has dedicated themselves to caring for these majestic animals as well as educating the public through free access to their educational interpretative visitor center at the sanctuary. For those who are interested in learning more, please visit https://www.windriverwildhorses.com/.

I can honestly say I would not have finished this story without the love and support of my family and friends. To Will, AJ, and Kaleb, thank you for carrying me through. To my sister, Erin, and my brother, Kyle... what a blessing to have siblings who are also my closest friends. To my father-in-law, Keith, and my mother-in-law, Wanda, thank you for always being willing to jump in and help so I can find the space and time to work.

This story would also not have been possible without the dedication of the best team an author could ever hope for. From the editing—waving at you Amy Pierpont and Sam Brody—to the cover design to the copy edits and proofreading to the marketing, publicity, and sales teams, I truly work with the best in the business. Thank you all! Last but never least, I'd like to thank my agent, Suzie Townsend, and the team at New Leaf Literary for making my dreams come true.

ABOUT THE AUTHOR

Sara Richardson grew up chasing adventure in Colorado's rugged mountains. She's climbed to the top of a fourteen-thousand-foot peak at midnight, swum through class IV rapids, completed her wilderness first aid certification, and spent seven days at a time tromping through the wilderness with a thirty-pound backpack strapped to her shoulders.

Eventually Sara did the responsible thing and got an education in writing and journalism. After a brief stint in the corporate writing world, she stopped ignoring the voices in her head and started writing fiction. Now she uses her experience as a mountain adventure guide to write stories that incorporate adventure with romance. Sara lives and plays in the Upper Midwest, where she still indulges her adventurous spirit, with her saint of a husband and two young sons.

You can learn more at:
SaraRichardson.net
Twitter @SaraR_Books
Facebook.com/SaraRichardsonBooks
Instagram @SaraRichardsonBooks

For a bonus story from another author that you'll love, please turn the page to read *Only Home with You* by Jeannie Chin.

Zoe Leung allowed her mother to pressure her into a safe, stable career path, but now Zoe's job search has hit a dead end, and she isn't sure what to do next. She fills her days with waitressing and volunteering at Harvest Home, her uncle's food bank and soup kitchen, while figuring out her next move. If she flirts with fellow volunteer—and her older brother's best friend—Devin James, who can blame her? He's only the subject of her lifelong crush. And finally looking at her like he returns the sentiment.

Construction worker Devin James has always thought Zoe was gorgeous, but he doesn't want to jeopardize his friendship with her brother or her family, who all but took him in when he was younger. But as much as he plans to stay focused on building his dream house, he can't stop thinking about Zoe. And the more time he spends with her, the more he realizes that the only home he wants is one with her.

FOREVER

Chapter One

Twenty-eight more months.

Devin James silently repeated it to himself with every crack of his nail gun. He moved to the next mark on the beam, lined up his shot, and drove another spike of steel into the wood.

Based on the numbers he'd rerun over the weekend, twenty-eight months was how long it was going to take him to save up for a house of his own. Still too long, but he was on target, putting away exactly as much as he'd budgeted for, paycheck after paycheck.

"Take that," he muttered, sucking in a breath as he kept moving down the line.

His dad had told him enough times that he'd never amount to anything. Devin tightened his grip on the nail gun and sank his teeth into the inside of his lip. What he'd give to get that voice out of his head. To show his dad he wasn't too stupid to do the math, and he wasn't too lazy to do the work.

He'd buy those three acres of land from Arthur. His mentor—and his best friend Han's uncle—had been saving the lot for him for three years now, and he'd promised to sell it to him at cost. Once Devin had the deed in his hand, he'd start digging out the foundation the next day. Between the buddies he'd made at construction sites and the favors folks owed him, he could be standing in his own house within six months. A quiet place all to himself on a wooded lot five miles outside of town. He'd get a dog—a big one, too. A mutt from the animal rescue off Main Street.

He'd have everything his useless old man told him he could never have. All he had to do was keep his head down and keep working hard.

He finished the last join on this section of the house's frame and nodded at Terrell, who'd been helping him out. The guy let go, and they both stood.

Adjusting his safety glasses, Devin glanced around. It was a cool fall day in his hometown of Blue Cedar Falls, North Carolina. The sun shone down from a bright blue sky dotted with wispy clouds. The last few autumn leaves hung on to the branches of the surrounding trees, while in the distance, the mountains were a piney green.

He and his crew had been working on this development for the better part of a year now. It was a good job, with good guys for the most part. Solid pay for solid work, and if he had a restlessness buzzing around under his skin, well, that was the kind of thing he was good at pushing down.

"Hey—James."

At the shout of his last name across the build site, Devin looked up. One of the new guys stood outside the trailer, waving him over. Devin nudged the protective muffs off his ears so he could hear.

"Boss wants to see you before you clock out."

Devin nodded and glanced at his watch. The shift ended in thirty. That gave him enough time to quickly clean up and check in with Joe.

He made a motion to Terrell to wrap things up.

"What's the hurry?" a voice behind him sneered. "Got to run off to Daddy?"

Devin pulled a rough breath in between his teeth. Head down and work hard, he reminded himself.

No punching the mayor's son in the face.

But Bryce Horton wasn't going to be ignored. He stepped right in Devin's way, and it took everything Devin had to keep his mouth shut.

"Isn't that what you call old Joe?" Bryce taunted. "*Daddy?* You sure come fast enough when he calls."

Devin's muscles tensed, heat building in his chest.

He kept himself together, though. Bryce had been like this since high school, putting everybody down and acting like he was the king of the hill. The entire hill was all sand, though. The guy never did any work. If *his* daddy didn't run this town, he'd have been out on his rear end ages ago.

As it was, Bryce'd been hired on as a favor to the mayor's office, and getting him fired would take an act of God. Didn't stop Devin from picturing it in his head. Daily.

Devin ground his molars together and brushed past him.

"Oh, that's right," Bryce called as Devin showed him his back and started to walk away. "Your real daddy left, didn't he?"

Red tinted Devin's vision. He flexed his fingers, curling them into a palm before taking a deep breath and letting them go.

It'd be so easy, was the thing. Bryce wasn't a small guy, but he wasn't a particularly strong one, either. Two hits and he'd be on the ground, snot-faced and crying. That was how bullies were.

That was how Devin's dad had been.

Without so much as a glance in Bryce's direction, Devin

shucked his glasses, muffs, and gloves, stowed his stuff, and headed over to the trailer. As he walked, he blocked out the sound of Bryce running his mouth. He blocked out the surly voice in his own head, too.

By the time he got to the door, his blood was still up, but he was calm enough to show model employee material, because that was what mattered.

With a quick knock, he tugged open the trailer door and poked his head inside. Joe was at his desk, big hands pecking out something or other on the keyboard.

"Hey." Devin kept his voice level. "Heard you wanted to see me?"

Joe glanced up and smiled, the lines around his eyes crinkling. "Yeah, hey, have a seat."

Devin closed the door and sat down. While Joe finished up what he was working on, Devin half smiled.

Joe was a good boss because he was one of them. He'd worked his way up the ranks from grunt to site supervisor over the last twenty-five years.

Didn't make the sight of his giant frame squished behind a desk any less funny, though.

After a minute, Joe squinted and hammered the return key before straightening and turning to Devin. "James. Thanks for coming in."

"No problem, boss."

"I'll cut to the chase. You're probably wondering why I called you in here."

Devin shifted his weight in his chair. He'd been so distracted by Bryce and then by watching Joe pretend he didn't need reading glasses that he hadn't given it that much thought. Business had been good, and Devin never missed a day. He hadn't screwed anything up that he knew of. Which left only one thing.

Something he'd dismissed out of hand, even as he'd thrown his hat in the ring.

"Uh..."

"You know Todd's retiring at the end of the month."

Devin nodded, his mouth going dry. He fought to keep his reaction—and his expectations—down. "Sorry to see him go."

"We all are, but he's earned it." Joe let out a breath. Then he cocked a brow. "Big question of the day is who's going to fill in for him as shift leader for your crew."

"You made a decision."

"Sure did." Joe kept a straight face for all of a second. When his face split into a wide smile, Devin mentally pumped his fist. Joe extended his hand across the desk. "Congratulations."

Devin didn't waste any time. He shoved his hand into Joe's with fireworks going off inside his chest.

Yes. Holy freaking hell, yes.

"I won't let you down, sir."

"Oh, believe me, I know it, or I woulda picked somebody else."

As he pulled his hand back, Joe started talking about responsibilities and expectations, and Devin was definitely listening.

He was also mentally updating all the numbers in his budget.

He'd never really expected to get the job of shift leader. There were older guys who'd put their names in. Heck, Bryce could have gotten it, and then Devin would have been looking for another job entirely.

But he knew exactly how much his pay was going to go up by. Every cent of it could go into savings. Twenty-eight months would be more like fourteen. Maybe even twelve.

One year. One year until he'd have enough for the land and the materials.

He couldn't wait to tell everybody. Drinks with his buddy Han would be on him tonight.

Arthur was going to be so proud.

Joe paused, narrowing his eyes at Devin and making him tap the brakes on his runaway thoughts. "It won't be an easy job, Devin."

Devin swallowed. "I'm up for the challenge."

"You don't have to convince me," Joe repeated, holding his big hands up in front of his chest. He set them down on the desk and fixed Devin with a meaningful look. "Just. Stand your ground, okay? Do that and I have every confidence you'll be fine."

Right.

Moving up would also mean being responsible for an entire shift crew of guys.

Including Bryce Horton.

That same hot, ready-to-fight instinct flared inside him, followed right after by the icy reminder to push it down. He smiled tightly. "Not a problem."

"All righty, then." The matter seemed settled as Joe stood. "I'll get the paperwork sorted. You start training on Monday."

Devin rose. "Thank you. Really."

Joe gestured with his head toward the door. "Go on. Have a beer or three to celebrate, you hear?"

Devin had no doubt he'd do exactly that—eventually.

With a spring in his step, he headed for the parking lot. He smacked the steering wheel of his beat-up bucket of bolts as he got in and slammed the door behind him. As the old truck lurched to life, he cranked the stereo and peeled out, triumph bursting inside him.

This was it. The break he hadn't dared to hope for but that he needed, the thing that was going to get him on the fast track to his goals.

And there was only one place he wanted to go.

The Harvest Home food bank and soup kitchen stood in a converted mill on the north end of town. Business in Blue Cedar Falls was generally good, and it had only been getting better since tourism had picked up on Main Street.

Main Street's cute little tourist district felt a long way away, though. Devin's wasn't the only rust bucket truck parked outside Harvest Home. On his way in, he held the door for a woman and her four kids who were coming out, each armed with a bag. He didn't need to peek inside to know they were filled with not just cans but fresh food, too. The kind of stuff that filled your belly *and* your heart.

Goodness knew Devin'd had to rely on that enough times when he was a kid.

He ran his hand along the yellow painted concrete wall of the entry hallway, his throat tight. He couldn't wait to tell Arthur.

But when he turned the corner, it wasn't Arthur standing behind the desk. Oh no. Of course it wasn't.

Devin's blood flashed hot. For one fraction of a second, he let his gaze wander, taking in soft curves and softer-looking lips. Dark eyes and long, silky, ink-black hair.

A throat cleared. A brow arched.

Like he'd been slapped upside the head, he jerked his gaze back to meet hers. She smiled at him mischievously, and he bit back a swear.

"Hey, Zoe," he managed to grit out. Silently, he said the rest of her name, too.

Zoe *Leung*. Devin's best friend Han Leung's little sister. Arthur Chao's beloved niece.

The one person on this earth he should *not* be getting caught checking out. Especially by her.

"Hey, Dev." The curl of her full lips made his heart feel like a puppy tugging at its leash to go run off into traffic. Only a semi was barreling down the road.

The past few months since Zoe had moved back home after college had been torture. Fortunately, he had lots of practice keeping himself from doing anything stupid around her. He'd been holding himself in check for years, after all. Since she was eighteen and he was twenty-two.

Because if he ever let go of that leash on his control? Gave in to the invitation in her eyes?

Well.

It'd probably be a whole lot easier if he just got run over by a truck.

Chapter Two

Zoe Leung's heart pounded as heat flared in Devin's eyes.

Only for it to flicker and then fizzle in about two seconds flat.

The whole thing made her want to tear her hair out.

Because she was a realist, you know? Sure, she'd had a crush on Devin since she'd realized that not all boys were slimy and gross (her brother Han definitely excluded). But she'd never expected anything to ever come of it.

To him, she was the bratty kid who used to follow her brother and his friends around all the time. Skinned knees and messy ponytails and oversize hand-me-down T-shirts did not bring any boys to the yard, and she'd made her peace with that.

Right until her high school graduation, four and a half long years ago.

Her mom had made such a big deal of it. Her last kid graduating from high school had combined with menopause in some pretty unpredictable ways. Finally, the nagging about wanting a good picture had gotten to be too much. Fed up with it all, Zoe had gotten her sister Lian to help her figure out how to do her hair and her makeup, and she'd actually worn a dress for once. It'd been a big hassle, but she'd had to admit that she felt and looked great.

At the party after, while Han and Devin and a few of their friends were tossing a football around in the backyard, she'd gone up to them to let them know the pizza was there.

She could see it all in her head so clearly. Devin had looked up. His eyes had gone wide.

Only to have a football smack him right in the head.

He'd never looked at her the same after that. Every time his gaze landed on her, it would darken. His Adam's apple would bob, and that scruffy jaw would tense, his rough, hardworking hands clenching into fists at his sides.

Exactly the way he'd been looking at her about two seconds ago.

An angry flush warmed her cheeks as he jerked his gaze away—probably checking to make sure her overprotective big brother, Han, wasn't going to materialize out of nowhere and throw another football at his head.

It was infuriating.

When he didn't have any interest in her, she could totally handle it. But now? This weird, intense game of sexual-attraction chicken he was playing?

What a bunch of bull.

The last time they'd run into each other at the drugstore, he'd done the same thing, heat building in his gaze right until the moment she'd stared back at him. She'd played it cool, hoping he'd say something. Instead, he'd grabbed the first thing he saw off the shelf and darted toward the checkout. Either the guy was super eager to get home with his novelty sunglasses or he was avoiding her.

After months of being back home spinning her wheels on her doomed job search, she was tired of spinning her wheels on whatever was going on between the two of them, too. She wasn't expecting him to drop down on one knee and ask her to marry him or anything. But she was into him, and it sure seemed like he was into her. While she was here, couldn't they, like, *do* something about it?

Enough playing it cool. Clearly she was going to have to be the one to make the first move.

Abandoning subtlety for once, she sauntered over to him. She put a little swing in her hips, just for fun. She'd come out of her shell a lot during the four years she'd been away. She could still rock a messy ponytail and an oversize T-shirt, but the snug top and short skirt she was wearing in preparation for her shift at the Junebug tonight were just as comfortable—and she knew how to use them.

"How's it going?" she asked, coming to a stop a foot away. Too close, for sure. The air hummed. He was tantalizingly warm, pushing heat into the tight space between them and making her skin prickle with awareness.

Licking her lips, she gazed up at him. She was all but batting her lashes here.

The darkness in his eyes returned as he stared down at her.

He had always been good-looking. Back in the day, it had been in a loping, gangly teenage way. His spots on the baseball and football teams had put some muscle on him, but whatever he'd been up to at his construction job had done even more. Under his jacket and tee, he rippled with muscle. His jaw had gone from soft to chiseled, and he kept his golden-brown hair shorter, too.

"Uh." He swallowed. "Good. Great, actually."

"Yeah?"

He still hadn't backed away. That was a good sign, right?

"Yeah." He nodded almost imperceptibly.

Something turned over, low in the pit of her belly.

He smelled so good, like man and hard work and wood shavings.

She wanted to ask him what was going on that was so great. She wanted to sway forward into him, tip her head up or put her hand on his broad chest and find out if it was as hard and hot as it looked.

He swallowed and shifted his weight, edging ever so slightly closer to her. Her heart thudded hard. Maybe he wanted her to do all those things, too. Maybe...

"Devin? What are you doing here?"

Crap.

The instant Uncle Arthur's gently accented voice rang out, Devin jumped back as if he'd been burned. The hot thread of tension that had been building between them snapped. A flush rose on her cheeks, almost as deep as the disappointment flooding her chest.

"Arthur! Hey, um." Devin glanced around wildly, looking at everything but Zoe. Honestly, it would have been less conspicuous if he'd come over and put his arm around her. "Do you have a second?"

"For you?" Uncle Arthur smiled, pleased lines appearing around his eyes and mouth. "Of course." He looked to Zoe. "You don't mind?"

Zoe forced a smile of her own. "Of course not."

With a smile of thanks to Zoe, Uncle Arthur led Devin back to his office. Zoe was tempted to follow and listen at the door, but that would be childish.

Instead, she sighed and retreated to the front desk. This was a slow hour. All the appointments for people to pick up goods from the food bank were over, but the soup kitchen hadn't opened for dinner service yet. Down the hall, pots and pans banged, though, so Harvest Home's two staff cooks, Sherry and Tania, must already be at work.

That didn't mean there wasn't anything to do, of course.

Ever since she'd slunk back to Blue Cedar Falls with the useless accounting degree her mom had talked her into, she'd been splitting her time between scrolling social media, waitressing at the new bar in town, and helping out here. Working at Harvest Home barely paid a pittance, of course, but she didn't mind. Uncle Arthur might be her mom's brother, but he was her exact opposite in terms of how he treated Zoe. He was cool and relaxed, and he trusted Zoe with real responsibilities. Watching him work his rear end off here—even though he was in his sixties and on three different high blood pressure medications—made her want to live up to his example.

She liked helping people. Sending folks off with whatever they needed to help get them through tough times gave her a warm feeling inside. Even the boring administrative stuff felt important.

With a sigh, she plunked behind the desk and got to it, confirming pickups, arranging deliveries, and checking in about volunteer shifts. When the crew of said volunteers helping out with supper tonight showed up, she showed them to the kitchen and placed them in Sherry's and Tania's capable hands. On the way back, she definitely did *not* linger outside Arthur's office, staring at the closed door as if she could burn through it with her laser eyes and find out what he and Devin were going on about.

Okay, maybe for a minute, but that was it.

As she returned to the front room and started in on labeling bags for the next day's pickups, the door swung open.

A telltale *tutt*ing sound announced who it was before Zoe could so much as look up.

"Zhaohui." Her mother came in carrying a box of extra

produce from their family restaurant, the same way she did every Tuesday—the one day of the week the Jade Garden was closed. She set the box down and came straight over, her tone as disapproving as ever as she snatched the marker from Zoe's hand. "You know Arthur likes black ink."

Zoe rolled her eyes. "Well, I like purple, and do you see Arthur doing the work?"

"I think the bags look great." Han had come in behind her, hauling another crate of soon-to-expire vegetables.

"See?" Zoe told her mom.

Her mom made that noise in the back of her throat that said nothing and everything as she waved a hand at Zoe and let her grab the marker back. She drifted away, and Zoe met her brother's gaze over her head.

"Hey." Han wrapped an arm around her shoulders to give her a quick squeeze in greeting. She rolled her eyes the way she was contractually obligated to as his little sister, but she appreciated the affection all the same. "How's it been today?"

"Not bad." Zoe finished labeling the bags—in dark, entirely legible purple—as she gave him a general rundown. She glanced at the clock. She didn't need to leave for her shift at the Junebug for another few minutes. Normally, with Han and her mom here to take over, she'd head out and get a few minutes of quiet in her car to decompress, but she eyed the back office again.

Before she had to make a decision, the door swung open, and her breath caught. Devin came out first. Uncle Arthur followed, patting his back. Both of them were all smiles.

As Devin spotted Han, his grin grew even wider. "Dude, I didn't know you were going to be here."

"What's up?" The two traded bro-hugs and smashed their fists together, and for a second it was like being twelve years old again, watching them and feeling completely outside it all.

Devin stepped back. "Guess who's moving up to shift leader next week."

"Whaaaat?" Han held his hand out, and they high-fived.

"That's awesome," Zoe interjected.

Devin's gaze shot to hers only to dart right back away.

Uncle Arthur clapped Devin's shoulder. "I knew it would happen."

The corners of Devin's mouth curled up, even as he shrugged and looked down.

Zoe's ribs squeezed. He might be trying to act cool, but Devin had been following her uncle around for even longer than Zoe had been following Devin. She knew the praise and faith meant the world to him.

"Your company hiring?" her mom asked Devin, her tone way too innocent. "Maybe in accounting department?"

Zoe glared at her.

"What?" Her mom put her hand over her chest. "I'm just asking." She raised her brows. "Someone has to."

Sure, sure. So helpful. Zoe clamped her mouth shut against the instinct to remind her mom that she'd been the one to push Zoe into accounting in the first place. Well, that or medicine or law, and accounting had definitely been the easiest option of those.

Zoe hadn't exactly had a strong sense of what she wanted to do, but it wasn't sit behind a desk crunching numbers all day. The fact that she hadn't been able to find a job in the field was salt in the wound. Did her mom really need to remind her of it constantly?

"I'll check, Mrs. Leung," Devin promised. He cast Zoe a sympathetic glance, and she couldn't decide if that was better or worse than him totally ignoring her.

Her mother cocked a brow, silently saying, *See?*

Zoe huffed out a breath.

Defusing things the way he always did, Han turned back to Devin. "We *have* to celebrate."

"The Junebug does two-for-one drinks before eight tonight," Zoe blurted out. Self-consciousness stole over her as all eyes turned to her, but screw it. She doubled down. "Plus, you know." She pointed her thumbs at her chest. "Employee discount."

Han looked to Devin, brows raised.

"Sure," Devin said slowly. He let his gaze fall on her for all of a second. There was that flare of heat again. But as fast as it had come, it disappeared as his eyes darted away. "Who doesn't like cheap beer, right?"

"Right," Zoe agreed. She smiled tightly.

Thanks to her entire freaking family showing up, this round of "Poke Devin Until He Cracks" was a stalemate.

But the good news was that she'd just earned herself another shot.

Chapter Three

So, how's it feel?" Han asked. "Mr. Fancypants promotion."

Devin shook his head. "I'm still having a pretty hard time believing it."

After a brief stop at home to change, he'd met Han at the Junebug on Main Street for the cheap drinks Zoe had promised them. Add in some burgers and the owner Clay's famous cheese fries, and this was basically Devin's ideal night out. He snagged another stick of greasy goodness from the basket in front of him and popped it in his mouth. It tasted like victory.

And cheese.

But mostly victory. After years of careful planning, everything he'd been working for finally felt like it was within his grasp. Arthur'd taken the time to rerun the numbers with him in his office, and twelve months was a solid projection. For years now, Arthur had been holding on to that lot on the outskirts of town for him. It was one of a handful of shrewd real estate investments he'd made decades ago. He'd been slowly selling off the rest of his plots as Blue Cedar Falls had grown and tourism had boomed, but not that one. It made Devin's throat tight, just thinking about it. The guy had so much faith in him.

Sure, he'd also somehow gotten Devin to commit to mustering up a volunteer squad from Meyer Construction to serve Sunday supper at Harvest Home—some church group had apparently made the finals in a choral competition and had to pull out at the last minute. But that was just more evidence of how much he trusted Devin.

Well, Devin was going to show him that he'd put his faith in the right man. He'd get enough guys from work to show up on Sunday—no problem. And twelve months from now, he'd make good on his promise to buy those undeveloped acres.

His own land, away from the crappy apartments where he'd grown up. Someplace quiet just for him, no nosy roommates or noisy neighbors upstairs. A home he'd build with his own two hands.

Just don't screw it up, a voice in his head whispered.

Devin bit the inside of his cheek. Ignoring the doubt in the back of his mind, he reached for his beer and took a good swig.

"How're you boys doing?" Zoe appeared at the side of their table in the corner. Heaven help him. She'd put on some lipstick or something since he'd seen her at Harvest Home. He couldn't stop looking at her red mouth, and his best friend was going to *murder him*. Oblivious, Zoe glanced between the both of them. "Y'all ready for another round?"

Devin drained the last gulp from his glass and thunked it down in front of her. "Sure am."

"Awesome."

Devin should probably be pacing himself. He had an early shift in the morning. But he was celebrating. Letting loose for one night wouldn't hurt.

Just so long as he didn't slip up and let himself look at Zoe's chest.

Crap. Too late.

He jerked his gaze away. "Maybe some water, too," he croaked.

Zoe nodded. "Probably a good call."

"Whatever he's having, put it on the house." Clay Hawthorne, owner and proprietor of the Junebug, wandered over. He clapped Devin on the shoulder, then shot a narrow-eyed glance at Han. "Not this guy, though."

"Hey," Han protested. "After all the free food I give you."

"Fine, fine." Clay held his hands up in front of his chest. "It's all on the house, but, Zoe, don't give them any top-shelf stuff, you hear?"

"Only the worst for my brother," Zoe agreed. "Got it, boss."

"You know I'm just giving you free stuff because it means I don't have to write a receipt, right?" Clay told them.

Han shook his head. "You have really got to figure that stuff out, man."

"I know." Clay scrubbed a hand through his red-brown hair. "But math is hard."

Devin gestured around. "When you get to big numbers like this it is."

"Doomed by your own success," Han sympathized.

Clay was a relative newcomer to Blue Cedar Falls, but you'd never know it. Devin didn't make it out to Main Street all that often, but whenever he did, the Junebug was hopping, drawing in the tourists that flocked to the area and locals alike. Clay seemed to know everybody on a first-name basis—or if he didn't at the start of the night, he did by the end.

He'd become good friends in particular with Han, which

was great to see. Han had been Devin's best friend since they were kids. He was a good guy—maybe the best. But he was so serious, carrying the weight of the world on his shoulders. He didn't get out a lot. The guy could use another friend in his corner.

"Tell me about it," Clay grumbled. "This place was supposed to be small, you know. Just a hole in the wall for me and maybe ten other people."

"Guess you should have told June that." Han tipped his head toward the front door, which had just swung open to reveal the lady in question.

Clay's complaining ceased, his whole demeanor changing as he lifted a hand to her in greeting. She smiled, too, broad and unreserved, as she crossed the space toward him.

Devin shook his head, rolling his eyes fondly as Clay swept June up in his arms. He'd never get over a big, gruff guy like that turning into a teddy bear whenever his girlfriend was around.

As they kissed, Devin looked away, because wow. They were really going at it. He happened to meet Zoe's gaze, and they shared a stifled laugh at the PDA.

Then Devin had to look away all over again, because sharing anything with Zoe—especially something related to kissing—was a terrible idea.

"Get a room." Han threw a napkin at Clay and June, and they finally broke apart.

Zoe swatted lightly at Han. "Don't listen to my brother," she told June. "He's just jealous."

"Ew." Han recoiled. "I definitely am not."

And okay, yeah, considering Han had dated June's sister May for approximately all of high school, that made sense.

"How's it going?" June asked, ignoring him.

"Fine," Zoe told her. "Just commiserating with Clay about how you ruthlessly turned his dive bar into the most popular spot on Main Street."

June shook her head and patted his arm. "Pretty sure that was mostly your doing." She gestured around. "Everything here was your idea. I just helped you put it all together."

"Okay, fine, it was a group effort," Clay said, his smile wry. He then pointedly steered the conversation away from how business was booming—and, Devin noticed, away from the jabs Han had been making about how he needed to get his accounting figured out.

If anybody else noticed, they didn't make a big deal of it, so Devin kept mum, too. They all made small talk for a few minutes. Inevitably, Zoe had to excuse herself to go check on her other tables. "You got everything under control?" Clay asked.

Zoe gave him a thumbs-up as she walked away. "On top of it all, boss."

"Guess we should head out." To Han and Devin, he explained, "Date night."

"Have fun," Han told them.

"And thanks again for the grub," Devin said.

Clay tipped an imaginary hat at him before turning and steering June toward the back.

Devin returned to his burger, but after a minute, it registered with him that Han's attention was decidedly elsewhere. And that he wasn't happy.

He followed his buddy's scowling gaze.

And kind of immediately wished he hadn't.

Zoe stood over by a table on the other side of the bar, her head tipped back in laughter as a group of guys gave her their orders. One of them had sidled his chair awfully close to her. Another winked.

Devin fought not to sigh.

"Don't do it," he warned.

Han's voice came out gruff and pinched. "Do what?"

"Whatever it is you're thinking about doing to those jerks."

The guy next to Zoe leaned over as if to pick something up off the ground, only there was nothing there.

Han bristled.

Zoe neatly sidestepped the creeper, but none of the tension left Han's frame.

"Seriously, dude." Devin shifted his chair to block Han's sight line. If it also meant he couldn't see Zoe anymore, well, that was just a bonus. "She can handle herself."

The opening night of the Junebug had proven that. Han had lost it on the guys leering at his little sister, and she'd put both them—and her brother—in their places.

"I know," Han grumbled. "But those guys are out of line."

He wasn't wrong, but still. "When it comes to Zoe, you think everyone is out of line."

"I do not."

"You absolutely do." Devin's throat tightened.

Han had always been overprotective. When they were kids, it was cool. No one at Blue Cedar Falls Elementary could mess with either Zoe or their middle sister, Lian. But as the girls had gotten older—and after Han's father died—Han's overprotective instincts went out of control.

"I just . . ." Han picked at his fries before pushing them away. "I know she's an adult, okay?"

"You sure about that?"

Han ignored him. "She's an adult, but she doesn't act like one. At her age, I'd taken over the restaurant. I was paying the mortgage, you know? She's living in the basement."

Ouch.

That wasn't exactly fair, though. Their father had died during Han's first term at the Culinary Institute in Raleigh. It'd been his decision to leave and help his mom out after.

It'd also been his decision to make sure Zoe and Lian wouldn't have to make the same sorts of sacrifices.

Devin raised a brow. "You think she shouldn't have gone to school?"

"Of course not." Han blew out a breath. "It's not even that I mind her living in the basement. It's just—those guys are dirtbags."

"Maybe dirtbags leave good tips."

"It's more than that," Han insisted. "It's like she *likes* dirtbags. You remember all the losers she brought home in high school. And none of them lasted."

"So she dated a few guys." Devin stared at Han pointedly. "*Most* people did."

Han narrowed his eyes right back. "This is not about me. Or May."

Han had been practically married to May Wu for the entirety of high school, and everybody knew it.

As Devin saw it, Han had never gotten over her, either. Just because he'd mated for life didn't mean he should expect everybody else to.

"Uh-huh."

"I didn't go nuts on Lian, did I?"

Lian had also been a lot less of a wild child than Zoe growing up.

"I'm telling you," Han insisted. "You know how Zoe and Mom would go at it. She's always been rebellious. Mom says turn left and Zoe heads right. Mom says get a job in your field, and Zoe ends up waitressing in a bar."

"In a job you got her."

"Beside the point—I just wanted to get her out of the

house, and Clay needed the help." Han picked up a fry and pointed at Devin with it. "The guy thing is just a part of it. She'll bring home anyone she thinks will piss Mom off."

Was that it?

Devin fought not to squirm. If so, how far did it go? Their mom had her opinions, and yes, she and Zoe bumped heads about them. But was Han any different with his overprotective crap?

Would Zoe do something just to piss her brother off, too?

Suddenly, Zoe going all seductive temptress on Devin back at Harvest Home that afternoon took on a whole new light.

Something in his stomach churned. He'd known better than to act on her flirtations—for a whole host of reasons. But if she'd been doing it to get a rise out of Han?

Devin took a big gulp of his water to wash down the bitterness creeping into the back of his throat.

It didn't matter. Han was Devin's best friend. If he didn't want anyone dating his little sister, Devin would respect that.

That didn't stop him from asking one final question.

"So what if she brought home someone you *did* like? Someone with good intentions, a decent job. Treated her well." Devin's voice threatened to tick upward, but he wrestled it down. "What would you do then?"

Han chuckled. "Sure. That'll be the day."

"For real, though."

"Look, I just want her to be happy. She brings home someone great, fine. But I don't see it happening. She's immature and messing with fire just to see if it'll burn. I'm protecting her from douchebag guys at bars, sure. But I'm also protecting her from herself."

"Who are you protecting from herself? Someone new?"

Crap, where had Zoe come from? She set a fresh beer down in front of Devin. She snagged the other one off her tray and held it over the table like she was seriously considering throwing it in her brother's face. "Or just me, like usual?"

Han reached out and grabbed the pint glass, but she pulled it away, keeping it out of his grasp.

"Way to prove how mature you are." Han stood.

She set the glass down with a thud. Beer sloshed right to the edge, but it didn't spill over. Clenching her jaw, she asked, "Anything else I can get you gentlemen?"

"Zo, don't be like that."

She ignored Han. "Devin?"

"Nah," Devin said carefully. "I'm good."

"Great, well, anything you need, you just let me know." She smiled at him way too sweetly.

He swallowed hard, his heart pounding. The full force of her attention on him affected him way more than it should. He didn't want Han getting a whiff of him being interested. He didn't want her getting an inkling about it, either.

Maybe her earlier flirting had been genuine. But her being sunshine and roses to him now?

Yeah. That was definitely for Han's benefit.

Which cast everything else in doubt, too.

Chapter Four

S top."

Zoe screeched to a halt with her hand mere inches from the knob on her family home's back door.

So close.

Her mother cleared her throat, and Zoe prayed for strength before turning around. "Yes, Mother?"

Her mom stood in the kitchen, brows raised, arms crossed. Ling-Ling, the shepherd mix Han had adopted after Zoe left home, sat at her heels. If it was possible, the dog bore the same judgmental glare. "How many résumés did you send out today?"

"Mom—"

"How many?" her mother repeated, firm.

Zoe blew out an exasperated breath. "I didn't, like, count."

"And why not? We paid for a degree in *accounting*, did we not?"

"Would you like me to send you a spreadsheet?"

Her mom scowled, and Ling-Ling made a little growling sound. "No need to take that tone."

Zoe could say the same herself. "Look—"

"You remember what we talked about earlier, right?"

How could Zoe forget?

"Yes, Mom." Zoe wasn't applying herself enough, wasn't taking her future seriously, wasn't considering enough options, blah, blah, blah. "Can I go now? I promised Uncle Arthur I'd open up Harvest Home for him."

The severe line of her mother's frown finally softened. "Fine." She made a little shooing motion with her hand. "Go, go."

Zoe turned to leave. "I just fed Ling-Ling, so don't let her con you into a second dinner."

Her mom never cut Zoe an inch of slack, but the dog walked all over her.

"You send me that spreadsheet tomorrow," her mom called.

"I was *obviously* kidding about that," Zoe cast over her shoulder, opening the door.

She kept walking right on through it, too, blocking out any further replies from her mother by swiftly—but gently!—closing the door behind her.

Still annoyed by the whole thing, she got into her sensible pre-owned Kia and started it up. Her fingers itched on the steering wheel, and the urge to put the pedal to the metal as she pulled onto Main Street tugged at her. She mentally shook her head at herself. The last thing she needed was Officer Dwight pulling her over and giving her a lecture, too.

As she begrudgingly maintained the speed limit, she ran over her mom's words again in her head. With every iteration, she got more worked up. Wasn't it bad enough that her mom had pressured her into going into accounting in the first place?

"Think about your future," Zoe mumbled, imitating her mother's voice. "You want good job, right?"

Fat lot of good the accounting degree had done her in that respect.

To be fair, Zoe hadn't exactly had a better idea about what to do with her life. But it would have been nice to have had some options other than doctor, lawyer, or bean counter.

She chewed on the inside of her lip. At a stoplight, she impulsively hit the button on the dashboard to make a call.

Her sister, Lian, picked up on the second ring. Long and drawn out, her voice came out over the car's tinny speakers. "Yes?"

"How did you know what you wanted to do with your life?"

"Well, hello to you, too."

"I'm serious," Zoe insisted.

Despite facing more or less the same pressure from their mother, Lian had forged her own path. She had a job as a teacher in the next town over, with a 401(k) and health insurance and everything and an apartment where no one harassed her every time she tried to get out the door.

Basically, living the dream.

"I can tell," Lian said dryly. There were rustling noises in the background. "Give me a second to think."

Zoe didn't have a second. The drive to Harvest Home took only ten minutes, and she'd squandered at least seven of them stewing. "I mean, you must have felt pretty strongly about it. Goodness knows it wasn't Mom's idea."

Lian laughed. "No, that it was not." She hummed in thought, then said, "I guess... When you know, you just *know*. You know?"

"Clearly not." Zoe groaned.

"Sorry, that's what I've got."

"You are so useless."

"Uh-huh. Which is why you always call me first when you're stuck."

"I'm not stuck." Okay, she was. Kind of.

She just didn't know what to do with her life or how to get her mother off her back. But other than that, she was fine.

No, she hadn't made any progress on Operation: Seduce Devin Until He Breaks, but she had her job at the Junebug, which was fun and paid well. Her leftover free time—when she wasn't applying for jobs or making pointless spreadsheets for her mother—she spent at Harvest Home, and it was... well, great.

She sighed. If only she could convince Uncle Arthur to take that well-earned trip to Fiji he was always talking about and let her take over there full time. She'd miss him, sure, and it wouldn't exactly be a fancy corporate accounting job. But if she could rustle up enough grants to pay herself a salary, even her mother couldn't give her a hard time about that.

As she turned into Harvest Home's parking lot, she finished up her conversation with her sister. Sherry and Tania arrived just as she was heading toward the door.

"Good afternoon, ladies," Zoe said, swinging her hair out of her face as she found the right key.

Sherry grinned. She was an older white woman who'd been cooking for Harvest Home since Arthur had founded it back in the late nineties. "Hey, Zoe."

"Arthur finally take a day off?" Tania asked. Tania was newer, hired when the place had expanded a few years ago, but now it was hard to imagine how they'd gotten along without her. She was Black and maybe twenty years younger than Sherry, and the two were a powerhouse team.

"Fingers crossed."

Tania threw her head back and laughed. "I give it an hour."

"Swear I'm going to tie that man to his recliner." Zoe shook her head and pushed open the door.

Uncle Arthur was tireless, and getting him to take an entire day off—much less a trip to Fiji—was a rare victory. She swallowed hard. The only person she'd ever known who worked harder was her dad, and everyone knew how that had ended. If he'd rested and relaxed more, would that have prevented him from dropping dead of a heart attack at forty-eight?

Who knew. Probably not.

But Uncle Arthur was sixty-five with high blood pressure. The guy deserved a break.

Heading inside, Zoe flicked on the lights and fired up the computer to check messages at the front desk. Sherry and Tania made their way to the kitchen. Absently, Zoe pulled up the volunteer schedule. It took its sweet time loading, so she called, "Any idea who's serving tonight?"

As paid employees, Sherry and Tania were the backbone of the organization's meal service, but they couldn't pull off feeding fifty people a day without an equally dedicated crew of volunteers. Businesses, churches, and schools fielded teams that came out to make the magic happen every night.

Sherry and Tania must have been out of earshot. Frowning, she wiggled the computer mouse and reloaded the schedule. Before it could come up, the door swung open. Zoe darted her gaze toward the entryway.

Only to be met with a pair of gorgeous blue eyes, a broad set of shoulders, a trim, muscular frame, and a bright smile.

"Meyer Construction, reporting for duty," Devin said.

Zoe's heart did a little jump inside her chest as she straightened up. "Oh, hey!"

"Hey." Just like he had the last time he strode through that door, he raked his gaze over her. She swallowed. She wasn't dressed to get good tips at the Junebug today. A flannel shirt over a T-shirt and jeans was hardly what she'd call sexy, but it didn't seem to matter, based on the way his eyes darkened.

"I didn't know you all were serving today."

Devin moved forward into the space, making room for a half dozen folks to file in after him. He shrugged, tucking his thumbs into the belt loops of his dark-rinse jeans. "Arthur talked me into it when I was here telling him about my promotion." One corner of his mouth curled upward. "Said it'd be a good use for my new leadership skills."

The last guy to come in groaned. "Are we ever going to hear the end of that?"

Devin stiffened and flexed his jaw. "I haven't even started yet, Bryce."

Ah, okay, now Zoe recognized the guy shouldering past Devin. The mayor's son, Bryce Horton, had been a couple of years ahead of her in school, but Lian had complained about him plenty at the time. He'd been a royal jerk, and it didn't seem like much had changed.

"Then why am I even here?" Bryce asked, pulling out his phone and plunking down in one of the chairs meant for patrons.

Devin's whole frame radiated tension, but however angry he was, he kept it out of his tone. "Come on. Kitchen's in the back."

Bryce rolled his eyes, even as he kept his gaze glued to what sure looked like a dating app he was swiping through.

Zoe resisted the urge to sneak a peek at his username—just so she could avoid it if she ever ended up on the same site.

Devin's voice dropped. "Now."

Grumbling, Bryce lurched out of the chair and followed Devin down the hall.

"Right behind you," Zoe called. She just had a couple more quick things to take care of out here.

Bryce looked over his shoulder at her and made a super-gross kissy face. Glancing back, Devin caught him, and his eyes narrowed, his hands curling into fists at his sides.

Interesting. When her brother shot his death glare at guys who were hitting on her at the bar, it made her want to strangle him. But when Devin did it?

A warm little shiver ran up her spine.

She probably shouldn't like it so much, but she did.

She swallowed, fighting to calm the flutters in her chest as she shot Bryce a glare of her own. No matter how much Devin's protectiveness gave her the warm fuzzies, she could handle herself. "Wasn't talking to you," she informed Bryce.

"Sure." He clicked his tongue and brought his hand to his ear like a phone and mouthed, *Call me.*

Devin bustled him along, thunderclouds in his eyes. The coiled strength in him gave her even more little flutters inside.

As soon as they disappeared around the corner, she put her head in her hands to muffle her groan. Getting the butterflies over this guy was pathetic. She was acting like a swooning schoolgirl with a crush again.

Sucking in a deep breath, she dropped her hands from her face. She was too old for this pining nonsense.

Resolve filled her. Devin showing up to volunteer tonight

might have taken her by surprise, but it was a golden opportunity. Han was working at the restaurant tonight, so he couldn't appear from out of nowhere, football in hand or no. Devin would have his guard down.

With so many people around, Zoe couldn't exactly seduce Devin. But maybe this was her chance to show him that she was so much more than a kid with a crush now.

And that the spark between them was real.

———

"Need any help?"

Zoe sighed and cast her gaze skyward but didn't stop busing dishes. "I thought you were taking the day off."

Uncle Arthur smiled. "Was just in the neighborhood and thought I'd stop in." He craned his neck to peer into the dining room. "Decent crowd tonight."

"Fifty-seven."

"Impressive." He pursed his lips. "Terrible, but impressive."

Nobody wanted to be put out of business more than Uncle Arthur. When his family had landed in this country nearly sixty years ago, they'd relied on soup kitchens. He'd come a long way since then, and he'd had some good luck with investments that had allowed him to found this place. He loved having a way to give back to the community here in Blue Cedar Falls that had taken him in. But if hunger and unemployment just disappeared, he'd be delighted to be out of a job.

Stir crazy and climbing the walls, looking for his next venture, but delighted.

"Late fall is always tough."

The weather here was warm enough that construction and tourism carried on year-round, but whenever the weather turned chilly, the number of people showing up at Harvest Home climbed.

"True." Uncle Arthur came over to squeeze her arm. "Knew you could handle it, though."

Her chest contracted. With no one else in her life trusting her to handle anything more than her TikTok account, that was way too nice to hear. She chuckled to hide the tightness behind her ribs. "Which is why you felt no need to check up on me at all."

"He's not checking up on you," Tania said, coming in from taking a load to the compost pile out back. "He just can't stay away from me," she teased.

"You know me," Uncle Arthur agreed indulgently, dropping his hand.

Sherry was right behind Tania. She shook her head at Arthur. "Held out longer than I thought you would."

Ignoring her, Uncle Arthur gestured toward the dining room. "I'm just going to quick make the rounds."

Zoe waved him along. On his way out, Arthur nearly bumped right into Devin, who had a crate filled with dirty dishes in his arms.

Devin's eyes lit up. "Thought you were taking the night off."

"Don't you start in on me, too." Uncle Arthur waggled a finger at him.

"You're working yourself to an early grave," Zoe called after him.

Uncle Arthur's finger shifted to point at her, but she just shrugged. She wasn't going to apologize for trying to remind him to take a break once in a while. He continued out to the dining room to do his usual thing, thanking volunteers and checking in on the guests. Sherry and Tania followed him with more milk crates to help with cleanup.

Rolling her sleeves to her elbows, Zoe started running the water.

Devin brought his crate of dishes over to her. "He's unstoppable, huh?"

"Seems it." She frowned. Her uncle definitely gave that impression, but he was getting up there, and she did genuinely worry about him.

"He's fine. There's a reason he showed up at the last possible second." Devin tipped his head toward the dining room. "He's not going to do any work. He just likes talking to everybody."

His voice was soft and full of affection.

"Right." Sometimes Zoe forgot that Devin's road to practically becoming a member of their extended family began right here at Harvest Home. Uncle Arthur didn't like to talk about it, but Devin had started out as a guest, coming by with his dad every week. Then by himself even more often than that. Sure, he'd become best buddies with Han by then, but it went deeper than that. Devin knew better than anyone how dedicated Uncle Arthur was to making people feel welcome here.

As he started unloading the dirty dishes, Devin's arm brushed hers, and a shiver of warmth ran through her skin.

Her throat went dry as she glanced up at him. They'd been working in close quarters all night, but any efforts to either seduce him or change his impression of her had taken a back seat to the task of getting dinner on the table for almost sixty people. In the end, this was the closest they'd really gotten, physically.

As if he could feel her gaze, he looked down. When their eyes met, heat flushed through her. How could a person's eyes be so blue? She got lost for a second, just staring at the gold-brown scruff on his sharp jaw, the soft red fullness of his lips, when everything else about him was chiseled and hard.

"Do you—" The huskiness of his voice only distracted her more.

"Huh?"

He pushed a plate toward her more insistently.

A different, embarrassed flush rose to her cheeks as she grabbed it and ran it under the water. "Right, right. Sorry."

He didn't need to stand so close as he passed her the next one, but she didn't tell him that. Wasn't she the one who'd started the game of trying to make him break? With the way he'd been looking at her, she'd taken it as a personal challenge to get him to make a move or at least admit that there was something brewing between them.

Now here she was, right on the cusp of cracking herself.

What would he do if she did? If she made the real first move and turned to him. Reached up to graze her fingertips along his cheek.

If she leaned forward on her tiptoes and tugged him down so she could taste his mouth...

She shuddered inside, blushing furiously as she placed another plate on the rack inside the dishwasher. She'd been harboring these kinds of fantasies since she was a teenager. It was hard to tell how much was actually possible and how much was just the same nonsense she'd been imagining for years.

Unwilling to shatter the moment, she set it all aside and concentrated on cleaning up. He seemed content to do the same. Even if his presence was making her heart do weird flips behind her ribs, she tried not to let it show.

They fell into a rhythm, like they'd been working together like this forever. That made sense—they'd both been volunteering here for years, but it still felt unfairly kismet, somehow.

"Thanks," she said after a couple of minutes. "By the way. For bringing in the folks from your company tonight."

"Happy to do it." He let out a rough sigh. "Well, for the most part."

It was clear who he was talking about.

Chuckling quietly, she shook her head. "Yeah, Bryce is still a piece of work, huh?"

"You have no idea."

The guy had barely lifted a finger the entire time he'd been here, and he'd eaten a solid dinner's worth of food meant for the guests.

"How does he get away with it?"

"You know." A dark undertone ran through Devin's words.

She shivered, reminded again of how much strength Devin kept contained inside himself. He never used it, though, no matter how frustrated he got.

It made her feel . . . safe. It always had. Even when they'd been kids messing around in Uncle Arthur's basement. Any time the other boys his age had gotten too rough around her, he'd stepped in and said something.

Which was probably part of how she'd ended up with this stupid crush on him in the first place.

"Yeah, I guess I do."

People filed in and out of the kitchen, bringing new loads of dishes through. Zoe was indulging herself, spending this time rinsing plates when she should be out there directing traffic, but between Uncle Arthur, Sherry, and Tania, there were enough people running the show for her to dawdle a little longer. And the chance to stand so close to Devin was just too good to pass up.

"So you've really gotten involved here, huh?" he asked, moving to her other side to help her start loading the second washer.

She shrugged and passed him a stack of silverware. "I have the time right now. And I like helping out. Working with the guests. Getting to spend more time with Uncle Arthur."

A smile stole across her face as she talked about it all. She'd missed everyone in her family while she'd been away at college, but her uncle was the only one who didn't carry any baggage—or seem to have some sort of agenda for what she should do with her life.

Devin hummed in acknowledgment, giving her space to keep talking. It was refreshing.

"This place," she continued, trying to sum it up. "The work we do here, the people we serve. It feels important."

"I get it," Devin said quietly.

He would.

But then one corner of his mouth tilted down. "You said you have the time 'right now.' You see that changing soon?"

"Ugh." Zoe huffed out a breath as she scrubbed at a particularly stubborn spot on a plate. "I don't know. Apparently, at some point I'm supposed to get a real job."

He chuckled and passed her another dish. "What? Overrated."

"Says the guy who just got the big promotion."

"It's not that big a deal," he said, rolling his eyes, but his posture straightened slightly. It was definitely at least a medium-size deal. Humble as he might be, she hoped he was getting some satisfaction from his work.

She considered for a second before asking, "How did you know? That construction was what you wanted to do?"

It was the same basic question she'd asked Lian earlier—unhelpful as that conversation had been.

"I don't know," he answered slowly. "I didn't exactly have a ton of options."

"Smart guy like you?"

He laughed, only it didn't entirely sound funny. "I like working with my hands. Got a decent eye for it. Pay's good, relatively speaking. Arthur was able to help me get my foot in the door when I needed—when I decided it was time to find a place of my own."

There was something he wasn't saying, his voice dipping low and pulling at something in her chest. Before she could probe any deeper, though, he looked at her.

"So, how are things going with the whole real job thing, then?" he asked.

Well, that was certainly a way to kill the mood.

"Ugh. Terrible." Her mom had laid into her just that afternoon, telling her she wasn't sending out enough résumés or casting her net wide enough, prompting her to waste a good hour or two rage-scrolling Monster. "I'm putting in applications for jobs pretty much all over the state at this point. A few in Atlanta, too."

His eyebrows pinched together. "You'd really go that far?"

"I don't want to." She liked it here. She always had. Things here were easy. Comfortable. Being close to her family—when they weren't driving her up a wall or dictating her love life and her job search, anyway—was nice.

But she'd do what she had to do. She'd always wanted to get out on her own, and this extended period of being between things was making her itch to be independent again.

It wasn't like it was with her brother. Han had come

home when their father died and had taken over—well, everything. His sense of duty was giving him white hairs.

She'd choose to stay here, too, if it worked out. But she had to keep her options open. She couldn't just be *stuck* here because she couldn't make it on her own.

"We'll see how things go." She shrugged. It was such an annoying platitude, but that was her life now.

"Well, I hope you stay close." The way he said it was so genuine, she jerked her gaze up to meet his, but he was pointedly studying the dishes. After a second, he smiled, his tone lightening as he darted a teasing glance her way. "I mean, how can Han kill anyone who dares to look at you if you live far away?"

That was it. She shoved him, and he laughed, plates clanking together as he bumped into them where they were so neatly stacked in the racks. He playfully pushed back, and then what choice did she have, with her wet hands and all, but to flick some water in his face?

He sputtered, the droplets clinging to his skin in interesting ways, and her breath sped up. She went to do it again, but she must have telegraphed her intentions too clearly, because he grabbed her wrist before she could. Her heart hammered in her chest.

She stared up into his eyes, and for a second, everything around them faded, because she had seen that look before.

About two seconds before he got hit in the head with a football.

"Someone wanna tell me why we're out there doing all the work while these two are messing around in here?"

Devin straightened, pulling away from her so fast, she had to catch herself from falling over.

Apparently, playing the part of the football tonight, Bryce came over holding one measly dish, which he popped—still caked in drying potatoes—straight into the dishwasher. Struggling not to let on how flustered she was by the unwelcome interruption, Zoe plucked it out and set it in the sink, shooting him a glare.

"Thank you, Mr. Horton," Arthur said delicately as he hauled a crate in and set it on the counter. He caught Zoe's gaze, and she huffed out a breath.

Bryce's dad was the mayor. The town gave Harvest Home a bunch of money and support every year. She would do well to remember it.

But wasn't that just how a jerk like Bryce got so . . . jerk-y? Everyone giving him a free pass because his father was a powerful guy?

She glanced at Devin. How did he do it? Constantly keeping a lid on himself when the guy kept asking to get punched in the face?

Before she could suss it out, a few more of the Meyer Construction volunteers came in with the last of the supper service cleanup.

Bryce gawked at the towering piles of dishes. "How are we supposed to get all this done? Some of us have places to be tonight." Winking, he elbowed one of the other guys, who subtly moved to put more distance between them. Not that Bryce noticed. With a leering smirk and a waggle of his phone, he added, "If you know what I mean."

Devin exhaled roughly. He threw his shoulders back. Instead of answering Bryce, he looked around and held his hands out expansively. "With a crew like this? We all pitch in and we'll have it done in no time."

"Uh-huh." Bryce kept scrolling on his phone.

"What do you say we put a little wager on it?" Devin's smile rippled with challenge. "We get out of here within the hour, and the first round at the bar is on me."

Chapter Five

This was going to cost Devin a small fortune.

It was worth it, though. At the hour mark, pretty nearly on the dot, his team had put the last clean pan on its shelf. The fact that Arthur, Sherry, Tania, and Zoe had thrown their backs into it, too, had helped a ton. Heck, even Bryce had cleaned a few tables. Free drinks were some powerful motivation.

Powerful, expensive motivation.

As the last guy put in his order, Clay whistled, punching in the numbers on the register.

"This sure seems like a nightmare for the bookkeeping," Devin tried in vain. "You should probably just give them to me for free."

"Nice try." Clay printed off the bill and handed it to Devin. "You wanna settle up now or start a tab?"

"Settle up now." Passing over his debit card, Devin eyed Bryce, who was standing by the pool table in the corner. Devin had promised the first round, and he was going to see it through, but he wasn't going to make it easy for anyone to try to turn it into two.

"Good choice."

He signed the slip, then joined the rest of his crew. He tried to pay attention to what they were saying, but his gaze kept drifting to the table in the corner where Zoe sat with Arthur, Sherry, and Tania. All four of them had been only too happy to take him up on the free drink offer, too, and he was happy to have them.

Probably too happy.

Working side by side with Zoe tonight had been an eye-opening experience. While her sexy waitress outfit had bowled him over the other day, this afternoon it had been her maturity—the way she'd known how to handle every situation that arose as they'd cooked and served. Even now, while he and his buddies from work stood around, shooting pool and playing darts and talking about yesterday's game, she was engaged in what looked like a deep conversation with Arthur, Sherry, and Tania. They regarded her with all the respect she deserved. Which he was starting to realize was a heck of a lot.

She'd really rolled up her sleeves tonight. She knew Harvest Home as well as he did, and despite mostly working in the front office, she wasn't afraid to get her hands dirty. Her eyes went all soft when she talked about the place, too. She might be the only person besides him and Arthur who understood it for the miracle it was.

She was funny and smart and beautiful and...

He cut off his train of thought before it could pull any farther out of the station. Jerking his gaze away from her mouth as she laughed at something Tania was saying, he took a big gulp of his beer.

Han wasn't here tonight, but the two of them had been friends for so long that the guy lived rent-free in his head. If anybody else was staring at Zoe the way Devin had been just now, Han would've been ready to deck him. Devin wasn't some dirtbag trying to get a peek up her skirt, but he needed to do a better job keeping his eyes to himself.

Before too long, Bryce gave one of the other guys a noogie before sauntering Devin's way. Devin crossed his arms over his chest, but his body language wasn't enough to keep Bryce from coming over and slapping him on the biceps.

"See you tomorrow, *boss*." He said it like an insult, but Devin wasn't going to take it that way.

"Bright and early."

The instant Bryce was gone, it was like someone had undone one of the knots in Devin's back. A few others filtered out not long after, and he thanked them each for coming out and giving a part of their day to volunteer.

Eventually, he and what was left of his crew drifted toward the pool table. They played a couple of rounds, but it was tough to focus. Every time he lined up a shot, he either had to face Zoe or put his back to her, and he had to get this under control. Being this aware of her wasn't right.

But it did give him a heads-up when she and the others started to gather their things.

Arthur was the one to approach first and clear his throat. Devin turned to find him jacket in hand.

Arthur clapped him firmly on the shoulder. "Good work tonight, Devin."

"Anytime." Then he remembered how Arthur had somehow managed to get him to agree to find a crew for this afternoon without his even fully realizing he'd committed until it was too late. "I mean, not *any* time, but..."

"I know what you mean."

Devin nodded at Sherry and Tania, who stood behind Arthur, clearly ready to go, too. "Glad you all could come out."

Tania grinned. "Any time you feel like footing the bill, you let us know."

They said their goodbyes, and the three of them made for the exit.

Which left Zoe. He scrunched his brows together. She wouldn't have just snuck out, would she? He would have noticed.

"Boo," she said from just behind him, poking his shoulder.

He didn't jump, but it was a near thing.

"Oh, hey." His voice came out rough. God, she smelled good. She was doing that thing again, getting up in his space, but unlike the other day, it didn't feel forced or unnatural. It felt like where she was supposed to be. Half hopeful and half ready to be disappointed, he asked, "You taking off, too?"

She had her flannel shirt draped over her arm and her bag slung across one shoulder, but there wasn't any sign of her keys. She cocked a brow and glanced behind him. "Actually, I was about to call winner."

Oh.

Oh, okay. This he remembered.

Devin and Han and some of the other guys used to play pool in Arthur's basement, days they couldn't mess around outside. Zoe would hang out there, too, and of course they couldn't tell Arthur's niece to scram. They only ever let her play if they needed an even number for a team. She was short and she scratched half her shots, and when she called winner, everybody had to pretend not to groan.

Unconsciously, he flicked his gaze over her form. His throat bobbed.

She was still short, but the confidence in her expression told him she'd learned a couple of things since she was twelve.

It was late. He should probably tell her he was just wrapping up here and ready to call it a night. If he was serious about not jeopardizing his friendship with Han, spending more time with his baby sister was *not* a smart strategy.

But there was something about the challenge in her eyes that was too enticing to resist.

For old times' sake...

Before he could second-guess himself any further, he lifted a brow to match hers. Without a word, he turned. He surveyed the table. His team was in good shape—just the eight ball left to sink, while stripes had three balls on the table. Sucking in a deep breath, he pointed toward the corner pocket.

He could feel her behind him as he lined up his shot. His skin tingled with awareness, but his vision went sharp. He pulled his cue back and nudged it forward, once, then twice.

The cue ball went spinning off across the felt, straight as an arrow. It rebounded, narrowly missing the ten before smacking straight into the eight. The eight shot toward the corner pocket, where it hovered for half a second on the edge before sinking right in.

He couldn't have done it better if he'd tried.

His partner held out his hand, and Devin slapped their palms together. He nodded at the guys he'd beaten. They shook their heads, but they took it just fine. He grabbed his beer and swallowed the last of it down.

Then he turned. He met Zoe's gaze again, and the heat in it went straight to the center of him.

"You want winner?" he asked, throat raw.

Her head bobbed up and down, her pretty pink mouth parted just the tiniest bit.

"Well." He swallowed deeply. This was a monumentally

stupid idea. But he was in it now. "What're you waiting for?"

———

Zoe was seriously starting to lose track of who was egging
on who. After she'd called winner, the other guys Devin
had been playing with decided to head out. At least one
of them had shot him a knowing look. Another had patted
him on the back and winked at her. She'd rolled her eyes
and sent them on their way.

Was the tension between them as obvious to the people
around them as it was to her? If so, it was a good thing
her brother wasn't around. She glanced toward the bar.
Clay didn't seem to be paying them any attention. His
girlfriend, June, had shown up a little while ago with her
friends Caitlin and Bobbi, and between pouring drinks for
everyone and chatting with them, he had his hands full.

Zoe still didn't completely trust him not to rat her out to
Han—intentionally or otherwise.

Whatever. All along, she'd said her brother should mind
his own business. She was a grown woman, and she could
do as she pleased.

And at the moment, what she wanted to do was Devin.

Only it wasn't quite that simple anymore, was it? Her
advances had sort of been a lark at the beginning, but after
spending time talking to him while cleaning up tonight,
she was starting to wonder if there might be more between
them than simple attraction. This wasn't a schoolgirl crush,
and it wasn't leading to just a single night of fun.

As to what it was leading to?

Little sparklers fired off inside her. She'd love to have
the chance to find out.

After she schooled him at pool.

She took a second to select a cue and chalk the tip as he went ahead and racked the balls. The sight of him in those jeans had her sucking her bottom lip between her teeth.

The guy was really just unfairly handsome, with that golden tan skin and clear blue eyes. The short-cropped hair that shone under the hanging lights and the scruff on his deliciously sharp jaw.

He smiled at her and gestured toward the table. "You wanna break?"

"Be my guest." That had been her plan, right? Getting him to break.

He grabbed his cue from where he'd leaned it. He set the cue ball down just to the right of center, leaned over, and lined up. She let her gaze move over his entire body as his muscles tensed.

With a sudden surge of motion, he fired off his shot. The crack of the cue ball hitting the one dead center rang out through the air. Balls scattered everywhere, while the cue ball spun in the middle of the table before coming to a halt.

"Nice."

He winked. "I've been practicing a bit."

Oh, she liked him like this. She'd always appreciated his serious side, but seeing him loose and playful and—dare she say flirty? It warmed her insides, even as it ratcheted up nervous anticipation about where this evening was going.

He called a shot and made it with ease. He sank two more before finally missing.

Zoe gripped her cue more tightly as she walked the perimeter of the table. Devin's gaze on her was distracting as hell, but she kept her focus.

He might have missed, but he'd done a good job setting her up for failure. Nice to know he wasn't going easy on her. She finally selected her shot and grabbed a bridge off the rack.

"You don't need that," Devin told her.

"Speak for yourself, tall person."

"Seriously." Then he was there, wrapping his hand around hers. "May I?"

Heat zipped up her arm. His warm scent surrounded her, and she got dizzy for a second, having him so close.

Which was her only explanation for why she let him take the bridge away. He guided her to the other edge of the table. She lined up her shot, and sure, she was closer to the ball now, but she didn't love the angles.

"I don't know." She shook her head, ready to stand and go back to her original plan, but he stopped her.

"Let me show you?" he asked.

Her whole body locked down as he stepped up behind her. He was so hot, bracketing her frame. His height swamped her, making it hard for her to breathe, and she was going to die before she even so much as managed to seduce him.

"See?" he asked.

Did he know what he was doing to her? She clenched down inside against a powerful wave of desire.

But he was still talking about pool. He placed his hand over hers on the felt, realigning her shot a few degrees to the left. Her breath caught.

Seriously. She was Going. To. *Die*.

She hovered there for just a second, soaking in the feeling of his body blanketing her, fluttering her eyes shut to bask in his closeness.

But as good as it felt—and as much as she never

wanted to move again, ever in her life—she couldn't stand there and take a crummy shot just because a hot guy was scrambling her brains.

Carefully, she stood up again. He moved with her. She glanced at him over her shoulder, and his face was inches from hers, his kissable mouth *right there*.

She stepped away. She got the bridge down from the rack. Her face flushed hot as she set up her original shot again. If she missed, she was going to feel like twice the idiot now, but she knew herself, dammit all. She knew her own mind, and she knew her body and her abilities.

No guy was going to waltz in out of nowhere and try to tell her differently before he'd even seen her play.

She ignored the pressure of his gaze. Then, with a breath and a prayer, she pulled the cue stick back.

The ball careened forward, banking off the far rail before heading straight for the nine. Everything in her tightened as the nine rolled toward the side pocket, slower than she would have liked. It hovered on the edge for an agonizing instant.

And then it tipped right on in.

She wanted to shout and scream—maybe jump and dance. As it was, she restricted herself to a single pump of her fist before locking her gaze with Devin's.

"Watch out," she told him, breathless—and not just from the score. "I've been practicing, too."

Chapter Six

Okay, for real, though, where did you learn to play like that?"

Zoe laughed as she braced her elbow against the bar. Devin settled onto the stool beside hers. His knee rested against hers, and she shivered.

They'd been getting closer and closer all evening. She wasn't complaining, but there was a tension inside her chest. This didn't seem like it could last. A half dozen games of pool and almost as many drinks between the two of them had them both loose-limbed and happy. After their last match, when someone else had asked them for the table, she'd kind of expected him to call it a night. It was late, after all. But when she'd started making her way over to the bar, figuring she'd check in with Clay before heading out herself, Devin had come on over, too.

Now here they were. Sitting together, fresh drinks in hand.

Zoe shrugged and took a sip of her cosmo. "There was a pool table in the basement of my dorm my first year of college."

"And a shark there to teach you all?"

"Don't underestimate bored teenage girls trying to avoid writing term papers."

He chuckled. "Fair enough."

She stirred her drink, probably a little too forcefully. "Turns out, hustling pool is one of the most useful things I learned at school."

"Oh?"

"I mean..." Releasing the tiny straw, she gestured around. She couldn't quite keep the sour note out of her tone. "See how far that degree has gotten me?"

"I don't know. Doesn't seem so bad."

She shook her head. "Try telling that to everyone else."

"You mean your mom?"

"Among other people. Han and Lian don't seem super impressed, either." Sighing, she looked away, to the bottles of liquor on the shelf, the taps, the specials she'd written on the big black board the day before. "I mean, I had a great time at college—don't get me wrong. But the whole grand compromise of it all—me going so far away, to a school that cost so much..." Even with aid and a bunch of money from her mom, she was going to be paying off loans forever. "Mom let me follow my dream, but she hammered home that if I didn't pick something practical, I'd end up penniless in a gutter somewhere."

"And that's how you ended up going into accounting?" Devin asked, leaning his elbow on the bar.

"Pretty much." She pinched the little straw from her drink again and stabbed at an ice cube. "I'm good at math, and after the first year, none of the courses were before noon. Seemed like a good deal at the time."

"What if you could do it all over again? Without your mom hanging over your shoulder. Would you pick something different?"

The question barely computed. Zoe's parents had always had strong opinions about her life. After her dad had died, her mom had become even more aggressive in trying to control Zoe's future. She'd clearly been grieving. Zoe had been, too. She'd fought back about some things, but on others, she got worn down and just got used to going along.

"I don't know," she said quietly. "Maybe? There wasn't anything I was super passionate about at school."

"Was there anything you were passionate about outside of it?"

"Not really." Usually, when people asked her questions like this, it made her uncomfortable, but Devin's expression was so open as he gazed at her. He'd known her practically their entire lives, but it felt like he actually wanted to know more. So she dug deeper. "I liked normal stuff—hanging out with my friends, watching TV."

"Making friendship bracelets."

"Shut up." She flapped a hand in his general direction as if to swat at him. Her cheeks flushed warmer.

One corner of his mouth lifted. "I still have mine."

"You do not." Oh wow. She'd made them for everybody one summer. She'd found a ton of old embroidery floss from some kit her mother had never finished. Bored, she'd gone to town.

She'd picked the colors for the one she'd given to Devin so carefully. Blue for his eyes, orange and brown for the Blue Cedar Falls team colors. Red for the hearts she secretly drew around his name in the back of her diary. Because she was super, super cool and not a dork at all.

"I do," he promised, and for some reason, she actually believed him.

Her throat tight, she looked down at her drink again.

Silence held for a second. Then she continued. "But yeah. Just normal teenager stuff, mostly. I mean, I liked volunteering at Harvest Home, too, but if I'd told my mom I wanted to work at a nonprofit or go into social services or something, I think she would have flipped her lid."

"Did you ever try?"

"What? No." The idea had never occurred to her.

But maybe it should have.

That was too much food for thought for this late into the night, though.

"How about you?" she asked. "You said construction was sort of something you fell into. Did you ever think about doing anything else? Going to school?"

The question seemed to take him off guard. Furrows appeared between his brows. She wanted to reach over and smooth them out, but even with the soft intimacy that somehow surrounded them now, it felt like too big of a line to cross.

"You mean college?"

She nodded, sipping at her drink.

"Sort of?" He lifted one shoulder before setting it back down. "Mrs. Jeffries in the guidance department thought I should, but it was never in the cards for me."

"How come?"

"Money." He said it without any bitterness to his tone. "There's a reason I started going to Harvest Home, you know."

Right. Crap. "Sorry—"

"It's fine. I could have maybe gotten financial aid or something, but I needed to be out on my own."

"I can drink to that." She lifted her drink, and he clinked his glass against hers before taking a deep pull at it and setting it down.

He still seemed calm, but a familiar stiffness settled into his shoulders. A far-off look came into his gaze. "My mom died when I was young, you know. Really, really young. I don't even remember her. But my dad—he was..."

As he searched for words, Zoe sat up straighter. A girl couldn't hang around her big brother and his best friend all the time without overhearing some stuff. She knew Devin's home life wasn't great, but he'd never talked about it in front of her directly.

"Yeah?" She held her breath and reached out, brushing her hand against his. His skin was warm and rough, and she wasn't oblivious to all the other, different ways she wanted to touch him. But she dropped her hand away after one quick, encouraging squeeze.

The point of his jaw flexed. His bright eyes met hers for a second, shadows forming behind his irises. Then he looked away. "He wasn't a good guy—let's just leave it at that."

He picked up his glass again. Zoe bit her lip. She should probably leave well enough alone.

But the book he'd started to crack open didn't feel shut quite yet. She couldn't shake the sense that he *wanted* to talk about this. How many times had she caught him holding himself back? Was this just more restraint?

What would it be like if he let go?

And honestly. Poking the bear had gotten her this far.

"You don't have to."

He lowered his drink and stared at her in question.

She took a deep breath. "You don't have to leave it at that. If you don't want to." Her face warmed, but she wasn't backing down. "I'm happy to listen."

He regarded her for a long, silent moment. The sounds of the bar around them filtered in. It had felt like they'd been in their own little world this whole time, but there were other people here. Not many. It really was late. But a few. Clay was still kicking around here somewhere.

No one else mattered, though.

As the moment stretched on, she held her ground, waiting patiently.

Finally, he grabbed his beer and tossed the rest of it back. He gestured at her drink. She was tempted to finish it, too, especially when he put on his jacket. The taste of it soured in her mouth. She'd pushed too far, huh? Sometimes she did that. She set her half-full glass on the bar.

But then he tipped his head toward the door.

"Come on. Let me walk you home."

The offer took her by surprise. Neither of them had had so much to drink that they couldn't drive. She probably *should* drive. Getting her car in the morning would be a hassle.

But walking home... walking home was good.

Letting *Devin* walk her home. Well, that was downright great.

When he extended his hand to help her up? No way that was an invitation she could refuse.

His calloused fingers were warm against hers. He gripped her tightly as she popped down from the stool. Was she imagining it when he held on for a second even after her feet hit the floor?

He let go, and she dropped her gaze. She untied her flannel from around her waist and shrugged it on.

Then she followed him out into the night.

It was chillier than she was prepared for, but between the Asian flush from the little alcohol she'd had and the heat Devin radiated at her side, she didn't mind. She crossed her arms over her chest.

Devin didn't have to ask where she lived, of course.

He'd been hanging out at the Leung house for a decade or two. They were both quiet as they headed north on Main Street.

The crisp air smelled like fall, the last few leaves of the season just clinging to the trees. She hugged herself more tightly. The dark sky above shone with stars and a half-full moon. Twinkling lights draped over the white fences all along Main Street gave everything a cozy feel.

She sighed. When she'd first realized she'd have to move home, she'd spent most of her time thinking about how annoying it would be to have to camp out in her mom's basement. She'd been right about that. Her mother's constant, snide comments about her prospects had only added to the ambience.

She hadn't been thinking about this, though. Blue Cedar Falls was beautiful by day, with the bright blue sky above and the mountains all around them. At night it was quiet and still, and it just felt like...

Home.

A tiny shiver racked her, followed by a pang. Getting a real job would be great, but the more time she spent here in Blue Cedar Falls—and with Devin—the less eager she was to leave.

Misunderstanding her shiver, Devin glanced down at her. "Cold?"

"I'm fine."

Stupid, chivalrous boy. He whipped off his jacket anyway, leaving his arms bare. Really hot, sexy, muscular arms, but it still seemed unpleasant for him.

"I'm fine," she protested again, but he was having none of it.

He draped the jacket over her shoulders. Instantly, heat blanketed her. Oh wow. His delicious scent wrapped around her even more thoroughly, making her whole body come into another, deeper level of awareness.

"Looks good on you," he said, his voice rough. He snapped his mouth closed as if he hadn't meant to say that, but it was out there now.

There was clearly no point arguing anymore, and anyway, now that she had his jacket, it wasn't as if she wanted to give it up. "Thanks."

"No problem."

They hit the end of the downtown strip and turned right together. As the businesses faded away into little houses, the quiet grew. She glanced up at him.

She met the soft blue gaze staring back down at her, and warmth fluttered inside her chest.

"Thanks," he murmured. He pointed with his thumb in the direction of the Junebug. "For what you said back there."

Right. Talking about his not-a-good-guy father.

She got her head out of the clouds of teenage crush land and mustered a smile. "I meant it."

"I know." He directed his gaze forward, ducking to avoid a couple of low-hanging branches on an old oak. "Sorry it took me by surprise. I work with too many guys. Some women, too, but they act even tougher than the men. Nobody gets touchy-feely on the job site."

"What about friends?"

"You mean your brother?"

"Okay, yeah, never mind."

Han was a cool guy, deep down. To hear Clay talk about it, he'd offered all kinds of great relationship advice back when he and June were getting their act together. But Han had never gotten over their father. He'd died suddenly, almost ten years ago. All Han's plans for his life had gone up in smoke when he'd rushed home, eighteen years old and determined to take up the mantle and become the man of the house.

The loss still hurt in Zoe's heart, too, of course. She missed her dad. Losing him had changed the entire family. It had harshened her mom and aged her brother. Fortunately, she'd had Lian and Uncle Arthur to lean on, both during that first tough year and after.

But Han hadn't seemed interested in leaning on anyone. He was too busy taking over the business and the house. Deep down, though, she knew her brother too well. He'd been devastated.

Talking about someone else's issues with their father? He couldn't have handled it. He probably still couldn't.

Devin's gaze focused on something far off in the distance. His jaw hardened before going soft—like he was building walls around himself only to have to consciously decide to let them down.

"He was a bully," he said quietly. "A mean old drunk who told me I'd never amount to anything in my life."

Zoe's heart squeezed. "Devin... That's awful."

"When high school graduation came around, I still half believed him." His smile was pained. "I told myself I didn't, but asking for people to give me money so I could go fail out of college just the way he always told me I would? Nah."

She shook her head, but he kept talking. As they turned onto her street, his pace slowed.

"It was all stupid head games, I know. In the end, it didn't matter. The best route to getting out of his house was getting a job." The sharpness in his gaze finally eased. "Arthur hooked me up, actually."

"Sounds like him."

"Yeah, it does." Unguarded affection colored his tone—with maybe a little hero worship mixed in there, too. "I was always handy. He got me an interview at Meyer, and the rest is history. I got a good-paying job and an apartment." His jaw flexed. "And I never looked back."

A different kind of darkness shadowed his eyes now. He clenched and unclenched his hands at his sides.

"Devin..."

"It's for the best. I'm saving up for a house of my own, too. In another year, it'll be just me and some mutt out on the edge of town, and no one will ever be able to bother me like that again." He looked down at her and blew out a breath. "I'm glad. Honestly."

"Okay." There was more to the story than he was telling, but even she knew when a bear had been poked too much. "Well, I'm glad you're glad, too." With a soft smile of her own, she bumped her elbow against his arm. "For what it's worth, I think you turned out pretty great."

His lips curled upward. "You didn't turn out so bad yourself, Itch."

"Hey!" She swatted at him. That's what he and Han and their friends had called her when she was really bugging them.

"Sorry, sorry!" He put his hands in front of his face as she swung at him again.

And she was just goofing around—really, she was. He was, too. But she rose onto her toes and reached up, aiming for a good smack upside his head. "Take it back."

"I take it back. I take it back." He grabbed her wrists in his big, strong hands. He held on to her, stopping her from taking another shot at him.

He was breathing hard. She was, too.

Suddenly, it dawned on her exactly how close they were

standing. Her chest was practically brushing his. Heat radiated off his body, soaking into hers, and out of nowhere,
she couldn't get enough air.

She darted her gaze to his. Surprise colored his eyes,
like he'd just realized the position they were in, too.

But he didn't let go.

Forget fluttering. Her whole chest was on fire. She was
dizzy with the unexpected rush of contact.

Of his gaze darting down to her lips.

A pang of wanting hit her so hard it took her breath
away. She looked to his mouth, too, red and soft. She'd
been dreaming about this since she was twelve, but this
was real. Devin James was really standing here with her,
looking at her.

"Zoe..."

Before he could move, a bright light suddenly blinded
them. Devin jerked away, shielding his eyes. Zoe cursed.

Right. Without her even really noticing, they'd arrived
at her house.

And the floodlights outside had just turned on.

Humiliated anger swept across her cheeks. She looked
at Devin, but he was backing up—fast.

"Sorry. Good grief, Zo."

"What—"

"You should go in." His throat bobbed as he gestured at
the house.

And it was hard to make out, given the glare of the
lights. But yeah. That was her mom standing just inside
the door.

She cursed beneath her breath. "Look—"

"You should go," he said again, firmer.

She wanted to laugh. Almost as much as she wanted
to cry.

Five seconds ago, he'd been looking at her like she was anything but the little girl she used to be. His gaze had been hot as fire, his hands grasping at her wrists like he had no intention of letting go. He'd been about to kiss her.

Her. A grown woman, fully capable of making her own decisions.

"Devin." She hated the shakiness in her voice.

"Keep the jacket," he told her, backing away. "I can grab it from Han. Later."

"Devin," she called again.

Regret flashed in his eyes.

And that was what did it.

She couldn't decide which was worse—him regretting getting caught or him regretting almost letting it happen in the first place. Either way, if he regretted it already?

It didn't matter how much she liked him—how much she had liked him since she was twelve freaking years old.

She deserved better than that.

He turned and walked away. She watched him go for a long minute.

Fuming, she turned and stormed toward the house. The door swung open before she could get to it, which only pissed her off more. With her mom holding the thing, she couldn't even slam it behind her.

"Late night," her mom observed.

"I've been home later." She worked at a bar, for Pete's sake.

"Zhaohui…"

She rounded on her mom. "Save it."

Her mom regarded her. Zoe was vibrating with anger. At her mom for interrupting. At Devin for walking away.

At every freaking person in her life who treated her like a kid, who didn't trust her to know her own mind.

Her mother made a soft *tut*ting sound in the back of her throat. She let the door swing closed. Lifting one brow, she leveled Zoe with her most skeptical gaze. "I hope you know what you're doing."

"Believe it or not, Mom," she gritted out, "I usually do."

Only in this case, even she wasn't sure that was true.

Chapter Seven

"Y ou want to talk about it?"

Devin looked up to find Arthur gazing at him across the worktable in the back of Harvest Home. He fought not to snap at him. Arthur didn't deserve any of his crap.

The only one who deserved that was himself.

"About what?"

Arthur just raised his brows, shifting his gaze pointedly to the mangled box Devin had been destroying in a vain effort to rip it open with his bare hands.

Okay, yeah, fine, so he was acting a little off.

Scrubbing his hand across his face, he grabbed the box cutter from the other side of the table and got back to work.

But Arthur wasn't going to leave this one alone. "Let me guess. Girl trouble."

Devin narrowly avoided slicing his finger off. Stupid. More carefully, he started again. "No."

"Boy trouble, then?"

Devin scrunched up his face in confusion. "What?"

"Never hurts to ask," Arthur said, waving away Devin's reaction. "Zoe yelled at me the other day, saying I'm too"—

he snapped his fingers a couple of times before finding the word—"'heteronormative.'"

"Believe me, I still like the ladies." There was nothing wrong with being gay, obviously, but Devin had known from day one that he was into women.

And what he was into right now, apparently, was a girl who was too young for him, a girl who got under his skin like nobody else. A girl who made it easy to talk about things he never talked about. His dad, his life, everything.

A girl with dark, sparkling eyes, silky hair, and the softest hands. A girl he'd come so close to ruining everything with on Sunday night.

He swallowed hard, putting down the knife and clenching his hands around the edges of the box. Ever since he'd been a kid, this place had been a second home to him. The Leung house had become a third. Arthur, Han, and everyone else in their family trusted him. How would they look at him if they found out he was having wildly inappropriate thoughts about the youngest member of their family?

What would happen if he got with Zoe for real? Even if everyone accepted it...if it didn't work out, if their relationship hit the rocks or went down in flames...

Arthur and Han cared about him. Deeply. But at the end of the day, faced with the decision, they'd choose their flesh and blood over some stray they'd taken in.

Acting on his attraction to Zoe was a nonstarter. It couldn't happen.

So why couldn't he stop thinking about it?

Even a couple of days later, he could feel her skin, smell the sweet scent of her wrapping around him and turning him inside out. In the driveway of the Leung house—right where he and Han used to hang out when they were kids, when Zoe was *literally* a kid—he'd been inches from kissing her. The moment they'd shared kept playing in his head on repeat, and all he could think was, what if those lights hadn't gone on? What if Zoe and Han's mom hadn't caught him ready to claim those soft, rose-colored lips?

When would he have stopped?

How much would he have risked?

He shook his head. Fury burned in his chest, almost as hot as his arousal whenever he let his mind drift back to that almost-kiss. He was an idiot to be even thinking about it, much less actively imagining it.

So why was he torturing himself like this?

And why was Arthur just sitting there instead of trying to get him to talk?

"Okay, fine," he exploded. He glared at Arthur. Patient bastard had always been good at waiting him out until he finally told on himself. "Let's say there is a particular lady in question."

Arthur set aside the inventory sheet he'd been working on and gave Devin his full attention. "Okay."

"But it's a terrible idea."

"Most love usually is," Arthur said with a sly smile.

Devin shook his head, gesturing wildly with his hands. "Like, natural disaster kind of terrible."

Arthur just raised his brows.

"Okay, fine, maybe not that bad, but bad. It would cause big problems."

"What sort of problems are we talking about? Legal trouble?"

"No." Though a half dozen years ago, it would have.

"Work trouble?"

"No."

"Then . . . ?"

Devin cast about for a second before landing on "Her family."

Of which Arthur was a member. This was so messed up.

"I can't believe they wouldn't approve of you."

"It's more complicated than that." Devin raked a hand through his hair. "But they'd have good reason to think it's a bad idea."

The Leungs had welcomed Devin with open arms. Here at Harvest Home, Arthur had taken Devin under his wing. As Han's best friend, Devin had free run of the Leung house. Sleepovers, afternoon hangouts. They trusted him.

Han trusted him. Han, who was so obsessed with keeping his family safe and secure. He'd always been protective of his baby sister. How many times had he confided in Devin about wanting to basically go check Zoe into a convent?

Devin hadn't been lusting after Zoe that entire time, but his attraction to her had grown and grown, from the spark he first felt at her high school graduation to this inferno now. The other night, first at Harvest Home and then later at the bar, he'd kept losing sight of who she was. She stopped being his best friend's sister or Arthur's niece. She'd become just...Zoe. Gorgeous, easy-to-talk-to, smart, funny, empathetic Zoe.

While Devin's thoughts spun out, Arthur kept regarding him with that steady, patient gaze of his. Finally, he sat back and exhaled long and low.

"Have I ever told you the story of how I ended up here?"

Only about a million times.

Devin managed not to thunk his head against the table. "Yeah."

"All of it?"

"I don't know," Devin said carefully.

"My family, when we came over, we started in San Francisco."

"Right."

"Moved to New York from there. It was crowded. Dirty. We worked hard, lived in a tiny apartment. Huilang and David and me with our parents." Huilang being Han, Lian, and Zoe's mom, and David their distant uncle.

"Okay..."

"I was the one who decided to set out and go somewhere else. Not an easy decision."

"I'm sure." There was no stopping Arthur now, so Devin strapped in for the ride.

"My father. He told me it would be big trouble if I left."

Devin perked up. This was a part of the story he hadn't heard before. "Really?"

Arthur nodded. "He had so many reasons it wouldn't work. He thought I was betraying the family by leaving them behind." He smiled, knowing and maybe just a little smug. "But I knew. There were more reasons to go. And you know what?"

"What?"

"I was right." He waved a hand around. "Look what I've been able to accomplish. I had a great career." He had, starting the Jade Garden restaurant. Socking away cash and making a whole series of unlikely investments that had enabled him to open this place and grow it year after year. "Brought my sister and her husband down here with me, and they've had happy lives. We all have."

"Okay..."

Arthur fixed him with a gaze like he could see right through Devin. Could he? Did he know more than he was letting on?

If he did, he kept it to himself. "You can't let fear push

you around. Worrying about what other people will think, what other people will do. It leaves you miserable. This girl—if she means enough to you, you go to her. You find a way to make it work. No matter what anybody else says, you hear me?"

For a split second, Devin considered it. He let go of all his concerns about Han and Arthur and Zoe's mom.

He let himself imagine going for it. Being with Zoe. Having her in his arms, talking to her the way he had the other night. Celebrating a great game of pool with a kiss.

Taking her to his bed.

A jolt of electricity zipped down his spine.

Yeah. He wanted that. All of it.

But before he could really talk himself into believing he could have it, a deep voice broke in.

"Wait—Devin's got a girl?"

All the hope that had started to rise in Devin's chest came crashing down. He turned to find Han in the doorway.

Right. Crap. It was Tuesday. Han or his mom or both—they always came by in the late afternoon.

Stupid. How could he have forgotten? How could he have asked Arthur of all people about Zoe—even in the most veiled of terms?

How could he have imagined this could work?

He forced out a laugh, but it was hollow to his own ears. "Nah, man. Me and Arthur—we were just talking."

Devin stood up, anxious, restless energy making it impossible to sit.

"Really?" Han asked, setting down a crate of leftover produce from the restaurant before wiping his brow. "Because it sounded like—"

Mercifully, Arthur stepped in to save him. "Your friend. He was talking in"—he cleared his throat—"hypotheticals."

Devin directed an appreciative glance his way. Leave it to Arthur to make Devin sound innocent without telling a single untruth.

But Han wasn't going to be deterred. "I don't know, man." He sized Devin up. "You have been a little weird lately."

"Work stuff." That wasn't an untruth, either. Taking over as shift leader had been great, but it had come with all the headaches he'd assumed it would.

Namely managing Bryce Horton.

But he wasn't here to complain about Bryce. Especially when Han was still regarding Devin with suspicion, and Devin was trying not to sweat.

Finally, Han gave him a playful shove on his shoulder. "Well, whoever the *hypothetical* girl is, I hope you win her over. Your dry spell has been going on for *way* too long."

"Like you're one to talk."

Han's gaze darkened. The fact he hadn't had a serious long-term relationship since he and May broke up after high school was a sore spot, and Devin had aimed right for it. "Whatever. Keep your secrets."

"No secrets to tell." And he was going to make sure it stayed that way. Needing some air after that close call, he grabbed a stack of inventory forms they'd already gotten through. "Gotta hit the head. I'll swing these by the front office."

"Thanks," Arthur said.

Han got to work. Relieved there wasn't going to be any more third degree, Devin headed out.

He had an ulterior motive for swinging past the office anyway.

The second Zoe came into view, his heart did something funny in his chest. She looked as beautiful as ever. She had when he'd first arrived, too.

She'd avoided his gaze in a way that was new, though. There'd been no flirty banter. She hadn't gotten in his space. She definitely hadn't come close enough for him to slip up and almost kiss her, and that was a good thing.

So why did it feel so awful?

Arthur hadn't known all the facts, so his advice hadn't been right, but there was one area where he'd been on the nose. Zoe did mean something to Devin. That meant he had to make this work between them. Not the kissing part, but the rest of it. He'd really started to think they were becoming friends. He wanted her, sure, but he also just plain liked her.

If almost kissing her meant losing her smiles and the way she looked at him and talked to him, then he'd screwed up worse than he'd realized. He had to make it right. Fast, before he messed this up for good.

He walked right up to the desk and put the inventory sheets in the bin. She glanced up at him. Her eyes sparkled for a second before darkening. Glowering, she looked away.

No smile. No "hello," even.

Guilt churned in his gut. She really was mad, and she had every right to be.

"You have a minute?" he asked. He couldn't keep the urgency out of his tone.

"Nope."

"Come on, Zo." He reached for her hand, only for her to snap it away.

"Uh-uh. No way." She darted her gaze around, but they were definitely alone out here. She still lowered her voice. "You of all people do not get to do what you almost did on Sunday night and then 'Zo' me."

Anger flashed in her gaze, only it was more than that.

She was trying to hide it, but she was hurt.

Was it possible to feel even worse?

"Just hear me out," he begged.

She narrowed her eyes. "Fine."

Crossing her arms over her chest, she stared up at him, fire and defiance in her gaze, and that really shouldn't get him feeling hot under the collar, but it did.

He didn't care that she'd just verified that they were alone. He did the same thing she had, glancing around, but he couldn't talk to her like this, one eye constantly looking over his shoulder.

"Come on."

He tipped his head toward the spare office behind the desk. Keeping her feet planted, she cocked a brow at him, and he shot a glance skyward before holding out a hand. "Please?"

With a gruff sigh, she rolled her eyes but then consented to follow him. Once they were both inside, he closed the door and flipped the lock.

He turned to look at her. Her posture was still closed and defensive, and he hated that. But what could he do? How could he get them back to the place they'd been the other night—all smiles and quiet confidences—without going too far?

"Look, Zoe." He was making this up as he went along, barreling ahead without a plan. "I'm sorry. Really."

"For what?" She tipped her chin up, the stubborn set to her jaw driving him to distraction. She started counting things off on her fingers. "For almost kissing me? Because if so, screw you. Or for jumping away from me like I'm a leper? Because if so, also screw you." She started advancing on him, her voice rising. "Or for treating me like a freaking child, the way everybody in my life does?" She was right in his space again, her eyes on fire. "Because if so"—she reached out and jabbed him in the chest—"screw"—she did it again—"you."

He grabbed her by the hand, and oh no. This was too much like the other night. She'd been swatting at him for his teasing then. She was righteously angry now. Guilt churned in his stomach, but his skin was prickling, her hand warm in his. He stroked his thumb over her palm, holding on even though he should let her go.

He should walk right out of this office. Out of this building and maybe off a short pier, but her cheeks were flushed, her eyes bright, and her soft red lips so wet and kissable, he was losing his mind.

"I can't," he said. "Your brother—"

"Isn't my keeper." She went softer against him, some of the anger fading out of her.

And it was like he couldn't stop himself.

He drifted closer to her, erasing the gap between them, licks of flame darting across his skin. "I don't want to be a bad guy."

He didn't want to take advantage. He didn't want to mess things up between them and lose the fragile friendship they'd been building—the one that had already come to mean so much to him.

What could they even have together besides friendship? Her time here in Blue Cedar Falls was clearly a stopgap. She was on her way to bigger and better things. His biggest goal in life was a house in the woods alone. If they crossed this line, it would change things forever. With her. With her family.

Keeper or not, he didn't want to violate Han's trust.

She gazed up into his eyes. The liquid brown of her irises melted something inside him. Reaching up, she grazed her fingertips across his cheek.

"You're not a bad guy, Devin." Her hand settled tentatively on the side of his neck, and the intimacy of it was almost too much. "I've been back home for months, and I swear you're the first person who's made me feel like you're actually listening to me. You care. A lot." She shook her head gently. "Bad guys don't do that."

He swallowed, scarcely able to think with her so close. Without his permission, his arm moved to wrap around her, and that felt so good. She was practically flush against him, warm and soft and smelling like heaven.

All his resolutions went up in smoke.

"This is a terrible idea," he rasped.

"Probably."

Then she rose onto her toes.

He was going to hell, because he met her halfway. Their mouths crashed together, and that was it. Something snapped inside him. Hauling her in against him, he let himself really feel her. Light exploded behind his eyes. Forget all his worries about the fact that she used to be a kid to him—Zoe Leung was all woman now. Her soft curves fit to his body like they were made to press together. She kissed like the spitfire she was, opening to him, nipping at his lips with her teeth, sucking on his tongue.

Groaning, he picked her up and sat her on the edge of the desk. This whole place was a disaster—the place they put stuff when they didn't know where it should go. Something clattered to the floor, but he didn't care. With a hand at the back of his neck, she reeled him in, and he went so happily. He lost his mind to the heat of her mouth, the warmth of her hips in his hands. Scooting backward on the desk, she folded her legs around him.

Alarm bells went off in his head.

What was he doing?

He tore himself away, only for her to drag him back in.

"Zoe," he gasped, kissing her again, but he had to stop.

She raked her nails through his scalp. "If you say one word about my stupid brother, I swear—"

"No." He laughed. "Just no."

But as he drew away, the kiss-bitten redness of her lips, her tousled hair, and her flushed cheeks told him the truth. They'd crossed a line. He knew how she tasted now, how perfectly she fit in his arms.

There was no going back.

But he wasn't a complete idiot.

"My place," he panted. "Not here."

She hooked her ankles behind his rear and pulled him in, and he saw stars.

He pulled away again and fixed her with a gaze that brooked no argument. "Not here."

She pouted, breathing hard, but she released him. He stepped away, and she hopped down off the table.

"Fine," she relented. She narrowed her eyes at him, but her voice shook. "No take-backs, though, okay?" She reached up to tap him on the head. "Don't overthink this."

Yeah. Like that was going to happen.

He grabbed her hand again. But instead of brushing her away, he held her gaze and brought the back of her palm to his mouth.

"No take-backs." He kissed the soft skin of her knuckles.

And seriously. He was going to hell.

But if the smoldering look in her eyes was any indication? It was going to be worth the ride.

Chapter Eight

Nervous anticipation and wary disbelief warred in Zoe's gut as she pulled up to Devin's building an hour later. Staying at Harvest Home and finishing the tasks she usually enjoyed had been pure torture—especially when Devin had slipped out. The dark look he'd given her on his way to the door had made her clench down deep inside.

But he'd been hot and cold over the past few days, to say nothing of the past few years. She had no idea what she was walking into here.

Still half expecting him to have changed his mind again, she got out of the car and headed up the walk. Bubbles formed and popped inside her chest. She was trying to keep her expectations in check, but his kiss had set her on fire. An hour of waiting had only stoked the flame. By the time she hit the top of the stairs, she was a riot of desire and nerves—if he turned her away after all that, she really was going to deck him. She reached the apartment number he'd given her, lifted her hand, and curled it into a fist. She took a deep breath, then steeled up her nerve and knocked.

The door swung open instantly.

Behind it stood Devin, and Zoe's stomach did a loop-the-loop.

Good grief, he was gorgeous. His sandy-brown hair was all mussed, exactly the way she wanted it to be after she'd been raking her hands through it all night. If it was possible, his jaw was sharper, the scruff there even more masculine. He stood there in a T-shirt and jeans, his feet bare on the hardwood.

His eyes shone midnight black with want, and just like that, all the doubt disappeared from her mind.

"Devin—"

"C'mere."

He reached into the space between them to drag her in.

She crashed into him with the same passionate, desperate need that had overcome them in the back office of Harvest Home. The kisses were just that bright and stinging, and she couldn't get enough. The door slammed closed behind her. With all his bulk, Devin pressed her into it, and oh *God*.

She'd known he was ripped, but feeling all that hard muscle awakened a need inside her. Wrapping her arms around his neck, she used what leverage she had to climb his body, and he helped her, lifting her up. She curled her legs around him.

The hot bulge of him against her center sent fireworks off inside her. He let out a noise that was pure sex as they ground together. She'd never gone from zero to sixty so fast. She was dizzy with it, barely able to think.

He moved them away from the door, holding on to her as he turned to carry her through his apartment.

She got only the most glancing impression of the place. It was neat but spare, no pictures on the wall. A plain beige couch, a glass coffee table, and a sage-green rug.

And then she didn't have time to even think about his

interior decorating, because that was his bedroom door he was hauling her through.

She pulsed deep inside as he practically tossed her down onto the big bed. He stood over her for a long moment, breath coming hard. Her entire body flushed. She liked being seen like this, liked the dark glint in his piercing eyes as he ran his broad hands along the tops of her thighs.

But the moment stretched and stretched. That same nervous flutter from earlier returned. "No take-backs?" she reminded him. She hated how it came out like a question.

He inhaled deeply. Then he nodded. "No take-backs."

Resolved, he climbed on top of her. As he kissed her again, slower this time, she wanted to pinch herself. There was no hesitation in him, and when she put her hands on his skin, under the hem of his shirt, he pushed into her touch. This wasn't some frantic, impulsive rush.

This was real.

Savoring every moment, she opened to him, curling her legs around his hips. The hot weight of his body settled over her. Every lick of his tongue and scrape of his teeth across her lips set her ablaze. Molten desire bubbled up inside her, and she wanted to take her time, but she couldn't wait.

She pushed his shirt up. Rising onto his knees, he grabbed the fabric by the back of the neck and tore it off, and holy crap. His muscles had muscles, all of him golden tan and smooth. A trail of hair led down to the button of his jeans, and she had to stop herself from ripping those open right away, too.

When he kissed her again, it was with a new intensity. A flash of burning arousal shot through her when his rough hands dipped beneath her top. She helped him take it off. Her bra followed, and he groaned.

"I've been trying not to think about these for so long." He buried his face in her breasts, and she laughed.

It didn't stay funny for long. Not when his hot mouth sealed over that tender flesh. Aching for more, she arched into him, running her fingers through his hair. Everything he did felt so good. Triumph had her flying high.

Until he started kissing lower down her abdomen.

"Devin," she moaned when he got to the waistband of her leggings.

Staring her straight in the eyes, he pressed one firm kiss to the very center of her through the fabric, and she practically came right then and there.

She reached for him.

He raced back up her body, sucking and biting at her all the way. As soon as he was close enough, she kissed him hot and deep, scrambling at his fly. She finally ripped it open and pushed his jeans and underwear down. The hot, hard length of him sprang free, and they groaned as one. He was huge in her hands, and she still couldn't believe this was happening.

As she stroked him, he tore at her clothes, too. She kicked off her boots, and it was all a mad dash until they were both naked. He paused just long enough to get a condom on. When he lined himself up, she had no doubts.

Still, he paused. "Zo..."

She sucked in a breath. Cupping his face in her hands, she brought his lips to hers for another, softer kiss.

"I want this," she promised him, and it was too true. With emotion she couldn't name, she told him, "I want you."

He closed his eyes.

His body sinking into hers turned her inside out. He felt so perfect as he ground against her, sending sparks surging through her.

"Zo," he repeated.

"I'm here." She was babbling. What was she saying? "I'm here, I'm here, I want you. I want this."

He pulled back, and she pushed into him until they fell into a rhythm. Pleasure started at the apex of her thighs, spreading outward until all she could see and feel and touch and taste was him. Over and over he drove into her, faster. She scrabbled at him, running her hands all up and down his back and shoulders.

"Zoe, Zo, I can't—you feel so good—"

"Devin, come on, please, I want—"

He slammed into her another half dozen times.

Her climax tore through her out of nowhere. Her vision flashed to black, and she squeezed every part of herself around him. Driving in deep, he called her name a final time. He pulsed inside her, and her entire world shattered.

Because this was *real*. She'd had sex with Devin James.

What had started as a challenge to see if she could get him to break had turned into a breaking down of her conception of the natural order of the universe.

She still had no real delusions that this could be more than a fling, but the impossible had already happened the instant he'd touched his lips to hers.

As she stared up at his ceiling in wonder, she pressed a hand to the center of his back.

Who knew? Maybe all her notions of what she could and couldn't have in this world were wrong.

Chapter Nine

W atch out!"

At the sound of Terrell's shout, Devin jerked his gaze up from his clipboard.

Half his people were raising a section of the house's frame, Terrell and Gene up on ladders while the rest supported and spotted from below, only something wasn't right. Devin shot to his feet, gaze swinging wildly, the entire site going into slow motion. There—crap.

Off to the side, Bryce had let go prematurely, and Devin lurched forward, calling his name, but it was too late. Terrell's grip slipped without anyone to back him up.

The whole thing came crashing down.

Devin raced over. "Is everybody okay?"

"Yeah." Terrell scrubbed a hand over his face.

Devin checked in with everybody else, and no one had gotten hurt, thank goodness. He appraised the rest of the scene. The damage to the section that had fallen wasn't that bad, either, but it was still going to set them back a couple of hours—and that was before the headache of writing this up.

"I swore I had it," Terrell said, climbing down. His eyes narrowed as he glared silently off to the left.

Following his gaze, Devin flexed his jaw. He patted Terrell on the back. "It's just about lunch time anyway. Take a break, and then we'll get this cleaned up afterward."

He and the rest of the crew nodded.

Reassured that they were all okay, Devin stalked to the other side of the building, grinding his teeth together hard enough to crack.

A week had passed since he'd moved up to shift leader, and for the most part it had been going great. The team listened to him, and he'd handled the couple of issues that had arisen without much trouble.

Except Bryce.

Mostly it was little things like unauthorized breaks or screwing around on his phone when he was supposed to be working. Some of it was more serious, like using inappropriate language when talking to the women on the crew. Devin had documented it all, slowly building a case that even the folks who protected him couldn't ignore.

But this?

"Horton," he growled.

Bryce looked up from his phone. "What?"

"Don't 'what' me." Devin wanted to grab the guy's phone and chuck it in the cement mixer, only that would make a defect in the next house's foundation. Workers on the site weren't forbidden from being on them or anything; this wasn't high school. But when your eyes and hands needed to be on the job, they needed to be on the job. "Where were you?"

"Right there." He gestured toward where the crash had happened. "Weren't you watching?"

Old anxiety rose in Devin. His dad used to do that, too—reframing everything to make it out like Devin was the one to blame. He had to remind himself that wasn't true today.

Devin had been doing his job, keeping an eye on his team while also seeing to the rest of his duties. "You weren't paying attention, and somebody could've gotten hurt."

Bryce rolled his eyes. "Terrell's butterfingers aren't my fault."

Forget a headache; the incident report was going to be a full-on migraine. Enough other people would back Devin and Terrell up that Bryce had been the one to let go, but the fact of the matter was that this never should have happened in the first place.

"You not doing your job is your fault." Devin kept his voice restrained but barely. "I'm not going to turn a blind eye to this BS."

"Sure you won't." Bryce's smile was mocking as he patted Devin on the shoulder.

Devin shoved him off automatically. He clenched and unclenched his jaw.

He walked away, hating the hot feeling in his chest and the hotter one in his face. The sense of helplessness ate at him, making him feel like he was twelve years old all over again.

Sure, he'd document this entire thing, but there was no satisfaction in that.

How did he protect his people? Stop giving Bryce any jobs where he could put the other members of his crew at risk? Stop giving him jobs at all? Bryce would love that.

The unfairness made him want to punch something.

Instead, he drew in a few deep breaths, trying to calm himself down before getting back to it.

On impulse, he popped his phone out of his pocket for the first time all morning. A handful of alerts greeted him, and he scrolled through them. When he got to the couple of texts from Zoe, the remaining tension bled out of his body, and he couldn't hold back the warm smile that curled his lips.

Ugh, remind me why I'm shacking up with a morning person again? I need coffee and it's all the way over theeeeerre

A photo came with the message, showing her in his bed, her hair a mess where it lay splayed out across his sheets, and he had to suck in a breath. There wasn't a single inappropriate thing about the shot, but it didn't matter. The sight of her, all rumpled and gorgeous and soft from sleep...It did things to him.

He just wished he could be there to take advantage of it. To roll her over and kiss that red mouth until they were both breathless.

Or maybe—if it was a day when he wasn't working...to go make her coffee. Pancakes. Breakfast in bed.

He mentally shook his head at himself. What a sap.

A week now they'd been doing...whatever it was they were doing together. Giving in to the overwhelming force of attraction between them had been the easiest thing in the world. When she was around, it was like all his worries disappeared.

He'd thought it would be weird, going from her brother's best friend to her friend to maybe something more, but it hadn't been. At all.

They'd never had to have any intense conversations about what was going on between them, either. Even that first time, when he'd been nervous about risking everything for a night of fun, it was like she'd been able to see right through him. Proving just how well she knew him, she'd just climbed right back on top of him and kissed him senseless, then wandered naked into his kitchen to fix herself a sandwich. She'd called out to ask if he wanted anything, too. Casual—like it was the most normal thing. And you know, he had been kind of hungry after working up an appetite like that.

So she'd just slipped into his life. When they weren't having mind-blowing sex, they were sharing takeout pizza or introducing each other to their favorite shows. He still wasn't quite sold on *The Bachelor*, but watching her yelling at the TV made him grin, and she was surprisingly receptive to reruns of *This Old House* playing in the background the rest of the time.

His crummy, boring apartment felt warm when she was in it. So warm that he almost forgot for hours at a time that his entire goal in life was to build his house in the woods and get out of here.

His only regret was the same one she had. She worked nights and he worked days, and so there she was waking up at—he checked the time stamp on the message—ten in the morning, while he was up at six.

Shaking his head at himself, he tapped out a quick reply. *Wish I could've gone and grabbed you one.*

Her answer came seconds later. *It's ok, I managed.*

The picture that followed was of her at Bobbi's bakery on Main Street. She was seated at one of the little tables inside, a latte and an empty plate set next to her open laptop.

His smile faded slightly. She'd kicked it up a notch on the job search of late. That or, now that he got regular updates about her life, he was just more aware of it.

Every time she talked about it, a little pit formed in his stomach. Which was stupid. He'd known from the minute she moved back home that it was temporary. She was only here until the right opportunity came along, and he could be a big enough man to hope it showed up for her soon.

Even if, deep down, he never wanted her to leave.

"Hey, James." Bryce's voice had Devin jerking his gaze up. "Your girlfriend's here."

For a second, Devin's heart lurched into his throat.

No way. Zoe had just texted him from the bakery, and even if she hadn't—they hadn't exactly talked about it, but the one time he'd tried to bring up how he'd prefer to keep whatever they were doing together quiet, at least for the time being, she'd just rolled her eyes.

"Don't worry. Your secret is safe with me," she'd said before kissing his cheek. "My brother murdering you would be a real bummer."

And then she'd started kissing *other* parts of him, and well, that'd been the end of that.

Long story short, she wouldn't just show up at his work unannounced, and Bryce wouldn't know to call her his girlfriend.

Before he could work himself up any further worrying, he spotted Han's car in the lot—not Zoe's. Relief swept over him, even as a new kind of nervousness started to intrude.

Flipping Bryce off for being a homophobic prick, he started crossing the site toward the lot. As he approached, Han got out of his car and held up one of the same chopped-up liquor boxes he used for Jade Garden deliveries, and Devin managed a smile.

"Hey, buddy," Han said as he hauled the food over to the picnic table by the trailer, where they usually ate.

"Hey."

He and Han did this once a week or so. Their schedules didn't match up much better than Devin's and Zoe's. Lunch on the job site was one of the easier ways to get together most weeks.

As Han started unpacking the containers he'd brought,

Devin pulled apart a couple of paper plates. His stomach growled as the mouthwatering scents of whatever Han had cooked up today hit him.

"The mango pork's new," Han said. "And I tweaked the ginger on the veggies."

"Yeah?"

Han might've had to drop out of culinary school when his dad died, but you'd never know it. He cooked all day, and then he cooked some more on his days off. He tried out new recipes—fancy "fusion" stuff that he and his mom had agreed didn't fit with the Jade Garden's brand, though he did manage to sneak a few of the tamer test recipes into the Chef's Specials "secret menu" now and then.

As Han plated up the food, he tipped his head toward the guys eating sandwiches and leftovers at the other tables. "So, how's it going?"

Devin rolled his eyes. "Same as usual."

"AKA, Bryce is being a jerk?"

Devin glared, but he knew there had been no one close enough to hear Han. "Yeah, pretty much."

Han scooped meat and vegetables onto a bed of noodles, then went ahead and sprinkled sesame seeds and scallions and drizzled some sort of orange sauce over it all, because the parking lot of a construction site was a five-star restaurant in his eyes. He passed the plate over, and Devin smacked his lips.

"I'm telling you." Han opened a set of wooden chopsticks and pointed them at Devin. "You gotta stand up to guys like him."

The same old discomfort churned in Devin's gut, but he pushed it down. "Sure, just like you did with all the mean kids back in high school."

"Shut up, man."

Neither of them had gotten picked on too badly when they were kids. Han stuck out, one of maybe four Asian kids in the school at the time, but he'd been as charming then as he was now—the bastard. Devin had held his own. He never started any fights, but when any came his way, he finished them. The two of them and the rest of the gang they ran with—they were fine.

But Han's girlfriend, May, had gotten savaged by the mean girl squad. She acted like it was no big deal, but whatever had happened, it had been bad enough that May had taken off after graduation. She'd come back for Han's dad's funeral and a visit or two here and there, and that was it.

Han scowled and nodded at Devin's food. "So? You gonna eat or just give me crap about things that happened a decade ago?"

"Like I can't do both." He tore open his own chopsticks. He'd never be as good with them as Han was, but he managed okay. He eyed the food. "Nice presentation."

"Obviously."

He tried the pork first, because how could he not.

"Get some mango with it," Han urged him.

Devin raised a brow. He didn't ignore the advice, though. He scooped up a noodle for good measure and shoveled the whole thing into his mouth.

His eyes slipped closed and he thumped his fist onto the table.

"Uh..."

"Shh." Devin put a finger to his sealed lips as he chewed. Once he swallowed, he opened his eyes.

"Well?"

"Man, that's good." Salty and sweet, rich but not heavy.

"The mango really makes it, huh?"

"Yup."

"You getting the garlic?"

"Uh-huh."

"But not too much."

"Close—I wouldn't do any more. But seriously. It's a keeper."

"Try the veg."

Devin forced himself to stop cramming delicious, delicious pork in his face. The vegetable was some weird green thing Han had been messing around with. It'd been a little bitter for his taste last time, but it'd probably go pretty well with the pork. He gave it a shot and nodded. "Yup. Cutting the ginger helped a lot."

"Thought so." Han flashed a smug, ever-so-slightly-secretive smile as he dug into his own plate.

"What're you up to?"

"Nothing."

"Yeah, I don't buy it."

Han had always had fun messing around with new recipes, but he'd been more intense about it of late. There was definitely something going on.

"You don't have to." Then his smirk deepened. "But maybe someday someone will."

Devin put down his chopsticks. "You aren't finally doing it."

Han had always idly talked about opening his own restaurant. It never came to anything, though. He was too busy at the family business.

"No." Han shook his head. "Not yet. But let's just say I'm working on something that might be a first step."

"Okay, you keep your secrets. As long as you keep the awesome grub coming, too."

Chuckling, Han nodded. "That I can do." He took a bite

of his own lunch and seemed pleased. "Speaking of which, I've got a few other things I'm ready to guinea pig. Dinner at my place tomorrow?"

Normally, Devin would jump at the chance, but heading to the Leung house made all the hairs stand up on the back of his neck. He cleared his throat. "Who all's going to be there?"

"Does it matter? Free grub, remember."

"I know. I'm just asking."

Han shrugged. "Bobbi and Caitlin probably. Clay if I can pry him away from the Junebug for a minute, and you know he'll want to bring June." He listed the names of a couple of other guys they hung out with regularly. Then he grimaced. "I think Zoe has the night off, so she'll probably invite herself."

"Oh?" Devin's voice came out strangled to his own ears.

"Maybe. Who knows."

Not good enough. But he couldn't probe any deeper without sounding suspicious. He rummaged around in his brain, trying to think of excuses why he couldn't go, but he came up with squat.

Zoe was a firecracker. She said their secret was safe with her, but she loved to push him, and he had to admit it—he kind of loved it when she did. But interacting with her at their family home, with Han right there? What lines would get blurred?

It wasn't just her he didn't trust. His fingers twitched. He was getting too comfortable hanging out at his apartment with her. They spent half their time naked or snuggled up or both. Reaching out and putting his hand over hers and pulling her into him was becoming second nature.

Would he be the one to slip up and give them away?

Oblivious to Devin twisting himself into knots, Han

pursed his lips. "Then again, she's been going out a lot recently."

"Yeah?" Devin's throat threatened to close again.

"It's super weird. She bummed around the house all the time when she first moved back in, but now it's like she's never there. I think she's sneaking out at night, too."

Devin tried not to choke on a piece of mango and pork. He coughed into a napkin.

"You okay?" Han asked.

No.

"Yeah, yeah." Fighting both to breathe and to come off as casual, Devin asked, "Is it really sneaking, though? She's in her twenties, right?"

"Fine, fine, whatever. It's still weird. I didn't think she had a lot of friends around here." He narrowed his eyes. "I'm pretty sure she's not dating anybody."

"Maybe she's just working late? The Junebug is a bar."

"Maybe." Han frowned. "You're right—it's none of my business. I just hope she's not doing anything stupid."

Devin's stomach flopped around inside his abdomen.

She was doing something stupid all right.

Namely him.

"I'm sure it's nothing," he lied.

Only he wasn't so sure of that.

He wasn't so sure at all.

———

"So...do you want me to stay away?" Zoe had her back turned to Devin as she brushed her hair, but her gaze flicked to his in the bathroom mirror.

He was a little groggy, still splayed out on the mattress, naked and boneless. She hadn't had to close the bar tonight, so she'd come over after her shift, which was great—he loved seeing her. But it was past his bedtime, and that last round had been particularly athletic.

There was something in her voice that told him he needed to pay attention, though.

He rose onto his elbows and rummaged around in his skull for enough brain cells to rub together. "What do you mean? It's your house."

Their pillow talk had inevitably turned to a discussion of the dinner party Han was holding at the Leung house. She'd seemed surprised to hear he was trying to find a way out of it.

"Yeah," she allowed. She set down her brush—one of a couple of her things that had somehow found a home for themselves in his bathroom this week—and came back over to the bed. As if she could tell that he wasn't at his best when she wasn't wearing any clothes, she pulled the covers up over her chest. "But Han is your best friend. I don't want to get in the way of that."

He wasn't quite tired or stupid enough to laugh. He'd only resisted her as long as he had because he hadn't been willing to risk Han's friendship or Arthur's welcome. Of course his being with her now was going to affect his relationship with her family.

He reached for her hand and held it in his, running his thumb along the lines of her palm. He should be stressing out right now, but it was hard to be anything but relaxed when it was just the two of them. She made talking about his feelings easy in a way no one ever had. "You aren't in the way. I'm just nervous he'll catch on to something being weird between us."

"Yeah…"

He closed his fingers around hers more firmly. "You know I don't like keeping this secret, right?"

"I know." She wasn't looking at him, though.

"It's just..."

"I get it. I'm probably not going to be here for long." She huffed out a breath and pitched her voice higher, putting on the fake-happy smile she always used when talking about her job search. "Fifteen more applications submitted today." She deflated back to a more natural tone. "No point rocking the boat for something temporary, right?"

Sourness coated the back of his tongue. This was good, them being clear with each other like this. It was smart and mature.

So why did he hate it so much?

He couldn't bring himself to agree with her, so he barreled on. "Look, I don't want you to feel like you have to stay away."

"And I don't want you to feel like you do."

"So we won't," he decided. "We'll both go—if that's what you want to do. And we'll just try to be normal. It'll probably be fine."

Her expression finally brightened. "Sure. We can do this."

"Of course we can."

"So, what do you think?" She scooted closer to him, and he breathed a little easier. "Does Han just keep living with our mom out of sheer martyrdom? Or is it because he's using her for her kitchen?"

Devin tipped his head back and laughed. Leave it to Zoe not to mince words. "He'd probably say it's to take care of your mom and save money."

"Martyrdom." She poked his arm with her index finger.

He took her hand in his and kissed her knuckles. "But you might be onto something with the kitchen." Devin had helped them redo it back a few years ago. "He'd never find an apartment with one as nice."

Gazing down at their joined hands, Zoe asked, "What about at your loner house in the woods? Any plans to build a giant kitchen there that he can use?"

"It'd be worth it just for the free food," he mused. But he shook his head. "I don't know. It's going to be a small place. Just me kicking around it."

"You don't think there'd ever be anybody else?" she asked quietly.

The question settled on him heavily. She was still studiously looking down. He brushed her hair back from her face, but it didn't let him see her eyes any better.

The answer should be simple. His whole life, he'd been dreaming of the day he could have a home of his own.

He glanced over at the bathroom, though. At the hairbrush and the toothbrush and the little bottles of lotion and soap.

He shrugged, noncommittal. "How about you? Gorgeous kitchen a must-have for your Realtor when you land your dream job?"

He kept his voice light, but forget heavy. This question sank inside him like a stone.

"Nah." She put her head on his shoulder. "It's not like Han would ever leave to come visit me."

I would, Devin didn't say. But her kitchen wouldn't have a thing to do with it.

Silence hung between them for a minute. He twisted his neck to press a kiss to her temple, but before he could come up with anything smart to say, a yawn snuck out of him.

She laughed and kissed him back before ruffling his hair. "Come on. Let's get you to bed. You have incident reports to write in the morning."

"Don't remind me," he groaned, flopping backward into his pillow.

She got up and turned off the lights, and wow, she was so great. As she slipped back into the bed beside him, he curled his arms around her. Even the prospect of dealing with more paperwork and more people letting Bryce off the hook couldn't bring him down.

Nope. Apparently, the only thing that could do that was the reminder that his time with her was temporary.

Which sucked. Because he was pretty sure he was going to get even more of those when he was pretending not to be sleeping with her at Han's party tomorrow night.

Chapter Ten

Y'all—don't even get me started on weird customers." June held a hand in front of herself, palm out.

Zoe raised a brow and took another sip of her wine.

Ten minutes into Han's dinner party, she, June, and June's friend Bobbi were standing around the island in the center of the kitchen, trading work stories. Over by the stove, Han prepped ingredients while trying to keep Ling-Ling from stealing any of them—with mixed success. Between fond rebukes to the dog, he kept a light conversation going with Clay, Bobbi's girlfriend, Caitlin, and a couple of guy friends.

"Ooh." Bobbi rubbed her hands together. "This is going to be good."

June smiled. "Let's just say there's a reason the Sweetbriar Inn now has an official policy prohibiting birds."

Zoe snickered, but before June could dive any deeper into whatever guest at her family's B&B had prompted that new rule, the doorbell rang, setting Ling-Ling off.

Zoe's pulse raced, and she put her glass down with a thunk. "I'll get it!"

"Seriously," Han called after her, "nobody's fighting you for it except the dog."

And okay, yeah, she was a little eager, racing to get the

door each time a new person arrived. But this time, she had extra reason to run. Devin was the only person they were still waiting for. This had to be him.

She skidded to a stop in the entryway, making sure her body was blocking Ling-Ling from getting out before flinging open the door.

And there Devin was. All six-foot-something glorious inches of him, his cheeks flushed from the chill outside, his blue eyes sparkling, and what was it about the way he lit up when his gaze fell on her? Her heart pounded, her ribs squeezing around it.

Her over-the-top reaction made no sense. He was just a guy, and she was in a weird, temporary place in her life. They'd basically agreed that whatever they were doing together was just for fun. The very sight of him shouldn't turn her to goo.

But she liked him so much.

She cast one backward glance over her shoulder before closing the door and launching herself at him. He caught her in his arms. Pausing only to set down the six-pack he'd brought, he pressed her into the freezing-cold siding of the house, and she didn't care about the temperature or the fact that he was so worried about getting caught.

His mouth was hot as it covered hers, his tongue commanding. She kissed him back with a hunger that had nothing to do with the promise of the upcoming meal. Running her hands through his hair, she soaked up every second of contact with him.

It wasn't enough. He jerked away, his breath coming fast, the darkness in his gaze pure torture considering what was coming next. "We should—"

"Go make out some more in your truck?" she suggested helpfully.

He buried his face in her shoulder, and she wrapped her arms around him as tightly as she could. "Don't tempt me, woman."

"Why not?" She gazed up at the stars and breathed him in. "It's so much fun."

"For you, maybe," he said, but there was a hint of darkness in his tone.

The corners of her mouth turned down. "I was just messing around."

"I know." Did he, though?

The mood broken, he gave her one last quick peck before letting go.

Stepping away, he gestured at his face. "Do I have any . . . ?"

"Just—" She reached up on her toes to swipe at the little smudge of lipstick at the corner of his mouth. Considering how they'd just been sticking their tongues down each other's throats, it wasn't bad. This long-wearing stuff was the best.

"Thanks."

"No problem."

He picked up the beer he'd set down and they headed inside. She stole another glance at him under the entryway light as he stopped to give Ling-Ling a quick scratch behind the ear. There was no sign that anything was amiss. The way she'd run her fingers through his hair could have easily been the wind. No one would know.

She tried to remind herself that that was a good thing.

"I'll, uh, show you where to put your coat." She started to lead him down the hall.

"Please," her brother scoffed, appearing at the top of the half flight of stairs. "It's just Devin. He knows." Han smiled at Devin. "What's up, man?"

"Nothing," Devin replied.

"Was starting to think you'd gotten lost out there."

"Nah." Devin brushed past her. Out of her brother's sight line, he gave her fingers a reassuring squeeze before continuing on. He held up the six-pack. "Almost forgot these in the truck and had to run back for them."

"Nice." Han accepted the beers.

But as Zoe followed Han and Devin into the kitchen, she caught June gazing at her appraisingly. Crap—she'd checked Devin for lipstick smudges but she hadn't checked herself. She casually glanced at her reflection in the hallway mirror. Nope—she was basically okay.

Well, whatever. June could give her weird looks if she wanted to. Zoe wasn't going to act like she had anything to hide.

To prove it, she snagged a fried wonton strip off one of the appetizer plates. She dragged it through the plum sauce dip and popped it in her mouth. She really didn't know what that was supposed to prove, but it was freaking delicious, so it didn't matter.

Around her, all signs showed this to be a successful dinner party. Han was doing his thing, cooking and putting on a show. If it weren't so clichéd—and if they were Japanese instead of Chinese—he could've had a heck of a career at one of those hibachi places.

Zoe shook her head, trying not to stare at Devin, who had joined the loose cluster hanging out over by her brother. Han's parties were never formal or anything, but people usually put in a little effort. Devin had traded in his work clothes for a sharp blue button-down that made his eyes look even brighter.

She wanted to peel it off him.

"So, you wanna talk about it?"

Zoe tried not to jump when June spoke from right beside her. "Talk about what?"

June's friend Bobbi snickered.

Zoe's face went warm. Crap. She was really bad at this secretly banging her brother's friend thing, huh?

"There's nothing to talk about," she said, more firmly this time.

June didn't seem convinced. "Uh-huh."

"He's one of Han's friends." Zoe swallowed past the lump in her throat. "Gross."

"Gross? I mean—" Bobbi gestured with her wineglass at the guys. Her girlfriend, Caitlin, stood over beside them. "I don't even like dudes, and I can admit he's hot."

"They're all hot," June said.

Zoe recoiled. "Ew. My brother is not hot."

Shrugging, June took a sip of her wine. "May would kill me for saying it, but it's true."

"Seriously, though," Bobbi said, leaning in. "Devin's been sneaking looks at you almost as much as you've been sneaking looks at him."

"Really?" Her voice came out too high. She retreated to the side a bit to reclaim her wineglass and took a gulp.

"Really," June confirmed.

Zoe had to stop herself from glancing over at him to verify. "It doesn't matter. Even if he weren't gross." He was so, so not gross. "It's like I said—he's my brother's best friend, and you know how Han is." Her mouth felt dry despite the wine. "If either of us made a move, he'd flip his lid."

"I don't know . . ." June mused.

"Well, believe me, I do."

Devin and Han had both been plenty clear. A bitter taste formed at the back of her mouth.

At first, the whole off-limits thing had been kind of fun. But the more time they spent together, the more it twisted her up inside.

Being someone's dirty little secret wasn't great for the ego.

Not that that was stopping her from developing—ugh—*feelings* for the guy.

Yeah, she might be in denial about a lot of things, but that was a tough one to get away from. She wasn't an idiot. The way his touch made her feel all warm and squishy inside, the way her thoughts kept drifting to him throughout the day...It was like her teenage crush, only times a million, because now she knew he liked her, too.

Maybe not as much as she liked him, but more than enough to keep throwing gasoline on the fire in her chest.

She was saved from having to downplay things to June and Bobbi any further by Han flicking off the burners with a flourish. "Okay, y'all, grub's up."

Zoe downed another gulp of her wine before excusing herself. This was old hat. Positioning herself at her brother's side, she passed him plates, and he portioned out the food.

Her mouth watered. Han had been refining his stable of experimental dishes for ages, and they just kept getting better. Tonight's menu included a rice dish with pickled ginger and edamame, plus seared scallops in a basil sauce she never would have thought would work, but it did. Baby bok choy that he'd cooked over a little electric grill, and some mystery egg tarts he'd done in the oven. He scattered the lot with a drizzle of vibrant green and white sauces, chopped nori, and sesame.

Devin stepped in to pass the completed dishes out.

"Wow," Caitlin said as she received the first plate.

"Let me know what you think."

Zoe frowned at her brother. His voice had a different pitch to it. He was always proud of his cooking, but the nerves jangling around in there were new.

She didn't have much time to think about it. Before she knew it, everyone had a plate in hand. As they found places to sit or stand, appreciative moans and compliments sounded out around the room. Han shone a sly smile as he started eating, too, Ling-Ling parked hopefully at his feet. He made a running commentary—he always did. What worked and what hadn't, though as far as Zoe was concerned, it was all a hit.

The regulars in Han's guinea pig squad were easy to spot as they echoed Han's comments. Devin was a down-to-earth guy, but he'd been hanging out with Han long enough to mention something about the butter-to-shortening ratio in the crust of the savory egg tart. Zoe shook her head and just kept shoveling it in.

One of Han and Devin's buddies, Terrell, snapped his fingers. "I know what this reminds me of. That thing you made for my sister's wedding."

Han tipped his head to the side. "Did I do shrimp for that?"

"No, but the sauce."

"That was totally different," Han said.

Devin scrunched up his nose. "It was kind of the same."

"You know what it reminds me of?" June interjected.

"What?" Han asked. "And please tell me you have a better memory than these guys."

"She usually does." Clay chuckled, and Devin elbowed him in the ribs.

"Graduation," June said, sure of herself. "Your year. That meal you did at our place."

"Oh." A shadow crept across Han's gaze.

Right. Any meal he would have made at the Wu-Miller house would have been because of May.

Devin looked at Han with the same concern Zoe felt.

As if realizing her mistake in bringing that up, June continued. "Though this is way better. I mean, the graduation meal was amazing, but these egg tarts are next level. What's in them again?"

Han rattled off some of the ingredients.

Devin cleared his throat. "I think it's more like that Thanksgiving you cooked—what was it? Twenty seventeen?"

Han pulled a face. "That menu was totally different."

"Yeah, but the basil—"

"Oh man," Terrell said, elbowing his buddy. "New Year's Eve, like, five years ago."

"Yeah!" The dude's eyes lit up. He waved a hand at Han. "The one you did at the park."

"Fried turkey," Han agreed. "Seriously, guys, that was nothing like this."

"Didn't you have little pastries? I swear there was, like, basil in them like this."

"The basil is in the sauce." Han was smiling again now, which was something.

"Oh! Oh!" Terrell held up a finger. "Wasn't that the year we were picking gravel out of the cupcakes?"

"Man, who baked those?"

"Pretty sure it was me." Bobbi grinned.

"They were so good, it was totally worth it, even when—"

Devin slammed his plate down on the counter. His fork clattered against the china. Ling-Ling whined.

Suddenly, everyone got quiet.

Zoe sucked in a breath. Devin's face had turned a shade of purple. Thunderheads colored his eyes.

"What?" she asked.

Devin's gaze connected with hers for a fraction of a second, and it was like an iron band closed around her heart.

Devin glanced away. "Excuse me."

He stalked off. Zoe put her plate down. The band around her heart released, but it was replaced by a freaking jackrabbit, jumping up and down on the insides of her chest so fast, she could hardly breathe. She gripped the edge of the counter she'd been leaning against until her knuckles turned white.

Everything in her told her to follow him. His gaze was seared into her. His eyes had looked so *angry*.

But more than that, he'd looked so...

Lost.

A door slammed in the distance, and Zoe squeezed the counter even tighter. Han smacked himself in the forehead, then reached over to cuff Terrell on the back of his head, too.

"Ow—"

"Devin's dad," Han hissed. "Remember?"

"Wait." Zoe should shut up, but she couldn't. "What—"

Han shook his head.

Wincing, Terrell scrubbed at his face. "Oh, right. Crap."

Quietly, Bobbi turned to Zoe. "Devin's dad showed up drunk. He knocked over the cupcakes."

"Said some really awful stuff, too," Han added.

Zoe stared toward the corner Devin had disappeared around. It was like she was being yanked in that direction. He'd told her the other night that his dad wasn't a good guy, but seeing his reaction to someone bringing up that memory now...

She bit the inside of her lip.

Was he okay? No, of course not. How could he be?

She wanted so badly to chase after him. If she were really his girlfriend, she would do just that. She'd put her arms around him and hold him tight, and maybe—maybe he'd even let her.

Her stomach plummeted to the floor.

The only problem was that she wasn't. If she gave them away, he'd be even more furious—furious at her.

But she couldn't ignore this *pull*.

"Shouldn't someone go after him?" she asked.

Han shook his head. "Just makes it worse."

Everyone seemed to take that as definitive.

Slowly, people started eating and talking again, but Zoe couldn't hear any of it. She was listening so carefully for any sort of sound from the hallway. When she heard the bathroom door open, her heart leaped.

Speaking to no one in particular, she said, "I have to . . ."

She pulled out her phone as if that would explain her needing to step away.

June gave her a knowing glance that bordered on encouragement. Accepting that unexpected morsel of support, she took off down the hall at a measured pace, but as soon as she was out of sight, she couldn't help it. She broke into an all-out sprint.

Only to almost crash into Devin. His jaw was set, storms still brewing in his eyes, and she'd just come out here to check on him.

But she couldn't stand this.

She grabbed him by the wrist and hauled him down the hall.

"Zo—"

He resisted, but he finally let himself be dragged into

the next available room with a door. It was Lian's old
room—now her mother's sewing room, but it would do.
Her mom was working at the restaurant tonight, so she
wouldn't notice.

As soon as the door was closed behind them, she
launched herself at him. She wrapped her arms around his
chest, but he was stone.

"You don't have to—" he gritted out.

"Shh."

He shook his head, but she wasn't having any of it.

She shushed him again. He stayed as stiff as a board
for a long moment. Crap. Maybe she'd misread this entire
thing. Maybe he didn't need comfort.

Maybe he didn't want any from her.

Well, too bad. She was giving it to him anyway.

She'd give him anything.

She clenched her eyes tight. That was probably so
stupid of her. He wasn't in this with her for real. Even if
he were—what kind of future could they have? He'd never
be willing to face Han's wrath or risk Arthur's judgment.
There wasn't any place for her in his lonely loner's house
in the woods. Who knew how long she'd be staying in Blue
Cedar Falls anyway? Getting invested was a waste, but she
couldn't seem to fight it anymore.

Finally, Devin let out a sigh. He curled his arms around
her, too. His posture softened as he pressed a kiss to the
top of her head. "I'm fine," he told her.

"I know." People banging dishes on counters and leaving
in a huff—that was always a sign that they were fine.

"I just..."

She leaned back so she could look him in the eye. The
anger had faded from his gaze, replaced by something that
made him look tired and older than he was. She sucked

in a breath. "Han said it was something to do with your father?"

Devin nodded grimly. He pulled her back into a hug, her face pressed to his chest. Normally, she wouldn't mind being snuggled up with his firm pecs, but it was clearly a way for him to avoid her gaze. She allowed it for now.

Exhaling, he said, "Yeah. Told you he wasn't a good guy."

"You didn't tell me he was the 'shows up drunk to parties and knocks over cupcakes' kind of bad guy."

He shrugged, but she could practically feel his wince. "They told you that, huh?"

"Yup."

"They tell you the part about him smacking me around?"

She drew back. "No."

His grimace deepened. "Can we forget I just admitted it, then?"

"Seriously?"

"He was a jerk," he said, as if that were some kind of explanation.

"But he hit you?" More rumors and hushed conversations floated into her memory. She hadn't understood them then. But Devin telling her this... It slotted an awful lot of things into place.

Devin rubbed his hands up and down her arms, and she didn't need him to comfort her. Not when he was telling her about his pain. "It's okay. I'm fine now."

"How?"

His throat bobbed. "I got out."

"How?" An intense need to understand this man clawed at her. She shouldn't pry, but she wanted to know everything. "I mean—if you don't want to talk about it—"

"Your family, for one." His gaze connected with hers, a little light coming back to his eyes. "There's a reason

I was always at your place or hanging out in Arthur's basement."

"Right."

"And then, as soon as I was out of high school, I packed my bag. Started working. Got an apartment. The rest is history."

Was it, though? The pain of it still seemed to live inside him.

She put her hands over Devin's chest, trying to take in the breadth of him. This strong, incredible man, who'd dealt with so much and who still stayed open and kind.

It occurred to her again, just like that night he'd walked her home after they'd hung out at the bar. Did he ever talk about what had happened to him? How did the pressure of keeping it all inside not make him explode?

Gazing up at him, she took a deep breath. "What happened to him?"

"I have no idea," he said quietly, ghosts in his eyes. "I assume he rotted in that house for a while. I never went back. He never came looking for me except a couple of times when he was trashed." He shrugged. "When he did, I just called Officer Dwight to take him home. Otherwise, I had nothing to do with him. Year or so after I left, I got a drunk dial from him. Said he was set up in a trailer park in Florida."

"You think he'll stay there?"

"Honestly, I don't care."

He meant it, too. The pain in his voice was like a hand reaching into her chest and squeezing.

Zoe's family was her bedrock. She defied them and fought with them, but deep down she loved them fiercely. She never in a million years could doubt they loved her, too.

Devin...he didn't have that.

Slowly, she skated her hands up his chest. She took his face between her palms. His scruff was rough against her skin. She stroked her thumbs just beneath his eyes. "I'm so sorry," she told him quietly.

"It's nothing. Old history."

She repeated it. More firmly this time. "I'm sorry." She reached up onto her tiptoes, pulling him down to meet her. She kissed his lips. "I'm sorry."

"Zo..."

"I'm sorry." She kissed him again, soft and slow.

He melted into it, wrapping his arms around her. Holding on to him, she tried to pour everything she was feeling into the motion of their lips. He didn't want her to comfort him or to let her tell him how her heart ached for him, and that was fine. She'd make him understand like this.

Because any of her ideas about not getting invested? Not growing *feelings* for this man?

They were out the window. She'd tossed her sense of self-preservation right along with them.

All she could do was hang on.

And wait for the crash when they all hit the ground.

Chapter Eleven

A couple of weeks later, Zoe sat on the kitchen counter, texting with June about grabbing coffee, Clay about whether or not she could open the bar tomorrow, Lian about how she wanted to bang her head against the wall over her job search, and a group of high school friends about a time to meet up for drinks later that week—all without accidentally sending any messages to the wrong person. She snickered to herself as she sent a reaction gif to Lian. Take that, accounting firm looking for "attention to detail."

No sooner had the thought occurred to her than her screen went blank, a call from an unknown number appearing over her fifteen messaging threads.

Her first impulse was to ignore it—she'd talked to quite enough people excited to offer her a free time-share or help her with a problem at the social security agency. But one of the worst things about being on a job hunt was having to answer every call.

Bracing for the worst, she tucked her hair out of the way and brought the phone to her ear. "Hello?"

A male voice replied, "Good morning. Is this Zoe Leung?"

She sat up straighter. "It is."

"Hi, I'm Brad Sullivan from Pinnacle Accounting, following up on a résumé we received."

"Oh, hi!" She scrambled down off the counter and over to her makeshift office set up on the end of the dining room table. Pinnacle, Pinnacle—oh, right. It was a firm in Atlanta she'd applied to last week.

"I was hoping to talk to you about your interest in the position. Do you have a few minutes?"

She blinked about fifty-seven times. "Of course."

"Great." With that, he launched into a quick overview of the job she'd applied for as well as a series of questions about her experience and training, which she somehow or other managed to string together coherent answers to.

Slipping back into the accounting persona she'd honed during her coursework and internship was harder than it used to be. Once upon a time, it had felt like a second skin. Now it felt like a wet suit that was three sizes too small.

"All right," Brad said, "sounds to me like you're an excellent candidate. Let me just talk to a few people and we'll get you set up for an interview with the rest of the team."

It was a good thing the chair she was sitting on had a back, because otherwise she might have tipped right out of it. "Oh wow, okay, great."

"Just one last question—this job does require you to be on-site in our Buckhead office. Looks like you're in North Carolina right now, but I'm assuming you're prepared to relocate?"

"Yes," she said, but as she did, a stone lodged in her throat.

"Perfect." He rattled off a few more details, and they said their goodbyes.

The whole while, the tightness in her windpipe grew and grew.

Atlanta was a four-hour drive from here. A few months ago, she might not have cared. She'd lived away from home when she'd gone to college. She'd always assumed she'd have to leave again to get a decent job that was in her field.

But her time back here in Blue Cedar Falls had changed her perspective.

She liked being home. She liked seeing Han all the time and being able to meet up with Lian now and then. She liked Clay and June and working at the bar. She loved getting to spend time with Arthur and helping out at Harvest Home.

She loved...

She clenched her phone so tightly she worried the screen would break.

She and Devin had told each other that their time together was limited. He wasn't interested in anything serious; all he wanted in this world was a house of his own outside of town, and he never imagined sharing it with anyone, least of all her. He definitely wasn't interested in upsetting the balance of his relationship with her family.

Ever since Han's dinner party, when he'd opened up to her about his dad, she'd known that eventually he'd break her heart.

She just hadn't been prepared for it to happen so soon.

Maybe it didn't have to. A bubble of hope filled her chest. Maybe she wouldn't get the job. Maybe she could just stay here forever, working at the bar and helping Arthur run the food kitchen and sleeping with Devin and it would all be okay.

Right.

The bubble popped almost instantaneously. She needed this job. If it was offered to her, she'd have no choice but to take it and go. This was the moment she'd been waiting for, working toward, training for.

So why did everything about it make her feel so terrible?

Before she could even begin to get it all sorted out, the front door opened.

"Crap."

Instinctively, she scrambled to look busy, but sitting at her laptop with her spreadsheet open was about as busy-looking as she could get.

"Oh, look, you're awake," her mom said, deadpan.

Zoe drew in a breath and forced herself to smile. She hadn't gotten home until two a.m. yesterday after closing up the Junebug. The fact that she was up before ten was a miracle.

Try telling her early-bird mother that, though.

"Han went to the restaurant already?" her mom asked.

Zoe shook her head. "Took the dog for a hike first."

"Good. Ling-Ling needs more exercise."

"Ling-Ling needs you to stop slipping her extra treats."

"Me?" Her mother put her hand to her chest dramatically. "Never."

Right. "How was brunch?"

Zoe's mother ate with May and June's mom and a few other old ladies almost every morning down at the Sweetbriar Inn on Main Street.

Her mom waved a hand dismissively. "Same as ever." She headed into the kitchen to start a pot of tea. Managing to sound both casual and pointed, she mentioned, "Mrs. Smith's son got a big promotion. Branch manager."

"That's great." Zoe dug her nails into the meat of her palm.

The competitive instinct in her told her to brag about the interview she'd just landed, but she knew better. Her mom would get obsessed with it and have her cramming for it like the SATs. Better to keep mum.

But as her mother puttered around, getting everything together for her tea, Zoe kept running around in circles inside her head. She wanted to talk this out with someone. Devin, namely. He was so grounded, and he asked her questions that made her see things in a new light. Could she bring up her mixed feelings about moving without letting on that she was getting too attached to him? Probably not. He was working right now anyway. So were June and Lian and pretty much all of her other friends she might try to talk to about this.

Which left her with her mom.

With her teapot and little porcelain cup and saucer balanced on a tray, her mother returned to the table and took her usual seat at the head. She put on her reading glasses and opened up the newspaper.

Zoe fidgeted, glancing between her open laptop screen and her mom, but she couldn't quite figure out how to open up her mouth and say what was on her mind.

Talking—really talking—with her mother had never been easy. Her mom had this unique way of shutting Zoe down and making all her ideas seem foolish. Sometimes Zoe had enough force of will to barrel right through.

And sometimes she ended up picking a stupid major she didn't even like anyway.

She still couldn't decide who she was more upset with about that—her mother or herself. Clearly her mom wasn't entirely to blame. Yeah, Zoe had gotten a different version of her mom's weird guilt-trippy style of parenting, considering how much younger she'd been than her siblings when their father died. But Han and Lian—they were doing what they wanted to do. Or at least some variation on it. They were happy.

"Something on your mind?" her mother asked, not looking up from her paper.

So many things.

But the one she ended up blurting out was, "How come you always rode me so much harder than Han and Lian?"

Her mother's rapid blinking was the only sign that the question took her by surprise. With deliberate slowness, she set her teacup down and dabbed at the corner of her mouth with a napkin.

Stalling. Zoe was used to it.

That didn't make it any easier to wait her mother out. Chewing on the inside of her lip, she put her hands under her thighs, literally sitting on them to try to give herself patience.

Finally, her mom put the napkin down. She fixed Zoe with an appraising stare that lasted way too long for comfort. Inside, Zoe squirmed a little, but she remained firm.

Shaking her head, her mother let out a breath and looked away. "I ever tell you about the first day I picked you up from nursery school?"

Zoe deflated. She pulled her hands out from under her legs. "Probably."

"You were a mess. Glitter everywhere. Your teacher apologized, but I knew. It wasn't her fault."

Great, so Zoe had been a disaster since she was four. Good to know. "Look—"

Her mom talked right over her, slow and steady. Like a Zamboni. "Whole ride home, you never stopped talking. Told me all the friends you made, everything you did. You couldn't decide if you liked Joey best or Kim. Or costume party or building with blocks. Everything was your favorite."

"Right, right. I was a happy kid. I know."

Her mom's lips curled into a smile. "Ray of sunshine." She turned her gaze from the past and back to the woman in front of her. Her smile faded. "You remember what you told me you wanted to be when you grew up?"

Had she ever known? "No."

"I remember. Clear as yesterday. 'Princess astronaut veterinarian ballerina.'"

Zoe's face flushed warm. "I mean, I was, what? Four?"

"But you believed it. With all your heart."

"Mom..." She was beginning to lose her patience.

Her mother's voice rose by a fraction, her tone growing serious. "Your brother, Han. Only thing he cares about besides his family is cooking." Her mother jabbed her pointer finger into the table. "Han is easy."

Zoe frowned. She wasn't so sure about all that.

But her mom was on a roll now. She tapped the table hard again. "Lian wanted to be a teacher since she was six. Easy."

"But what about all the stuff you told me?" Zoe asked. Bitterness seeped into her tone. "Pick any career you want, just make sure it's comfortably middle class."

How many times had Zoe come home from school excited about some project in her communications elective or jazzed about a fundraiser Uncle Arthur was going to let her help out with at Harvest Home, only to be met with her mother's dismissive *tut-tut*ting?

"You." Her mother shoved that finger in Zoe's direction this time. "You were never easy."

"Great," Zoe grumbled.

"You weren't. Still aren't."

Zoe's cheeks warmed, and she squirmed inside. Clearly she'd been selling her mom's passive-aggressive streak short, because this direct insult approach was no peach. "Okay, okay, I get it."

Her mother shook her head. She was fluent in English, but she still muttered a few words to herself in Mandarin. It was one of her only tells that she was getting flustered.

"That's not a bad thing, Zhaohui. You always make it out like I'm attacking you."

"Uh, you kind of are." How else was she supposed to interpret her mom telling her to her face that she was, always had been, and always would be difficult?

"You were not easy, because you actually wanted to be princess astronaut veterinarian ballerina!"

"Who wouldn't?" That sounded awesome.

"You have your head in the clouds. Someone has to help keep you here. On earth where you belong." Fire burned in her mother's gaze.

And okay, Zoe knew her mom loved her and that she'd fight off an invading horde for her. But she occasionally forgot that the overbearing stuff was love, too.

Annoying, frustrating, occasionally infuriating love.

"You don't have to," she insisted.

"I do." Her mother reached across the table, and for the first time in what seemed like a long, long while, it felt like she was looking at Zoe. Not past her. No snide remarks, no judgment. She held out her hand. "I know it, because that's what your father did for me."

Zoe's eyes flew wide. Her mom almost never talked about her dad. "Wait—"

Her mother shook her head, her whole expression softening. "So like me, sometimes, my Zhaohui. I don't want you to learn lessons the hard way like I did." She extended her hand an inch farther, and Zoe slipped her fingers into her palm. "You have to be practical. You have to survive."

And Zoe would probably never fully understand her mother, but for one moment, she wondered if maybe she was right. If maybe they did have more in common than had ever been keeping them apart.

Her mother gave her hand a gentle, reassuring squeeze. "Look. I make you a deal."

"Okay..."

"You ever find job opening for princess astronaut veterinarian ballerina *with* pension and health insurance? I promise I stop riding you so hard."

Zoe laughed, and she swabbed at her eyes. This was making her way too emotional—especially considering her mom had basically just promised to never, ever give her a break.

She had about a bazillion other questions, but before she could figure out a way to give voice to them, the actual, honest-to-goodness phone on the wall started ringing.

Her mother patted Zoe's hand before letting go to stand and answer it.

"Hello—" She barely got through the word. A muffled voice came over the line.

Then all the color drained from her face.

———

"For crying out loud, James." Bryce looked up from the same set of joists he'd been supposedly assembling for the last hour now. "Your mommy calling you or something?"

"Mind your own business." Devin ignored his phone buzzing in his pocket again. This was the third time, and no, it wasn't his mommy. Dead women didn't call.

He was starting to get a little worried, though.

He drove the last nail home in his set and looked up, meeting Terrell's gaze. "You got this for a second?"

"Sure, man."

"You heard him," Bryce said, dropping his nail gun. "That's five, everybody."

"You already had your break, and you don't have time to take another." Devin gestured at the work still to be done.

Bryce pantomimed a yapping mouth, and Devin gritted his teeth.

The guy had been giving Devin a hard time since high school. Ever since Bryce had come on at Meyer Construction, it had been the same—like Bryce resented that a guy as powerful as the mayor's son had to stoop so low as to be working alongside schlubs like Devin. Devin's promotion had been salt in the wound. The backtalk had gotten worse and worse, and Devin had tried to turn a blind eye to it. He'd focused on the job and the work and let the personal stuff slide.

Goodness knew there was enough to focus on work-wise. Ever since the disaster the other week when Bryce had let half a wall collapse, the higher-ups had taken a personal interest in Devin's crew. Devin had shown Joe all the documentation he'd been gathering about Bryce's sloppy work, and Joe had been clear that Devin had his support. He just needed to keep collecting evidence to build a case that could hold up against whatever scrutiny they might get if and when the time came to finally give the boot to the mayor's son.

Ignoring Bryce, Devin made sure he was out of everybody's way before pulling out his phone.

Only to find three missed calls from Zoe.

His heart thunked around in his chest, thrown by a

whole warring set of reactions. Pleasure at hearing from her. Surprise, because she never called unless it was too late to come over and she still wanted to tell him something dirty.

Worry.

He tapped on her number and brought his phone to his ear. As it rang, he glanced around. The rest of his crew was still working. Bryce was continuing with his little tantrum, but he'd actually nailed two pieces of wood together, so who cared.

On the third ring, Zoe picked up.

"Hey—" he started.

"Devin."

He straightened, adrenaline rushing his system. Her voice was all breathy and watery and wrong. "What happened."

"Uncle Arthur. He had a heart attack."

A ten-ton weight fell right on Devin's chest. He changed direction midstride. "Where is he?"

"Pine Ridge."

"I'll be there in ten."

"You don't have to." She sniffled. "I just—I thought you should know. Arthur—"

Arthur was like a father to him. A better one than his own had ever been, but Devin couldn't focus on his own concern right now.

Zoe put on such a front. She acted carefree, like nothing could touch her, but under all that she was tender and soft, and he knew her well enough now. The raw emotion in her voice reached into his chest and squeezed.

"Who's there with you?"

"Just my mom. She's trying not to freak out, but it's not working. Han's on his way, but Lian's car broke down, so he had to drive out to Lincoln to get her."

Right. "I'll be there in ten."

"Devin..." The way her voice broke made him stop.

He exhaled out, deep and rough. He covered his eyes with his hand. "Do you not want me to come?"

Everything in him was itching to go. A crisis demanded action. This was Arthur they were talking about.

"I just...If you don't...You're working."

She'd called him three times. She'd reached out.

"Tell me not to come."

"I—"

"Tell me explicitly, specifically, that you do not want me there, or I am getting in my truck."

Silence held across the line. A sob broke it.

"I want you to come," she whispered.

He dropped his hand from his face. "Ten minutes." His voice was still too hard. With a deep breath, he forced himself to be soft for her. "Hang on, baby."

Then he hung up.

It was fifty yards to the trailer. He crossed it in big strides.

"Hey, James, you okay?" one of the guys called.

"Family emergency," he barked out. He tossed open the door to the trailer, but it was empty. He backed right out. "Where's Joe?"

The couple of guys gathered around shook their heads and shrugged. "Maybe down at corporate?" one of them offered.

Devin shucked his safety gear. "When he gets back, tell him I had to go."

"Okay..."

"Terrell? You're in charge."

And then a voice came from behind him. A stupid, teasing voice. "What did your mommy want, James? Need you to come home and have your bottle?"

Devin ignored Bryce. He didn't have time for this.

But as he headed for his truck, Bryce followed him. "Real nice, ignoring your employees while you're running out the door halfway through your shift. Super responsible. I can see why you got the promotion over me."

Real nice, ignoring your father. Worthless sack of—

Devin's father's words had no place in his head. Not now when he was on his way to help Zoe, to help her family, who had been better to him than his own flesh and blood had ever been.

"Maybe I'll fill out one of those write-up forms you keep doing for me—not that anybody reads them." Bryce leaned against the side of Devin's truck as Devin went to open the door. "You know that, right? That nobody listens to you?"

Just try to report me. Devin's dad had been stumbling, slurring. *Nobody's going to listen to you.*

"Get out of my way." Devin managed to keep from growling, but it was a narrow thing.

"Make me."

Devin hauled open the door of his truck and got in, but when he went to pull it closed behind him, Bryce was still there.

"Seriously, James. I want to see you do it." Bryce was in the way now, making it impossible to close the door. "Or are you too weak? Weak guy trying to boss everyone around." His voice dropped. "Not a great look. Think all of them will still respect you when they see me walk all over you?"

Devin looked past Bryce's shoulder before he could stop himself. Terrell and the rest of the team were back at work, but people were looking. Was that Bryce's angle? Trap him like this? Make him back down? Rub it in his face the next time Devin tried to call him out?

When would it end?

All Devin's life, he'd tried to keep his head down, work hard, stay out of trouble, and for the most part, it had panned out just fine. He had a great job, great friends. For the moment, at least, he had Zoe.

But what if it wasn't enough to keep quiet and do things the way they were supposed to be done?

What if he'd stood up to his dad a long, long time ago?

Righteousness surged through Devin's veins. "Move." When Bryce didn't budge, Devin turned. He got out of the truck, and that put him right in Bryce's face, and he didn't care. "Go back to work now or pack up your things."

"Whatever—"

And that was it. Devin was done. "You're fired."

For the first time, Bryce flinched. "Wait."

"Get off my site. Don't come back."

"You can't—"

"I can." Devin took a step forward, and as Bryce retreated, power filled Devin's chest. He didn't have to keep his head down. He didn't have to stay silent when people were treating him like crap. He was in charge. People trusted him to make the right calls.

And this was one of them.

"Terrell?" Devin shouted.

"Yeah?"

"Call security to escort Mr. Horton off the property."

"With pleasure."

"My father—" Bryce tried.

"Doesn't have any authority here. And if he shows up and tries to pretend he does, then I'll stand up to him just the same."

Devin had heard enough. This guy didn't deserve his time. He had to get to the hospital, had to find out if Arthur was okay. Zoe needed him.

He climbed back into his truck and slammed the door shut behind him. He put the key in the ignition, and the engine roared to life.

From the other side of the window, Bryce shouted, "My dad is going to destroy you. One word from me and you can kiss this job goodbye. That little piece of land you've been saving up for? You can forget it. My father—"

Terrell appeared behind Bryce, two security officers in tow. "Oh, shut up already, Bryce."

One corner of Devin's lips curled up. They'd all been tiptoeing around Bryce forever, but a dam had just broken.

He should have told Bryce off years ago. It hadn't even taken a punch or a shove. Just evidence and words and an unwillingness to be pushed around anymore.

But he didn't have any more energy to waste on that guy now.

Arthur was in trouble. Zoe was reeling. Han was on his way.

The most important people in his life were waiting for him.

And he'd do anything for them.

Anything.

Chapter Twelve

Ok, class is covered, Han's here, be there in 20

The text from Lian allowed Zoe to let out a sigh of relief.
Drive safe, she replied. She trusted her brother and all,
but the look in his eyes as he'd taken off to go get their
sister had shaken her.

It was the same look he'd had after their father died.
Devastated. Determined. Hard.

She put her phone away, only to pull it back out again
two seconds later. She couldn't focus on anything. The
waiting room wasn't big enough for her to properly pace,
and if she drank another cup of stale coffee, she'd shake
right out of her skin.

The elevator at the other end of the room dinged, and
she looked up. This was getting ridiculous. She'd been
snapping her gaze to see who was arriving every time,
but inevitably it was a group of doctors or nurses. Maybe
another worried family with food from the cafeteria, a
bouquet of flowers, or balloons.

Except this time, when the doors slid open, they finally
revealed the face she'd been waiting for.

She leaped to her feet as Devin scanned the area. He

spotted her immediately. Their gazes connected, and something inside her broke down. He ate up the space with huge strides and pulled her right into his arms.

A sob erupted from her. She clung to him, which was stupid—everyone could see.

When she started to pull away, he only held her tighter, though, and she couldn't help herself.

She'd been trying to keep it together since the moment the phone had rung.

Uncle Arthur was in his sixties. He had high blood pressure. He was fit enough, but he never stopped, never took care of himself. Others always came first.

"Shh, I got you," Devin murmured.

Tears were leaking down her face. She breathed through them. "He's fine. He's going to be fine."

So why was she losing it like this?

Maybe it was because she finally had the option to.

On the way to the hospital, she'd had to be the one to drive. Her mother had been even more of a wreck than her, so Zoe had been strong. It made sense. Uncle Arthur was her mother's big brother, after all. They'd been through so much together.

Devin rocked her back and forth, whispering reassurances into her ear the entire time, and she melted into him.

It seemed like it took forever, but Devin's steady strength slowly seeped into her. The tears ebbed. She pulled away, reaching into her purse for yet more Kleenex. Dabbing at her eyes, she shook her head. "Sorry."

"Don't be."

She blew her nose, but her mouth started wobbling all over again. He was being so nice to her, when he must be all shaken up, too.

Sitting back down, she beckoned him to take the seat beside her.

"What happened?"

"Heart attack. Partial, they said?" She gestured at the door her mother had disappeared behind a few minutes before. "They let my mom go see him before he heads up to surgery. They're doing that—that balloon thing." Angioplasty? "And a stent. They think his prognosis is good." She waved her hands at herself. "I don't know why I'm freaking out."

"Hey, hey." He grabbed her hand out of the air and squeezed it. "It's okay."

"I just—" She forced herself to stop and take a few deep breaths. As she stared up into his eyes, an unshakable sense of safety wrapped around her. It made her mist up all over again, but it was better this time. Shaky, she buried her face in his shoulder. "I'm just really glad you're here."

Too glad. Good grief. She needed to pull herself together. Han would be back with Lian soon. Her mother would be coming out before she knew it. The moment any of them returned, Devin would pull away. The idea of having him so close but unwilling to actually touch her made a fresh wave of misery crash across her chest.

"Come on." He held her close, rubbing her back. "You said it yourself. He's going to be okay."

"I know," she said, but the reassurances rang hollow. The only thing that helped was him holding her, so she clung to him, trying to soak in his strength while she could.

Far too soon, the elevator let out another chime. When she looked toward the opening doors, a different sort of nerves stole over her.

There they were. Han and Lian. Ten minutes ago, she would have been trembling with relief.

Ha.

She dropped her face into Devin's neck for one last

breath. Then she tore herself away, and it actually hurt. She met his concerned gaze, and she hated having to do it, but she nodded toward her brother and sister.

Devin glanced in the direction of the elevator. He had to see them, but he didn't let go. Instead, he turned to Zoe. He stared deep into her eyes. A dozen emotions flashed across his face.

But the last one—the one that remained…

It was resolve.

———

Enough.

It was the same feeling that had come over Devin back at the construction site. When he'd been pushed too far, and he finally pushed back. He'd made himself heard.

And it had worked.

A strange, ringing silence eclipsed the riot of voices in his head.

He wasn't powerless. He wasn't unworthy of love or acceptance.

He wasn't going to hide what he wanted. How he felt. From anyone.

Least of all his best friend.

Least of all when it was going to hurt someone he cared about, someone he…

Well.

For a long moment, he gazed down into Zoe's deep brown eyes. She was shaking. Just minutes ago, she'd been crying. She'd gone soft in his arms, molding herself to him, leaning into him, and this wasn't about sex anymore. This wasn't some game to her. All his doubts about what she was doing with him finally melted away.

He held out his hand to her.

Without hesitation, she slipped her fingers into his palm, her eyes going wide as she sputtered, "But—"

He shook his head and raised his brows.

Her mouth snapped closed.

Like she understood him, she wordlessly rose to stand beside him. Their gazes held, and the rightness in his chest was so hot it burned. He curled an arm around her. Bending down, he pressed his lips first to her forehead. Then to her mouth.

He turned forward.

Lian spotted them first. Her eyes flew wide, and she started to divert Han, but Devin shook his head.

The second Han caught sight of them, he waved. A relieved grin crossed his face, only to fade in the next instant. His pace slowed, his brows furrowing.

A few feet away from them, Han came to a stop. "Devin." His mouth drew into a frown. "Zoe."

Zoe fidgeted the way she did when she was nervous, but Devin felt steady as a rock. He gave her fingers a reassuring squeeze.

"Hey there, Han."

Slowly, deliberately, Han darted his gaze between the two of them and their joined hands. "What's going on?"

Lian practically bounced up and down.

Maybe that shouldn't have given him confidence, but it did.

"Before you say anything," he started.

Han's complexion darkened. "Say anything like what?"

"We're in a hospital," Zoe interjected. "You try to murder us and they'll fix us up." She snapped her fingers. "Like that."

"Devin."

And Devin was standing his ground. He was refusing to let anyone push him around anymore. He wasn't going to live in fear of his best friend, and he wasn't going to hide the way he felt. He couldn't.

"I didn't mean for this to happen," he prefaced.

The vein in Han's temple started to bulge. "She's my *sister*, man. You were supposed to help me protect her."

"I am," Devin said helplessly. "I will." A lump formed in his throat.

Because he would. He'd protect her from anything that could possibly threaten her.

Even Han.

"I don't need protecting," Zoe insisted, because of course she'd never step back and let two men argue about her.

In the far reaches of Devin's brain, he registered the sound of Han laughing, but he couldn't focus on that right now.

This was Zoe he was talking about. The little girl he'd bickered with as a kid and the feisty, incredible, kind, wonderful woman he'd come to know since. She'd drawn him out of his shell over these past few weeks. She'd helped him let down his guard and see the world beyond the little piece of it he'd carved out for himself.

She made him happy. She made him want things he'd never even considered before.

He wanted them all with her.

"I love her," he blurted. The pressure behind his ribs popped, and he could breathe again.

Lian squealed, her hands over her mouth. Han looked like he might need heart surgery, too, but they were in a hospital. He'd be fine.

Zoe whipped her head around to gawk at him.

This wasn't how he'd wanted to tell her. He hadn't realized he wanted to tell her how he felt in the first place, but now that it was out there, he wouldn't take it back. Its truth radiated through him.

"I do," he confessed. "Sorry, but—"

"Oh my God, shut up, I love you, too, you idiot." Zoe flung herself at him, and if Han murdered them this second, it would be worth it.

Devin caught her in his arms and kissed her hard and deep. All this time, they'd been acting as if they were both okay with being casual, but apparently the only person he'd been fooling had been himself. Nobody made him laugh or turned him on or pulled him out of his head like she did.

For years now, he'd had dreams of building a house in the middle of nowhere, but those dreams had been about running away from the unhappy home he'd grown up in.

He wasn't running away from anything now.

At the sound of Lian clearing her throat, Devin tore himself away from Zoe. All around them, people cheered. Zoe hid her face in Devin's shoulder, blushing but happy.

He looked to Han.

The man had been Devin's best friend since they were in elementary school. They'd been through everything together.

But Devin had never seen Han's jaw come unhinged like this before.

"Wait—" Han held up a hand in front of himself. "Who said anything about love?"

"This guy." Zoe jabbed a finger into Devin's chest.

"Ow." He caught her hand and brought it to his lips.

He couldn't quite get a real lungful of air, though. Not while Han was looking at them like this.

"How long has this been going on?" he finally asked.

Devin looked to Zoe, who lifted a brow. "About a month?" he answered.

"Or maybe forever," Zoe said.

"Uh, but not like creepy forever, right?" Lian asked.

Devin scrunched up his face. "No."

"No." Zoe rolled her eyes. "Definitely not 'creepy forever.'"

He'd never laid a hand on her until this fall. But the truth of what she was saying smacked him upside the head all the same. He'd been looking at her differently since her high school graduation. Every time they'd hung out in the years since, he'd enjoyed her company more and more. The way they felt about each other now—yeah, it had been building for a lot longer than a month.

"I'm not even going to touch that one with a ten-foot pole." Han scrubbed a hand over his face. Then he let out a rough breath. "You're both happy."

"Yeah," Devin answered, automatic and sure. He glanced down at Zoe, and she nodded.

"Really, really happy," she promised.

"Well, that's good enough for me." Lian broke the tension by swooping in and hugging them both. She whispered something to Zoe that made her blush deeper. Pulling back, she smiled at Devin. "Welcome to the family."

Oh wow. That part hadn't even occurred to Devin. He'd been too busy worrying about how pissed Han would be.

His gaze shot to Han. It was too early to be thinking about this stuff, but if he and Zoe worked out...if they went the distance...

They'd be brothers. For real.

Han shook his head. As Lian backed away, he held out his arms. There was still a certain wariness to him, but any fury had left him. "Dude. You've always been family."

With that he came in and awkwardly hugged them, too, and it was like a ten-ton weight suddenly floating off Devin's chest.

Zoe squirmed away from her brother, leaving Devin and Han in a weird side-to-side bro-hug. Han took advantage of the opportunity to haul Devin down into what Devin was going to choose to assume was a joking headlock. He ruffled Devin's hair, and yeah. He was definitely playing at the edge between teasing and menacing.

"Seriously, though," Han muttered under his breath as he let Devin go. "You ever hurt her, and I will kill you."

Devin straightened up and cleared his throat. Han's smile was warm, even as he cocked a brow in genuine warning.

Devin looked at Zoe. It was so clichéd, but his heart swelled.

Beautiful, incredible Zoe. Whom he loved and who loved him. He couldn't help but smile.

Devin bumped his hand against Han's. "I'm going to hold you to that."

Something in Han's gaze shifted. His mouth curled at the corners. He bumped Devin's hand right back, and even more relief flooded Devin's chest.

They were going to be okay.

It wasn't going to be easy, but for the first time since Zoe had arrived back home...Devin was starting to think this all just might work out.

Chapter Thirteen

Read 'em and weep." Zoe laid her cards down on the table, showing her three of a kind.

"Ugh." Han tossed his cards aside.

Devin groaned and pushed the impressive pot of five sticks of gum and a half dozen of the wrapped hard candies her mom kept in her purse Zoe's way.

"Your deal." Her mom nudged the deck toward Lian. The two of them had been smart enough to fold as soon as Han and Devin started raising each other peppermints. Knowing exactly what she had in her hand, Zoe had stayed quiet and let them bid each other up.

Uncle Arthur had been in surgery for an hour or so now, and they'd had to dig deep into the well of ways to distract themselves—if for no other reason than that their mom was going to get herself kicked out if she bothered the nurses station anymore.

As Lian started shuffling, Zoe's phone buzzed in her pocket. She pulled it out.

Oh crap. "Sorry, gotta take this."

"Sure, sure," Han said. "Wipe us out and then walk away."

"I'll be right back."

Devin tilted his head in question, but she shook her head, telling him that everything was okay.

Despite the thread of dread spinning in her gut, she was even pretty sure it was true.

Demonstrating exactly how distracted she was, her mom didn't even question her retreating toward the elevator bank. Zoe turned away from her family before accepting the call. "Hello?"

"Hi, Zoe. It's Brad from Pinnacle Accounting again. I just reviewed your file with the team, and we're excited to get you scheduled for that interview. How does Thursday morning work for you?"

Zoe opened her mouth. All the mumbo-jumbo accountant-drone speak she'd managed to summon to the tip of her tongue while talking to him earlier that morning was right there, ready to come spilling out again.

But she closed her mouth.

She turned, looking back across the waiting room at her mom eyeing the clock, her brother and sister fighting over a couple of Werther's.

Her Devin, who was holding his cards close to his chest, literally. But figuratively, he was staring right at her with all of them right there for the entire world to see.

Sudden certainty filled her chest.

"Zoe?" Brad asked. "You still there?"

"Yeah, Brad." She gripped the phone more tightly. "I'm right here."

Still holding eye contact with Devin across the space, she took a couple of deep breaths.

Every time she'd discussed her job search with him, he'd asked her questions she hadn't been ready to answer. Questions about what she wanted, what she loved, what had motivated her to go down the roads she'd chosen.

She'd answered the best she could, but deep down, she'd known that she'd been hiding the truth, both from him and from herself.

She didn't care about some big corporate accounting job. She didn't want to go to Atlanta or Charlotte or Savannah.

She wanted to be here. With him. Working with Arthur and Clay and just living her life. Not the one her mother had charted out for her the second she'd been born.

She may be a dreamer, just like her mom said, but her head wasn't in the clouds. Her feet were firmly planted on the ground, and she was ready to stand tall.

"I'm sorry, Brad," she said. "But I've decided not to pursue this opportunity after all."

As she said the words, the rightness of them sank into her bones. There'd be consequences to this decision, but she was prepared to face them.

If Devin could stand up to Han for her, then Zoe could stand up to her mom. She could fight for her own happiness—and for a chance at a future for the both of them, here in Blue Cedar Falls, where they belonged.

———

"How is he?" Zoe practically bounced to her feet as Han and Lian returned to the waiting room after getting to go in and see Uncle Arthur in person.

"He's good," Han assured her.

"If already getting annoyed at Mom." Lian rolled her eyes.

Zoe could only imagine. She'd spent enough sick days at home with her mom—and her delightful bedside manner—to empathize.

"Can we . . . ?" Devin asked, standing and gesturing toward the door. Zoe's mom had wrestled her way back to sit with Uncle Arthur the second he got out of recovery, but outside of her, they were only letting folks in one or two people at a time.

Han nodded. He reached for his jacket. "I should go check on the restaurant."

Thank goodness they had employees who could open the place.

"Call if you need anything," Devin told him.

"Will do." Han looked to Lian. "You want to stay or go?"

"I'll stay awhile." She tipped her head toward the door before sinking into one of the seats near where Zoe and Devin had been sitting. "Go on."

As he pulled out his keys, Han paused for a moment. "Hey, Zo?"

"Yeah?"

"Thanks." His gaze met hers, and it wasn't as if it was the first time he'd made eye contact with her since he'd found out about her and Devin, but there was something different about the way he regarded her. Like he was acknowledging her as an equal and not some kid sister he had to protect. "Mom told me how you held things together this afternoon, when I was off picking up Lian."

Zoe smiled. "No problem."

Han nodded, new respect in his eyes, and it was too much to hope that he'd start letting the rest of his family help carry some of the responsibility he was always lugging around with him. But a girl could dream, right?

As Han took a backward step toward the elevator, Devin held out his hand. Another little thrill ran through Zoe as she slipped her palm into his.

And hey, the vein in Han's temple bulged only a little, so that was progress, right?

A nurse was kind enough to show Zoe and Devin to Uncle Arthur's room, but they didn't really need the guide. Her mother's voice rang out as clear as day the moment they rounded the corner. "*Jeopardy!* gets you too worked up."

"*You* get me too worked up." Her uncle muttered a more colorful rebuke in Mandarin.

Zoe shook her head and sighed. Well, at least it was good to know he was feeling better.

She knocked on the door, eyebrows raised. "You two playing nice in here?"

Her mother and her uncle both looked up and smiled. Zoe didn't miss the way they were still silently wrestling over the remote, though.

"Zoe," Uncle Arthur said, swatting at his sister's hand. "Devin." Then he seemed to notice the fact that they were holding hands, and his head tilted in question.

"Uh..." Devin rubbed the back of his neck.

Her mother followed his gaze and did a double take, though she recovered quickly. Letting Uncle Arthur have the remote, she stepped back, one brow raised.

With Han finally in the know, Zoe and Devin hadn't held back on the casual PDA while they'd been hanging out in the waiting room, but they hadn't made an announcement or anything, either. Her mom was usually uncannily observant, but apparently she'd been too busy pacing a hole in the carpet to notice all the shared glances or the occasional moments when Devin would put a hand on her back or her knee.

Zoe's face warmed, but she held her head high, meeting her mother's gaze.

Her mom clicked her tongue behind her teeth and shook her head fondly. "Guess you did know what you were doing after all."

Zoe huffed out a breath. "Sure did."

"Good," her mom said, firm. A sly smile curled her lips, and Zoe's throat went tight.

It would scarcely count as approval from anybody else's parent, but for Zoe's mom? She might as well have thrown her a "Congratulations on Nailing the Hot Guy" party.

Uncle Arthur's reaction wasn't nearly as subdued, his pale face eclipsed by a bright grin. "About time."

"Hey," Devin protested.

"'Theoretical,'" Uncle Arthur scoffed, tucking the remote under his leg to make air quotes.

Zoe didn't know what they were talking about, but that was all right. Letting go of Devin's hand, she stepped forward to kiss her uncle on the cheek.

He squeezed her palm and winked. Quietly, he murmured, "Good choice."

"I know."

She moved aside, and Devin took his turn giving Arthur a careful hug.

Her mom slung her purse over her shoulder. "I'll give you two a minute."

"Really?"

She patted Zoe's hand. "Just a minute. I'm starving. Did you know vending machines here charge two dollars for a Kit Kat bar?"

Okay, yeah, her mom running to the car to grab a free snack from the stash she kept there made a lot more sense than her actually giving them privacy. "Outrageous."

Her mom made a disapproving sound in the back of her throat, calling out Zoe's sarcasm, but with a quick pat to Zoe's shoulder, she kept walking.

Zoe turned her attention back to Devin and Uncle Arthur, who were engaged in a little sidebar of their own.

She rolled her eyes. "You don't have to threaten Devin if he hurts me. Han's already got that covered."

"You?" Uncle Arthur huffed out a breath and waved a hand dismissively. "You can fend for yourself. I was telling Devin that if you hurt him, you'd have to deal with me."

Devin looked kind of embarrassed about it, if secretly pleased.

Good. He deserved someone looking out for him.

Zoe dropped into the chair her mother had set up on the other side of Arthur's bed. As she did, Arthur struggled to sit up. She shook her head at him. "Relax."

"Your mother wouldn't let me have my phone."

"Nor should she have."

"I have to call Sherry." He scrubbed a hand across his forehead. "Ten people had appointments at Harvest Home today. Supper service—"

Zoe grabbed his hand and held on tight. "Is handled."

"The key—"

"Sherry already came by to pick up mine."

"Deliveries—"

"Have been postponed until tomorrow. All today's pick-ups, too."

"But—"

"Uncle Arthur." She gripped his hand in both of hers. "I've got it."

She sucked in a deep breath. Instinctively, she glanced up at Devin, but he just stood there, silently supportive. Because he was the awesomest dude in the world, and she was so freaking glad to have him at her side.

"Zoe…" Uncle Arthur started.

"Trust me." That's what she'd been asking everyone in her life to do since she graduated.

She could make her own decisions about who she wanted to date.

And about what she wanted to do with her life.

"I've been doing a lot of thinking." She stopped her uncle before he could interrupt again. "Not just today, but for the past few months. About my future."

That finally got him to let her speak. His mouth drew down into a frown, but she had his attention.

"You've been doing too much."

He shook his head, but she looked pointedly at the hospital bed he was all but strapped into.

"You do too much," she insisted again, "because you care too much. You take care of everyone all the time. Well, it's time we all took care of you." She cleared her throat. "It's time I did."

"Zhaohui?"

"I'm taking over Harvest Home." She kept going, putting it all out there before he could try to contradict her. "You'll still be in charge, obviously. It's your baby. But from now on, the day-to-day operations are on me."

"But your job—"

"Will be fine." She'd already talked to Clay about adjusting her schedule. It wouldn't be a problem. And she had some other ideas she was going to run past him, too.

Arthur started again. "Your job *search*. You had all those leads in Atlanta, Charlotte—"

Zoe shook her head. "My job search is over."

"But—"

"I don't want to be an accountant. And I don't want to leave Blue Cedar Falls," she said firmly. She looked at Devin, asking him to hear the weight of her words.

She was done worrying about what everyone else expected her to do.

Devin's own actions, telling Han about them, had been an inspiration. He wasn't going to let other people's opinions hold him back anymore. So neither was she.

"I like it here." She squeezed Uncle Arthur's hands. "I'm happy here. I have friends, family." Leaning in conspiratorially, she murmured, "And a really nice boyfriend."

Devin smiled, and her heart glowed. He wasn't going to fight her on this. Good.

Because she would fight. For her family and for her future and for her vision of how she wanted to spend her life, now that she'd finally figured it out.

"You don't have to..." Uncle Arthur put his other hand on top of hers.

"I want to. So you just focus on getting better. Leave all the worrying about Harvest Home to me."

Uncle Arthur finally smiled. "I wouldn't trust it to anyone else."

The warmth in her heart only grew.

"There are some grants we can apply for," he said, that gleam appearing in his eyes, exhausted as they were. "So we can get you a salary. If you go to my desk in the back office—"

"After you get out of the hospital," she assured him, reaching in to fluff his pillows. "Until then, you just rest." She nodded, both to him and to herself. "I've got everything under control."

Chapter Fourteen

Epilogue

*O*ne month later...

"So, as you can see in Figure C in your handout." Zoe clicked a button on the remote for the LCD projector she'd borrowed from Lian. She arched a brow toward her audience as the spreadsheet she'd meticulously compiled came into view. "Taking into account average rent for a one-bedroom apartment, food, gas, personal expenses, and an acceptable rate of savings for a person in my age bracket..."

At the back of the room, June silently wiggled her hand, reminding Zoe about the laser pointer in her other hand. Right. Thank goodness the two of them had practiced this together last night.

She aimed the little red dot at the total at the bottom of the column. "Projected monthly expenses can be satisfactorily accounted for with projected earnings."

"Hold on a second." Clay held up his hand.

"I know exactly what you're going to say, Mr. Hawthorne." Zoe flipped to the next slide. "Income is broken out in Figure D." As the assembled crowd all turned the pages in their handout, she moved the laser pointer to highlight each number as she explained it. "Earnings fall into two major categories. The first is the modest salary I'll be able to begin drawing from Harvest Home once our grant applications to expand our staff are accepted."

Uncle Arthur nodded, leaning forward to agree. "The grant proposals are very good."

"Thank you, Mr. Chao." Zoe shifted the pointer. "The second category is income from my part-time position in the hospitality industry."

"You mean waitressing," Clay said.

"Waitressing, hostessing"—she set down the pointer and remote to begin counting on her fingers—"bartending—"

"Okay, okay," Clay interrupted. "You're good, but—"

"And bookkeeping."

His mouth snapped closed. "Wait."

"Admit you need the help," June said from the back.

"Hey—"

"With these additional responsibilities, I've determined that I'll be earning a twenty percent raise."

"Twenty percent!" Clay balked.

Zoe's pulse ticked up, but she had full confidence in her value to him. She arched a brow. "You think you can find a new server who's as good as me *and* who can start doing your books for you?"

"She's got a point, man," Han agreed.

"This is a setup." Clay looked around at everyone with suspicion in his gaze. There wasn't any malice, though. The guy had been to war and ended up with a knee full of shrapnel and so many trust issues he might as well have gotten a subscription, but he knew he was among friends here.

"Of course it's a setup," Zoe's mom agreed. She gazed at Zoe with a knowing curl to her lips. "But you're not the one she's setting up."

Zoe's heart pounded harder as she met her mother's gaze.

Oblivious, Clay continued, gesturing at the screen. "She just gave herself a twenty percent raise."

"That I'm going to earn," she promised, still looking at her mom.

"You sure about this, Zhaohui?" her mother asked.

Clay sat back in his chair, arms crossed. "I'm not sure about it."

"Yes, you are," Zoe and her mom both said as one.

"I guess that settles that," Clay said.

June stepped forward to put her hands on his shoulders. She pressed her lips to his temple. "Accept when you're beaten, dear."

"Fine, fine."

As they spoke, Zoe and her mom continued their silent staring contest. Zoe could hear all her mother's doubts, and she expressed her confidence back to her, even as neither of them said anything at all.

This plan was going to work. She'd draw a low but respectable salary managing the day-to-day operations of Harvest Home. She'd augment it by continuing to work at the Junebug and taking over Clay's accounting. She liked both jobs. Her work at Harvest Home fulfilled her, while waitressing at the bar was both lucrative and fun. Doing a little bookkeeping would maintain her skills and her résumé in case she ever changed her mind. Uncle Arthur would be less stressed, and if he ever decided to retire, she'd be ready to step up and slide right into his place. It was a win-win-win-win.

Finally, Zoe's mother raised a brow. "Princess astronaut veterinarian ballerina?"

"Princess astronaut veterinarian ballerina." Zoe let out a rough breath as lightness filled her chest.

"Well, then." Her mother smiled. "I suppose I can't argue with that."

———

"Hey—James!"

At the sound of his last name, Devin looked up. Joe stood outside the trailer, waving him over.

"Got a sec before you head out?"

"Sure." He finished the last couple of joins he'd been working on before nodding to the crew. It was a few minutes early, but they'd made good progress today.

He helped with cleanup, but once it was all in hand, he patted his buddy Terrell on the back and gestured at Joe's office.

Terrell nodded. "See you in the morning, boss."

Devin took off, a spring in his step.

It still amazed him how peaceful the entire site felt now that Bryce was gone. The guy had talked a big game about getting his father to retaliate, but it had been precisely that: talk. Sure, the mayor's office had made a few overtures, hoping to get management to reverse his dismissal, but Joe had stood behind Devin's decision. In the end, Bryce had been more of a liability than he'd been worth. Last Devin had heard, the guy was heading back to community college. Devin hoped he learned some things while he was there, but as long as he didn't show up on Devin's job site again, he honestly didn't care.

Inside the trailer, Joe was perched behind his computer, same as always. He smiled when Devin knocked and let himself in, gesturing for him to have a seat.

Joe folded his big hands on top of the desk. "Just wanted to ask how things are going."

"Good." Devin pointed his thumb toward the door behind him. "We're on schedule out there, maybe even a little ahead."

"I know that. I meant with you."

"Me?" Uh... "I'm good."

Great, actually. He couldn't stop the little smile that curled his lips.

Work was less stressful. The bump in his pay from the promotion had finally started showing up in his bank account. Arthur's recovery was going well.

And then there was the conversation he and Arthur had had the other night.

His leg bobbed up and down in anticipation.

He couldn't wait to tell Zoe about it. He was leaving after his shift to go pick her up, and he was going to do just that.

It had only been a month since he and Zoe had gone public, but it had been the best month of his entire life. It was like the thing with Bryce; Devin hadn't grasped how much strain all the secrecy and sneaking around was putting on them both.

But that was behind them now. They were happy and in love. Han was still his best friend—even if he did look at him kind of funny now and then.

Well, he'd get used to it. Devin was in this for the long haul.

And after what he planned to show Zoe this evening, hopefully by the end of the night he'd know she was in it for the long haul, too.

"All right, all right." Joe shook his head. "I get it— you're a private guy. Well, I just wanted to let you know that we're real pleased with how you've taken over as shift leader. Your crew's doing good work. Word on the street is you've really turned things around."

"Oh. Thanks."

Joe's raised brows were pointed. "Wasn't an easy situation you inherited with Horton on your crew. But you handled it like a pro." With that, Joe pulled open the top drawer of his desk and fished out an envelope. He passed it over. Nodding at it, he said, "Little token of our appreciation."

Devin blinked in surprise. He glanced at Joe, who motioned for him to go ahead and open it. The check inside stared back at him, and his jaw dropped. "I—I mean—"

People got bonuses pretty regularly around here when things were going well, but this was generous, to say the least. He sputtered for another few seconds before Joe took mercy.

"'Thank you' is the phrase you're looking for, I think."

Right. "Thank you."

"You earned it." Joe closed the drawer and gestured toward the door. "Now get on out of here."

"Will do." Devin tucked the check in his pocket. He rose, turned to leave, then stopped and twisted back around. More fervently, he repeated, "Really, Joe. Thank you."

Devin didn't think he'd ever fully get rid of his old man's voice in his head, telling him he'd never amount to anything. But he had a lot of evidence to say otherwise of late. This bonus...the pride in Joe's eyes...They were the icing on what was already a pretty flipping amazing cake.

By the time he got back outside, the cleanup job was basically done, and folks were getting ready to head out. Devin gave everything one last check over before making his way to his truck. He drove the familiar route to Harvest Home, where Zoe stood outside waiting for him.

She hopped in the cab of the truck and leaned over the gearshift. He threaded his fingers through her silky hair, closed his eyes, and kissed her, and he was really never going to get over that, was he? How good she felt, how sweet she tasted.

How much he loved her.

"Hey," he managed when she pulled away.

"Hey, yourself."

The flush to her cheeks and the glazed darkness in her eyes almost derailed him, but he managed to keep his focus. "How'd it go?" he asked. "Your presentation?"

"Good. Really good." She rolled her eyes. "Clay's on board with the promotion, and Uncle Arthur was super supportive."

"And your mom?" That was the part she'd been worried about.

"I'm going to go with 'begrudgingly accepting.'"

"Hey!" Devin grinned. "So basically wild enthusiasm?"

"Next best thing."

"Good." He leaned in and pressed another firm kiss to her lips. "Knew you could do it."

Curling a hand in the collar of his shirt, she kept him close for a second. "Thank you," she said quietly. "For believing in me."

They kissed again. He tucked a bit of hair behind her ear. "Always."

She let him go and settled back into her seat. "So, what's the plan?"

The nerves he'd felt earlier while thinking about this moment melted away. "You mind going for a drive?"

She scrunched up her brows at him. "Uh...okay?"

Once she was buckled in, he put the truck back into first and steered toward the road. While he drove, he asked her about her day, and he told her about his. They commiserated over how tough it was to get Arthur to delegate and rest. She spoke with pride about her juggling act taking over for him.

But she had good people with her. Sherry and Tania had been only too happy to start managing the supper service by themselves most nights. Volunteers had come out of the woodwork to lend a hand, because that was what people in Blue Cedar Falls did. They took care of one another.

As he glanced over at her, warmth grew in his chest.

He was so glad to call this place home.

He was so glad she was going to stay. Here. With him.

Clearing his throat, he forced himself to focus on the road. Before long, he turned off onto the country route leading out of town.

Zoe shifted beside him. "You're not taking me out into the middle of nowhere to act out some weird serial killer fantasy, are you?"

Devin laughed. "Is that really the first thing to pop into your mind?"

"I mean..." In his periphery, she waved a hand at their surroundings.

"Not much farther," he promised.

Five minutes outside town, he put on the blinker.

"Wait—isn't this...?"

Zoe held her tongue as they took the gravel road he'd been imagining driving down for the last three years. He came to a stop where the road ended.

It wasn't much. Just a small clearing in the wooded lot. He pulled the keys from the ignition and reached behind his seat for the camping lantern he stowed there. He turned it on and flicked his headlights off. Twilight settled over them, quiet and peaceful. Exactly the way he liked it.

He opened the door on his side. For a second, Zoe sat there, gazing out the front windshield.

"You coming?" he asked.

She looked at him. "This is Arthur's place, right? The old lot he snatched up in his real estate phase."

"None other."

"What are we doing here?"

"Just come on."

She followed him out, wary but smiling. Maybe she had a clue. They went to the center of the clearing. He breathed in the woodsy scent of the air. Tipped his head up at the stars just beginning to come out.

"I know you've been doing a lot of soul-searching lately," he told her. "I did some of that myself a while back."

"Yeah?"

"You know about my dad. I was...kind of directionless for a long time after I got out of his house. Just so glad to be on my own, I wasn't thinking about what I really wanted, you know?"

"Sure," she said slowly. "I can see that."

He held out his arm, and she came into his embrace. The warmth of her against his side heated him all the way to his core. "Your uncle Arthur—he was a big part of helping me figure it out. I decided my goal was a place of my own. Not just a roof to live under that wasn't my old man's. A home."

His pulse sped up a tick, his mouth going dry. Getting nervous talking about this didn't make sense, but he couldn't seem to help it.

"Arthur promised me then and there that as soon as I could save up the money, he'd sell me this lot—at cost."

Zoe scrunched up her brow. "But he bought it twenty years ago. He must've paid, like, nothing for it."

Devin let out a quiet laugh. "It was a little more than nothing." A lot less than it was worth now, but on Devin's income, it was still a chunk of change.

A chunk of change that had taken him three whole years to save.

He was still a little shy, even with his promotion and his bonus. But that didn't matter.

"The other night, when I was keeping him company, he changed the deal."

"Yeah?"

Devin shrugged. "Apparently a heart attack gave him some new perspective. He doesn't want to make me wait anymore. He trusts me. Knows I'm good for it."

And he was. With the new promotion and the bonus he'd earned this afternoon, he'd be paying Arthur everything he owed in six months.

Pulling Zoe closer in against his side, he looked around. "He's signing it over to me next week."

"Devin. That's amazing."

It was. A kid like him who'd grown up with nothing, living off what he could get at the local food bank. Cowering in a dark house with a dad who made him feel like dirt.

And now he was here.

He had the Leungs for his family. He had Zoe tucked beneath his arm.

He had this land.

His voice went hoarse. "This weekend, I was wondering if maybe you'd want to look at some building plans with me."

"Sure, I mean—"

"For when you move in here with me." He didn't want her mistaking him. He wanted to be clear. Looking down at her, he swallowed back his last remaining doubts. "I know it's soon, but I know what I want."

Her bright, beautiful gaze met his through the dimness. Her lips curled into a smile, and her eyes shone. "Devin..."

"Building a house. It'll take time. This isn't right now, but—"

"Yes," she said. She rose onto her toes and kissed him. "Of course, absolutely, yes."

He clutched her in his arms as tightly as he dared, returning the kiss with all the wonder in his heart. "I love you," he managed to get out.

"I love you, too." She pressed her mouth to his once more before pulling back. "There's just one tiny thing you're wrong about."

"What's that?" He was having a hard time concentrating. She felt so good pressed against him.

But then she grinned. "The soul-searching. The figuring out what I want with my life."

"Oh?"

"I'm done with that." Her smile widened, and he felt it in the center of his chest. "I'm exactly where I want to be."

And just like that, so was he.

Here. In this home that they would build.

Together.

About the Author

Jeannie Chin writes contemporary small-town romances. She draws on her experiences as a biracial Asian and white American to craft heartfelt stories that speak to a uniquely American experience. She is a former high school science teacher, wife to a geeky engineer, and mom to an extremely talkative kindergartener. Her hobbies include crafting, reading, and hiking.

You can learn more at:
Website: JeannieChin.com
Twitter @JeannieCWrites
Facebook.com/JeannieCWrites
Instagram @JeannieCWrites

Enjoy the best of the West with these handsome, rugged cowboys!

NATIONAL BESTSELLING AUTHOR
SARA RICHARDSON
BETTING *on a* **GOOD LUCK COWBOY**

BETTING ON A GOOD LUCK COWBOY
by Sara Richardson

Single mom Tess Valdez is determined to honor the memory of her late husband—so when she hears the wild horses he loved will be culled, she swears to protect them. She'll need the help of Navy SEAL Silas Beck, but Silas is leaving. He may have started working for Tess to honor his fallen friend, but now he's fallen for her, hard. He vows to finish one last mission, then go…but can Tess say goodbye to the man who opened up her heart?

MONTANA PROUD
by R. C. Ryan

Get swept away with two cowboys in the McCords series. In *Montana Legacy*, a reserved rancher is content to live alone years after the one person he ever let in suddenly left. Now she's back, and he's determined to resist her charms. But soon he must protect their very lives—and growing chemistry—from an unseen enemy. In *Montana Destiny*, a woman who lives for trouble stumbles upon a clue to the legendary McCord gold. Now she's in a mysterious killer's sights—and the arms of an irresistible McCord playboy who claims he finally wants to settle down. Trust is the one thing she can't easily give…but when danger closes in fast, only surrendering to each other can ensure their survival.

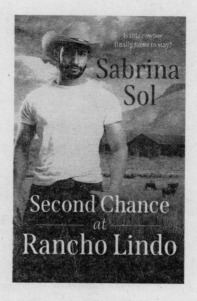

SECOND CHANCE AT RANCHO LINDO
by Sabrina Sol

After being wounded in the military, Gabe Ortega has returned home to Rancho Lindo. But he plans to leave as soon as possible—despite his family's wishes—until he runs into a childhood friend. The beautiful Nora Torres is now a horticulturist in charge of the ranch's greenhouse. She's usually a ray of sunshine, so why has she been giving him the cold shoulder? As they work together and he breaks down her walls, he starts to wonder if everything he'd been looking for has been here all along.

SECOND CHANCE COWBOY
by A. J. Pine

Ten years ago, Jack Everett left his family's ranch without a backward glance. Now what was supposed to be a quick trip home for his father's funeral has suddenly become more complicated. The ranch Jack can handle—he might be a lawyer, but he still remembers how to work with his hands. But turning around the failing vineyard he's also inherited? That requires working with the one woman he never expected to see again.